I0699813

afterlight

afterlight

CASSANDRA PINE

Published by Laureano Creative Media LLC
P.O. Box 460241
Aurora, CO 80046, U.S.A.
laureanocreativemedia.com

Cover design by Hillary Manton Lodge Design. Images from iStock
and Adobe Stock.

This story is a work of fiction. Where real people, events, establishments,
organizations, or locales appear, they are used fictitiously. All other elements
are products of the author's imagination.

ISBN 978-1-960079-10-7 (sc)
ISBN 978-1-960079-09-1 (e-book)

103025

While this book does not contain explicit material,
it does include themes that could be upsetting to some
readers. For a full list of content warnings,
please turn to page 417 of this book.

chapter one

September 2025, Los Angeles

They said that over time, my grief would lessen, but five years later, it's still the first thing that hits me as I open my eyes. The loss isn't as keen as it once was, but I know the truth all too well: sometimes dull blades leave messier wounds than sharp ones.

I push myself upright amid my fluffy comforter and swing my legs over the side of the bed, taking a moment to take stock of the sensations in my body. No dizziness, no blurred vision. I reach for the blood pressure machine on my nightstand, wait patiently through the tourniquet tightness until the screen flashes up a respectable 128/85, HR 92. Not my target, but I'll take it. I won't need to cancel any of my sessions today. Which is good, because my private clients are the bulk of my business, the vast majority of my income, and the reason that I've been able to stay put in this overpriced apartment in this quiet and walkable neighborhood of Studio City.

Now that I know I'm not likely to collapse on the way to the shower, I push myself off the bed and bend forward slowly, stretching my hamstrings until I can wrap my arms around my calves and rest my nose on my shins. It may not be strictly necessary, not with my performance days far behind me, but that flexibility was too hard-won to give it up so easily.

Besides, I have a lifetime of habit behind me.

It's that habit that propels me through my morning routine. Except instead of twisting my hair up into a bun out of the shower, I spend the twenty minutes it takes to blow out the coppery red strands smooth and sleek, then gather it all up into a high ponytail. Instead of pulling on my favorite leotard and tights, I select a coordinated outfit from my wardrobe of chic fitness wear and slide it on. And then, because low blood-sugar is one of my triggers, I force myself to make a smoothie out of whole milk, fresh fruit, with a big scoop of protein powder and a drizzle of hemp oil. I pour it into a travel cup to take with me and set it on the entry table in my apartment while I pull on my walking shoes and grab the bag that contains everything I need for the day. At the last minute, I spot my white long-haired cat, Misha, already sunning himself in the window, and give him a quick stroke. He offers me a lazy meow before his blue eyes drift closed again.

After witnessing my unvarying routine, my best friend once asked me if it was hard to adjust to living with my condition. And while it's not exactly a pleasurable experience to feel all the blood take a downward journey to my feet every time I stand up, it's not as if my routine has changed much. In my fourteen years as a ballet dancer, five of them as a professional, there was not a single day when I didn't wake up and catalog what hurt, what I needed to be concerned about, how much I'd be capable of that day. I was eight when I noticed that my belly poked out in profile when standing at the barre; that night, I sneaked my mom's nutrition book off the shelf and looked at how many calories and grams of fat my favorite foods contained. I was twelve the first time I knowingly danced on an injury. By the time I was sixteen, my measure of my condition was not what hurt but how much I could push myself through without collapsing.

I'm not saying it was healthy, I'm just saying it's how it was. In comparison to the way I've lived the majority of my life—pained, bloody, bruised, and starving—a blood-pressure check and a few extra minutes for breakfast doesn't even really register as a hardship.

By the time I reach the street below my apartment and put on my sunglasses against the bright wash of Southern California sunshine, the tightness in my chest is already loosening. It's not as if I spend all day cataloging everything that I lost to COVID—my boyfriend, my health, my career. It's just that for that one split second, before I come fully to consciousness and remember where I am, I'm still okay, six years in the past with only good things in my future. I like my life now; it just always takes me a few minutes every day to remember which one I'm living. New York versus California. Professional ballet dancer versus master Pilates instructor. Engaged-to-be-engaged versus very, very, *very* single.

Okay, that last one still stings.

My apartment is only a ten minute walk from my studio and I keep my pace slow, cataloging my breathing, glancing at my heart rate on my fitness watch. Everything is as it should be, which means that it's going to be a good day. I smile to myself, my spirits lifting even more. Monday is the busiest day for Marquee Pilates, the business that I own with my best friend, Amira, but it's barely after eight and my first client doesn't arrive until after ten. That means I have time to complete my own workout, do a little barre, and otherwise mitigate the fact that while I might *teach* fitness for a living, the reality involves a lot of standing and not all that much moving.

When I arrive at our bright, shiny storefront on Ventura Boulevard, the front door is locked but the lights are already on inside, a sign that Amira has once again beaten me here. I quickly let myself in and flip the lock closed behind me, breathing in the scent of lavender from the essential oil diffuser already going in the corner, and take a satisfied look around the space. It's spotless as usual, thanks to our cleaning crew and Amira, who manages everything that is not specifically teaching. Maple and shining steel apparatuses stand on antique Persian rugs; vintage Hollywood prints decorate the maple-paneled wall. I left the design to Amira, given that she and her trust fund bankrolled the whole thing, and I couldn't love it more. The whole place is an oasis of health and serenity.

Almost. The air-conditioning is already working overtime, trying to get ahead of the September afternoon heat that will eventually bake the studio through its plate glass windows like a blast furnace, and above the rattle of the commercial system pulses a heavy dance beat. I can't understand the lyrics, not because of the noise from the AC, but because they're in Korean.

"A little early for K-pop, don't you think?" I call, dropping my bag behind the front desk and taking the phone off voice-mail.

Almost instantly, Amira appears from the office in back and does a little spin and a shimmy, what I can only guess is part of the official choreography for the song currently playing, and then turns and throws it back, which I'm fairly certain is *not* part of the choreo.

I laugh—she's not a dancer in the same way I am, but she's certainly almost always in motion. Her mane of thick dark hair sways around her shoulders as she struts toward me, a pretend-seductive look on her face. She puckers up, and I push her away with a grin.

"Stop. I can't look at you when you do that."

"First, you need to lighten up. Second, it is *never* too early for K-pop. And third, I'm just warming up for the concert tonight." She fixes a stern look on me. "You did bring your clothes, right? We have to leave directly after your last client."

I nudge the bag on the floor with my foot. "Packed and ready to go. Anything I should be aware of today?"

Amira shifts into business mode immediately. She's always silly first thing in the morning because she knows I start the day rough, but she is the most professional and focused person I know. For one thing, she handles all the business stuff for the studio, from marketing to accounting to scheduling. For another, she got her business degree from UCLA while simultaneously working a full-time job. Her friendly, bubbly exterior is just a veneer over an extremely driven personality.

"Alison rescheduled today's one o'clock session for Wednesday—she got a last minute audition. And Deirdre from the Pilates Festival sent another email about you giving the day two keynote."

I make a face. "I already told you. I don't do public speaking. The stress, the standing. . . I'm not so sure that collapsing in front of a couple hundred people is the boost we want for my career."

"Please. We can always ask for accommodations. Sit on a stool behind the podium. Talk about what it's like to be a Pilates teacher with a disability. For that matter, talk about what it's like to teach Pilates to *people* with disabilities. You're poised to make an impact, especially considering how ableist sections of this industry can be."

I just shake my head, and Amira sighs, but she doesn't press. She doesn't understand how someone who made a living as as performer can be so insistent about staying out of the public eye, but there's a difference between stepping onto stage, well-rehearsed and in full control of your physical faculties, and putting yourself on display when you have no idea if you'll even remain upright. At least here, my clients know about my issues, and they understand that sometimes I have to adapt.

More than that, I hate having to explain why I no longer do the thing I love and instead do the thing I settled for.

No, that's not fair. I love what I do now. Pilates was the thing that saved me immediately after my diagnosis when I could barely stand up and I thought I would spend my twenties bed-ridden. The intricacies of my teacher's programs built on my innate understanding of kinesiology acquired from decades of ballet training and reminded me that at one point, I'd thought maybe I'd become an orthopedist or physical therapist. There's always more to learn, and I keep in touch with friends from my master teaching program who now live all over the world.

It's just that, all things being equal, I would much rather be in the studio, sweating through a rehearsal, my brain and my body strained to its very limits.

Enough. *Enough.* It's much too easy to spiral when I'm in this kind of mood, and I've got four clients today who are counting on me to be focused and upbeat. I pick up my bag and shift past Amira to go into the office where I drop my bag, pull on a pair of grippy socks, and shrug out of my windbreaker. Two minutes later, I'm on the Reformer—a bed-like contraption with a moving carriage attached to springs—working my way methodically through the advanced classical series.

Forty-five minutes after that, everything feels warmed and aligned, so I swap the socks for a pair of canvas ballet slippers and move to the barre attached to the long, mirrored wall on one side of the studio. I can feel Amira's eyes on me as I melt into the first set of plies and quickly move through an abbreviated barre. I don't know if she's monitoring my physical state or just watching. It's only when I'm through the first several exercises and moving into développés, my foot drawing up one leg and unfolding at head height before me, then shifting to the side above my ear, that I glance her way again and catch her pained expression.

Whether it's the sudden jolt of embarrassment at her pity or actual overexertion, my watch beeps an alert. I shift my leg behind me into a graceful arabesque before I call it. My heart rate is too elevated for mere barre work. Years ago, this wouldn't be enough effort to get me breathing hard and now my pulse is pounding a warning in my throat. My muscles might still work they way they used to—and I work hard not to lose that strength or flexibility—but my autonomic nervous system doesn't always play along.

"Trina," Amira begins, but I wave her off and stride toward the back to clean up for my first client.

Don't focus on what you can't do. Focus on what you can do. Wise words from my therapist.

How I hate them.

But I wipe away my regret and frustration, fix my hair, and swipe on one more layer of deodorant before I zip up my sweatshirt and prepare for my first client of the day.

Despite the repeatedly rough start, the day moves by swiftly. My ten o'clock is a lovely older woman named Delores with a killer physique and an even better singing voice; she was a Broadway actress in the seventies and now mostly does commercials to keep herself busy. I work her hard but carefully, and when we finish, she regales me with stories of her naughty Maltese puppy who is determined to make a shambles of her 1920s bungalow. She kisses both my cheeks in farewell and gives me a saucy little wink before she saunters out of the studio.

Eleven-thirty is a fifteen year-old-girl whom I've been only training for the last couple of weeks. Millie just landed her first real role as a supporting character on a teen drama, and it takes me only minutes into our Reformer session to know that she's starving herself. Her muscles shake and she's breathing harder that she should be for the level of exertion, especially considering she used to play soccer and softball before she decided to make a go at Hollywood. I don't say anything, but I turn down the intensity of the session. Before she leaves, I dip behind the counter and scrawl a name and a phone number on a sticky note.

"Call this nutritionist," I say in a low voice, extending the note on a fingertip. "She'll help you get the weight off safely. You can't starve yourself if you're in this for the long run. It just gets harder and harder."

She flushes pink, but she gives me a grateful nod and a hug before she darts out to where her mom waits in a battered Audi station wagon at the curb.

Amira comes up behind me. "I can't believe you just told a fifteen year old to see a dietitian. She's perfectly fine the way she is."

"Of course she is," I say flatly. "She's also ten pounds over what the studio wants her at, whether they say it or not, and she's going to do real damage to herself trying to lose it. Wouldn't you rather her have professional help?"

Amira sighs, but she says nothing. This is the one thing she hates about the fact we've built our clientele off performers; ironic considering this niche had been her idea. Her dad is a well-known producer, so she grew up going to pool parties at Aaron Spelling's house and eating at the studio commissaries while her dad did business. She knows better than anyone what the ridiculous body standards do to performers' psyches, and it's why she can't understand why I haven't gained more than five pounds since I stopped dancing. She just doesn't say anything anymore. She called me skeletal once, and I didn't talk to her for three days.

Since my one o'clock session was canceled, we dip out for lunch at the pizza place down the street, and neither of us talks about anything that happened that morning while she digs into a loaded slice and I eat the best Italian chopped salad in the San Fernando Valley. Instead, she starts giving me the low-down on the K-pop group we're going to see tonight at BMO Stadium. I listen with half my attention. It's not that I don't like K-pop or concerts, it's simply that Amira knows *so much* that her primer is more like a private detective's dossier. Helios has only five members—who are called *idols*—but she knows everyone's real names, stage names, city of birth, blood type, when they debuted, and which languages they speak. That last part is pretty impressive, considering that everyone is at least bilingual if not multilingual, and here I am still struggling along with a handful of pathetic high-school Spanish. But it's not until she drops another fact that I interrupt.

"*What exactly,*" I ask, "is a supergroup?"

She gives me a look that tells me she's already explained this once, if not more. "It's a group formed with already successful idols. Two of them are from groups that have disbanded, one is on hiatus because everyone else in his group is finishing their military service, and two left active groups to go solo."

"So it's the K-pop equivalent of an All-Star Team."

Amira grins, pleased that I've caught on. "Exactly. You're going to love it."

I'm sure I will. I love live performances, no matter what kind, and Amira assures me that this is more like a musical theater experience than an ordinary concert. I'm actually kind of excited, even though I don't tell her that. I haven't seen any live dance or theater since I retired—it's still too hard to walk into an opera house—but a live pop performance in a soccer stadium isn't in the same universe as the Met.

But first, I have my last two sessions for the day—an R&B singer getting back into shape for her world tour and a six-foot-eleven basketball player trying to increase his flexibility after injuries benched him for most of last season. As soon as he leaves, Amira locks the door and flips off the lights. "Hurry up and change," she says. "Our ride is going to be here in seven minutes."

I rush into the office and strip off my workout clothes, but once I slide into the baggy jeans and boots I'd brought, I realize my mistake—neither the tank top nor the leather jacket I thought I brought are in the bag.

Because they're hanging on the hooks by my front door, where they wouldn't get rumpled in my bag.

"Uh, Amira, I have a problem."

Amira rushes in. "No. No problems. We don't have time for problems. We're already barely going to make it on time, and trust me when I say that unlike Western concerts, this show will start *on the dot*. No opening acts."

"I'm thinking that the dress code probably requires a shirt, and I can't pull off my workout top with these jeans."

Amira sighs and looks around, then snatches something off the desk. It's a sample sent to us from a clothing line who wants us to carry their stuff in the studio—basically a long-line sports bra with a strappy back. It just doesn't cover much.

"Here, wear this," Amira says. "It's perfect with those jeans. Very '90s hip-hop."

I shoot her a look.

"Okay, sort of '90s hip-hop, but if I had your abs, I would be showing them off at every opportunity. Put it on, throw the jacket on over top or tie it around your waist and you're great."

She's right. We don't have time for me to be having a wardrobe crisis, and what does it matter anyway? It's not like anyone is going to be looking at me. They're going to be staring at the five gorgeous men on stage—she showed me photos, so I know this for a fact. I strip off my tank top and pull on the bra top thing. Amira looks me over approvingly, and then at the last minute, she takes the gold threader earrings out of her ears. They have little gold suns dangling from the end of the many chains. *Helios.* Cute.

"Here, put these on. And appreciate the sacrifice I'm making for you because I bought them specifically for this concert."

I laugh and poke them through my piercings, then grab my cross-body purse out of the bag. Amira glances at her phone. "Rideshare's here. Let's go."

I don't even have time to glance in the mirror before we're out the door and locking up behind us to jump in the shiny blue Toyota waiting at the curb. Just before we climb in, Amira throws an arm around my shoulder and winks. "Just wait. This is going to be life-changing."

I laugh, but inwardly, I hope it's nothing of the sort.

I've had enough changes for a lifetime.

chapter two

Two hours is not nearly enough time to get anywhere in LA, but certainly not when a big event is going on. We creep down the 101 Freeway at a speed that a ten year old on a skateboard could beat while Amira wiggles her crossed legs fitfully and checks her phone every few minutes. We've finally made the transition to the Harbor Freeway when my phone buzzes in my pocket. I pull it out and see the name *Jackson* on the screen. I send it to voice mail and then immediately tap out a message.

TRINA

Can't talk now, what's up?

Amira throws me a questioning look.

"Jackson," I explain.

She frowns. "He's actually still around? You haven't talked about him in ages."

"He's been in Taiwan on business for the last few weeks."

"And his phone miraculously doesn't work in Asia?"

I just shake my head. Amira can't understand my on-and-off relationship with Jackson Childers, and to be honest, neither do I. We met at the grocery store of all places—he was trying to figure out what he could substitute for garam masala, I happen to like Indian food, we got talking and he suggested that we hit up India House and skip the whole trouble. I turned him down, but I liked his low-key humor and calm way of speaking enough to give him my number. He waited exactly twenty-four hours to ask me out for Indian food again, and this time I agreed.

That was six months ago, and while I like him, we've yet to make any real progress in our relationship. He's a manufacturing engineer and so he spends two weeks a month out of the country, auditing factories and supervising production runs. I still have no idea what exactly his company manufactures.

> JACKSON
> Back in town for a bit. You
> free for dinner and maybe a
> movie this week?

I start to tap out a reply, but inexplicably, I erase the characters and turn off the screen, not sure how I want to respond. It's not that I don't find him attractive, because I do. It's not even that I think he's boring—he may be an engineer, but he loves movies and music and can actually speak intelligently on all of the above. When we're together, we have a nice time. He's a good kisser, but he hasn't pressed for the relationship to progress to the bedroom. Amira insists that he's probably gay and closeted, but I think mostly he's just smart enough to know that I'll stop taking his calls if he pushes too hard.

Bottom line, there's nothing at all wrong with him. It just feels like . . . there's something missing. And I have no idea what that is. On paper, we probably make sense, but in person it's like there's some essential connection that isn't there.

Amira throws me a knowing look, but she doesn't say anything. She doesn't have to. I already know what she's thinking.

Somehow, thanks to some warp in the space-time continuum and our rideshare driver's questionable grasp of traffic law, we pull up in front of the stadium twenty minutes before the concert is scheduled to start. I try not to think about how absurdly expensive that fare must have been and instead manage to be grateful that we didn't have to find parking—because we would definitely be late. As it is, by the time we find our seats, the crowd is getting restless and my watch tells me it's only three minutes until show time.

But . . . whoa. When Amira said she got us good seats, she meant it. I heard *arena* and thought we would be up in the bleachers, looking at the stage from a distance. But no. One of the narrow ends of the arena has been turned into the main stage, with a thrust stage that projects out into the field, and our seats are on the floor, directly at the intersection of the two. As in, were there not a proper barricade, I could probably reach out and touch the performers.

"You went all out," I said, pitching my voice beneath the vibrating hum of the crowd and the music playing in the background.

"Had to," she said. "Their contract is up this year and no one knows whether they're going to exist in a few months."

I suppose I can't blame her for that. There's always something ephemeral about live performances, and knowing that this could be among the last handful of times that *anyone* has a chance to see them makes me happy to be here, even if I know nothing about them.

I scan the crowd around me. Ninety percent of the audience is female, more than half are teenagers, and they're dressed in a dizzying array of outfits ranging from leather and chains that I imagine echo the group's costuming to homemade black-and-gold bedazzled T-shirts with photos of the group on the front and back. Some of the audience members are waving wands with a 3D sun embedded in a glowing globe.

"Light sticks," Amira explains when she sees me looking. "They sync to the music via an app. It's pretty cool, actually."

Clever. As is the fandom name—apparently Helios fans are called Hellions, and it makes me smile because this group is about as threatening as a scooter gang.

And then there's no opportunity to talk, because the second my watch turns over the hour, the background music fades out and the stage lights shift. Instantly, the entire stadium erupts into screams. Amira digs in her small purse and hands me a pair of earplugs, which immediately takes the noise down to a bearable din. She grins and then before I can comprehend what's going on, she's jumping up and down with the rest of our section, chanting something that I don't understand. I have to resist the urge to join them, having been warned that this show will be over two hours and I'll be on my feet for most of it. So instead, I pull out my cell phone and press *record* to capture the screaming, churning masses.

I have been transported to an entirely different planet. I'm not going to lie—I like it.

The first strains of music—a metallic hum, really— vibrates through the arena as dry-ice fog slowly rolls across the surface of the stage. It takes me a moment to make out the platform slowly raising the five members from beneath the stage. The audience erupts.

The singers are all dressed in tough-looking variations of leather and black denim and chains, skin-tight and sporting rips and missing pieces that show off a surprising amount of skin. One member has platinum blond hair and another cotton-candy pink, but as the music builds and they slowly turn, I realize that every one of them is impossibly, ethereally beautiful.

I lean over and shout to Amira, "I see the appeal now!"

She laughs and grins at me. "Just wait!"

One by one, they step off the platform into formation and only then do I notice the band at the back of the stage, the musicians blending into the black backdrop. The music builds into a pulsing rhythm, and then a black-haired singer in leather pants and a shredded, skin-tight black top steps forward, raises his microphone, and belts a high note so spectacular the crowd goes wild again.

That was the cue to launch into motion, and it takes me all of twenty seconds to become hooked. The song is a blend of rock and dance music, but I'm enthralled by the choreography—an addictive combination of hip-hop and jazz and street dance that they make look easy because of their perfect synchronicity. Amira is singing along next to me in English and Korean, but I'm just marveling over every intricate hand motion, every bit of footwork, their seamless formation changes as they swap positions along with lines in the song.

I don't want to admit that I was skeptical before, but now I'm sold. They're incredible.

"Which one is yours?" I ask Amira, my eyes still fixed on the stage. I know she has told me who's her favorite, but I have no frame of reference, especially considering in the photo she showed me, he had blue hair.

"Jae," she says immediately. "The one without a sleeve."

The one who hit the high note then. He's undeniably gorgeous, and he has a beautiful voice with an impressive range, but my eye keeps going to the pink-haired guy who's taken the center position in the dance break. There's something mesmerizing about his movements, perfectly controlled and precise. I almost ask her his name, but she's back to being fixed on the performance and I don't want to distract her.

They finish the song, back in formation, heads bowed and hands clasped in front of them, and now I'm screaming and cheering as loudly as the rest of the arena. So I'm surprised when the pink-haired guy steps forward, adjusting his head mic, and calls out "Hello, Los Angeles!" in American-accented English. The crowd roars back.

I throw a surprised look at Amira, and she grins. "Seojun. He grew up near here."

Seojun. Well, at least I know his name. His gives the usual spiel about how happy they are to be back in their favorite city, how glad he is to be back in his hometown, delivered in a smooth, surprisingly low voice. That earns another round of screaming and a teenage girl near me screams, "I love you, Seojun!" I throw another grin at Amira. It's been a while since I've witnessed this sheer intensity of adoration.

And then Seojun is strutting back to the group in his painted-on denim, and as soon as he takes his place in the formation, the second song starts.

I'd thought it would bother me that I didn't understand any of the lyrics, but I'm swept up in the performance as much as anyone around me. Besides, there's enough English peppered through the songs—even whole choruses—that I can understand the general meaning of the songs. And even if I didn't, I couldn't care less. I'm enthralled by the performance, the sheer fact that they sing, dance, and in some cases, rap, so well while being so singularly pretty, and I get why they call them idols. The image they project is definitely superhuman.

There are more rock-inflected songs, some that are straight up dance pop, a smooth R&B number that has my eyebrows lifting at just how sexy the choreography is. Thanks to Amira's shouted guidance, I know that Jae is the leader, and he challenges the rapper—Hyunsoo, I think—to freestyle over a beat that he arranges with the band on the spot.

I've been so fixated on the performance that I haven't noticed that the sky has deepened into an inky blue and the brilliant stage lights are splashing the space with red and gold. I pull on my jacket against the sudden cool bite of wind while the lights go down and two huge screens on either side of the stage play videos of the group—mini-movies for which I completely lack context. Then more songs that are so catchy I know I'll be humming them for the rest of the night. I'm starting to feel tired after the day I've had, but I'm having too much fun to sit down.

Hyunsoo and Seojun leave the stage while the other three perform what Amira calls a unit number, and then the lights all fall dark. When they come back up it's just the lights at the front of the stage, where Seojun sits reversed on a wooden chair, his arms folded over the back and his head bowed. He's changed into a white suit over a black mesh shirt that, from where I'm standing a mere twenty feet away, might as well be non-existent. The first strains of what sounds like another ballad comes up, and he lifts his head as he begins to sing.

I find myself losing breath at the first touch of his liquid baritone—the group's pop and rock songs didn't do his voice justice. It's . . . incredible. I can't understand the words, but I know it's a love song of sorts as he gazes out onto the audience with a sincerity that's impossible not to get drawn into. Then, the tempo shifts. He draws his leg around behind him and twists so he's rolling up out of an impressive backbend, and the stage lights come up to reveal five backup dancers all in black, seated on similar chairs.

I laugh as I recognize the reference. Seojun's voice turns sultry as they launch into a sexy cabaret number straight out of a Fosse musical—assuming that Fosse choreographed hip thrusts and body rolls. Once more I'm mesmerized. There's no way this guy isn't classically trained. It's evident in every line, the way he uses his hands and head . . . and a sudden, unexpected ache strikes soundly in my chest.

Amira nudges me, and I blink at her, the complicated emotion vanishing as quickly as it began. "I knew I'd get you eventually. He's amazing, isn't he?"

I nod, attention fixed on the stage. I'm so enthralled that it takes a long moment to realize that the woman in black standing in the aisle between me and the barricade is trying to get my attention. When I turn to her, she shouts, "Do you want to go on stage?"

I blink again. "What?"

Amira is crowding me in an instant, giving me a shove. "Oh my God, he's actually doing it. It's his turn tonight. Go!"

Now I'm absolutely baffled, but there's no time to argue, because Amira is pushing me and the woman with the headset is taking my arm and guiding me to the barricade a few feet in front of us, through an opening blocked by two security guards. One of the backup dancers is there on the stairs to grab me by the hand and lead me to Seojun's vacated chair at the front of the stage.

It's all happened so fast that it's not until I'm seated that I realize I'm looking out over what must be thirty- or forty-thousand people, cell phones and light sticks forming an ocean of fireflies. Lights beat down on me, though thankfully there's no spot, and it takes me the longest time to focus on Seojun where he's singing out on the catwalk, his head thrown back to reach an extended high note.

Suddenly, he swivels and stalks back toward me, his attention fixed on me. I freeze in the chair, suddenly feeling exposed, uncomfortable, as if he's drawn the gazes of every person in the stadium to me—which he probably has. Blood rushes to my face and it takes all my effort to not squirm, to keep my expression level and blank. He circles me as if I'm some sort of prey, fingertips drifting over the back of the chair inches from my shoulders. Only when he performs an impressive coupé turn, spinning five or six times on one foot with the other at his ankle, then drops to one knee in front of me, do I see the slight vacancy in his gaze.

It's an impressive effect, the idea that he's fully focused on me, but I can see him calculate the angle of his head so the camera catches him best, judge how this position on his knees in front of me must look to the audience, and oddly, the realization drains all the tension from me. As he slowly rises, I feel a smile coming to my face, and for a split second, he really does see me. Surprise flickers in his expression before he's whirling away again, behind me, his hand tracing up from my wrist to my shoulder and up my neck. Then his hand grips my jaw to tilt my head back in a gesture that is much gentler that it probably looks to the audience. Even though I'm inwardly shocked that he's touching me, I play along and let my head fall back against his torso as the crowd erupts into thunderous screaming.

I should be panicked or embarrassed, but for a split second, all I can feel is the exhilaration of having been on stage again, having been a tiny part of his re- markable, provocative performance. Seojun circles in front of me and holds out his hand, and I smile at him again as I rise.

And feel the downward rush of cold that indicates disaster.

Understanding registers on his face for the briefest moment before his smile returns, and he pulls me to his side to half-guide, half-drag me forward to the edge of the stage as if to show me off. Sparks are starting to interrupt my vision, my heart rate climbing with every passing second, but I manage to stumble forward with him and try not to look like his arm around my waist is the only thing keeping me upright. Then he's guiding me to the stairs on the opposite side of the stage from which I entered, covering his headset mic with one hand as he hisses to a staff member at the bottom, "Get her! Now!"

The man scrambles up and slides his hand around my waist just as Seojun lets go, then supports my weight all the way down the stairs. The minute I reach the ground, I try to pull away. "I'm okay," I say. "I just need to sit down. I'll be fine."

But I must not look all right, because I clock the horror on the staff member's face as he takes my arm and guides me behind a tall barrier at the side of the stage. I've barely passed beyond the meager conceal- ment before my vision goes white and I fall.

chapter three

March 2019, Lincoln Center, New York City

I stand on the edge of the stage just inside the second wing, nervousness twisting my stomach. There's normally some comfort in standing among my sea of fellow dancers, all dressed the same as swans or flowers or spirits, our identities hidden by our duplicated clothing and identical hairstyles. But tonight, for the first time, I'm alone. Once the heavy red curtain lifts to expose the stage to the house, all eyes will be on me, both critical and curious, waiting to make their own determination about my worth. Or perhaps, waiting for me to make a big mistake.

I push away those dark thoughts as I shake out my hands and arms, roll my neck, press the arches of my feet against the shanks of my pointe shoes one after the other, hoping that I haven't softened them too much for the one-act ballet. There's a fine line between breaking them down enough to mute their impact on the stage and leaving myself enough support to get through the difficult series of turns and balances at the end of the ballet—given that this is the first time I've performed this ballet for an audience, I won't know if I've gambled right until its over.

It doesn't help that an hour before curtain, someone had left the magazine in my shared dressing room, right beside my stage makeup. Only a half-page, little more than a blurb, but the subtext had been clear. Any time a dancer rises through the ranks of a world-class company like New York Theater Ballet as quickly as I have, there's going to be scrutiny. Discussions of whether I have the talent to back up my big roles. Speculation about whether company politics are supplanting another principal in order to give the lead in a brand-new ballet to a nearly unknown soloist.

They are, of course, far more circumspect than the speculations that go through my own company about how I got here, and I don't even have any way to dispel them.

Except I do.

Because once I go out on stage and show what I'm capable of, there will be no doubt.

It's that determination that singes my veins and burns away my nervousness. I have not slaved away in a rehearsal studio for two months, perfecting every step and motion and glance of this ballet, to let my nerves get the better of me now. They want to know how a virtually unknown twenty year old became Philip Barbier's muse, the reason he decided to choreograph a new contemporary ballet after five years of focusing only on dancing classical roles.

I'll show them why.

Across the stage in the opposite wing, I glimpse Philip talking to my partner, Michael, his hands pinwheeling animatedly in emphasis to his French-accented English. I'm not sure if he's giving last minute instructions or telling him to behave himself, but when Michael turns my direction as if he senses my attention, I can see the dislike plain on his face. Which means that he must be taking

Philip's lecture to heart, because Michael doesn't just dislike me, he hates me.

To be fair, when his partner of fifteen years took maternity leave, he didn't expect to be paired with an twenty-year-old soloist who never had a ballet set on her before. But I can't help the fact that Philip plucked me out of relative obscurity, citing the fact that I was just the ingenue that this passionate love story called for. And to be fair, at thirty-five, Michael is a seasoned professional; he does his job and he does his job well. He won't drop me and he won't hurt the performance because of his personal feelings. I simply don't have enough experience with acting not to feel the whiplash between the narrowed dislike he throws at me now and the adoration he'll show me on stage in just a moment.

Beyond the curtain, I can hear the orchestra finish their warm-up, and the butterflies strike again. I shake out my limbs once more, test my shoes, touch the pins that hold the top half of my hair away from my face while the rest spills down over my shoulders. And then the stage lights go down and the curtain begins to rise, just as the first strains of violins drift through the air.

I walk on stage in a stylized ballet walk, my head bowed, my hair falling around my face and my shoulders. This piece is mostly abstract, about feelings and emotions, though there's a very loose story at its center. I get caught up in the mournful strains of the strings as I step onto pointe in an arabesque, my back arched while my arms hang loosely by my sides. Then I'm slicing across the stage in a whirl of chiffon and red curls, spinning in precise turns that spiral into leaps with wild abandon. Michael enters from upstage right, his arrow-straight patterns of powerful movements and impossible jumps bringing him close to me, but ever out of reach. Until my spirals and his diagonals collide and we jolt to a stop in the precise center of the stage, just inches from each other. The orchestral score soars in contrast to this moment of stillness, both our chests heaving from exertion, and in that still, small moment, I almost believe the look of stunned wonder on his face as he stares down at me. He lifts his hand and trails a gentle finger down my shoulder to my hand.

But before he can clasp it, I'm backing away and our arcs are separating once more. We move in intersecting patterns, his straight lines contrasting with my curved ones until we catch up in the center once more. This time, I let him take my hand and I step into a yearning arabesque that seems as if it should be the first movement of a pas de deux, but before it can develop, a rush of dancers—six men and six women—sweep onto stage and catch us up into their motions.

It's a short ballet as far as ballets go—only twenty-six minutes—and Michael and I are whisked on and off stage by the dancers, meant to represent the vicissitudes of fate. Sometimes I'm in the center of a precise arrangement of female dancers, moving through choreography as formal and precise as a military formation; other times, I'm ducking and weaving through a half-dozen men, moving quickly enough that they can never catch more than a whisper of my passing, sometimes flirting and sometimes asserting my will. Michael is tempted through a series of seductive pairings, but always his focus is in the wings and not on his partner, as if he's looking for me. It's an impressive bit of technique, supporting the women so well without looking at them, and once more I'm reminded of why he's regarded as one of the top dancers of his era.

In the last part of the ballet, he and I join the other dozen on stage, his movements stiff and mine weary, pushed ever closer by the group choreography until suddenly, miraculously, the others melt away and it's just the two of us facing each other under the spotlight once more. We stand there, inches apart, but this time we just stare at the ground, neither of us moving. We are both broken down and weary, the tender moments of flirtation and excitement from the opening now lost in the experience of time. And then, the most subtle movement, just a twitch of his hand at his side has me lifting my face to his with the first twinge of hope.

The pas de deux that ensues is achingly beautiful, a bit of genius that rivals anything I've ever seen, and I let my body expand to feel every bit of music, every emotion that we convey through halting touches and frightened glances, even while a never-ending litany of technical data filters through the back of my mind. Present the heel here, don't over-arch the back, let him come to me instead of reaching for him, remember to breathe in the promenade. My attention is split between the physical sensations and the need to emote, and the last two minutes of the ballet fly by in a blink.

Until we form the last image—I pose stretched in a reaching arabesque, my standing leg thrust out in front of me with my weight dragging me back, only the counterbalance of Michael's deep stance and his grip on my hand keeping me upright. And then, a split second before the stage lights go down, he lets go.

chapter four

When I come to again, I'm lying flat on the ground, my head pillowed on something soft, light searing my retinas. I blink and try to turn my head away—only then do I realize a paramedic is leaning over me, checking my pupillary response.

Instantly, everything comes rushing back to me—having been drawn up on stage, how I almost collapsed in front of forty thousand people—and my heart rate jacks again. It's my worst nightmare come to life, and I wonder if I've just spoiled everything.

But no, the concert is still going on—I can hear the music, see flashes of the dancing on stage just at the edge of my vision—and it takes me a few seconds to realize the EMT is talking to me.

"I'm fine," I manage. "I have POTS. The heat and the excitement and the stage lights . . ."

He doesn't seem to register what I'm saying, so I try again. "Postural Orthostatic Tachycardia. Sometimes when I stand up, my heart rate spikes." I look down and see that there's a pulse oximeter clipped to my left finger. My oxygen sats are at 99%, predictably, but my heart rate is still 140. Good enough. I push myself up.

The EMT protests, but I shake my head. "I need to sit up and take my beta blocker. Can I have some water?"

He studies me, no doubt judging whether or not I know what I'm talking about, but finally he and a female EMT help me to my feet and guide me to a metal folding chair at the entrance of the tunnel that leads under the stage. The woman disappears and a few seconds later returns with a warm bottle of water. I dig in my purse for my pill bottle—showing the EMT the label before he asks—then shake a tablet out and swallow it down.

"I'd really rather you stay here where we can monitor you," the woman says, glancing at her partner.

I don't say that they don't have a choice, that I'm not in any condition to return to Amira on the floor and then blanch. Amira. She's probably wondering where I am right now. "How long was I out?"

"Ten, fifteen seconds, maybe," the man says. "Not long."

"Did anyone see?"

They both shake their heads. "Only the performers."

Great. Most of the audience members would kill to catch the eye of Helios, and I had to do it by nearly collapsing on stage. Not the kind of attention I really wanted tonight.

I dig in my pocket for my phone, thankful it didn't fall out, and check my messages. There's almost a dozen, starting giddy and turning worried.

AMIRA
That was amazing! OMG!
Where are you?
Trina, are you okay? What's
going on?
Come on, Trina, I'm worried

Quickly, I type out a message that explains everything.

TRINA

Syncope. EMT won't let me
leave yet.

Almost instantly, her reply comes in.

AMIRA
Stay right there. I'm coming.

My heart sinks. I didn't ruin the performance, but I am most definitely ruining the night for Amira.

TRINA

No, stay there and enjoy
yourself. I'm fine. Took my
meds. Besides, I can see the
stage from here. I'm closer
than you.

I add a tongue-sticking-out emoji, though it isn't going to fool anyone, least of all Amira.

AMIRA
Are you sure?

TRINA

Of course I'm sure. Have
fun. I'll be out when I can

But we both know I'm not going anywhere, and by the time the meds kick in and I start to feel better, the main show is over and the guys are coming out for their encore. Disappointment that I've missed the last third of the show, foiled by my own stupid body, sinks in, but I push the sensation away and instead focus on the memory of being on stage for Seojun's solo. I was mostly too surprised and overwhelmed to truly enjoy it, but in retrospect, it was kind of hot. I hope Amira got it on video.

And then it's all over and Amira is texting me.

AMIRA
I'm at the barricade.
Have someone tell them to
let me in.

I gesture to the EMT and tell him that I need my friend to come get me. He relays the message and a few minutes later, Amira is running toward me, her expression worried. She drops down beside me and grabs my hand. "My god, Trina, I'm so sorry. Are you okay?"

"Fine," I say helplessly, and it's as true as it ever gets. It's not as if my condition is truly dangerous—I've been to enough cardiologists to know that my biggest risk is falling and hurting myself on the way down. "I'm so sorry. I ruined everything for you."

"Of course you didn't! I'm just sorry you missed the show! But. . .whoa. Can you believe it? He had his hands all over you!"

It's a bit of an exaggeration, but I laugh anyway. "I know. My single claim to fame. Manhandled by a boy band member."

"Manhandled by an *idol*," she teases, but it's just a way to hide her worry. "I got the whole thing on video, by the way."

"I knew you would. You're an angel. I'm going to have to replay that about a million times tonight."

She laughs. "You and like six million other people. It's already on YouTube and Instagram." She pulls up her phone to show me the clip that's been uploaded, and holy hell, it already has almost fifty thousand views. How can a fan-provided clip go viral that quickly?

My heart sinks and my face goes cold, and for a second, I think I'm having another episode, but no, that's just good old dread. "Can you identify me?" Not that I'm famous enough for anyone to recognize, but AI is so good these days, it can tag just about anyone with a public profile. It's LA, so it wouldn't be the end of the world, but I still try to keep my public profile scrubbed of anything personal.

"I don't think so. The lighting kind of shadowed your face and he was in front of you a lot of the time anyway." She grins at me. "Good call putting your hair down though."

I reach up and touch my hair, out of its ponytail. I don't remember taking it down, but now I'm glad I did. Quickly, I grab a spare elastic from around my wrist and smooth it back from my face.

I glance at my watch and see that my heart rate has dropped several dozen points, a good sign that I can make it out of the building without incident. I signal to the EMTs that I'm going to leave, and they nod. The concert is over and their job is done anyway. But I barely make it out of the chair before the same woman who had pulled me from the audience strides over to us.

"Seojun would like to see you backstage if you have a minute?" It's phrased as a question, and I almost laugh, because I doubt anyone turns down that kind of offer.

Still, I turn to check with Amira, and she gives me her internally screaming face. I laugh, even though exhaustion is hitting me hard. I turn to the staff member. "Sure, thanks."

"Give him a couple of minutes and I'll be back for you," she says. "What's your name?"

"Uh, Katrina," I stammer.

It's more like twenty minutes by the time the woman returns to retrieve us, and my heart is fluttering in a way that I can't quite identify. Having a medical condition makes it surprisingly hard to distinguish between actual symptoms and just regular feelings. We follow her beneath the stage and then intersect with the tunnel I assume leads back to locker rooms and things—I actually have no idea how they repurpose a sports arena for concerts. It doesn't matter, though, because we're no more than twenty feet into the tunnel, where staff members mill around on their varied business, before I see him.

Seojun is staring blankly at the ground, still dressed in his white suit and twisting and untwisting the cap on a massive bottle of water. We're within a few feet of him before he registers our presence, and I can see the immediate shift between the exhausted performer to the polished idol. He extends a hand, his expression sincere and concerned.

"Katrina. Are you all right? I was so worried."

Damn, he's good. The use of my name gets me immediately, as if we know each other, and I instantly want to believe his concern is real. More likely, though, his management has pushed him to reach out in case I'm upset about having been dragged on stage.

I nod, my eyes searching his face—for what, I couldn't say. Off stage, he seems smaller. He's still tall, probably close to six feet, but in stillness I can see how slender he is, the mesh shirt between the open lapels of his jacket outlining every muscle in his torso. Beneath the heavy makeup airbrushing already flawless skin and accentuating his eyes, I also realize he's older than I thought, probably rounding thirty. Don't get me wrong, he's blindingly beautiful, but without the glow of his stage presence, I can recognize that he's just another performer trying to hold it together for his audience until he can go back to his hotel and collapse for the night.

I let out a long breath, my tension going with it. "I'm fine, thank you. It wasn't your fault. I have a medical condition, and it didn't occur to me that the stage lights might trigger it." An abbreviated explanation for sure, but he didn't need my medical history.

His shoulders slump forward, and with surprise, I realize he was truly concerned. "I'm so glad. You were great, by the way. Most people freeze. Thanks for playing along." A smile edges onto his face. "I might have . . . gotten a bit caught up in the moment."

He glances away, his ears turning pink with embarrassment, and now I want to know what he'd *actually* intended to do. Maybe that's why I'm here. Maybe he's worried because he touched me. But I can't think of how to respond, so I just smile blandly like a fool.

The moment stretches awkwardly, and he clears his throat. "Do you . . . want a picture or something before you go?"

"Oh!" I shake myself. "Sure, thanks. That would be great." I dig for my phone in my purse and hand it to Amira, then shrug off my jacket and move to his side. To my surprise, he puts his arm around me—or rather, mimes putting his arm around me. He's not actually touching me. Amira takes what must be ten or twenty or a hundred photos until I wave her off.

"Can we do one with Amira?"

Seojun smiles and nods. "Sure."

I expect him to hand the phone off to a staff member, but instead he takes it from Amira's hand and flips the screen to selfie mode. We crowd together in the screen, and he tilts his head and holds up two fingers in a sideways V, then takes what must be another twenty photos of the three of us cheesing it up. He hands the phone back to me, holding my eye.

"I'm glad you're okay. Thanks for coming backstage."

"Thanks for . . . the great concert. And the photos."

He steps back and gives us both a slight bow; it strikes me as automatic. "Nice to meet you, Katrina, Amira." And then he's gone, striding down the tunnel and disappearing around the corner.

Amira turns to me, her face frozen in a silent scream, and then starts giggling. "Oh my God, we just met Seojun."

I laugh, but now that it's over, I'm too tired to feel much of anything. "Yes. Yes we did. And got about a hundred photos with him, if I estimate correctly."

"You have to send me all the selfies." Amira links my arm with hers as our staff escort begins to usher us back out onto the field. No doubt to be sure we actually leave.

"Done. Is your brother picking us up?"

"Yep, he's on his way."

Amira would never say as much, but she conceived the rideshare/pickup plan so that I wouldn't have to walk to the back-forty parking lot. Maybe she didn't anticipate an episode, but she always thinks ahead for me. I'm struck by a rush of love for my best friend, and I squeeze her arm to my side.

"I love you, babe. I'm not sure what I would do without you."

"You wouldn't be meeting hot K-pop idols, that's for sure." She grins at me, and I know this is just a way to lighten the mood, to take the emphasis off of what actually happened to make that meeting occur. "So what was it like, being up there on stage with him?"

"It was . . . fun."

"Just fun?"

"Okay," I relent. "It was kind of amazing. The view out onto the audience . . . there's nothing like it."

It's the truth, but I'm glad that Amira is too enveloped in concert adrenaline to pick up on what I'm not saying. There really *isn't* anything like it.

I've spent the last six years trying to forget what it felt like to stand on stage, to convince myself that I don't need it, that I don't want it, that I don't miss it.

And it took all of three minutes to bring all my convictions crashing down.

chapter five

Amira's twenty-year-old brother, Tommy, shows up about ten minutes after we reach the exit of the arena, and we pile into his 1988 BMW coupe with groans. Even though I'm the first stop, I squeeze into the cramped backseat and lean my head against the headrest. I'd feel bad about dragging him from his dorm at UCLA on a Monday night, except three minutes after we leave the parking lot, he sheepishly admits that he's headed to a party in Van Nuys after he drops us off. We're more or less on his way.

Tommy couldn't care less about a Korean boy band, but Amira rattles on about the concert all the way back to the valley, I suspect simply to make him turn down the heavy metal blasting from the car's mediocre speakers. Weariness overtakes me, even though my heart rate still hasn't returned to resting, and I turn my head away from the window and close my eyes. What feels like moments later, Amira is shaking me awake, leaning over the folded front seat.

"Hey, babe, we're at your place. You need help up to your apartment?"

I yawn and stretch, instinctively taking stock of how I feel, and shake my head. I'm tired, but the beta blocker did its job. Now all I need is rest. Slowly, I climb out of the car, and Amira returns her seat to its original position.

"Call me in the morning if you don't feel up to coming in. I'll cancel your sessions. It's a light day anyway."

"I will," I say, hiking my purse over my shoulder. "Thanks again."

Amira winks at me. "Text me those photos of the three of us together before you crash out, will you? People pay a fortune just to high-five an idol, let alone take a hundred and ninety photos with one."

I laugh and nod because it's not all the far from the truth. I love that Amira is so unashamed of her enthusiasms. Turning thirty this year has done nothing to dampen her zest for life, and I wish I had half of her courage. Of course, I can admit that it's easier to be courageous when you have a trust fund backing your decisions; failure doesn't mean the same thing for her as it does for me.

I make it up to my second floor apartment without incident and text Amira.

TRINA
Here safely.

She doesn't even try to pretend that she wasn't waiting for it, because she replies immediately.

AMIRA
Okay love you good night.

Misha meets me at the door, meowing insistently as if he didn't have plenty of food left in his bowl. I take off my boots and then move to the dish, shaking it so the bottom is covered; he immediately digs in. Cats. It feels like too much trouble to go back to hang my purse on the hook, so I leave it on the kitchen counter and stagger into my bedroom. After I've had an episode, I'm running on low-power mode with minimum energy, so I decide that brushing my teeth is more important than washing my face or combing my hair. Then I stumble back into my bedroom and fall onto my bed fully clothed.

Except while my body feels like it's been through the wringer, my mind is now fully awake. I prop my feet up on pillows to help get blood back to my heart and brain and my heart rate back to resting. And then I open my photo app and text the best of the selfies to Amira.

I linger over the rest. Amira is a genius at cell phone photos. Both Seojun and I look fantastic, and the angle she's taken it at makes it look like he has his arm around me. Only I know that my smile is about as false as his probably is; we were both playing a role to get through the night. Still, I find myself zooming in to convince myself that he isn't as perfect as I'd initially registered. And while there is definitely some excellent makeup going on there . . . nope. He really is that good-looking.

Amira's response comes through.

AMIRA
Thanks. Are you obsessing
over the photos?

TRINA
Of course not.
I'm obsessing over NOT seeking
out every instance of the video.

> AMIRA
> I'm not sure how to tell you
> this, but that's going to be
> difficult. You're already a
> meme.

And then an image comes through. It's a still from the final pose of the performance. My back is arching away from the chair, my head tilted back against Seojun, and the angle makes it look like he has his hand around my throat.

Shit, that's a lot sexier than I thought when it was happening. No wonder the crowd went wild. Once more, I'm impressed by the level of craft and professionalism inherent in the stage performance. I'm also completely helpless against the urge to watch the original.

It takes exactly twenty seconds to figure out the right searches and hashtags to bring up more than a dozen fan-uploaded videos of the performance. I select the one that looks like it's closest to the stage and learn that the song was called "Burn." I take a second to browse the comments and find out that it's been rumored to exist—Seojun once sang a few bars from it on a live stream—but never has it been performed or released as a single. I also find the lyrics helpfully translated in comments by a bilingual fan.

Below it, users duke it out in comments about the meaning of the song—whether it's about obsessive love, wanting anything that's not good for you, or purposely returning to the same mistakes over and over again, despite your best intentions. I can't deny it's good songwriting if it stirs this kind of passion in a mere three hours after its first performance.

And now I know I'm just stalling because I'm afraid to see the video. I take a deep breath and press play.

The first half of the song is just as good as I remember, maybe even more so because my eyes aren't solely fixed on Seojun and I can appreciate the very definite nods to the musicals *Cabaret* and *Chicago* in the staging and choreography. And then my heart rises into my throat as I glimpse myself being led onto the stage and seated in the vacant chair.

I can exhale a few moments later, though, because it's clear that the stage lighting is in my favor: between my hair hanging down and the angle of the lights, my face is mostly in shadow or I'm being blocked by Seojun. And by the time he's circled around behind me, my head is already tilted back, my features obscured.

But damn. . .there's no question that's a sexy moment. And because I'd decided to play along, my body language makes it look like I really have just been seduced on stage.

I click off the video and toss my phone away on the bed next to me, feeling suddenly vulnerable, as if I was somehow taken advantage of. But that's completely ridiculous. I was caught up in the moment, I decided to play along, and the result was. . .more than he'd probably hoped it would be. From what I'm learning about the Helios fandom—the *Seojun* fandom—it would have gone viral either way, but at least if I'm going to be a meme, I look absolutely incredible.

My phone rings a moment later, and hesitantly, I reach for it. Amira. I pick up. "Hey."

"Are you freaking out?"

"No." I take a breath and then admit, "A little. I didn't think it would be so. . . ."

"I know. It really is. But you look amazing even if you can't see your face. People are saying it was planned."

"I think I'm going to go to bed now. I don't have the energy for this tonight." Or ever.

"Don't obsess, Trina. Just appreciate the fact that you basically helped create one of the most iconic K-pop performances in history."

That feels like overstating things by a lot, but when Amira gets like this, there's no convincing her otherwise. I promise to call her first thing in the morning with a status report and finally summon the energy to drag off my jeans. It's definitely too much work to put on pajamas, so I slide beneath the sheets in my boy shorts and the bra top and click off my bedside lamp.

Where I lay there, the siren song of my phone calling me.

I feel almost as guilty as I would if I were looking up deep-fake porn when I type *Seojun Helios* into my browser and bring up an ungodly number of results. I click on the first one, which is some sort of K-pop repository, and in less than three minutes, pick up the man's entire bio. His real name, it turns out, is Simon Yang. He is thirty years old. He was born in Ventura, California, where he lived until he was accepted as a trainee with Titan Entertainment and moved to Seoul at fifteen. He debuted with his first group, Hyperion, as a main dancer when he was eighteen and stayed with them until they disbanded nine years later.

He speaks English, Korean, Japanese, and a little Tagalog. His blood type is O, his MBTI type is ISFJ, and he has four piercings, one in his right ear and three in his left. He is best known for his dancing, his distinctive baritone voice, and his abs, which he has the habit of showing off at least once a show. The site has helpfully provided a gif as proof.

"Oh my god," I murmur. "What am I doing?" I realize this is a public site, but after having met the man, it feels like reading a private investigator's dossier. I click away

from the site, but the other results are either embarrassingly giggly or list known facts with clinical detach-
ment, complete with sources in the footnotes.

At least there's no talk of his underwear preferences.

No, scratch that. Seojun—Simon, if you will—
prefers boxers. The reason I know this is because there
is a site dedicated to analyzing idol clothing and linking
to the original retailers.

I screenshot the page and text it to Amira.

> TRINA
> Why why why?

> AMIRA
> How is this going to sleep?
> You fell down the fandom
> clickhole, didn't you?

I don't dignify that with an answer, even though it is
absolutely true, then click over to YouTube to search
for dance videos. After all, ever since I saw him perform
that perfect turn on stage—in boots, no less—I have
been utterly convinced that he was a ballet dancer at
some point. We know our own kind. I lose track of the
number of hip-hop and jazz-pop videos I peruse before
I get to a John Legend contemporary dance cover that
his company has posted on his behalf.

He's . . . amazing. Fluid, graceful, flexible. Great
articulation of every part of his body, but I'm especially
taken with how graceful his hands are. It's one of the
things that always tells me if someone has had classical
training. I tap the share button and send it to Amira.

> TRINA
> Wow.

She just sends back a smiley face. She knows I'm hooked now.

I'm about to close my phone when an Instagram message notification pops up. I think it's from Amira for a second, but the handle is @*SJY_1995_* which I don't recognize. Curious, I tap it.

> SJY_1995_
> Hey, it's Simon. I'm sorry if
> this is weird, but I wanted
> to check on you.

My whole body goes cold again, and I check my watch to make sure my heart rate hasn't suddenly jacked itself back up. Every bit of me goes on alert.

> KATBA_91602
> Who is this really? How did
> you find me?

This account is private and separate from my studio account, so there's no way anyone should have been able to track me down so quickly, even from the video. There's nothing identifying to match.

> SJY_1995_
> Amira tagged you in our
> photo from the concert.

With trembling fingers, I flip over to my notifications, and sure enough, she's tagged both me and the official Helios account in one of the photos I sent her. Okay, so clearly someone has made the connection between the redhead on stage and the one in the photo and thought they'd scam me.

KATBA_91602
Don't believe you.

SJY_1995_
You smiled at me on stage
after my turns.

That gives me pause, but there's a good chance that
someone had a better angle of the stage than the videos,
so that doesn't prove anything. This is almost certainly
a scammer, so I might as well mess with him.

KATBA_91602
What color are my eyes?

SJY_1995_
Bad question.
1) I wasn't paying attention
to your eyes on stage.
2) Anyone can see from the
photo that they're blue.

Yeah, that was dumb.

KATBA_91602
You're going to have to do
better than that, then.

SJY_1995_
Okay, give me a few
minutes.

But minutes tick by with no reply, and I'm satisfied
that I've put an end to this. How stupid would I have to
be to think that an idol would go to the effort of

contacting me after a stage performance that he probably spared no more than five minutes thought on afterward? I roll my eyes and check to make sure my alarm is still set for 7:00 a.m., then stretch to put my phone on the wireless charger by the bed.

The screen lights up, and this time the notification is from the official Helios account. I click on it with a trembling finger.

> TITAN_HELIOS
> Seojun wanted me to
> confirm that he's
> communicating from a
> private account.

Holy shit.

I don't consider myself the type to get starstruck. I work with actors, athletes, and celebrities of all types all the time. But they don't contact me on their personal accounts for personal reasons. This is just . . . *weird*.

The SJY_1995_ account comes through again almost immediately.

> SJY_1995_
> Did my manager message
> you?

His manager.

> KATBA_91602
> Tell me you didn't actually
> have to call Korea to make
> that happen.

SJY_1995_
No. Worse. I had to wake
him up in the room next to
me.

A disbelieving laugh slips out of me. This is insane.

SJY_1995_
So, back to my initial
question. Are you okay? You
didn't look okay backstage
and I . . . feel responsible.

I take a long moment to consider my answer, even
though I feel like I'm having an out-of-body experience.

KATBA_91602
I'm fine. I mean that.
I'm just a little out of it after
I have an episode. It had
nothing to do with you.

A long pause has me glued to my screen.

SJY_1995_
Okay, good. I feel bad. That
last part wasn't scripted,
but I thought . . . you smiled
at me and it felt a bit like
you understood what was
going on.
That sounds stupid. Sorry.
You know what I mean.

Is this guy actually. . .insecure? Or shy? Wild, considering what I just saw, but then again, some of the most commanding performers I know can barely hold a conversation with a stranger. Or is he just making sure that I'm not going to sue him because he gave me heart palpitations or something?

I ponder my reply for a minute now that I realize there's a chance someone from his management might see it. Finally, I settle on a response.

KATBA_91602
I was just acting, too. I used
to be a performer. No harm,
no foul.

I send it before I can rethink and then wince. No harm, no foul? I'm being contacted by literally the best-looking man I've ever seen in real life—and trust me, I've seen a lot of good-looking guys working in the entertainment industry in New York and LA—and my response is *no harm, no foul?* Not something flirty like, *You were very convincing* or *Does this mean we have to call off the engagement?* No, not that last one. Amira has told me about stalker fans—*sasaeng*, they're called—and he'd probably block me in a second.

SJY_1995_
Okay. I hope you feel better
soon. Thanks for playing
along. You were great.

It feels like the end of the conversation, but somehow I can't resist the impulse to reply, to have the last word. Or maybe the chance to keep the conversation going.

KATBA_91602
You too. Merde for your
show in Vegas.

I wait longer than I'd like to admit for an answer, but it never comes.

That's that, I guess. The whole thing is so bizarre, it feels like a fever dream. I should really screenshot this conversation for Amira, but I can't bring myself to do it. I put my phone on the charger and roll over, but it still takes far longer than I'd like to admit for sleep to come.

chapter six

March 2019, Lincoln Center

As much as I would love to bask in the success of my principal debut and remember what it felt like to soak in the applause of four thousand people, I have to perform in two other ballets tonight. It's a one-act bill featuring original works choreographed by members of the New York Theater Ballet, and I've got a demi-soloist role next, followed by a corps part that requires me to be on stage for the majority of the final ballet but do very little actual dancing. As soon as the heavy curtain goes down on the apron, I'm tearing off to stage left and heading for the dressing room where I have less than five minutes to get my hair up into a proper ballet bun. Fortunately, my current makeup will do and I only need to strip off this costume in favor of a nude leotard. I will, however, need to switch to another pair of shoes that I've painstakingly reinforced for this ballet with layers of floor wax and Jet glue in order to make it through the seemingly endless series of turns and hops on pointe. All of course, on my right foot, which is already twinging ominously at the top of my instep.

I've already stripped off the chiffon, toweled myself off, and squeezed into the nude leotard and a faux-corset when a knock comes at the door. All of my dressing roommates have already headed for the stage, but I have another two minutes. I squeeze my throbbing foot into my pointe shoe and quickly tie the ribbons. "Come in."

I'm shocked to find Michael standing there, shirtless but still in his tights, holding a bouquet of flowers. I blink at him before grabbing my left shoe. "Yes?"

"I just wanted to say. . .you were. . .impressive tonight."

I freeze. An actual compliment was the last thing I expected from him, but I don't have time to process it right now. I quickly tie my ribbons and hop to my feet, testing the feel of the shoes. All fine. With forty-five seconds to spare. "Thank you," I say finally. "You too."

He holds up the flowers. "These are for you."

I waste two seconds with shock before I manage a small smile and take the flowers from him, then set them aside. "Thank you." Even though it's strictly practical and I'm not trying to make a point, I take the smallest amount of pleasure in his surprise when I push past him out the door into the hallway. I clatter through the cement-brick corridors and then down a flight of stairs and across to the stage, where I can hear the first strains of music from the orchestra.

I make it through my solo without a problem, but despite the fact that my time on stage is only forty-eight seconds, my foot is throbbing by the time I exit again. I hover in the wings for the next twenty minutes while I wait for the curtain call, take my bow—soloists get their individual moment in the spotlight, otherwise I would have already gone to change—and then half-limp, half-run back to the dressing room to change out of this costume and climb into a proper romantic tutu. This time the dressing room is crowded with the five other women I share it with—all soloists, but I'm the only one donning the corps costume. I feel suddenly self-conscious when the conversation mutes at my entrance.

Janine, the most senior dancer in the group—and one of the most senior dancers in the company at thirty-four—is the one who breaks first. She gives me a quick hug. "You were amazing," she whispers in my ear. "Don't let those fuckers get you down. They couldn't have pulled that off at your age."

I bark out a laugh and grin at her as I pull away. "Thanks, Janine."

She winks at me and motions for me to turn around, unhooking me from the corset and taking it back to the rack while I strip out of the leotard and climb into the white bodice and skirt for my final costume change. I wipe off my pink lipstick, apply red to match the other girls and quickly set everything with one more round of powder before I'm back out the door and headed for the stage again.

Fortunately, I wasn't joking about doing nothing but standing around in the last ballet. It's a typical white ballet, a modern ghost story, and there's a lot of running around in formation and posing in arabesque, fortunately mostly on my left side. The little bit of dancing I have to do is simple bourées and some graceful hand-waving. When we finally take our bow, I'm grateful to limp off stage and back to the dressing room, where I can put my feet up.

It's already cleared out, including Janine, and I let out a huge sigh of relief as I remove my costume and collapse into a chair, topless in my tights and pointe shoes. I throw my right foot up on the dressing table, grab my water bottle, and tip my head back against the chair.

And then I let myself grin.

It wouldn't have done to pat myself on the back before I danced my last role, but now that I'm free, I let the elation wash over me. Tonight was incredible. Was I perfect? Absolutely not. There were definitely a couple of moments where Michael saved me from disaster with his expert partnering, hands on my waist correcting my placement, adapting to the occasional count too early or too late. But considering that this was a world-premiere and choreography had continued to change up until a week ago, it couldn't have gone any more smoothly.

I finally lever myself off the chair and untie my ribbons, grimacing at the swelling in my right foot, then take off my tights and reach for a tank and panties. Only after I massage away my stage makeup with cold cream and brush my hair out do I throw on jeans, a scarf, and my leather jacket and grab my bag.

I haven't made more than two steps outside into the cold, dark night before a blur of motion slams into me.

"You were incredible!" a feminine voice squeals.

I laugh and disentangle myself. My younger sister, Maddie—a member of NYTB's studio company—grins as she detaches from me and steps back.

"I told you you didn't have to wait," I scold her half-heartedly.

But she's beaming. She waves the program in front of my face. "And miss being the first person to con-gratulate you on your debut in a *world-premiere original ballet*? Not a chance. Kat . . . you were . . . ." She breathes out and claps a hand to her heart. Of the two of us, she's always been the more emotional, the more theatrical. She's the one who lives and breathes ballet. She's the reason I'm here, in fact. But I just wait for her to find the words until she gives up and laughs. "I cried."

"Well, of course you did, because you're a big

sentimental idiot." I sling an arm around her shoulder and squish her close.

"I was thinking we should go celebrate. I have some—"

"Kat!"

I drop my arm and turn to find Philip striding from the stage door, beaming at me. He's dressed in a dark suit and an open-throated white shirt, elegant, graceful, and handsome, and his eyes are fixed on me and me only. He sweeps me up into a giant hug, lifting me off the ground. "You were astounding."

My heart picks up a rapid rhythm, but even so, I'm not prepared for him to take my face in his hands and plant an enthusiastic kiss on my lips. Heat rushes to my face and I see Maddie's shocked expression from the corner of my eye. Even so, I could probably explain this away as Gallic enthusiasm if it weren't for the way his hands grip my hips or the possessive glint in his eye.

"Let's go open a bottle of wine and celebrate the beginning of a long and fruitful partnership together."

I'm too stunned to know what to do. As far as I knew, we were keeping our relationship under wraps. Yes, there have been plenty of rumors, but rumors are different than openly flaunting the fact that I'm dating a man who is both a principal dancer at my company and the choreographer who plucked me out of relative obscurity. I clear my throat and throw an apologetic look at Maddie. "I'll meet you at home a little later, okay? I want to celebrate with you. I do."

But before she can reply, Philip is gripping my hand and propelling me across the square. I dare a look back at my sister. I can't tell whether the look on her face is stricken or disappointed, and I don't have time to decipher it or feel guilty before she disappears from view.

I have plenty of time, however, to feel guilty the

next morning. I roll over in Philip's dark gray sheets and reach for him, only to find the space next to me both empty and cold—he's been up for a while. Slowly, I push myself to a sitting position, holding the sheet against my chest and call out, "Philip?"

No answer. Gingerly, I push away the sheets and swing my legs over the side of the bed, feeling the room spin around me. Too much wine, undoubtedly—never mind the fact that I'm still a year away from legal drinking age, I already know I can't hold my alcohol. I blink away the grogginess long enough to focus on the throbbing in my right foot. It's swollen—I told Philip I needed an ice bath, but he was too high on excitement from the successful debut to listen to much I was telling him. It's only when I begin to push myself to a standing position that I see the beginnings of a purple bruise on my inner thigh.

I swallow hard and avert my eyes from it, instead wrapping the sheet around myself as I stumble from the bedroom. My clothes are undoubtedly somewhere in this apartment, but they're not here. Nor, it seems, is Philip.

On the kitchen counter, next to an espresso machine, is a note in his beautiful script. *Early breakfast meeting. Stay as long as you like. Just press start. XOXO Philip*

The knot in my stomach eases as I see the cup sitting in the bottom of the machine. I press *start* as instructed and it whirs and hisses to life before dispensing a perfect ristretto shot into the little cup. I dilute it with hot water to make an Americano and then take it with me back to the bedroom, where I take my time in his renovated shower, washing my long hair with his expensive French shampoo and conditioner. I try to ignore the evidence of other bruises—my memory is too foggy from wine to know how they got there—and overlook all the other places that feel tender this morning as well. When I'm clean and my hair is braided neatly away from my face, I finally locate my tank top near the sofa, my jeans by the bedroom door, and my panties peeking from underneath the bed.

I half-doze on the subway ride home and drag myself the eleven blocks to the apartment I share with Maddie. Of course we can't afford to live in Manhattan like Philip, but at least with our parents still subsidizing Maddie's rent, we have a decent little two-bedroom in Jackson Heights. It's wildly inconvenient in terms of commute, but our parents insisted that we weren't going to live in Hell's Kitchen or Washington Heights as long as they were helping to pay the rent, so Brooklyn it is. By the time I get up the stairs to our third-floor unit, my foot is throbbing again and all I can think of is sitting down.

Maddie is curled up on the sofa with a book and a cup of coffee, her kitten, Misha, happily kneading the fuzzy blanket over her lap.

"Hey," I say cautiously as I close the door behind me and drop my bag in the entry.

She doesn't even look up from her book.

"Maddie, I'm sorry. I didn't know about Philip's plans—"

"Well that makes us even," she says, still not looking at me. "Because I didn't know about Philip."

I bite my lip and toe the gap between the boards in our oak floors. "I'm sorry I didn't tell you. I thought you might . . . overreact."

"Overreact? Why would I do that? He's what? Forty?"

I snort. "Hardly. He's thirty-three."

Maddie shoots me a look that says she doesn't think it's much of a distinction, and to be fair, she's sort of right.

"Okay, I know it's unconventional. But . . . I like him. He likes me. He says I'm his muse." I'm not explaining this right, and I can tell because she throws off the blanket and tucks the cat under her arm like a football.

"I've got Pilates this morning before I go to the theater. I'm performing this afternoon, in case you forgot." And without waiting for an answer, she stalks out of the room to her bedroom.

I sigh. I screwed this one up royally. I don't know if she's more pissed about the fact I blew her off last night, that I didn't tell her I had a boyfriend, or who that boyfriend is. Regardless of the answer, I know my sister well enough to know she's not going to listen when she's angry; I'll wait by the stage exit after her performance today and beg her forgiveness. Or bribe her with sunflowers and chocolate, two of her favorites.

In the meantime, however, I grab the red plastic bucket we keep in this kitchen, fill it with ice and then water, and lug it carefully back to my room. I have to get this swelling under control before class tomorrow. I'm sure that Maddie wasn't the only one who saw Philip's blatant PDA after last night's performance, and now that it's out in the open, I have no choice but to continue to prove myself. To work harder than everyone else, to work through the pain. To show that I belong at NYTB.

The ice bath is as miserable as it sounds, but I can feel the swelling begin to subside in minutes. It's about the only thing I can feel as my feet go completely numb. While I'm perched there on the end of my bed, I open my phone and text Philip. *Hope the meeting went well. You have time for a quick lunch before the show?*

I pretend that I'm not waiting for a response, but I still check my phone every five minutes as if I could miss the obnoxious chime that indicates a text message.

Finally, a little before noon, the check mark next to the message turns blue, indicating he's read it.

I wait for as long as I can before going to the theater, but when I leave the building in my sundress and comfy boots and leather jacket, he still hasn't replied.

chapter seven

When the alarm on my watch vibrates me awake at 7 a.m.
I feel like I've been hit by a truck. The pain in my chest
is gone, but my body still aches and a heavy sense of
exhaustion lies over me, making movement difficult. The
fact that I barely got five hours of sleep by the time I
managed to drift off isn't helping matters either.

But when I do my regular blood pressure and heart
rate check, things aren't all that far off from normal, so
I can't justify lying in bed all day. I reach for my phone,
intending to text Amira, but somehow my fingers tap my
Instagram account instead and check messages, almost
like they've been waiting to do that since I opened my
eyes.

My last message to Simon stands unread.

I shake my head at my own stupidity. Of course it
does. His response was obviously a farewell; as far as he's
concerned, he's fulfilled his duty and there's nothing left
to say. I close out of the app and open text messaging
instead, firing off a quick *See you at the studio at 8* message
to Amira. Whether or not she shows up is another thing;
I only book sessions in the morning because we rent out

the space to another teacher in the afternoon. Consequently, she usually works from home on Tuesdays and Thursdays.

Though knowing her, she'll be there to keep an eye on me, just in case I need her.

I'm about to close the app when I glimpse the message from Jackson, left on read. I consider for a moment, then quickly type out a reply.

TRINA

Sorry about that. Amira and
I were at a concert. I'm free
tonight or Friday.

By the time I get out of the shower, there's a reply.

JACKSON
No prob, hope you had fun!
Either works for me but I'd
rather not wait to see you.
Pick you up at 7?

Ugh. He's so nice, it makes me feel guilty that I purposely ignored him last night. I waste no time tapping out my reply.

TRINA

Sounds great! See you then!

I finish my morning routine more slowly than usual, feed the cat, and then remember I left my bag at the studio last night. Good enough. Everything I need is already there. I slip on my outside trainers and then very carefully walk down the stairs.

I'm winded and aching by the time I reach the studio,

which Amira senses the minute she sees me push through the door twenty minutes late.

"What are you doing here?" she demands immediately. "You should be in bed."

"I'll teach from a stool today," I say, waving her off. "I don't feel bad enough to cancel clients."

"This is exactly why we schedule your Tuesdays light with your understanding long-timers, Trina."

"So I can bail when I've stayed up too late in a K-pop clickhole?" I shoot back.

Amira just rolls her eyes, sensing that I'm going to be difficult about this one. I can't help it. Dancers don't call in sick because they had a bad night or because they don't feel 100 percent. We drag our butts into the studio, put one hand on the barre, and start working. Just because my body doesn't remember those rules doesn't mean that I have suddenly become a completely different person in the last five years.

The fact that Amira and I met after my career was over means that she never really saw that part of me. Doesn't know that I performed with a stress fracture in my left foot for six weeks because I was afraid that Philip would never cast me again. Has no idea that I once danced the Nutcracker with pneumonia, running off stage to throw up in a trash can, take a hit on my inhaler, and then go right back on again.

I don't need to ask her to know she would not approve.

I also know she doesn't approve when I climb on the Reformer as usual, even though I do a much-abbreviated version of my workout and stick to exercises that can be done flat on my back. Even then, my watch beeps at me angrily and I have to cut it short.

Fortunately, I have only two clients this morning and they're two of my favorites, dancers I've been training since we opened the studio nearly three years ago. Maria is a retired Russian ballerina who now runs the pre-professional program at one of the biggest ballet schools in LA—if there is a client I vibe with, it's her. She's no-nonsense and focused with both a wicked sense of humor and a very balanced outlook on our former careers. She also has some mind-blowing stories of dancing in Russia, each of them more insane or unbelievable than the last. Today's story involves an attack on a choreographer by a dancer's boyfriend after the aforementioned choreographer implied he would only cast her if she provided certain sexual favors. As if that wasn't bad enough, the guy tried to frame one of his girlfriend's rivals for the attack.

This is the stuff of legends. While I've seen my share of destructive behavior, the reports of ground glass in pointe shoes and backbiting in American ballet is largely overblown. We had—have—plenty of problems, but generally not on the scale of felony assault.

My second client is Jeremy Kane, better known by his stage name, Hera Kane. He takes a single look at me perched on my rolling stool and whistles. "Good night or bad night?"

"Bad night," I say.

He shakes his head. "If you're going to come in rough, you have to make sure it's worth it."

I laugh. "It was worth it, even though it was a bad night. We went to the Helios concert downtown."

"I was there!" And then he gasps, his mouth dropping open. "It was you! On stage!"

I shush him and look around wildly even though we're literally the only two people in the room. "You can't tell anyone."

He gives me the side eye and another whistle. "Girl, you were on fire. That was the sexiest thing I've ever seen."

"It was all of thirty seconds!"

"And there was not a single person in the entire stadium who wouldn't give their right arm to be you for that thirty seconds. Including me."

As he grins at me, I wonder what he would say if I told him that Simon—Seojun—had actually messaged me last night. Of course, I keep that to myself; I haven't even told Amira, and I don't know why. The whole thing is just so surreal, if I didn't have the record of it in my inbox, I'd think maybe I dreamed it.

Jeremy is a dedicated, long-time practitioner, so we work through the super-advanced exercises on my extended-length reformer to accommodate his six-foot-two frame. He takes cues like the dancer he is, making it easy on me—I don't even have to touch him or stand to correct him. Still, by the time I say goodbye and flip the lock on the door, I feel as wrung out as an old washcloth.

Amira is right there to stare me down. "You're going home to lie down, right?"

I glance at my watch. "Yeah, I have some time. Jackson is picking me up at seven for dinner."

I can tell by the twist of her mouth she's not pleased by that answer, but I don't know whether it's because of Jackson or because she thinks I need to rest. In any case, she says nothing, just picks up her purse. "Come on. I'll drive you home."

It's only three and a half blocks, but right now, even that seems beyond me, so I nod. I follow her out back to the alley parking and climb into her Audi wagon, which is already about three hundred degrees inside even though it's not yet one o'clock. Valley summers are no joke, and the heat only makes me feel worse. When she drops me off outside my apartment building, she gives me a stern look. "Don't kill yourself."

I flinch, even though I know what she means. "I'll do my best. Thanks, babe."

Amira winks at me and watches as I climb out carefully and close the door, but I can see the concern etched in her face. I wish I could erase it—it's not like my situation is going to change anytime soon and she's taking on far too much responsibility for me. I know she loves me—just like I love her—but most days I feel like it's an unequal trade for her.

I let myself in, and Misha must sense that I'm not feeling well, because he immediately pads to my side and winds his way around my legs. I stop in the kitchen to fill my giant hospital cup with ice water so I don't have to get up again—I'm going to have to pee before I have to go get a refill—and on second thought grab a protein bar from the cabinet. Then I climb into bed still dressed in my workout clothes and wait while Misha gets settled, curling up next to me.

I almost don't realize I'm doing it until my phone is out and I'm checking my Instagram messages, which of course has shown no change since the last time I checked this morning. It was stupid to expect otherwise.

I sigh and throw it aside, then close my eyes.

I doze on and off for the rest of the afternoon, but I feel only marginally better by the time my alarm goes off, alerting me that I need to get ready for my date. Even the word *I* feels unfamiliar in this context. Is that what Jackson and I are doing? Dating? For lack of a better word, I suppose it's the truth, but this feels much more like the textbook definition of *hanging out*. We see each other when we have time, we make out a little, he hangs in there because we have fun and he hopes he might get laid at some point.

Aside from the fact I'm still not sure if I'm into him enough to consider sleeping with him, I haven't told him how my condition may or may not affect that whole situation. The discussion on the Reddit POTS sub has me terrified of what might happen if I try. At best, it might be bad and . . . unsuccessful . . . for me. At worse, I could have another episode and permanently traumatize the guy. I haven't been willing to entertain either possibility. I've never been a casual sex kind of girl, and when it comes down to it, I don't know if I want Jackson to be my first test run in this aspect of my new, chronically ill life.

It's all a moot point anyway, because I don't even have enough energy to shower, let alone get freaky. I sit on the edge of the bathtub while I French braid my long hair and do my makeup, then slowly walk to my closet and select a flowered sundress from the overstuffed interior. Guys think we wear dresses for them, but in truth, it's because it's literally the least amount of effort we can put into a clothing choice. And thanks to the built-in cups, I don't even have to wear a bra—not that it's usually an issue considering the ballet gods blessed me with a small chest.

I'm about to select flat sandals to go with it, but for some reason I reach for the black Chelseas and then grab the washed leather jacket I'd planned on wearing to the concert last night. The effect is tougher than I usually go for, but I like it. It feels like armor. I don't think about what exactly I'm protecting myself from, considering Jackson is not what I would call particularly aggressive.

When my doorbell rings at 7 o'clock on the dot, I'm already waiting. I open the door to him with a smile and stand aside for him to enter.

He's a big guy, over six feet with a stocky build that's at odds with his generally mild-mannered look. Dark hair, brown eyes, typical California corporate-guy wardrobe—tonight he's wearing a pair of dark wash jeans with a navy button down shirt and good shoes. He looks me over with a smile and then bends to kiss my cheek.

"You look nice," he says. "Are you ready to go?"

I grab my purse from the hook on the wall and gesture for him to precede me out the door, then lock up behind myself. We're nearly to his car—a Lexus SUV—at the curb when he turns to me and asks, "Sushi all right?"

"Sushi sounds great," I say automatically, mostly because I don't care. At least sushi is an easy date option—I can just order a single roll and there's no massive plate of leftovers to give away the fact that half the time I have no appetite. There's nothing worse than going out to a really expensive steakhouse and then looking rude because I can't stomach more than a few bites.

We're quiet in the car until he's made a few turns and rejoined Ventura Boulevard. I turn to him. "So how was Taipei?"

He throws me a smile. "Good. Long days in the factory, but I did have a chance to do a little sightseeing on the weekends." He regales me with stories of hiking in Yangmingshan National Park to Seven Stars Mountain, which apparently gives a spectacular view of the city. "I'm sure you'd love it," he says, his grip easy on the steering wheel. "You said you liked the outdoors, didn't you?"

I did, but I meant things like picnicking in the park, not clambering over rocks and risking total collapse. I don't want to spoil the conversation—it's not as if we're going to Taiwan together anytime soon anyway—so I just nod. "Sure. It sounds like fun."

The sushi restaurant isn't very far away, and it

conveniently has valet parking, so we don't even need to walk. I climb out when the valet holds my door open for me and wait for Jackson on the curb. He puts his hand on the small of my back to guide me inside the restaurant and speaks quickly to the hostess of the small space. Apparently, he's made a reservation already—I wonder what would have happened if I said I wasn't in the mood for sushi.

We're quickly seated at a table for two in the corner, and I immediately pick up my menu even though I already know that I'm going to order a single Philadelphia roll and some edamame and call it good. I make a good show of perusing the options before I mark exactly that down on the little card at the table.

"That's all you're going to eat?" Jackson asks skeptically.

"Yeah, I'm not all that hungry tonight. The heat."

To his credit, his expression shifts to understanding. "It makes your condition flare up, right?"

I nod. "Yeah. I had an episode at the concert last night and I'm still not completely recovered."

"You should have told me! We could have rescheduled if you're not feeling up to it."

"No, it's fine," I say quickly. "I wanted to see you. I wanted to get out."

The server comes over to our table, and Jackson hands the card to her, then asks for two glasses of ice water and a bottle of sake. Then he turns back to me. "What kind of concert was it anyway? I didn't know there was anything good in town this week."

Normally, I'd brush off the question, but for whatever reason, I sit back and look him in the eye. "We went to see Amira's favorite K-pop group."

A smile tips up the corner of his mouth. "Really? You're into that?"

Before last night, I would have said no, but now I'm feeling defensive. "Sure."

He must pick up something in my tone, because he simply says, "Cool," and I think that will be it. But then a moment later, he says, "I thought it was only guys who were into K-pop? Like, pretty Asian girls in school uniforms?"

"Actually," I say casually, "It was a boy group, and they were amazing. Best show I've ever been to."

I can tell he's taken aback, but I don't know why. He didn't bat an eye when I waxed eloquent over seeing Lena Carter on her last tour. But the idea of delving into his feelings on the subject are far beyond my energy level, so I just change the subject. "So tell me more about Taiwan."

This time, he's describing the incredibly stringent factory conditions and despite the fact that it should be boring, Jackson is a good storyteller. Our food comes a few minutes later, and he pours me a cup of sake without asking, which I don't touch. Instead, I eat my roll very slowly while the conversation shifts to a Japanese horror movie he saw on the plane and by coincidence, I happened to stream last week.

"I swear, that last jump scare almost made me pee my pants," I say with a laugh. "I've never been so freaked out in my life, I had to sleep with the lights on."

He smiles vaguely, and I don't know if it was the casual, thoughtless mention of bodily functions or the fact that a grown woman is scared of horror movies, but now I'm uncomfortable. Obviously, he is too, because he folds his napkin. "Will you excuse me for a moment?"

I watch him wind his way through the dark interior of the restaurant to the restroom and decide that it was definitely the pee comment that got him, especially if he wouldn't even use the word *restroom*. I sigh and after a moment, pull out my phone, debating whether to text Amira and ask her to message me in an hour to give me an out. This evening has been uneven from the start, and apparently I'm just not in the mood for company.

But the minute I unlock the screen, I see that I have an Instagram message from SJY_1995_.

My heart rises into my throat with a dull thud, and I click on the notification. My stomach jumps when I see it's a photo, the *Welcome to Las Vegas* sign at the Harry Reid International Airport, followed by several lines of text.

> SJY_1995_
> Viva Las Vegas.
> FYI, we don't say merde. We
> say 화이팅. Which, in the
> event you don't read
> Hangul (I don't want to
> assume because you strike
> me as a woman full of
> surprises) means "fighting."

A smile forms on my lips as something bubbly swells in my stomach. Maybe I'm reading too much into this, but that parenthetical feels downright flirty. I think for a moment on how I want to respond, then tap out a reply, copying and pasting the Korean characters.

> KATBA_91602
> 화이팅 then. I don't want to
> be the reason you're
> anything less than your
> usual impressive self.

As soon as I've sent it, I regret it, but it's too late to take it back. I don't know if deleting a message on

Instagram just deletes it for me or both of us, and then there's that awkward possibility that he might think what I deleted was worse than it actually was. Quickly, I add:

KATBA_91602
After all, you can't
disappoint your fans.

"What's so funny?"

Jackson's voice makes me start and I click the screen off without thinking. He's looking down at me with a fond smile that makes me instantly feel bad about the fact I'm corresponding with another guy—however innocently—while I'm on a date with him.

I clear my throat. "Friend send me a message. Are you ready to go?"

"Whenever you are."

The drive home is quiet, but not uncomfortably so. Streetlights crawl across the tinted windows of his car, and I stare out at the shops and restaurants on my side of Ventura. When he parks, he reaches for the key. "I'll walk you up."

It's a question couched in politeness, and I know I have to shut it down immediately. "It's not necessary. I'd invite you in, but I have a long day tomorrow and I should get to bed early."

"Of course." Not even a flicker of disappointment shows on his face as he leans over and kisses me, just the lightest press of lips on mine. I know that should I lean in to him, it will turn into more, but instead I pull back and smile.

"Thanks for dinner. I had a nice time. Maybe next time we should find a horror movie to watch."

He laughs. "It's a date. Sleep well."

I climb out and shut the door, then give Jackson a little wave as I walk up the path through the manicured front garden to the main door of the building. By the time I reach the second floor, though, I know the truth.

There won't be a next time.

Amira is right. I should have cut Jackson loose a long time ago. I'm simply not into him the way I should be if I'm going to keep seeing him. And it's not even that he's a bad guy or a boring one—we simply don't click. We tolerate each other's enthusiasms out of politeness, and while that's fine for distant family members at Thanksgiving, it's not really the best foundation for a relationship.

I don't want to think about why it took a message from a stranger to make me come to that realization.

I manage to ignore my phone while I undress and take off my makeup. I suppose my rest this afternoon did pay off, because I have the energy to slip into a cute summer pajama set and make myself a cup of tea before I retreat to my bedroom again. I turn on the TV and prop myself up on pillows before I let myself unlock the screen.

There's a message from Amira.

AMIRA
How was the date?

TRINA
Fine.
I'm going to have to break
up with him.

AMIRA
WHY??? What did he do?

> TRINA
> He didn't do anything,
> really. You're right. There's
> just no . . .

AMIRA
Chemistry?

> TRINA
> I was going to say spark, but
> yeah, chemistry.

AMIRA
Good. You're way too young
and talented and hot to
waste your time on a guy
who doesn't appreciate you.

That isn't exactly the situation, but I'm too distracted to reply when another Instagram message pops up from SJY_1995_. It's another photo, this time of a sea of what must be thirty or forty identical Samsonite luggage cases next to a baggage carousel.

While I'm watching, another message pops up.

SJY_1995_
I know we're on tour, but
this feels a bit like overkill?

I lower the phone. I know he's not texting me real time updates from the airport. Is he? Why would he?

Maybe he's bored. Maybe he knows he'll get a reaction out of me. But surely, *surely*, there are dozens of other people he could be sending this message to besides me. What game is he playing?

I consider long and hard before I reply. If I were smart, I would say something noncommittal, like *I'm sure you probably need it all.* Or *tell the truth, those all belong to your staff.*

I am not smart. Because what I type out is:

> KATBA_91602
> A bit? You don't wear
> enough clothes on stage to
> justify half of that.

I press *send* before I can overthink things and then proceed to chew a hole in my lip while I wait.

Shit. He's not replying. That really was over the line. I groan and throw myself back against my pillow. There's something about the unreality of this whole situation that is making me say and do things I would normally never dream of. I pick up the remote control and surf around channels before I settle on a nature documentary, but I couldn't tell you what it's about on pain of death because three-quarters of my attention is on my phone.

Another message comes through, a string of laugh-crying emojis. And then the dots that indicate he's typing.

> SJY_1995_
> Yes, but the other half is
> Jiho's skin care routine.

I laugh out loud in surprise—I now know that Jiho is the visual of the group, the one considered the best looking, so that tracks—but before I can even think of replying, there's another one.

> SJY_1995_
> Don't tell him I said that.

KATBA_19602
How would I ever tell him
you said that? You are the
only mega-famous Korean
pop star I correspond with
on the regular.

I'm already regretting the comment before it's even marked *sent*, but I half-expect a flippant answer like *Oh, so you only correspond with Japanese pop stars?* or something equally vague and flirty. Instead what I get back is one word.

SJY_1995_
Good.

I stop, my heart fluttering. What is that supposed to mean? Surely there's more. Maybe he just meant that he's glad I'm not a stalker fan. Maybe he was actually replying to the first part of my message, when I said I'd never have an opportunity to speak to Jiho, and I'm just reading too much into it.

I wait and wait for some sort of elaboration, illumination, but that's it.

It's near midnight when I pull the plug on the nature documentary *and* my pathetic waiting and go to sleep.

If Amira thinks I'm wasting my time on a guy who doesn't appreciate me when he's in the flesh and making an effort to see me every time he's in town, I can't imagine what she would say about this.

chapter eight

March 2019, Lincoln Center

Maddie is, predictably, stunning. An original ballet set on the studio company closes the one-act bill this afternoon, and she is the star. She might not have my fluidity or extensions, but she's an allegro dancer through and through, and she flits across the stage like a bejeweled butterfly, barely alighting before she's springing off elsewhere again. When the entire company comes back out onstage to take their bows and she steps forward, beaming, I feel tears prick my eyes.

This is what she's always wanted, and I can't help feeling emotional that I'm here to see it.

I wait for her outside the stage door, clutching the bouquet of sunflowers, but once the steady stream of dancers—some of whom stop to chat briefly with me— slows, I start wondering if maybe I've missed her. I wait for another half hour outside the closed door before I lower the hand holding the roses. She's making a statement. She doesn't want to see me.

I'm halfway to the subway station, preparing to ride back to our apartment when my cell phone chimes. I pull it out to see that Philip has responded to my text with a single line: *Come over?*

I hesitate. Part of me wants to go back in case I just missed Maddie, but I also know that she probably went out to eat with her friends after the show and I'll be sitting home alone with Misha. Cuddling a cute, fluffy kitten doesn't seem like a bad way to spend a Sunday evening, but while I'm still contemplating it, Philip sends another message. *I already miss you.*

I sigh and shake my head, but the smile is already coming to my lips. I'll catch Maddie later tonight when I come home. I veer off toward the 59th Street station instead so I can catch a train uptown. I'm halfway tempted to ditch the flowers somewhere, but something keeps me clutching them in the crook of my arm.

The door opens on Philip's apartment before I can even knock, and he favors me with a big smile. His eyes flick downward to the flowers. "For me? You shouldn't have."

I chuckle. "They were for Maddie, but I missed her."

I expect him to ask about the show, but instead he only takes the flowers from my hands and tosses them onto the entryway table. He pulls me to him as he pushes the door closed behind me, and before I can speak, he kisses me.

"Philip," I whisper when I come up for air, "wait. Can't we just—"

"I can't stop thinking about you," he says with a groan. "It killed me to leave you this morning." He hikes my leg up around his waist and presses against me, pushing me back against the wall.

I'm still sore from last night and the last thing I'm in the mood for is sex, but there's something about his desperation for me that numbs my worries over Maddie and what she thinks of this whole situation, so I say nothing when he starts unbuckling his belt. I just tip my head back against the wall, clutch his shoulders for support, and ignore the insistent throbbing in my foot from my walk from the station.

A few minutes later, when I'm lying on the sofa with my foot elevated on a cushion, he sprawls beside me and pulls out his phone. "I'm thinking Italian. What do you think?"

"I'm not a huge fan," I say. "Dairy doesn't sit well with me."

"Oh, but you've never had real eggplant parmesan. Trust me, the cheese is minimal. And Mama Estella is iconic." He taps on his screen a couple of times and then sets his phone aside. "It'll be here in thirty minutes. You want some wine?"

"No, thanks. I drank way too much last night and I can't afford to be wrecked in company class tomorrow. You know once this gets out, I can't be seen to be slacking even a little or it will kill my reputation in the company."

He quirks his head at me. "Once *this* gets out?"

"Yeah, like, the fact we're seeing each other. Maddie's already pissed that I didn't tell her."

"*Maddie*," he says deliberately, "is just jealous because your star is rising. As far as the others, don't worry about them. You proved why you earned the role. You don't need to do anything else."

It's the reassurance I wanted, but somehow it doesn't make me feel any better. He's been at this too long, I think. His start as a dancer was similar to mine, if not even more dramatic—he came in as something of a prodigy and rose rapidly through the company, making principal dancer at twenty, a rank he's held for the last thirteen years. He was given his first opportunity to choreograph a ballet for the company at twenty-four, though after a flurry of impressive creations, he took a long break to focus only on dancing the great roles of classical ballet. I suspect it's because people were starting to call him a one-trick pony, saying he was gravitating toward contemporary because he didn't have the acting chops for the Albrechts and Siegfrieds and Conrads of the classical ballet repertoire. He, of course, proved them wrong and was happy with that course.

Until me.

He won't say this outside this apartment, but the idea for the storyline came to him in the months after I joined the corps de ballet. Our paths only barely intersected—I'd be leaving rehearsal as he came in, we had places on opposite sides of the studio during company class . . . until one day we literally ran into each other in the corridor outside the dressing rooms. And just like in the ballet, we came to a stark standstill, staring at each other as if we'd never met.

After that day, I felt his eyes on me in class or in rehearsal. He made a point of offering me a piece of fruit between rehearsals or commenting on my performance. It was enough that curious eyes started turning toward me as well, but not enough to start rumors flying. Until the cast list of *Intersections* was posted.

Philip turns on the TV, but he's really not watching it as he scrolls on his phone. I really could use an ice pack or a couple of ibuprofen from my purse, but my feet are now propped comfortably in his lap, so I don't really want to move. Instead, I stay there and stare at the ceiling, ignoring the throbbing, until a knock comes at his apartment door. The Italian.

He's right—the eggplant parm is excellent, though I can feel my stomach churn almost instantly in response to the mozzarella threaded throughout. I say nothing, even when he pours me a glass of wine, which I sip at just enough to not seem like I'm refusing. When he gets up from the sofa to retrieve some paper towels, I call after him, "Could you get my purse from the entry? I need some ibuprofen."

He comes back a minute later with both my purse and two pills shaken out in the palm of his hand, along with a glass of water. I take them gratefully and gulp them down. He sets my glass aside and slants a concerned look at me. "Maybe you should get that looked at. It could be a fracture."

"Doesn't hurt that bad," I lie. "I think my pointe shoes are just putting pressure in the wrong place and making the swelling worse. I'm going to remove the drawstring for class tomorrow and see if that helps."

He looks skeptical, but I refuse to let him think that this is anything but a minor injury that's treatable with ice and NSAIDs. I have an understudy for *Intersections*—a soloist named Miranda—and she would just love to see me out with an injury so she can take over. Not to mention the fact that, unlike me, Michael actually seems to like Miranda, so he would probably be thrilled to have me sidelined.

There is no way I'm going to miss out on dancing this ballet for the next six weeks because of some stupid minor injury. I just need to take care of myself the best I can. In fact, I probably shouldn't dance on pointe in class at all for the next few days, give my foot a rest until I have to perform again on Friday and Saturday nights.

I normally help wash dishes, but he waves me back down to the sofa and disappears into the kitchen to rinse off our plates. When he comes back, he's holding a cannoli in one hand. He waves it tantalizingly in front of my face.

I laugh and snatch it from his hand, then take a big bite. He reaches out to swipe the cream from my lip, then changes his mind and leans in for a kiss. "Stay tonight," he whispers. "I like having you here."

"I should probably go home. I never did manage to see Maddie."

"Okay." He sits back on the sofa. "If that's what you want. I was going to offer you a massage . . . and I'm absolutely famous for my massages."

I'm not sure I really want to think about who he's famous *with* for those massages, but it's tempting, especially considering how much my whole body always hurts, particularly after a performance. He doesn't press though, and I dither around the idea until my eyes start to drift closed on the sofa and the twilight turns outside the window to full night.

"If you're going to go home, you should probably get going. I don't love the idea of you walking back from the station too late."

He's right. I should go. If I don't go now, I'm going to have to go home in the morning and then come *back* to Manhattan for class at ten. I keep a couple of leotards and tights in my locker, but I don't have any of the other things that I find essential for company class and rehearsal. But it feels like too much effort to get up.

As if he's sensing my debate, he drags my legs back into his lap and slides one strong hand up from my ankle to my calf. I groan as his fingertips dig into the tight muscle. He wasn't joking. He really does have a magic touch.

"I'll make sure you get up in time," he murmurs, throwing me a heavy-lidded glance that I recognize. "I promise you."

I hesitate for another moment, the image of any number of other dancers in this same position, his hands on them, but I shove it away and nod. There may have been others before me, but I'm the one he's with now. His muse.

That should be enough for anyone.

● ● ●

Philip is true to his word—just before seven, he wakes me with a kiss to my cheek, curling his warm body around me. "Wake up, Sleeping Beauty."

"I believe the role you're referring to is Aurora," I mumble. "And that was not nearly the hundred years of sleep I was promised."

He huffs a laugh in my ear and pinches my buttock lightly. "Get out of my bed, princess. You still have to go home and change before class."

I groan and mumble in irritation, but he's right. I push myself up and reach for my clothes, but I'm aware of his gaze on me as I slip the sundress over my head. "What?"

"I was just thinking . . . you've started spending a lot of time over here. Maybe you should just leave some stuff here? Just to save time. I hate the idea of you wasting half your morning on the train to Brooklyn."

I turn and freeze—he's serious, his handsome face earnest and his gaze steady.

"You want to give me a drawer?"

"Well, maybe more like half a drawer and a cubby under the bathroom sink? This is New York. But yeah. I like having you here with me. We're close to the studios . . ."

I turn away so he won't see my expression. I should be elated, but this is . . . moving fast. We've only been together for a few months, and until this weekend, we'd only slept together a couple of times. Now he's offering me the step before moving in with him?

"You're right. I'll think about it. I'm still responsible for Maddie, you know."

"She's eighteen," he says dismissively. "She's fine."

"She doesn't turn eighteen for another month, and technically, I'm the adult on the lease. So I really don't feel right about not being there overnight."

"Then that gives me a month to clear that drawer and the cubby for you." He winks at me and throws the covers off. "I'm going to take a shower. Feel free to make a cup of coffee before you go."

I watch him stalk naked to the bathroom and then shut the door behind him. I don't know why, but it feels like a dismissal. I take a deep breath, then move out to the living room to collect my boots, purse, and jacket. I don't, in fact, make myself a cup of coffee—the machine is far too complicated for me to operate without an instruction manual—but I at least have the presence of mind to stop in front of the entry mirror and tie my hair back into a ponytail. It'll be impossible to make this look like anything but a walk of shame— the mascara flaking under my eyes makes that pretty obvious—but I've seen worse on the train back to Brooklyn.

It's only as I'm about to reach for the door that I notice the sunflowers I bought for Maddie, wilted and abandoned on the entry table.

When I get back to the condo over an hour later, it's still and quiet—Maddie nowhere to be seen. My heart rises into my throat at the idea she didn't come home last night and there was no one to know, but then I see the note taped to the refrigerator: *Staying at Delaney's tonight. Be back tomorrow.* I let out a sigh of relief.

I shower quickly, shove several changes of rehearsal clothes into my bag, and then pack my lunch from the odds and ends in the refrigerator. We hardly ever cook—we go out if we're going to eat full meals—so mostly it's a mishmash of grab-and-go items like yogurt and hummus cups and hard-boiled eggs. I glance at the clock on my phone and swear. I'm not going to have time for the full warm-up before class that I usually need. I grab a protein bar on the fly and wolf it down on my half-walk, half-limp to the train station.

By the time I get to work, change, and enter the large studio where class is held, the entire company is already assembled and going through their warm-ups, clustered around their spots at the bar. One of the ballerinas, Deirdre, is practicing finger turns with her partner while another dancer films it on her phone for Instagram—even we aren't immune to the necessity of social media. I posted a clip from *Intersections* and gained eight thousand followers this week. Which doesn't sound like much when you consider that the most popular dancers have well over a million, but for someone who was just recently lifted out of obscurity, my forty-thousand followers feel like an army.

I'm distracted by everything that's going on, the throbbing in my foot, and the idea that I've missed out on my opportunity to get in a decent warm-up this morning, so I don't notice the additions to our class until Janine nudges me. I whip my head around to see four of the studio company members clustered around the free-standing barre in the middle of the room—the space no one likes because the view in the mirror is horrible. It takes a moment longer to register that one of them is Maddie.

My eyes widen and I try to meet my sister's gaze, but she's either too focused on her own warm-up or she's purposely ignoring me, because she doesn't glance my way once. She looks beautiful and very, very young in her gray-and-black floral leotard beneath her baggies, the water stains on the shiny peach satin of her pointe shoes telling me she's breaking in a new pair. I wish I knew what this was about. I don't want to jump to the wrong conclusion and be disappointed if this turns out to be some sort of . . . audition . . . or something. I was never in the studio company; I was taken directly from the school to the corps de ballet of the main company, so I have no idea how this works.

I don't have long to wait, however. I've barely managed to get a little movement into my joints and muscles before Alec Visser, the company director, walks in in his usual tight-fitting black T-shirt and sweatpants. He claps his hands together sharply and everyone stops what they're doing.

"Good morning," he says warmly, his Dutch accent prominent. "As you have no doubt noticed, we have some changes. Please help me welcome the newest members of the corps, Luke Baumer, Delaney Fischer, Eric Yoo, and Madeline Barbas."

The company gives a round of warm, but restrained applause, smiles thrown in the direction of the newcomers, and Maddie bows her head beneath the welcome. Still, she doesn't look my way, instead smiling at her friends while she works her high-arched feet against the stiff shank of her shoes. There's no time to congratulate her or do anything else besides take my usual spot at the bar before Diana Morozova, the company's ballet mistress, takes her place at the grand piano and begins to mark out the opening exercise.

I'm still distracted, throwing glances at Maddie every few bars, but she's assiduously focusing on her technique, something I should be doing. I work carefully, listening to what my right foot is telling me, working the muscles of my feet through my soft canvas technique shoes. It doesn't feel as bad as I feared; relevé on that side still hurts, but not as much as it does on pointe. I get through barre more or less intact, and while Diana sends me a searching look, she doesn't say anything. I manage to get through adagio and pirouettes without an issue, beg off petit allegro completely and limit grand allegro to my left side so I don't need to land any jumps on my right foot. That's the advantage of getting to the professional level; begging off exercises or doing your own thing may get you some curious looks, but everyone trusts you to manage your own training.

Sitting out does give me the chance to watch Maddie, though, and a warm glow builds in my chest as I do. She's . . . ethereal. Sparkling. Even in class, she evokes this brightness that draws the eye. I'm not surprised she got raised to the main company; she's more than ready—her technique solid, her musicality undeniable. I let the pride swell in my chest, and it must show in my face, because Deirdre pauses as she crosses back to the other side of the studio and follows my gaze. "She's lovely."

I don't know if it's a kindness or a jab, because Deirdre isn't my biggest fan—there was a time when she would have unquestionably been selected for *Intersections*, even though she's currently dancing Kitri in *Don Quixote*—but I take it at face value. "She is. She's always been beautiful."

A tiny smile lifts her lips. "He certainly thinks so."

I follow her gaze across the studio to where Philip is standing with another of the male dancers, and he is indeed watching my sister with an appraising look that I can't quite interpret. When I look back, Deirdre is walking away with a satisfied look on her face, her mission accomplished.

Not a kindness then.

But almost as if he senses my eyes on him, Philip finds me across the studio and gives me a wink and a thumbs up, then nods in Maddie's direction. I hate myself for how much relief I feel, that he's not trying to hide anything, that Deirdre is just stirring up shit because of her own jealousy. I come back to the center for the final exercise and reverence and then grab my things to wait by the door.

There's no way that Maddie can get away without seeing me now, and this time she doesn't try. She just tucks her foam roller and her discarded warm-ups beneath her arm and looks at me.

"Congratulations," I say.

"Thank you." She looks at me coolly for a long moment and says nothing else. This one is all on me.

"I take it that's what you were trying to tell me after the show? It wasn't just celebrating my premiere?"

"Now you're intuitive?" She arches an eyebrow, but she must see something in my face, because she breaks. She pushes past me through the door and gestures with her head for me to follow. "I found out on Friday, but I didn't see you. I thought maybe it would be a nice thing to celebrate together."

"I'm sorry," I say quietly. "I wish I had known."

"And I wish you had told me about you and Philip." She turns to me. "You know, the rumors made it all the way to the studio company, and I defended you. Because I figured if there was anything going on, you would have told me."

Her reproach strikes hard. I can't look her in the eye. "Maddie . . ."

Other dancers are lingering nearby, listening but pretending not to as they putter around on their way back to the dressing rooms or the lounge area to eat lunch before afternoon rehearsals start. She pulls me aside. "Listen, I didn't want to do this here, but since I don't know when I'm going to see you at home—"

That was definitely a jab.

"—we should probably discuss what to do with the lease."

I blink at her. "The lease."

"Yeah. The lease is up next month on the condo, and I turn eighteen in two weeks." She looks me straight in the eye. "I'm moving in with Delaney."

I'm still blinking like I've got something in my eye. "What?"

"You're never there anyway. Delaney lives in Manhattan, so she's closer to the studios and the theater. She needs a roommate, I'm tired of living alone. . . it just made sense."

The statement lands like a blow: *I'm tired of living alone.* I know I've been absent lately—mentally if not physically—but I didn't know she's been feeling like this. "Maddie—"

"Listen, I'm not trying to make you feel bad. You're older than me, I get that you don't want to be saddled with taking care of your little sister. Well, I'm going to officially be an adult. Mom and Dad said they'd pay for my rent for another year to let me build up some savings and then they're pulling the plug. This makes more sense."

For her. It makes more sense for her. For me, it just means that in a month, I'm going to be homeless. The fact she made her decision in isolation, without discussing it with me, stings, and I think she intended it to. She figures that if I've been cutting her out of my life, she's going to do the same to me.

Which would be fair if she and her dreams weren't the whole reason I'm here.

"Fine," I say tightly. I'm not going to try to guilt-trip

her into living with me. I've been keeping everything to myself for this long, what's another forever? "If that's what you want."

"It is." At the last minute, she softens. "I mean, it's not like we won't see each other. We'll see each other every day at work at the very least."

"Right," I say, giving a definitive nod. "It's fine."

She nods too, but she gives me a lingering look and I don't know if she expected more push-back or if she *wanted* more push-back. Either way, it's too late now. Neither of us are going to budge; we're both too proud and stubborn, and neither of us wants to admit that we need the other. So she just throws me one last smile before she turns and joins her newly raised corps friends as they move back down the hallway.

Philip must have been waiting for me to finish, because he appears at my side and places a hand on my arm. "Everything okay?"

"Yeah," I say. "Everything's fine. You know, considering I have to find a new place to live in a month."

He winces. "Moving in with friends, huh?"

"You heard?"

He nods. "Yeah. It'll work out. Don't worry." His hand slides down my arm and our fingers interlace. "We'll figure it out."

I smile up at him and try to push down the unease that inexplicably creeps in at the statement.

chapter nine

I am so distracted the next morning as I putter around the studio that even Amira notices.

"What is wrong with you?" she asks bluntly. "Is it about Jackson?"

I startle, because truthfully, I've forgotten about Jackson, and that right there is the perfect illustration of my problem. I exchanged five lines of text with a stranger last night and somehow that eclipsed the fact that I'm going to have to break up with a real, flesh-and-blood man sooner rather than later.

"I feel bad," I say finally. "I like him. On paper, he makes sense. He's smart and fun and attentive. He has a good job. He likes to travel . . ."

Amira just looks at me, and I sigh.

"I know. The fact I have to list his good qualities like a résumé is probably an indication it's not the right match. It's just . . . the attention is nice."

Amira walks over to where I've plopped myself on a rolling stool near the equipment and squats down in front of me. "I know. But the right guy will be more than just nice. The right guy will make you feel more like yourself than you've ever been, like you don't have to hide. You've had to settle too much already. Don't settle on this, too."

It's wise and sweet, and love for my best friend swells up inside me. I think back to last night and suddenly laugh. "You know what actually did it? When I told him what concert we went to and he acted like it was funny."

"Oh, well, I would have dumped him right there. Any man I date has to know that if Jae comes calling, he's out."

I laugh, though it isn't without an uncomfortable twinge. "I'm being serious! I don't like the idea that things I enjoy are simply something to be tolerated. Or worse yet, an endearing trait he uses to describe me to his friends."

"It's infantilizing," Amira says.

"And just . . . sad. I do the same thing with him. He loves hiking, but he still hasn't put together that I will never be that girl. He thinks because of how I look, someday I'm going to climb a Taiwanese mountain with him."

"That alone would have me dumping him," Amira says, winking at me as she rises. "Sounds like too much effort."

That's the signal that Amira is done with feelings for the morning and we have to get down to the real work. Wednesday is another heavy day with repeat clients from Monday, including my cancellation. Instead of working on the Reformer, I spend some time with them on the Cadillac, a trapeze-type apparatus that allows for inversions and hanging exercises. When I have a short break for lunch, Amira orders in to save me the walk down the street, and I sit in the corner of the office browsing social media while I work my way through an enormous bowl of greens with chicken and blue cheese crumbles.

I'm about to toss my bowl in the trash when a message from Simon comes through—another photo.

It's the view of a stadium from a stage, and this one looks twice as big as the arena in which Amira and I attended their concert. The message below it pings me again.

SJY_1995_
Sound check. Not a bad
view.

I smile to myself and shake my head. I regularly performed at the largest opera house in the world, and that topped out at just under four thousand seats. There must be over sixty thousand there, and I don't need to Google to know that Helios probably sold it out. What exactly do you say to someone who looks at a football stadium as "not a bad view?"

Impulsively, I duck out of the office. Amira is nowhere to be seen, so I take a photo of my studio and quickly send it with a message.

KATBA_91602
My view. Not as impressive,
but I still like it.

SJY_1995_
Pilates?

My eyebrows lift. I'm impressed.

KATBA_91602
A man of taste and culture,
I see.

> SJY_1995_
> A man of many injuries.
> When I'm home in Seoul, I
> go two days a week just to
> stay functional.

I shouldn't be surprised—it's common dancer cross-training—but I am. Before I can reply, he sends another message.

> SJY_1995_
> Your studio?

> KATBA_91602
> Amira and I own it together.
> She's my business partner.

> SJY_1995_
> Nice.

And that's it. Nothing else. I sigh and put my phone away. I'm beginning to expect these short bursts of conversation—though I question why I should *expect* anything—and I can only guess that he's messaging me in small pockets of downtime.

I'm not sure I like the warm feeling that gives me. This is a false connection. Seojun—Simon—contacted me out of guilt, but I can't fathom why he's continuing the conversation. This is a guy about to perform for sixty thousand people tonight, who is surrounded by managers and staff and fellow group members. He has no shortage of people in his life. So why is he reaching out to some random stranger he met for ten minutes at his concert?

But even as I'm thinking it, I know that's the whole

point. His group members are his coworkers, or maybe they're more like friends and family. The rest of them are employees.

I am . . . separate.

I'm not a fan, not exactly. I haven't asked him for anything. I've just replied like a normal human being, albeit one surprisingly unfazed by his fame.

The fact is, I deal with people way more famous than him on a daily basis, though their fandoms aren't nearly as rabid or boundary-pushing, so the sheer fact of being beloved by millions isn't as off-putting to me as he might think. Besides, even though I wasn't nearly to his level of notoriety, I had almost a million followers on Instagram when I retired. I spent all my time in the studio and with other dancers, and my only exposure to people outside that bubble was social media. The problem was, most of those comments were bots, thirsty men who liked to comment on my body, and young dancers desperate for a connection to the ballet world.

So maybe I understand a little. As absolutely bizarre as it feels, maybe Simon Yang—idol, couture ambassador, style icon—just wants a real friend.

I can do that.

I feel better when I put away my phone and prep for my next client—at least, I feel better emotionally. Physically, my body still aches, and both my hamstrings and hip flexors are protesting at the fact I haven't done my personal workouts for the last two days. I stand for part of the next session and then finish my day by sitting and scooting around on my rolling chair. No one says a word, no one even thinks twice about it, and everyone leaves happy. By the time we shut down the studio at 6:00 p.m., I'm dreaming of a cool bath and a few episodes of the K-drama Amira got me hooked on.

Some people would call it self-care, but these days it's just basic maintenance.

"You want to come over tonight?" Amira asks. I suspect she's thinking I might be sad about Jackson, but she might just want company. As an extrovert, she doesn't particularly enjoy being alone, and she hasn't had a boyfriend in a minute.

"Thanks, but I think I'm just going to hit the sack early. Still trying to recover."

"Okay. Call me if you need me."

I hug her goodbye and turn down her offer of a ride, then strike out down Ventura in the waning sunlight. The evening is still warm, verging on hot, and I have to dodge pedestrians as I go. If I lived somewhere other than this part of LA, not having a car—or rather, not being willing to risk driving one—would be more than an inconvenience; it would be nearly impossible. But I was used to walking in New York, and except for my very bad days, I don't miss driving. I suspect my experience of Los Angeles is much narrower than that of the people who spend all their time commuting in a high-speed metal box, but I'm not sure that's a bad thing.

I commence my evening plans with a long cool bath, my wireless earbuds pressed into my ears. Tonight I'm not listening to Helios, but Hyperion, Simon's first group, and I find that I can easily pick his voice out among the other seven members. He's the only baritone, for starters, though his range is deceptive; mostly it's a certain liquid quality, a lightness to it despite its depth, that makes it stand out.

It's rare for someone to have world-class talent in one area, even rarer to be outstanding in multiple areas, so I'm impressed but not surprised when the internet later informs me that he's one of the most popular—*biased*, in K-pop parlance—performers of his generation.

I'm certainly biased.

I fall asleep halfway through the third episode of the drama, and I can't even pretend that I was just resting my eyes, because I certainly can't follow subtitles with my eyes closed. When I wake, it's after midnight and Netflix is asking me if I'm still watching. I click *no* and shut off the TV, then reach over to put my phone on the charger. Only to see there's a message from Simon waiting. Just a single line.

SJY_1995_
You still up?

I fumble the phone as I try to quickly type out my reply.

KATBA_91602
Sort of? Fell asleep
watching a K-drama.

He replies immediately, as if he was waiting for my response, despite the fact his message had come through an hour ago.

SJY_1995_
Which one?

KATBA_91602
A Love Like Rain.

SJY_1995_
Oh, I haven't gotten to that
one yet!
Any good?

KATBA_91602
So far. I think? I fell asleep
in the last episode.

SJY_1995_
That is not exactly a vote in
its favor.

KATBA_91602
No, it wasn't the show. I was
just tired. As you probably
are. How was the concert?

It takes longer to respond this time, and I find myself wondering why. I don't have long to wait.

SJY_1995_
Sorry. Hyunsoo at the door,
asking me if I want to go out.

KATBA_91602
You should go!

SJY_1995_
☺

KATBA_91602
Not a night life person?

SJY_1995_
Not remotely. Introvert who
likes his K-dramas.

KATBA_91602
Got it. Show?

SJY_1995_
Oh, it went well.
Hellions seemed to enjoy it
(far more responsibly than
the name would suggest).

I laugh, because it's exactly what I had thought at
the concert.

KATBA_91602
You perform Burn again?

SJY_1995_
Why? Jealous?

I have to think about how I'm going to reply to that one.

KATBA_91602
Should I be?

SJY_1995_
No.
Not considering I haven't
performed it again.It was
Jae's turn for a solo stage.

KATBA_91602
So when do you perform it
next?

SJY_1995_
Chicago, I think? But it will
not involve audience
participation. Management
was not happy with me.

KATBA_91602
Is that slap on the wrist
unhappy or threaten your
job unhappy?

SJY_1995_
Mostly the former? They
want us to sign again, so
they're not going to be too
forceful, but apparently an
audience member
collapsing after
"unapproved touching" is
not a good look.

KATBA_91602
They actually used the term
"unapproved touching?"

SJY_1995_
In translation, yes

That's right. He's a native English speaker, so it's always jarring for me to remember that he probably conducts most of his life in Korean. Not just bilingual, but bi-continental. Bi-cultural.

KATBA_91602
Did you explain I had a
medical condition?

SJY_1995_
Unsurprisingly, that did not
help my case.

I can't help laughing again. I've only met him once and he was fully in idol mode, but I've now seen enough content of him goofing around with his group to be able to read that in the wry tone he uses in English when his members are annoying him. I'm slightly embarrassed at how much video I've watched, but now I'm rather glad for it.

KATBA_91602
Well, I'm sorry I caused you
problems. I should have just
sat there and looked
petrified.

SJY_1995_
Oh yes, that would have
been MUCH better. They
may have slapped me on
the wrist, but the official
video had 400k views the
first hour it was up

Shit, really? I flip over to YouTube and find the Helios account, and sure enough . . . it's the top of the list and right now it's sitting around 2.1 million. Incredible.

KATBA_19602
A lot more than that now.
Over 2m. To be fair, it looks
much hotter on video than
it felt at the time.

SJY_1995_
Always does. You're taking
2m views of yourself pretty
well, all things considered.

KATBA_91602
It's 2 million views of you.
I'm just the convenient self-
insert lucky fan.

It takes a long time for him to reply, and I wonder if he's had another member try to talk him into going out again. Or maybe he's fallen asleep. Or maybe he's just tired of the conversation. I roll over onto my side and snuggle into my pillow, ready to close my eyes again, but then he's back.

SJY_1995_
No, you made that
performance for me. You
were a dancer, right?

I sit bolt upright so fast that I tweak a muscle in my back and fall back onto the bed with a groan. He checked me out.

Well, of course he did. He probably wanted to know that I wasn't a psychopath with a history of stalking celebrities or something. I breathe in and out a few times, considering how to frame the answer. I go with the simplest, least embellished version.

KATBA_91602
I was. I retired a few
years ago.

SJY_1995_
I gathered as much. Injury?

KATBA_91602
Chronic illness.

SJY_1995_
I should have guessed. I'm
sorry. You're really talented.

Okay, now I'm curious. How much digging did he actually do? I throw out the bait.

KATBA_91602
Oh? Which was your
favorite?

SJY_1995_
I know I should say Sleeping
Beauty, because obviously
that's the most impressive.
Rose Adagio, etc etc
But I really liked you in In the
Middle, Somewhat Elevated. It
takes real presence to hold the
stage in a leotard
contemporary. Not to mention
perfect technique.

I'm stunned, not just because Simon dug up an obscure performance of mine—one that happens to be my favorite, in fact, because William Forsythe is a genius—but because of his very specific industry terminology. My enthusiasm spills over before I can consider.

KATBA_91602

I knew it! I pegged your
classical training the
minute you came out on
stage.But even if I hadn't,
your solo made it obvious.
Where did you train?

SJY_1995_
Before Korea? SAB.

I'm bowled over. School of American Ballet. He wasn't just a dancer, he was a *good* dancer.

SJY_1995_
But only for the summer.
They invited me for the
school year and I had to
decide between that and
becoming a Titan trainee.

I shake my head. There is so much that I want to ask, but I can't do it over text, certainly not after midnight after he's just performed on stage for three hours.

KATBA_91602

I'm impressed. Any footage
of you from those days?

It takes a minute, but then I get a YouTube link, a private one. I click on it and it takes me to a clip of a baby Simon—maybe thirteen or fourteen years old— wearing the ballet boy uniform of black tights and white t-shirt. He starts a bravura pirouette preparation, then casually tosses off about six turns before he closes in fifth position and then performs a double tour en l'air to one knee.

Damn. He was really good.

KATBA_91602
Only six?

SJY_1995_
Give me a break, I was
twelve.

Wow. If that was him at twelve, he was really, *really* good.

KATBA_91602
What made you give up the
glitz and glamour of
professional ballet for the
dull life of an idol?

SJY_1995_
Trust me, I wonder that all
the time.

I pause. He's just joking, certainly. The man is on a world tour right now, and he's wondering if he made the right decision? Look, I'm not one of those people who think the idol life is easy. I'm a dancer—my life back then probably wasn't *that* much different than his is now, with the exception of the lack of privacy. And the touring. And the millions of adoring fans. But even then, I still wouldn't trade the experience for anything. In fact, there's a lot I would trade to go back to that life this very second.

Katba_91602
You shouldn't. If there was
anyone cut out
for this job, it's you.

It's absolutely the wrong thing to say, because it takes him forever to answer, and when he does it's just a single line, the implied tone muted.

SJY_1995_
I think I can sleep now.
Good night, Katrina.

I want to apologize, but I really have nothing to apologize for, other that perhaps insensitivity. Instead I settle for the obvious.

KATBA_91602
Good night, Simon. 화이팅

chapter ten

October 2019, New York Theater Ballet studios

I get to the studio late, courtesy of my bi-weekly Pilates class and physical therapy, but in truth, I'm not in much of a hurry. Today is casting for Philip's new ballet, a stripped-down minimalist rendition of *Sleeping Beauty* using a rearranged version of Tchaikovsky's original score. Contrary to the rumors that swirled immediately after announcement of the new ballet, I know nothing about what he has planned, or more importantly, who he has it planned *for*. Even though I moved in with Philip a little over a year ago and our ongoing relationship is common knowledge in the company, I'm not privy to any more insider knowledge than any other dancer. No one believes that, of course, so I stopped protesting a long time ago.

Because the fact is, everything I do these days is scrutinized. If Philip bypasses me for another dancer— which he did for his follow-up to *Intersections*, it's a sign that our relationship is on shaky ground. If he casts me as the lead, it's because of his bias. Never mind the fact that my role in *Intersections* got stunning reviews, calling me the "brightest new star in the NYTB firmament" or the fact they lauded the piece as a "fresh new installation among the company's classic ballets." Both of those things were enough to get me a promotion earlier this year, the company's youngest female principal ever. I actually danced Myrtha in *Giselle* a month ago, a role usually reserved for a more mature ballerina with well-developed acting skills.

I hate my new position as much as I love it.

In any case, the cast list is already up when I get into the building and walk down the hallway toward the dressing room. The minute eyes turn toward me, I know what the results are, and my heart skips a beat. A crowd of corps de ballet dancers make room for me as I move to the bulletin board and stop in front of the cast sheet. And there, right at the top as I both hoped and feared is the line: *Aurora — Katrina Barbas.*

I control my expression even though my heart beats wildly in my chest as I scan the rest of the cast list, and I let out a little relieved breath when I see the prince casting: *Désiré — Anthony Liebowitz.* A smile comes to my face. I'm too new to the principal position to only have a single partner—I don't do leads in enough ballets yet—but of the three men I'm paired with, Anthony is my favorite. Tall and elegant with an uncommon maturity on stage for twenty-four, he partners me the best—people are already talking about how we could be one of those classic pairings like Fonteyn and Nureyev or Baryshnikov and Kirkland.

I barely have time to inwardly celebrate the casting before an arm snakes around my waist and a chin rests on my shoulder. I recognize Tony before he plants a kiss on my cheek. "Congratulations, princess."

I laugh and turn to throw my arms around his neck, and no one bats an eye. Perfectly matched on stage as we might be, Tony married one of my other partners,

Damien, last year. Our little love triangle is an ongoing joke within the company.

"I'm so excited," I say. "I'm glad it's you."

"Did you get a chance to see the rest?" he asks, nudging me back toward the cast list.

I blink for a second before I scan the rest of the casting. And there, halfway down the cast page, is what I'm looking for: *Florine — Madeline Barbas.*

I look at Tony, wide-eyed. "Bluebird?"

He grins at me and nods.

"Does she know?"

He nods again. "She's warming up in the studio."

I bypass the dressing room and go straight to the studio where Maddie is standing at the center barre, doing slow relevés on pointe. I barely give her time to register my presence before I pick her up and spin her around. "Bluebird!" I shriek.

Her startled expression melts into laughter, and her cheeks color. "I can't believe it."

"I can't either," I say. "I had no idea."

Now her expression shifts to caution. "Really? I thought Philip would have told you."

"No, I didn't even know *my* role until now. He's annoyingly closed-lipped when it comes to casting."

She lets out a breath. "Oh good. I thought. . . I thought you might have put him up to it."

Now I snort. "As if I have that much influence over him? I can barely convince him what to order for dinner."

Something flits over Maddie's face, but I dismiss it when she's swept back up into excitement. "Do you really think I can do it?"

"Of course you can," I say automatically, but I know it's not the answer she wants. Florine—and the Bluebird pas de deux—is both beautiful and one of the most energetically and technically demanding roles in the entire ballet. Everyone stays clear in the wings for that variation, because it's better than even odds that the dancers will go straight to the trash can to vomit when finishing. Even though Philip will be changing the choreography, I know him well enough to know that he's not going to make it *easier*, just different.

"You'll need to up your cardio," I admit finally. "And probably add some more strength training. But you can do it once you build the stamina. It suits you perfectly."

Maddie lets out a relieved sigh and then nods. For a second, it feels like it's a year ago, when we were still close, when we shared a house and a dream, before we became just colleagues in the studio. She reaches for my hand and squeezes. "Aurora. Congratulations."

"Thank you."

"I'm not surprised."

Now my smile turns wry. "Yeah, I don't suspect anyone is."

She shakes her head. "Not that. Your Myrtha was brilliant. You deserve it. Only principal roles for you from now on." She clears her throat and gives me a shy look. "I'm proud of you."

I'm stunned for a moment, and I have to blink a sudden swell of tears from my eyes. I clear my throat. "Thanks."

"You should go change and warm up," she says. "It's going to be a long season."

I start to turn away, but impulsively, I turn back and give her a fierce hug. Then I'm rushing out of the studio and down the hallway, blinking back tears for reasons I can't explain.

No, I can explain it. It feels like a year's worth of worries have sloughed off my shoulders. Not worries for me, but for Maddie. When we lived together, even if I was often absent, I could keep track of her and her mental health. But this past year, I've seen her struggling in class, her look of frustration when she couldn't get her body to move like she wanted it to. She got a late growth spurt just after she was raised to the corps, and while she's still thin, she filled out in ways that made her look stocky rather than slender. Slowly, from my spot across the room, I saw the weight come off her, just as I saw a little of the sparkle leave her movements, some of the light leave her eyes.

But any attempt to talk to her about it was met with a brush-off or outright hostility. When I chose Philip, I lost any right to talk to my sister. Even if I still didn't quite understand why.

But this. . .this is what she's been working for. Acknowledgment. It's a soloist role, a huge encouragement for a dancer still in the corps de ballet, and if she can pull it off, one that will allow her to distinguish herself in the company and to our audience.

The knot that's been drawn tight in my chest for the last year eases. Maybe I will finally have the chance to unpick it completely.

The dressing room is empty when I enter it—again, I'm late—so I quickly strip off my street clothes and shove them into the locker before I slip on my canvas flats. I'll change into pointe shoes for center. The stress fracture in my foot has mostly healed, but it still twinges when I spent too much time on pointe, so I try to save that for rehearsal when I can. I know very well that the best thing for me would be to take some solid time off from dancing, but I also know that's not something I'm willing to do. I've gotten it down to a manageable, if chronic, low-level pain, and while I know that's technically not wise, I also know that every single one of the other principals is dealing with something just as bad or worse. It's an occupational hazard.

Eventually all our bodies will give out, it's just about how much we can wring from them in the meantime.

I'm about to leave the dressing room when I hear murmurs just outside in the hallway. And though I know I shouldn't, I crack the door and listen.

". . . idea how he thinks she's going to pull that off," a female voice says. Deirdre. I recognize her snotty tone instantly. "She can barely make it though allegro these days."

"Maybe she's fucking him too," comes the smirking reply—I don't even need to guess to know it's Deirdre's partner in crime, Sophie.

Fury wells up inside me. I'm used to the snottiness and the speculation and the gossip, and while I can't exactly call it good-natured, Deirdre and Sophie escalate it to downright toxic. I yank the door open violently and enjoy their startled jumps back, the way they eye each other as if questioning whether I heard their words.

I won't give them the satisfaction. Instead I just smile sweetly. "I saw the casting. Congratulations, Deirdre. Lilac again. I can't wait to see what you do with the role after you've danced it so many times." And then I brush past them and move down the hallway, enjoying the sensation of their shocked stares on my back.

It's a pitiful jab, but one that I know will hit—dancers who get typecast in a particular role almost never move into the lead. I just told Deirdre it's too bad she'll probably never dance Aurora. It gives me little pleasure, though, knowing that the cast list just went up and already they're doubting Maddie's ability.

And yet I put on a happy face as I enter the studio, winking at Maddie as I move to my place at the barre and begin to work through an abbreviated version of my usual warm-up. Philip catches my eye from across the room where he usually stands, eyebrows lifted as if to ask what I think. I place my hand over my heart and bow my head briefly, a gesture of gratitude, and only then does he wink at me. I don't bother to look to see who witnessed the exchange.

And yet when the ballet mistress enters to start class and I shift to face the barre for the opening exercise, I can't help but feel like some of the joy had been sucked out of the announcement.

Even as I move through the opening pliés and tendus and relevés, when I should be focusing on the sensations in my body, asking myself what I need from the class, there is only one question circulating through my mind: what will it take to feel genuinely, unequivocally happy about the life I've chosen?

chapter eleven

Thursday is another light day, due to our rental agreement with the other teacher, but even so, I'm distracted enough that Amira shoots me concerned looks at me for a full hour before she finally approaches me.

"Okay, spill. What's going on? You're walking around like a cat on razor wire."

I'm not sure which to address first, the unusually folksy saying or the fact that she knows me so well that she can pick up my angst. I woke up hoping for something from Simon and simultaneously cursing myself for being invested enough in this. . . running conversation . . . that it's the first thing on my mind. I've been over the messages more times than I care to admit to myself, and as far as I can tell, my only misstep was glossing over his feelings about his career.

He's entitled to be conflicted about his career. There is literally no job on the planet that is as rosy as it looks from the outside, and what little I know about the K-pop world makes me think those drawbacks are turned up to eleven. But still, I meant what I said. There are good-looking guys, there are great dancers, there are even astounding vocalists. But rarely do you get that all in one package, combined with stage presence that draws your eye like a magnet. This is literally the only time I can say that a young prodigy devoting himself to a ballet career would have been an enormous waste of talent.

But he probably doesn't want to hear that. And now I get to sit around and find out exactly what Simon wants from me. If he's simply trying to cultivate a sounding board to tell him what he wants to hear or if he's actually interested in getting to know me.

I'll leave the question of why to another time.

"I'm fine," I say finally, remembering Amira's question. "I just didn't sleep well."

"Did you break it off with Jackson?"

"No, not yet."

"Girl, what are you waiting for? It's going to eat you up inside until you get it settled."

I shake my head. "I'll do it. I just need to figure out the right way. Besides, that's not why I couldn't sleep. I fell asleep watching Netflix and when I woke up to turn it off, I was wide awake."

"It's Seojun." She winks at me. "Tell me the truth, you fell down a YouTube clickhole again."

I grimace because she's not that far off, though in my mind he's already shifted to being Simon. "Kind of. I was right . . . he was a ballet dancer. I found a video." Okay, *found* is stretching the truth a bit, but sharing that little tidbit makes me feel less guilty about how much I'm hiding from my best friend . . . particularly because I still don't understand why I'm doing it.

I expect her to scold me, but she just grins. "I should have known I could get you hooked with a dancer. Had I thought of it earlier, we could have had so much fun at concerts and conventions this whole time!"

"You got me." I don't tell her that I'm not interested in idols as a whole, just one particular one, though I can admit to streaming a K-pop playlist while I was getting ready this morning.

"I've got a video you're going to love!" Amira exclaims, and then her whole demeanor shifts to friendly professionalism as my ten o'clock walks through the door.

I would love to say that's it and I get my act together and don't think about the man on the other side of my Instagram messages, but that would be a big fat lie. No, instead I do what every stupidly obsessed woman does . . . I check my phone compulsively while trying to hide said compulsive behavior from my friends. Or friend. Amira is the only one at present, if we don't count Jackson, which I don't.

He hasn't texted me since our date, by the way. I'd like to believe that maybe he's going to ghost me and save me from the whole "it's not you, it's me" talk, but I'm not that lucky. This is just his regular routine. He's a bit of a workaholic and we haven't reached the level in our relationship where we text each other mundane daily details. Nor will we, if I put on my big girl panties and do what needs to be done.

Ugh. Amira's right. I need to get this over with.

I brush off Amira's invitation to come over after work, citing that I need to rest—which is true. It's been so long since I've had a full blown syncope episode that I forget how much it takes out of me and how long it takes to reach equilibrium again. At least the muscle pain is going away, and I was able to stand for both my sessions. Baby steps.

But none of those things are the reason I turn her down. I need several hours to psych myself up for the call I'm going to make and then a couple of hours afterward to convince myself I did the right thing.

I take a long nap when I get home and then scrounge up some boiled eggs and fruit from the refrigerator as a meal while I wait for the clock's hands to edge toward six o'clock. Then I screw up my courage and press the button to call Jackson.

He answers on the fourth ring. "Hey, Trina! How are you?"

"Uh, I'm okay. Are you busy?"

"No, I just got home from work. What's up?"

My brow furrows at his casual tone, but I plow on anyway. "I needed to talk to you."

His tone shifts. "Okay. That sounds ominous. Is there a problem?"

"I've enjoyed spending time with you, but last night . . . I just realized . . . I don't think this working."

Silence stretches over the line. "You don't think *what* is working?"

"You and me. Whatever *this* is."

He clears his throat uncomfortably. "Okay, this is awkward. I . . . I didn't meant to give you the impression . . . I mean, we've just gone out a few times. We're not . . . like, in a relationship? I'm . . . seeing other people too."

Heat rushes to my face, and I slump back into the sofa. Oh my god. This is so humiliating. But he's given me the perfect out. I let out a long breath, like I'm relieved. "Oh good. I was afraid maybe you thought it was more . . . and . . . well, you're a great guy, but I'm never going to be that girl who can hike a national park in Taiwan with you."

"Are you . . . saying you don't want to see me because you think your illness bothers me? Because that's obviously not true. It doesn't matter to me at all."

There. Right there is the issue. It doesn't matter to him, but it matters a lot to me. My diagnosis is such a big part of my life that it colors every decision I make, guides every choice I have. Being flexible isn't enough; I need someone who is considerate.

But there's nothing to be gained by voicing that. "I know. It's been really nice getting to know you, but I think it's best if we don't see each other any more."

"Okay," he says, still with that tone of surprise. "I'll see you around. Or not, I guess."

I hang up and sit there with the phone in my hand, not sure which I'm more surprised by: the fact that he's been seeing other women this whole time or the fact that I didn't assume as much. It lets me off the hook, of course, but now I feel like a fool for thinking I'm the only person he's been dating.

My eyes widen. Maybe I'm the only person he's seeing *here* but considering he spends a good chunk of time in Taiwan, what's to say he doesn't have a woman there, too?

I break out laughing and then text Amira.

TRINA
Well, that was easy. I'M THE
OTHER WOMAN!

AMIRA
WHAT?????

TRINA
Okay, not really, but
Jackson sounded surprised
that I was breaking up with
him. In his words "We're
not, like, in a relationship."
He's seeing other people.

AMIRA
What a dick! Good riddance.

But I can't even be mad at him. He's right. We've gone out, what, twelve times over the course of eight months? It's barely enough to know if we like each other, and I'm kind of amazed that it lasted as long as it did. It probably only lasted that long because one of the other girls is putting out.

I immediately feel bad about the thought and pick up the phone again.

TRINA
Nah, it's okay. Glad it's done.

AMIRA
You want to come over?

TRINA
No, but are we still doing brunch on Sunday morning?

AMIRA
You bet. Charlie's, 11am. Sharp. Ish.

I smile and shove the phone into my back pocket and then begin to search the kitchen for something to eat for dinner. It takes about five minutes to figure out that not only have I not ordered groceries for the week, I don't like anything in the freezer either. I pull the phone back out and prepare to order in.

You'd think by some obscure dating law of the universe that now that I've cleared the romantic dead weight from my life, there would be a message waiting from Simon.

There's not.

In fact, two entire days go by with the Instagram chat silent, my farewell message left on read. By the time I finish my single group class on Saturday, I have to admit to myself that the whole thing was a lovely little interlude that someday I'll tell as a story at a dinner party—that time I fainted coming off stage at a concert and chatted with a celebrity before he got bored or tired or busy and ghosted me.

I try to be sanguine about it, because it's not like this was anything real. If I thought it was the start to a friendship, I read far too much into it. He was probably trying to be nice. Who knows, maybe he thought he would give a fan the thrill of a lifetime by sending her on-the-road photos. It makes sense now why he's tried to stay vague and there have been no actual selfies or personal information. He couldn't be sure that I wouldn't rush to post it on fan forums.

So when my phone beeps after midnight, while I'm dozing to the same exact episode that put me to sleep earlier this week, I fully expect it to be Amira or some random notification.

Instead, it's the notification for my SJY chat.

My stomach leaps and twists and I catch my breath as I open the message. Just a single word.

SJY_1995_
Hey.

Cautiously, I type back.

KATBA_91602
Hey?

The dots dance, indicating that he's typing, and I settle back against my pillows, not sure what to expect.

SJY_1995_
Srry ghsoted you. It's
been...interesting

> KATBA_91602
> Ooh, that sounds ominous.
> Show tonight? Where?

SJY_1995_
Phoneix. Shitshow. Tech
problems. Dead mic. Missed
an entrance. Everything hurts.

His terse responses unsettle me, since I have no frame of reference for them. In his previous messages, he's always been relaxed, playful. This is...frustrated? Angry? Exhausted? I'm not even sure whether he's talking about literal or figurative pain, but it's the thing I can latch onto.

> KATBA_91602
> What hurts?

SJY_1995_
Entire fcking body.
Sorry shit. Whiskey kicking
in. Let me get my glasses.

I huff out a little laugh. Somehow, glasses don't figure into the perfect image that he's cultivated, but it makes me soften a bit toward him. At least there's something about him that's not perfect.

A minute later, he comes back.

SJY_1995_
Better. I think. Still whiskey
problems though.

I shake my head. He's definitely well on his way to
drunk from his phrasing.

KATBA_91602
You want to tell me?

SJY_1995_
Details don't matter. We
made it through. Still pissed
about the missed entrance. I
was swapping battery packs
and I missed my lines. Joon
had to pick up for me.

Joonwoo—Jae, their leader. I remember that much.

KATBA_91602
So, no harm, I guess?
What about being hurt?

SJY_1995_
Not hurt. Just old. It's
harder this year.

I can relate to that. I retired at twenty-one, but even
then, the chronic injuries were starting to creep up on
me. I wasn't able to throw myself at choreography cold
like I could in my teens . . . it took a full class and a few
rounds with a foam roller to get my full range of

motion. If I remember the stats correctly, Simon is coming up on thirty this year.

Twenty-some years is a lot of dancing, particularly with the kind of choreo he performs daily. Ballet is difficult because of its extreme demands, but his K-pop choreography involves a lot of hard-hitting hip-hop moves. No doubt it takes a toll.

KATBA_91602
You have a physical or
massage therapist on tour
with you?

SJY_1995_
Both. Or same. Same
person. Tomorrow.

KATBA_91602
Ice?

SJY_1995_
Working on an ice bath right
now. Joon bringing me
more.

Well, at least he has someone looking after him tonight.

KATBA_91602
Okay, call me back when
you're done.

SJY_1995_
Call?

I flush at that slip.

> KATBA_91602
> I meant message.

SJY_1995_
You won't keep me company?

The flush deepens.

> KATBA_91602
> We're not at the texting
> while naked level yet.

SJY_1995_
How do you know? I could
have been texting you
naked this whole time.
Shit. Sorry. Whiskey again.

I can't suppress the laugh that bursts out of me. Drunk and flirty Simon is hilarious, and I dearly hope he's sober enough to remember every minute of this tomorrow. It takes him so long to come back that I think either he's fallen asleep, passed out, or decided to take me at my word and message me back once he's done with his bath. But no, about four minutes later, he replies.

SJY_1995_
Joon back with an entire
bucket of ice. I look like a
victim of an illegal organ
transplant.

Now I'm laughing so hard I'm crying. I'm also trying

not to think about the fact that he is indeed most likely naked while texting me.

KATBA_91602
DO NOT SEND ME A PHOTO.

SJY_1995_
You should not have issued
a challenge. WHISKEY.

Not five seconds later, a photo comes through and I experience a full-body cringe, praying I'm not about to see something I'll regret. But it's only a photo of a vacant hotel bathtub filled with ice and water. I exhale. He's been messing with me.

KATBA_91602
You scared me.

SJY_1995_
Not that stupid.

KATBA_91602
Afraid I'll alert the press?

SJY_1995_
Afraid I'll get hacked.
Careers ruined for less.

I exhale and shake my head, but it's getting harder to ignore the truth.
I really like this guy.
Katrina, he's looking for a friend. He just has no filter tonight.

KATBA_91602
For real, though, are you
actually okay? Okay people
don't take ice baths.

A long pause. I imagine him stepping into the bath and then push that image out of my head.

SJY_1995_
Real talk? I don't know how
long I can keep this up for.
Thirty is ancient for an idol.
My voice is in top condition.
My body feels like a fucking
Volvo. No, what's that car?
The communist one?
Yugo.

I snort-laugh—*whiskey*—but inwardly, I empathize with what he's saying. Still, I'm not going to make the same mistake I made last time.

KATBA_91602
You want sympathy or
advice?

SJY_1995_
Both maybe? Sympathy first.

KATBA_91602
Let's go for empathy. I
performed for six weeks
with a stress fracture in my
right foot, and after that it
never felt the same.

SJY_1995_
😐

KATBA_91602
So I get the whole performing through pain thing. NSAIDs and ice are your friends. So is your physical therapist, massage therapist, and Pilates instructor. (That was the advice part, btw.)

SJY_1995_
Good advice.

Another pause so long that I feel compelled to check in.

KATBA_91602
You okay there?

SJY_1995_
Yeah. I'm so cold I can't feel my . . . You know what? I'm going to stop now.

KATBA_91602
Because whiskey.

SJY_1995_
Yep.
Thanks, K. I mean it.

KATBA_91602

Sure. Any time. Seriously,

bodywork tomorrow, before

you travel.

SJY_1995_

Promise.

KATBA_91602

화이팅

I lay there in my bed, staring at the ceiling and ignoring the show that has been playing unwatched in the background this whole time. This is okay. I shouldn't read anything into this. He's a nice guy, probably a little lonely, knows I'm a dancer. I can commiserate with him better than anyone outside his fellow members, and maybe he can be more honest with me because there's literally no way this can come back on him. He's been very circumspect, with the exception of whiskey and nakedness. Even if I were to screenshot any of this, there's nothing to prove his identity.

Regardless of what his intentions might be with this conversation, he'll be okay.

I, on the other hand, am absolutely not.

chapter twelve

January 2020, New York Theater Ballet studios

"No! No! Why can't you fucking understand?"

I fall off pointe at the same time the accompanist breaks off his playing as Philip's aggravated voice cuts through the studio space. We've been rehearsing the Rose Adagio for almost two hours now; my lavender leotard is soaked through with sweat and my foot is beginning to throb and swell over the drawstring casing on my pointe shoe. I swipe my forehead with the back of my arm and try to look attentive for the criticism to come, even though his tone shoots me through with anxiety.

Philip marches across the room, his dance sneakers squeaking on the Marley floor, and runs a hand violently through his hair. He nudges me out of the way and steps into an arabesque, grabbing the hand of Damian—one of my four partners in this pas de deux— as he demonstrates. "You look like a robot," he says, exaggerating stiff shoulders and arms. "It needs to be fluid, like your costume. You're not wearing a tutu, for Christ's sake."

This shouldn't help me, but strangely—tone aside—it

does. At least it shows me what he's looking for. It doesn't, however, make it any easier to execute. The traditional choreography calls for Aurora to be partnered and promenaded by four suitors in turn, which makes it a foot-burning and calf-cramping series of balances as the men switch places with one another. But not only are all the balances on my bad foot, but he doesn't want to see the rigidity that's necessary to maintain my one-legged posture throughout the segment.

I can't even begin to guess how I'm supposed to execute what he's asking for.

"Do you see?" he snaps, at he steps back.

I nod, even though I don't. Boyfriend or not, you don't talk back to the choreographer or répétiteur in a rehearsal. You keep working until you execute their vision, however impossible it might seem. He claps his hands and strides back to the front of the room, then signals for the accompanist to begin again.

I step into the arabesque once more, this time trying to focus on reaching both up and out with my body, lifting as much as I can to give a sense of lightness and movement, even while I'm balancing in stillness. This time Philip just watches in silence as the first and second suitors take their turns moving me in a circle before handing me off to the next. I think I've finally got it, but once we get to the fourth, the pain in my foot is too great and I fall forward off pointe. Eli catches me before I smack the ground.

"Jesus Christ," Philip swears, shaking his head. "I thought you had it for a second. Get to the gym and gain some core strength so you can actually execute the fucking movements. *Moving on!*"

I let out a silent sigh of relief, pretending not to see the sympathetic look that Eli shoots my way. Philip has been on a tear this whole week. We've got eight weeks left until opening night, and from what I've heard from the other dancers, their rehearsals have been just as fraught. The best I can describe his vision is an oil painting reproduced in watercolors—this *Sleeping Beauty* has the overall outline and shape of the original, but softened and modernized, sometimes in ways that seem physically impossible.

When it works, it's stunning.

When it doesn't, it's an outright disaster.

More than half the corps de ballet has been in tears, and from what I understand, Maddie hid in a toilet stall for an hour after her first turn at Florine. I can empathize with them, because these rehearsals are pushing me to the brink as well. More than once I've questioned my ability to execute this role. It's the first full-length principal role that requires me to dance in nearly every act, and rather than getting better, it feels like I'm getting worse. Clearly I'm not the only one who thinks so. I mentally debate when I can get into the gym for some balance training on the bosu.

Fortunately, Philip means what he says and moves on to the next section after the balances, which goes more or less smoothly. This time he has some stern words for the cavaliers, but it's far less heated than moments ago. When we conclude thirty minutes later, I'm exhausted, pained, and drenched in sweat. My fellow dancers compliment my work, but I don't miss the sympathetic glances sent my way as they pack up their things and leave me alone with Philip. At least this is a private rehearsal, not requiring the presence of the whole company. They don't need to see how much I'm struggling.

I collapse on the floor under the barre and suck down water before bending forward and plopping my forehead on my knees. My back is to the rest of the rehearsal room, but I still hear Philip's soft approach behind me. Unconsciously, I tense.

Except a gentle touch lands on the bare skin exposed by the low back of my leotard. Philip's strong hands move over my back, thumbs digging into the tight muscles on either side of my spine until they relax. I let out a reluctant, shuddering breath.

"What do you think?" he asks softly. "Greek for dinner?"

I slowly sit up and turn toward him. "Excuse me?"

"You've been saying you want to try that new Greek place down the street from my apartment. I think you deserve a treat after that rehearsal. You were magnificent."

I stare at him. "You've been yelling at me all night."

He sits back on his heels and cocks his head to study me. "Because you needed the motivation. You're brilliant, Kat, but you can get lazy. I don't want you to rest on your very impressive laurels."

Lazy? I've been working my ass off every day for him and he's calling me lazy?

Except, if I really think about it, maybe I am being lazy. I'm calling on my previous knowledge of the choreography—I performed this adagio twice as a student—instead of listening to his cues and trying to understand his vision for the ballet.

I crumple in on myself and rub my forehead wearily. "I know. I'll do better."

"That's my girl." He leans forward and kisses me softly, and when I respond after a few seconds, his hand slips into the low cut front of my leotard. "I promise, I will reward you in all the ways I know how when we get home."

I sigh and pull back. The last thing I want to think about is sex, but I can probably parlay this into one of his absolutely fantastic full-body massages. And as much as I sometimes hate his timing, he always makes sure I'm satisfied in the end. Still, I'm not going to be bought that cheaply. "But first, Greek. You promised."

"Anything for my brilliant girl." He stands and holds out a hand to hoist me to my feet. My knees wobble for a second before I steady myself. He plants a kiss on my forehead. "Go change. I'll meet you in the lobby."

We hardly ever shower at the studios, but tonight I'm going to make an exception—I have a feeling I'm not going to get the chance when we get home, and I can't stand the feel of six hours of sweat on my skin. Fifteen minutes later, I'm clean and dressed in street clothes, my wet hair twisted into a figure-eight on the back of my head and secured with a big clip. Philip is waiting for me in the lobby of the building as promised, bundled in a coat against the winter cold. He slips an arm around my shoulders and guides me out into Lincoln Center.

I think we're headed for the subway station as usual, but instead, Philip hails a taxi at the curb and opens the door for me to get in. Gratefully, I climb into the back seat and scoot over for him, the tension leaving my body now that I know I'm not going to have to walk another half-mile on my throbbing foot tonight. Philip gives the address of the restaurant and is tapping in an order on his phone before we even leave the curb.

"Souvlaki?" he asks.

"I don't care," I say wearily, tipping my head back against the seat. "Whatever you want." He has a habit of doing whatever he wants anyway; this way, he gets to feel like he's taking care of me. And right now, I don't mind. I'm too tired and pained to take any responsibility for anything right now.

Fifteen minutes later, we're walking into the Greek restaurant to pick up our food; fifteen minutes after that, we're sitting cross-legged in front of the coffee table wolfing down keftedes and spinach rice and lemon potatoes with pitas. I eat like I'm starving—for sure I've burned twice as many calories as I've consumed today—and Philip spoons food onto my plate every time it empties. Finally, I push it back. "Enough. I'm so full I can't breathe."

He slings an arm around me and presses his lips to the top of my head. "I like watching you enjoy food. I like just about everything about you."

"Except my balances in the Rose Adagio."

"Except your balances in the Rose Adagio," he agrees lightly. "But I have faith that you'll get it together in time for opening night."

There's something about his tone that sets a nervous quiver in me, but I just smile up at him instead. When he leans down to kiss me, his tongue slipping into my mouth, I push him away playfully. "Don't get ahead of yourself. I want a massage."

His hand skims over my body in response.

"Not that kind of massage. A proper one. Your famous one."

He grins at me and then kisses my nose. "I'm at your service. Go get ready for me."

I push to my feet and head to the bedroom, where I strip down to nothing but my panties and climb into bed. I'll be lucky to get what I want out of this exchange before he gets what he wants, but if I can keep him on task, it will be worth it.

As Philip enters the room and turns down the lights and puts something soft and soothing on the speakers, an errant thought enters my head, one that's appearing more and more frequently these days.

All this sacrifice, all this work. This life.

When *will* it feel like it's worth it?

chapter thirteen

I actually feel somewhat normal when I get ready for my brunch with Amira, and it definitely does not have to do with the good night sleep I most certainly did not have. In fact, I've been jittery and uncertain since I ended my conversation with Simon last night, and I force myself not to look at my phone until after I get out of the shower.

And regret it, because for the first time, he has continued the conversation in the morning.

With a selfie.

From the looks of the mirrored and paneled background, he took it in an elevator. He's wearing a bucket hat that mostly covers his pink hair, a black surgical mask, and heavy black-rimmed glasses, along with a nondescript white T-shirt. He's holding up his hand with his thumb and forefinger crossed in a sign I don't understand. Money, maybe? Is it suppose to mean this is the money shot?

I'm not sure what to think or where to look first. I hope he's on the way to his massage therapist or PT like he promised, but at least there's no sign of a rough night in the photo. I can't see his mouth, but the lift beneath his eyes tells me that he's smiling.

Smiling is a good sign.

The fact that my heart is palpitating because of a guy who is literally only showing his eyes and one hand in a photo is not.

I put the phone aside while I finish getting ready, putting on a bit more makeup than I normally do, then slip into cute jeans and a white lace blouse. Inexplicably, I reach for the same leather jacket and boots that I wore out with Jackson, and I can only conclude that all the leather in the videos I've been watching of Helios and Hyperion have done some sort of permanent damage to my psyche. I am just swiping on a last coat of coppery-red lipstick when Amira messages that she's waiting for me downstairs.

It's time to go, but before I let myself out, I pull my phone out and do the thing I knew I was going to do from the start, even if I didn't admit it to myself. I find a spot with good natural light, hold the phone out and snap a selfie.

No, I snap thirty selfies and then pick the best out of the bunch—one where my lips are turned up just enough to look like a knowing smirk, my eyes crinkled a tiny bit at the corners. I look particularly good today, so I know exactly what response I want when I attach it to the chat and press send.

I'm downstairs in two minutes and when I yank open the car door and climb in, Amira lets out a low wolf whistle. "Dang. You look hot today. What's the occasion?"

I blow her a kiss. "Just trying to look good for my best girl."

Amira laughs and glances over her shoulder as she pulls away from the curb. "You seem like you're feeling better. No more dizziness? Body aches?"

"No, doctor, I feel just fine." Amira throws me a glance at my flippancy, and I sigh, turning serious. "Still a little tired, but I'm mostly back to normal. As long as I avoid unexpected trips on stage, I think I'll be okay. How was your night?"

I've been in my own little post-episode fog, combined with my Simon fixation, and with a note of shame I realize now that I can't remember what she had planned for the weekend.

"We had dinner at that new Mediterranean place on Vine I was talking about, and then we hit the clubs. It took us all about an hour to realize that Megan wasn't drinking and then she dropped the news on us."

Amira throws me a significant look, and I quickly piece together my jagged memories. That's right, she's told me at least a million times; she's a bridesmaid in a college friend's wedding, and last night was the woman's "hen night." Obviously, Megan is British.

"She's pregnant?" I guess.

"Just found out. She spent half the night running back and forth to the bathroom, poor thing." Amira laughs helplessly. "We all ended up going back to her place and watching movies while she ate candied ginger."

I groan in sympathy. "So much for her last hurrah."

"Oh, the last hurrah was a long time ago. They've been practically married since college. It was fun. And the restaurant was good, at least. We should go. You'd enjoy it."

It's an olive branch of sorts, Amira's attempt to include me. I know it bothers her that I spend so much time alone, but despite the fact I enjoy the interaction with her and my clients, I need my down time. Even when I didn't need so much rest, I always preferred a quiet night in with friends to hitting the town. People always thought that I was bold because I enjoyed performing so much, but there is a distinct difference between the character I put on when I stepped onto stage and the person inside.

Not surprisingly, my thoughts flicker back to Simon, and I push them down. But now that I'm thinking about it, I have to ask the question. I hold up my hand, crossing my thumb and forefinger like he had. "I've been meaning to ask you. What does this mean?"

Amira draws to a stop at a light and glances at me. I see the flicker of amusement on her face; she thinks I've been doing a deep dive into K-pop content, which to be fair, isn't that far from the truth. "It's a finger heart."

I look at my hand. "How do you figure?"

"From a certain angle, I guess. You'll see idols doing this"—she makes a heart with both hands against her chest and then her cheeks—"but the finger-heart is kind of a subtle appreciation to fans."

Fans. That doesn't make me feel good, but I'm probably reading too much into it. "Oh, okay. Just wondering."

Amira doesn't say anything as the light changes and she speeds up again. I can tell she wants to laugh but she doesn't want to put me off my newfound interest. I deserve it. I've given her crap—lovingly, of course—about her obsession with pretty Korean men every since I've known her, so I more than deserve it. It wasn't that I shamed her for her interests or didn't share them. I simply had no margin in my life to think of anything but getting through each day.

When we finally get to Charlie's, a brunch spot in a dusty corner of Calabasas, the gravel parking lot is already packed with cars and a few Harleys. We climb out of her wagon, and I snag a rare free spot on one of the benches outside the rustic wood-and-glass building while Amira goes inside to give her name to the hostess. Several minutes later, she comes out holding two curvy glasses with umbrellas and colored straws—a mimosa for her and a non-alcoholic version made with sparkling water for me. I drink rarely and definitely not during the day; alcohol makes my symptoms worse, so it's usually not something I want to risk.

I take the glass from her with a *thank you* and scoot over to make room for her on the bench. We sip quietly for a few minutes, but it doesn't take long for me to pick up the discomfort radiating from her.

"You might as well spit it out," I say, leaning back against the wooden slats of the bench. "I can practically hear you thinking."

Amira throws me a look. "Am I that obvious?"

"Let's say subtlety is not your strong suit." I smile to temper the statement, and her expression softens.

"I've just been worried about you lately. Ever since the concert, you've been . . . withdrawn, maybe? Distracted? You've worked so hard to get where you are, and I'm afraid that this one setback might have . . . thrown you off."

My eyebrows fly up. I have been admittedly distracted, for obvious reasons, but I didn't think I was coming off as withdrawn. I reach for her hand and squeeze. "I'm okay, I promise."

Her eyebrows lift, mimicking my expression perfectly. "Really?"

"Really." This time I put some firmness into my tone. "I haven't been obsessing"—not over my health, at least—"I've just been trying to take care of myself. You know I need my alone time."

Amira doesn't seem to believe me, but she also doesn't seem to be inclined to argue with me. We talk about other things, but I don't think I'm imagining the faint undercurrent of discomfort between us, something that I've never before felt with her. I'm glad when our names are finally called and the hostess leads us to a small table deep in the open-air patio.

After perusing the menu, I order Eggs Florentine with a side of fruit and black coffee, knowing that I'll be lucky to be able to eat half of it. Amira orders their famous sausage breakfast sandwich and a latte before she starts talking to me about her ideas for adding more group classes on the weekends. It's Sunday, but considering we work together all week and take time off when we need it, there's really no such thing as work/life boundaries in our relationship. It all blends together.

"I like it," I say finally. "You know I trust you. If we have money in the budget and room in the schedule, let's do it. I've been wanting to expand our community offerings. And if Regina is willing to teach those classes, it doesn't put any extra pressure on me."

"Good. I'll start putting it together then." She relaxes, and I think maybe I misread her concern. Was she worried about what I'd think of her ideas? I've always trusted her implicitly when it comes to the business and marketing side of our studio; if I had to focus on all those aspects along with teaching, we wouldn't be nearly as successful as we are.

We're finishing up our food—or at least, she is; my stomach warned me about a quarter of the way through my eggs that it would be accepting no further deposits, so I set it aside to box up for later—when my phone beeps in my purse. I try not to react, but I must flinch, because Amira's eyes narrow again. "Do you need to get that?"

"Probably junk," I say, but I reach for the phone anyway and swipe the screen.

Message from Simon. I tap it reflexively and find that it's a photo of him in the airport. Or at least it's a photo of his feet in Converse, propped up on a battered leather duffel bag, an airplane visible through the window beyond. *Next stop: Dallas*, says the caption.

I think I've done a good job at hiding my reaction, but something must give me away—a slight smile, a softening of my expression—because Amira crosses her arms on the table and leans over to me. "Okay, that does it. Now I know you really are hiding something. What's going on, Trina?" She lowers her voice. "Are you seeing someone else? Is that the reason you dumped Jackson?"

"No, of course not," I say. "It was just a message from a friend."

"A friend who makes you blush?"

Damn. That has always been my worst tell. Call it the curse of the redhead; my pale skin shows every single thing. It was only because of stage makeup that I didn't look like a beet when I finished a full-length ballet.

"It's nothing," I say firmly, sliding my phone back into my purse. But I'm so flustered that I fumble it, and it hits the cement patio and bounces under the table.

Amira reaches it first, an automatic reaction, as is her instinct to glance at the screen as she does. It's still open to my Instagram messages, and her eyes flick between the photo and me. "What is this?"

My blush turns into a blaze, and I reach for the phone. Amira gives it up immediately. She really didn't plan on invading my privacy, but now that she's seen the photo, she's not going to give up. I hold the device in my lap while I try to think of an answer.

There's nothing but the truth. I don't know why I feel so embarrassed, so protective. Maybe because up until now I didn't have to think about what this actually is, what it means, and now I'm going to have to explain why I'm suddenly so invested in a person I don't know.

"It's Simon," I say simply.

She blinks at me. "Simon?" And then she seems to recall the airport photo, the comment about the next stop, and her eyes widen comically. "*Seojun?*"

Slowly, I nod.

"How? When? How? He doesn't even have an Instagram account. He's said publicly that he doesn't like social media."

"It's private." I shrug, more casually than I feel. "He messaged me after the concert to make sure I was okay."

"From a private Instagram account."

"Yeah."

Amira's face shifts into something approaching pity. "Oh, honey."

Cold slides down from the crown of my head, and for a second, I think it's my condition, but no, this is just run-of-the-mill humiliation. "What? Don't look at me like that."

She leans forward, lowering her voice. "Are you sure you're not being catfished?"

"Yes! Of course. That was the first thing I thought. I told him to prove it, and he had his manager confirm it through the official Instagram account."

While that relaxes her a degree, she still looks skeptical. "How do you know it wasn't hacked?"

"I mean. I don't, I guess, but. . . ." I shake my head sharply and give up. I unlock the phone and shove it across the table to her. "Fine. Judge for yourself. Scroll all the way up to the top. It's not like we're talking about anything all that private."

Slowly, she takes the phone and flicks her fingertip along the screen. I glance away while she reads, watching birds hop along the concrete just outside the railing that marks off the patio, even though the tips of my ears still burn. I turn my head when I hear her huff out a little laugh. "What?"

She's repressing a smile. "Whiskey."

I bite my lip. The whole exchange was pretty funny, and I'm still surprised he didn't acknowledge it this morning. Or maybe he was in full control of his words and just using whiskey as an excuse.

Now Amira outright laughs.

"Yugo?"

"Yeah."

Finally, she's done and she pushes the phone back to me. "I have to admit. It's convincing."

"Convincing? You still don't believe it's him."

She hesitates, and I know she's trying not to crush me. I can already feel the sick, squirmy roots of doubt growing in my stomach. Is that why I didn't tell her? Because I didn't really believe any of it?

"It sounds like him," she says slowly. "Believe me when I say that I know these guys better than any stranger has a right to. It feels . . . on brand. But if I know that, so do the scammers."

"What scam? He hasn't asked me for anything."

"Yet. Some of these are long games, Trina. You wouldn't believe the sophistication of the AI deep fakes going through the K-pop world. People who speak perfect Korean using voice changers and posing as idols. They strike up personal conversations with fans for days, sometimes weeks, and then when they're hooked, they say that their managers are hassling them and in order to continue, they need to pretend like they're paying for fan calls. Things like that."

I swallow, the manager comment hitting home. Wasn't that one of the first few things that he'd mentioned in his messages?

And yet this is all predicated on her belief that there is no way that Simon—Seojun—cared enough to reach out, that someone could know what happened to me on the side of the stage and was able to track me down through the video and the one photo that Amira posted, and then immediately put together a scam within three hours.

I suppose it isn't impossible. Scammers are notoriously resourceful. . .but even for them, this is an awfully elaborate scheme.

"Fine," I say. "Let's see." I pull out my phone again and type out a blunt message.

> KATBA_91602
> Amira is convinced you're a scammer running a long con on me. Convince her otherwise.

I think about adding a happy face, but at the last minute, I leave it off. If this really is a scam, better they figure that I've caught on than think they can continue to lead me along. I stare at the screen for a second, but an immediate response would make me more suspicious than not. Given that he was sitting at the gate when he took the photo, he could already have his phone off and be seated on the plane right now. I shove my phone in my bag.

"That's done, then. Only time will tell the truth."

Amira nods and finishes her coffee, but she can barely look me in the eye. She knows that for a little while, I was happy, and she's just potentially ruined it for me. I can't hold it against her, though. She always has my best interests at heart, and she'd never forgive herself if I was taken in by a scam that she could have prevented. Just in time, our waitress comes to our table with the check and asks if we need boxes. Amira pulls out her card, waving me off when I try to pay, then looks at me with an overly bright smile.

"So. Sunday afternoon. What do we want to do next?"

If I were a better person, a stronger person, I would say that we should drive down Malibu Canyon and along PCH . . . walk on the beach . . . head into Santa Monica and find something to do. But I'm not, and the seeds that she planted have grown into twin vines of doubt and shame. I swallow hard and avert my eyes.

"I should go home. Tomorrow's a busy day."

I can tell Amira is disappointed or maybe worried, but I don't have the heart to put up a front anymore. I *am* tired. But I don't know if it's physical tiredness or just weariness over what my life has become.

chapter fourteen

I would like to say that I go home and never think about the unread message sitting in the conversation thread. Alas, I am neither that strong nor well-adjusted. After I check my phone about a hundred times over the course of thirty minutes, I purposely put it on the charger in the bedroom and then change out of my brunch clothes into a pair of leggings and a tank top. Then I roll my yoga mat out on the rug in the living room and stretch out on top of it.

Slowly, carefully, I begin my floor barre routine, mimicking the exercises that start every ballet class in a prone position, muscles engaged, legs turned out from my hips. For nearly a year after I was diagnosed, this was the closest to ballet I could get, lying on my back to keep my heart rate down, desperately trying to keep my muscles limber and flexible and keep the range of motion in my joints. It cut a lot of time off my rehab, but there's still something that feels defeating about having to retreat to this option five years later.

Amira once asked me why I bother. POTS is considered controllable, but not curable, and once you have it, you have it—it's hard to tell when symptoms will flare or an episode will occur. Sure, I have triggers that I try to avoid, but it became clear to me pretty quickly that any dreams I might have had about getting back on stage or even into a ballet studio are futile. *Why do you do it if it just reminds you of what you lost?* she asked.

It's hard to explain to anyone who isn't a dancer that class isn't about performing, it's about the discipline. The routine. I started dancing seriously when I was seven years old, and even now, retired, I never feel so much myself as when my hand rests on the polished wood of the barre and my feet turn out into first position. Being in the studio, starting my pliés like I have every day of almost my entire life, is the closest that I feel to whole.

It wasn't just the stage that got taken away with my diagnosis. It was part of my soul.

Unexpectedly, tears prick my eyes and spill from the corners, making small trails across my temples. I blink them away and continue, my arms rounded above me, my leg lifting in front of me, stretched and extended. By the time I'm finished, I'm panting and my muscles are trembling, but I feel like I accomplished something. Took something back.

It's about the discipline and not the result.

I have to engage that discipline when I push myself up off the ground and roll up my yoga mat. I have to engage that discipline to walk into the bathroom and take a shower, even though I end up sitting down in the porcelain tub to finish it. And I most certainly have to call upon it to leave my phone where it is without checking to see if Simon has responded.

I reheat my leftovers from this morning and eat them on the sofa in front of the TV. I'm still ignoring my phone, so I put on Netflix and choose a sitcom I've watched start to finish half a dozen times, just for the noise. My stomach grumbles at me, a sure sign that I ate too much, so I stretch out on the chaise part of the sofa to relieve the pressure on my midsection and zone out. Somewhere after dusk, I fall asleep. It's only when I drag myself back into the bathroom to brush my teeth and crawl into bed do I allow myself to pick up the phone.

One message.

AMIRA
Just checking on you. You
ok?

Her concern usually feels like a warm blanket, but tonight, it feels invasive, intrusive. I put the phone back without responding, flip off the light, and pull the covers up to my neck. I can deal with it all tomorrow. It will still be there. It always is.

• • •

The next morning I wake feeling physically good but emotionally spent, and I have to power through my morning routine just to get myself out the door on time. For some reason, Misha decided to take up residence under the sofa—it must be cooler under there, considering his long-haired coat—and never crept into my bed in the middle of the night like he normally does. I leave him a scoop of food and refill his water bowl, then grab my smoothie cup and my bag and head to the studio.

Monday. I try to psych myself up for the long line of privates that I have scheduled, but the enthusiasm just isn't there and I don't want to explore why. I'm not even sure it's about Simon. Sure, I'll be disappointed if he never responds . . . or rather, proves that it was never him in the first place. I will probably even feel the loss like getting dumped by someone that I had a few dates with. But it won't crush me.

So why can't I shake this morose feeling today?

Amira is late for a change, so I turn on all the lights, flip on the air conditioning, double-check the condition of the studio to make sure it's sparkling clean and ready for my clients. It is, of course, so I slip off my shoes and head to the barre in my slippery socks. I only get through my third exercise, tendus, before my watch beeps its angry reminder at me and I have to shift to the floor instead. I stretch my muscles thoroughly, then grab a foam roller from the corral on the wall and roll everything out for good measure.

Why do I continue to maintain my flexibility and my physique?

Because I earned it and it's mine to keep or lose. It's my choice whether I'm going to let circumstances crush me and make me settle. It's that thought that levers me up off the ground and shoves my feet back into my shoes. By the time Delores walks through the door, I wouldn't say that I feel cheery, but I feel quieter. Centered. Determined. I put on a pleasant smile and greet her as I always do, then start moving through the classical series with her as we do each week.

When Millie shows up a little early in her cute workout outfit, I greet her warmly and look her over surreptitiously. If I'm not mistaken, she seems a little thinner through the waist and her face is a little slimmer; I don't want to ask if she's consulted the nutritionist I suggested. When I settle her on the Reformer and start the beginning series with her, however, she seems stronger and more energetic than she had last week. I can only hope that she took a little bit of what I said to heart. I can understand the need to fit standards, but I've seen too many performers damage themselves through starvation diets and eating disorders to wish it on anyone.

I send her off with another hug and good luck wishes, then steal into the back of the studio to eat the salad Amira ordered for me. She came in briefly to pick up some stuff from the office, ordered lunch, and then ducked out as soon as it arrived. I don't know if she's avoiding me because she feels bad about yesterday or if she just has things to do and I've been too occupied with clients to ask her directly. Only then do I realize that I never responded to her text the night before and she probably thinks I'm mad at her. I'll need to give her a call later and smooth things over.

I'm somewhere between exhausted and trashed when I lock up the studio for the night and push around the soft mop to dust the wooden floors before I go. Normally, I'd have Amira drive me home, but since I've burned that bridge, I navigate Ventura Boulevard slowly and carefully, trying not to breathe in the exhaust from passing cars. I have to rest halfway up the flight of stairs to my second-floor apartment, and I don't even make it to my bedroom once I'm inside. I just kick off my shoes and flop down on the sofa.

This sucks.

Every time I think I'm back to normal, I get slapped in the face that I will never be normal.

I let myself rest for about an hour on the sofa, and then I pry myself up and find an all-natural frozen meal to put in the microwave. That four minutes and thirty seconds proves to be taxing, so I lay down on the kitchen floor, justifying it with the knowledge that I just cleaned it last week and I don't wear outdoor shoes inside.

I eat dinner leaning up against the cabinet just so I don't have to get up, walk to the living room, and then back to the kitchen when I'm done. I toss the fork into the sink from a seated position, lean over to toss the container in the trash, and then push myself up slowly.

It's not until I've completed the daunting task of brushing my teeth and collapsing into bed that I remember I still haven't responded to Amira.

I tap out a quick message.

> TRINA
> Sorry, I forgot to reply last night. Good day today, though. See you at the studio tomorrow?

Almost immediately, I get a reply back.

> AMIRA
> No problem, glad to hear it.
> See you tomorrow!

Before I put my phone on the charger, I quickly check Instagram, just in case there has been some glitch involved in the notification system.

My last message still sits there, but this time it has the little checkmark that says it's been read. Read and ignored.

It seems like things are finally back to normal.

Whatever normal means.

● ● ●

I have always known that I'm not a person who does well with ambiguity and uncertainty. That sounds strange for someone who pursued a career whose outcome was far from guaranteed. At least when you spend your teenage years in high school and college, if you work hard, you're somewhat guaranteed a job when you finish. There are no such guarantees in ballet, where you can work your entire youth away just to find out your extension is too low, your feet are too flat, your talent is insufficient. You have to be able to pivot.

And yet for all of that, there is control in the grind, in the way you show up to class every day, try to perfect one more step, force your turnout an extra degree, stretch your feet for a little bit more arch. There is control in your relationship with food—which unfortunately can backfire—and there's control in how you compose yourself.

There is very little control over anything that happens this week.

Tuesday is fine. Amira and I make up, and after we close the studio to hand it over to our afternoon teachers, we go out to lunch and chat like there was never any tension between us at all. Wednesday is another long day, and I make it through my sessions even though I have to sit for all my afternoon privates. Thursday, I can barely get out of bed without my heart rate spiking and I have no idea why. I call Amira and have her cancel everything. Friday, I'm exhausted as if I had another syncope episode, but my blood pressure, heart rate, and vision are all fine.

What. The. Hell.

And through it all, my message to Simon remains read but unacknowledged. In the back of my mind, I think it's the stress over that one simple message that's causing my body to behave like a toddler having a temper tantrum, and then I feel foolish that I'm letting something so stupid wreck my week. Then I'm stressed out over my foolishness and mad that the stress is exacerbating my condition.

I'm a mess.

It all comes to a head on Friday afternoon after my last session when Amira comes up to me and says, "Okay, you and I are going to have a come-to-Jesus talk. You're spinning out."

I swallow and close my eyes. "You're right. Lay it on me."

"You didn't think you were in love with this guy, did you?"

I snap my eyes open. "No. Of course not." That has not even once entered my mind. That he was my friend, yes. That I liked him and maybe would like the opportunity to get to know him better, however that might look? Certainly. But it wasn't more than that.

"Then what's the deal?"

I take a long, deep breath and sort through my feelings before I can settle on an answer. "I swore to myself that I wasn't ever going to trust so easily again. That I wouldn't be fooled again. And now I feel like an absolute idiot that I was taken in so easily." My voice drops to a whisper. "And I feel even worse that you were the one who had to break it to me."

Inexplicably, tears are back in my eyes, and Amira practically crumples in front of me. She pulls me to her. "I love you, babe. I know you hate that I hover over you, but someone needs to. Not because you're not capable, but because you deserve it. Okay?"

I nod against her shoulder—she's a lot taller than me—and then pull away, wiping my eyes with the back of my hand. The tears still make me feel weak but there's not much to be done about it.

"I have a solution," she says, "but you're not going to like it. Even if it is the best way to handle it. You know what I'm going to say."

I do. Because I've been contemplating the same thing all week, I just haven't been able to summon the courage to do it. I've been holding out hope for some proof that I haven't been taken in as badly as I think I have.

I pull out my phone, tap the screen a few times until I get to the message and hover over SJY's profile. Then I tap *block*.

It takes me longer to decide on the next step, and I have to restrain myself from opening the message or downloading the photos.

Instead I hover on the message thread for a long moment and press *delete*.

I feel vaguely ashamed to admit how much that unanswered message has been affecting me, given that I am a grown woman in full possession of her faculties. Okay, *full possession* is overstating things in every sense of the word, but still, it's not like I'm some emotionally stunted child. And it still takes me the rest of the night to get my head back into the right place.

I lay on the floor, staring at the ceiling and psycho-analyzing myself even though I'm quite literally unqualified for the effort in every single way. I've spent most of my life *not* analyzing myself, because analysis has the tendency to shine lights in the ugly little corners of your profession that you don't want to think about. The only way you can keep going is by letting those remain in the dark and focusing on what you can control.

But now?

I have to admit that whatever I'm doing, I'm not actually *living*. There's only so long that a person can do nothing but get up, go to work—even if it's work they enjoy—go home, eat dinner, and go to bed before the routine starts to make them insane. And yes, I realize it doesn't sound much different than what I left behind, but there was a payoff at the end. A goal. A successful performance, a packed house, the applause of the audience. The exhilaration from the result of all that practice.

But here, I'm just churning day after day with no end in sight.

"Simon" had added into my day something to look forward to, false as it may have been, a variation on the stale life I've been living for years. He—whoever he was—shined a light on the fact that there was something missing in my life. For that, I should feel more grateful than foolish.

But identifying a void is different than knowing how to fill the vacancy.

On Saturday night, Amira invites me over to her house to hang out, order a pizza, and watch a movie. The pizza is good, the movie less so, and halfway through I turn to her and say, "I think I'm bored."

She laughs. "Okay? We can do something else if you want. It's not a great film."

"No, I don't mean that. I mean, I do mean that. . . this movie is objectively awful. But . . . I need something different in my life."

"What you need is a boyfriend." She raises her eyebrows at me significantly. "But that would require you actually leaving the house and meeting people."

"No, that's the very last thing I need." Actually, she's not wrong, but that isn't the *only* thing I need, and in this context, it just exacerbates the problem. I don't want one more focus that depends on someone else's response. "I need some sort of goal. Some sort of endgame."

"Like, I don't know . . . speaking and teaching at a Pilates Conference this winter?"

I stop and look at her.

"I mean, it's a challenge. You'll have to take very good care of yourself for once"—she fixes me with a stare, though what I did to deserve it, I don't know—"and it means developing an entire speech as well as a class that you can give to a group of mixed-level, mixed-ability students. In a little more than four months."

I'm sure that wouldn't be much of a challenge for someone else, but to me it feels daunting. It means not only planning the actual event but for all the eventualities, including what I'm going to do if I wake up feeling like a train hit me.

So, basically . . . exactly what I'm looking for.

Amira is smiling at me as if she can see what's going through my head. "Should I call them on Monday and tell them you're in?"

Slowly, I nod my head. "Yeah. Let's do it."

The movie doesn't get any better, but when Amira drives me home, there's a lightness in my heart that's been absent for some time. And while I go straight to bed, my hips aching for absolutely no good reason, instead of going straight to sleep, I pull out a notepad and start to write.

Which I continue to do all day Sunday, with a brief break at a bistro down the street for a grilled chicken sandwich and the best seasoned fries I've ever had.

When I return to the studio on Monday, energized, Amira laughs at me. "You're such a masochist."

"Of course I am, I'm a dancer. Besides, I prefer *goal-oriented.*"

"I'm going to call them in a little bit and tell them that you would be delighted to accept their invitation."

And I am. Truly. When Amira comes back and confirms that they've slotted me in to deliver the day two keynote, which is focused on adaptations for different client needs—something that my program well prepared me for—I only freak out for about twenty minutes before a calm comes over me. I don't know why

I've been panicking so much. I have the knowledge. I have the discipline. I don't love public speaking, but I'm certainly not bad at it.

There is nothing about this that I can't do.

Because I'm certain that repeated rehearsal is going to be the key to my success, I turn my attention to getting the polished speech completed. Each night for the next week when I leave the studio, I go home and sit on the sofa or my bed with my laptop and outline, write, add, and delete, until I finally have a finished draft. Nothing near polished, of course, but at least it's something to work with. *You can't edit a blank page*, Amira repeatedly tells me.

Apparently, I can't edit a filled one either, because instead of being motivated to edit it into shape, I just stare at the word salad on my screen. Finally, when Friday edges towards midnight after two hours of this, I email it to Amira with the subject line: *Help*.

I'm surprised when I immediately get a message back.

AMIRA
Happy to help. On MONDAY.

I can't blame her for enforcing boundaries, but I understand when she sends me a selfie along with a *very* good-looking blond guy, both of them looking sweaty and maybe slightly inebriated, the lights and crowds behind them indicating a club.

TRINA
Good for you.
Have fun, be safe.

She hearts my comment in response, and I assume, gets back to Hot Blond.

I don't know if it's the feeling that I'm still missing out

on my life—not that a club hookup is my idea of fun—or loneliness or sheer boredom, but for the first time in a week, I find myself opening my phone and searching for Helios. There are official recordings of certain songs from the Phoenix shows—the opening number, Jae's solo stage, unreleased songs, the encore—but instead I find myself clicking on a shaky full concert upload taken by a fan somewhere near the front of the stadium.

Five minutes in, I have to respect their dedication—the fan must have held their phone up over their head for the entire concert in order to capture this particular view. And despite the fact that the jerky motion occasionally makes me sick, I sit there and watch the entire thing.

I want to say I feel absolutely nothing, but that would be a lie. I was mesmerized the first time I saw this show because of the sheer talent and mastery on display. Now, I'm impressed by their consistency. I have a flawless memory for choreography and everything is just as I'd remembered it, down to the angle of arms and heads, the shifting of formations. And I know now that even if I hadn't been pulled up on stage, my eye would have gone repeatedly to Simon.

Seojun.

Because Simon, at least the version of Simon that I know, doesn't exist.

It's not until I finish the entire two and a half hour video that I understand what I've been looking for the whole time. A broken headset mic, a missed entrance, lines sung by Jae that should have been sung by Seojun. A reason for the drunken frustration that I'd witnessed in an Instagram chat.

But, for all that I could tell, their performance was flawless.

chapter fifteen

January 2020, New York Theater Ballet studios

Over the next two months, I work harder than I ever have in my life. The closer we get to opening night, the more tense and demanding Philip gets. I can't even blame him. Now that we're in full cast rehearsals, putting all the moving parts together, I understand his vision. And it's astounding.

Big, lavish ballroom scenes. Technically demanding choreography that reimagines the classic sequences through the swing and flirtation of the jazz age. Even I'm awed, watching the corps de ballet rehearse the first act from the edges of the studio. Philip has engaged a jazz drummer to accompany our pianist, and the energy in the room is palpable.

But that doesn't mean it makes my part feel any more achievable. I'm still struggling with the Rose Adagio and my third act variation isn't coming along any better. Every time I take the center of the room, I can feel the eyes of the other company members on me, assessing, judging. Wondering if Philip made a mistake in casting me, if it has less to do with my talent and more to do with the fact I'm sleeping with him.

So I work harder.

Every moment that I'm not in the studio, I'm in the gym, lifting weights or doing training on the bosu ball, or I'm with one of the company's Pilates trainers, working out the imbalances in my body that are starting to show as I struggle through the choreography. There's not a day that I get out of bed without pain, and while that's not really an unusual feature in my life as a dancer, I start to wonder if it's an indication that I'm overtraining. My entire life becomes monitoring my diet, managing my workouts, and assimilating every last correction that Philip gives me in rehearsal. By the end of the day, I'm so tired I can barely drag myself out of the studio.

But Philip must be able to see how hard I'm working, because he hasn't yelled at me like he did that first day. He gives me calm corrections, and while irritation might creep into his tone, he no longer raises his voice. For my part, I'm downright meek in rehearsals, doing what I'm told, making minute adjustments until he's perfectly happy with how his steps sit on me. At the end of the night, he calls a taxi for us, picks up food on the way home, and prepares an ice bath for my still-problematic feet. Neither of us could be doing any more to make this ballet work.

So it comes as a surprise when we finish rehearsal one night and Philip comes over to where I'm slumped beneath the barre. He glances at his watch. "I have a dinner meeting tonight. Don't wait up for me."

I unfold myself from my forward stretch and look up at him in surprise. "Oh? Did you tell me about it? I must have forgotten."

He frowns at me and his face twists into something alarming. "I didn't realize I had to clear my activities with you."

I blink at the sudden change in tone. "Of course you don't. I just thought maybe I'd . . ." My voice trails off under his hard stare. "I'll just order something in then."

"Don't forget to ice your feet. You were struggling in the balances again." He moves to my side and I think he's going to bend to kiss me, but instead he just places a light hand on top of my head. "Get some sleep. Tomorrow is a long day. Full first act run-through."

I stare at Philip's departing back as he leaves the rehearsal room, his stride quick and confident, and slump back against the wall, too tired to even remove my pointe shoes. The rehearsal room is draining of the other dancers as they collect their various warm-ups, bags, and props, leaving only me in the silent space, my form reflected tiny and forlorn in the mirror across from me. It's tempting in this moment to think about other choices I could have made. Had I not accepted that first dinner from Philip, Maddie and I might still be living in the cute condo in Brooklyn, friends and sisters rather than virtual strangers who exchange pleasantries at the studio. We'd order in Japanese food, curl up on the couch, and watch something on Netflix while Misha purrs happily, draped over one or the other of us.

But that's just exhaustion talking. I'm not the one who broke things between Maddie and me. She's the one who decided that she didn't need me in her life anymore, despite the fact that I came to New York for her. She's the one who decided that hiding a relationship I knew she wouldn't approve of was the unforgivable sin. She's the one who has never once asked me how I'm holding up, even as she sees me being crushed beneath the pressure of this role, even though I do occasionally catch sympathetic looks when Philip is being particularly critical.

Philip, on the other hand, has been here every step

of the way. There hasn't been a night when he doesn't wait on me, massage out my overworked muscles, make sure I eat, take my vitamins, drink enough water. The only reason he didn't see fit to tell me about his meeting tonight was because he's just as stressed over the slow progress of the ballet as I am.

I untie my pointe shoe ribbons and pull my shoes off, wincing at the slight swelling in my right foot, then slide my feet into soft crocheted slippers and start to gather my stuff. I can shower at the apartment, so I just make a quick stop at my locker, trade my leotard and tights for my street clothes and pack my bag. The studios have cleared out quickly this late, and all the office lights are off as I walk down the deserted hallway toward the exit.

Or maybe it's not that deserted after all. I almost groan when I catch up to a familiar willowy form near the exit. Deirdre.

She pushes through the door, and to my surprise, holds it open for me. I step through and give a nod of thanks, but I don't wait up for her as I head across the square. We might manage to be civil in rehearsals, but she's never made it a secret that she thinks I slept my way into my current roles, and I haven't made it any secret that I think she's over the hill and losing her technique. Suffice it to say, at this point, it's a mutual dislike.

But to my surprise, she catches up to me. Her voice is casual when she asks, "Going home alone tonight?"

I slide her a suspicious look. She doesn't sound like she's being catty, but I don't trust it. At this point, all our out-of-studio interactions are more cutting than a fencing match. "He had a meeting."

"Ah, yes," she says knowingly. "The *meetings*."

I frown at her. Even though I know I shouldn't take

the bait, I can't keep myself from asking, "What do you mean by that?"

"Nothing." She shakes her head and thrusts her hands into her sweatshirt pockets. "Honestly, he lasted a lot longer than I thought he would. I was beginning to think you had him under some sort of spell with how devoted he's been to you."

"We're perfectly happy, thanks," I say, even though her use of past tense hasn't escaped me.

"That's good then. I've always said that the only way his relationship would last is if he found someone who could overlook his indiscretions. I honestly didn't think you would. Girls your age are usually romantics."

Now I know she's just trying to get under my skin; it's what she does. And yet I still find myself stopping in the middle of the dark cement square, turning to her. "If you want to say something to me, just say it outright. Stop dancing around the topic."

Deirdre shrugs, but there's a hint of a smile on her face when she says. "I'll put it simply for you. Philip is fucking other women."

I laugh and turn away. "You'll have to do better than that. He's always with me. When would he have the time?"

"When indeed? Unless of course, it's someone at the company. And he's not with you right now, is he? Did he tell you where he was going?"

"He doesn't have to," I grit out. "I trust him."

Deirdre lets out a long breath. "Ahh. So you are one of those romantics. Listen, I know you think I'm just telling you this because I don't like you, and that's true. But I'm also telling you because it's painful to watch from the outside. At least in my case, I didn't want a relationship with him, and he was good enough in bed to make it worth my while."

With that blunt statement, Deirdre turns on her heel and strides away, leaving me staring in shock at her departing back.

Deirdre. And Philip. Together. Even though I know it was probably long in the past, the revelation at this moment, when he's out somewhere else with God knows who, shakes me, just as she intended it to. It's not like I thought he was an angel; hookups are pretty common in the company, and we deal with the ends of relationships with a certain laissez-faire attitude. But he and I aren't just hooking up. We're not just dating. This is a committed relationship. We're *living* together. My mail comes to his place. I file my taxes under his address.

Shit. This is not something I need in my head, not when I'm this tired and vulnerable. She was probably lying anyway. As she said, she has reasons not to like me, and she never passes up the chance to get in a dig.

But the suspicions won't go away, even as I make the quick trip home via taxi, the cityscape silently sliding by in the dark. They persist when I walk into the pristine and empty apartment. They nag at me when I order in Greek food again, and they linger while I climb into the big, lonely bed by myself. Where is he exactly? What kind of meeting starts at nine o'clock? Will he even come home?

Except when I wake up the next morning, I'm not alone. Philip is snugged up behind me, an arm slung over my hip, his head tucked onto the pillow beside mine. All my tension melts away, and I let out a huge sigh. I shouldn't have let Deirdre get to me. I should have trusted the man who has been on my side since the beginning, my champion at the company and the reason I have the career I do now, not the dancer who is jealous of my success.

I can tell by the color of the light coming through the window that it's still early, so I try to extract myself from the bed without waking him. But the minute I start to slide away, Philip's arm tightens over my midsection.

"Where are you going?" His sleepy voice carries a familiar tone that I can't possibly miss.

"I thought I'd get to the gym a little early today."

He tugs me back to him and grinds his hips against my buttocks, his intentions unmistakable. "I promise you, I'll give you a workout at home."

And even though I want nothing more than to take a shower, eat a leisurely breakfast, and spend some time in the sauna before I go to class, I know he's not going to give up that easily. So instead, I turn in his arms, tuck my head into his shoulder and plant a sweet kiss on his neck.

"I missed you last night," I say, my tone leading.

"I missed you too, angel." But he volunteers nothing, instead busying himself by sliding off the sweat shorts I slept in last night. And like I always do, I stay quiet and let him.

chapter sixteen

"Hey, did you look at the schedule for today?"

Amira catches me the minute I walk into the studio on Tuesday two weeks later, my bag slung over my shoulder and a spring in my step. I finally feel like I've shaken the fatigue that's been dogging me since the concert, and I don't know if it's just because I've finally rested myself into recovery or if Amira's assumption about the real source of my exhaustion was correct.

I drop my bag behind the front desk while I take the phone off voice mail. "No. Why?"

"New client came in through the referral booking portal."

Now I frown at her. "I didn't even think that was up and running." With addition of the weekend classes that Amira has been setting up, we've now gotten so busy that the only way to book private sessions without going on a waiting list is through a special, referral-only site. I know that Amira was working on it, but not that it had gone live.

"Well, it's been up and running for a while now, but there's hardly anyone who has the link. Just the members of your teacher group I got the idea from; we haven't sent it out to any of your regular clients yet."

"Huh. Strange. Did you recognize the name? Maybe one of the teachers is coming into town and wanted to book a session while they're here?" It's not unusual for me to get calls and messages from my friends in the industry who want to use the studio while they're on vacation. Usually, though, they just want a spot on a piece of equipment to do their own workouts rather than an actual session.

Which is fine. Worst case scenario, I miss out on the fee for that hour and get to catch up with an old friend.

"No, it wasn't one I recognized, but I don't know everyone in that group. Let me go look at the name real quick . . ."

I wait, but the phone rings in the back and I hear Amira talking, so I assume she's not coming back. Instead, I kick off my shoes and climb onto the Reformer to start my personal workout for the day. I'm still taking it somewhat easy compared to usual, and instead of following up with barre work, I just stretch and roll out my muscles.

Amira still hasn't emerged when Maria shows up, and we get a late start because she begins to tell me a story about the time a notoriously nicotine-addicted dancer lit the scrim on fire while trying to sneak a backstage smoke. This one I'm not entirely sure I believe, but then again, she was in Russian ballet for decades and I imagine that customs were different over there in the seventies. As usual, I'm impressed with how well the woman has maintained her strength and flexibility all these years. She's part of my inspiration for staying on top of my own conditioning. If I'm half as fit as she is when I reach her age, I will consider myself successful.

After Maria leaves, I take a quick bathroom break

and retrieve my water bottle. I'm refilling it at the filtered water fountain in the back when I hear the jingle of the front door open. Shoot. This would be my 11:30 and I've forgotten to get the new client information from Amira again. I poke my head into the office, but she has the phone pressed to her ear. She holds up one finger. I'll just have to wing it.

I grind to a stop, though, as soon as I reach the main studio. A tall, slim man stands near the front door, looking around uncertainly, as if he's not sure he's in the right place. I frown. "Can I help you?"

He takes off his sunglasses, and I freeze, cold starting at the crown of my head and creeping down my body.

"Hey," he says, his voice a little raspy.

I'm absolutely certain that I must be imagining things because there's no way that Simon Yang is standing in my studio right now in sweatpants, a hoodie, and a ball cap, looking like a little boy about to be scolded for being late to dinner.

I open and close my mouth a few times, but I'm saved from having to form actual words when Amira comes out of the office, breathless and apologetic. Just as quickly, she skids to a stop beside me when she sees Simon.

"Oh," she says. "SJ Simmons . . . is . . . you?"

It might be the first time I've ever seen Amira speechless, and I'm all too aware that we're both gaping at him like fish out of water, but I can't seem to get my mouth reconnected to my brain. When I say he is literally the last person I expected to see in front of me, I'm not using the word incorrectly or hyperbolically. I have been so absolutely convinced that the SJY conversation was a scam that I never once entertained this possibility.

Simon whips his hat off and runs his fingers through his hair. The cotton candy pink has given way to a light brown. "I'm really sorry for the deception.

But . . . you blocked me. And I wasn't sure if you would see me otherwise."

Amira looks at me, her mouth open, then shakes herself. "I'm just going to go in the back and do . . . work. Call me if you need me, I guess." She turns away, but not before I see her stifle what could be a grin or a laugh or maybe both.

It breaks through my stupor, and I take a few steps toward him. "So it really was you?"

He frowns. "Of course it was me. I verified it, remember?"

"Yeah, but . . ." I shake my head. "You never responded to my message. And when you didn't, I just assumed that I'd been catfished."

Simon grimaces. With makeup, he is almost unnaturally pretty. Here, barefaced, I'm struck by his fresh, boy-next-door attractiveness. "I'm really sorry about that. There were issues."

"Issues? Issues that made it so you couldn't reply for a week?"

He comes a little closer and glances back toward the office, as if he knows Amira is eavesdropping, which of course she is. He stops a few feet away from me and rocks back on his heels. "I took you seriously when you said you wanted proof. I said something to my manager and he . . . flipped. Apparently, when I woke him up to send that message to you, he'd taken something to sleep and didn't even remember he had done it. So when I mentioned I was going to contact you outside of social media, but I wanted to be sure that, I don't know, you weren't a *sasaeng*—"

"—he wanted to know who I was." I close my eyes and shake my head. "Did you get in trouble?"

Simon makes a face that clearly means *yes* while he wants to say *no*. "Let's just say it turned into a conversation with my manager, the group manager, the division manager . . ."

"Over you chatting with a woman."

"Over me chatting with a perceived fan, who was on stage with me, who I touched in a suggestive manner, who then collapsed as she was going off stage. That woman."

Okay, so I can see how that might have turned into a problem for him. "How did you leave it then?"

"I promised that I would not continue this conversation with the aforementioned woman for the duration of the tour, and then I was going on vacation as planned and I would do whatever the hell I wanted while I was not officially representing the group." He smiles, but I can hear the compressed frustration behind the wry tone. "Which I went to tell you and then found myself blocked."

I rub my forehead. "Yeah."

"Listen, I am so sorry."

"You're sorry? It sounds like I'm the one who almost got you fired."

He scrunches up his nose again. "I didn't almost get fired. They're not going to fire me. 'Burn' now has over five million views."

"Okay, then," I say.

"Okay?"

I nod and glance at my watch. "It's 11:30. You can put your stuff in the locker on that wall. Bare feet or grippy socks, either are okay."

He doesn't move.

"You booked a session with me, did you not? You're going to get your session, and from what I recall, you could probably use it."

"Yes, ma'am." He gives me a slight bow, which once again seems automatic, then finds an open locker, drops his bag inside and replaces his running shoes with sticky socks. At the last minute, he strips off his joggers and sweatshirt so he's left wearing long athletic shorts and a body-skimming tank top.

I'm torn between admiring his very nice musculature and noting that he looks even thinner than when he was last in LA. Touring has taken a toll.

"By the way," I ask while he's folding his stuff neatly on the single shelf in the locker, "how did you get the link to book?"

He twists toward me, mischief sparkling in his eyes. "Hayun says hi."

I cock my head. "No . . . your teacher isn't . . . you study with Lee Hayun?"

"I checked you out, saw that you two went to the same school about the same time. So I messaged her and she said yes, she knows you. No, you're not the sasaeng type. In fact, had I just asked her rather than my manager, I probably could have avoided a lot of drama. She made me promise to stop in for a session with you while I'm in LA because you definitely know your stuff."

I'm not sure whether to be flattered—I got along very well with Hayun, who was a year ahead of me in our training—or impressed that he checked me out through my Pilates contacts. "If you study with her, then I assume you know what you're doing. Classical series level?"

"Advanced."

"Okay. Then let's start with a roll-down before getting on the Reformer."

I can see him shift from flirtation to focus mode when he approaches the Reformer. He turns to me at a 90-degree angle, assumes the foot position, and then starts the roll-down to the floor, articulating his spine all the way down and back up. I note the hitch in his movement and file it away for future reference. Before I can direct him, he's mounting the apparatus—properly, I note—and putting his feet on the footbar to start footwork.

I guide him through the sequence using cues but minimal corrections. Since he's been working with Hayun, he has very few bad habits, not to mention an excellent understanding of his own biomechanics. I manage to view him as simply another client, but just barely . . . every once in a while the less evolved part of me wants to shift my focus away from his technique and onto the fact he's a very attractive man.

Not until we get to the short box where he has a leg extended upwards—impressive flexibility—while he rolls his spine back down straight do I finally say something. "How long have you had problems with your L4 and L5?"

He curls back up, his nose going to the shin on his raised leg. "Since I was eighteen. Slipped discs. Still give me issues when we tour."

I make a note of it, but I don't say anything about it again until he's removed the box and we've transitioned into another exercise. "Can I touch you?"

He throws me a glance and I see that same glimmer of mischief in his brown eyes. I don't know if it's just the general phrasing of the question or if he's thinking about the "unapproved touching," but I give him a mock-stern look until he caves and nods. I place the first two fingers on each hand opposite each other on his abdomen and spine. "Lengthen through here when you extend the carriage. Lift your glutes. Don't dump into your back."

I step back, and he tries again, better this time. "Good. Less pressure on those vertebrae?"

He nods. "Yeah. Thanks."

The hour flies by, and we finish the entire advanced series with a couple of minutes to spare, so I put him through some split stretches. It's been ages since I've taught anyone, let alone a man, who can do full splits in all directions. I wait until he does the roll down again, noting that the articulation in the problem area of his spine has improved, then ask him, "What is your PT doing about your hypermobility?"

He rises back up and pushes his hair back from his face. "My what?"

"Your hypermobility?" I give him a wry look. "The fact you bend in directions you shouldn't be able to bend in?"

"I thought that was just being a dancer."

"Hypermobile people self-select for dance," I say. "It's probably why you hurt so much all the time. Your muscles might be compensating for the fact your tendons and ligaments are extremely elastic." I extend my leg in front of me, fully pointed, to show my hyperextended knees, then do the same with my arms. "I have a lot fewer problems since I started focusing on joint stabilization. I should have done it younger."

"Yeah," he says darkly. "Apparently me too."

"Well, how long will you be in LA? I can probably make some room in my schedule for you. We can do some mat work so you're able to keep it up when you're not near Hayun's studio."

"I'm here for almost a month," he says. "But. . . I didn't actually come here for classes."

I've been dancing around this topic, but now that it's here, I want to hear him say it. "Why *are* you here then?"

He doesn't hesitate. "I wanted to see you. Can I take you to lunch? Or coffee?"

"I. . . have another session in half an hour." I push down the flutter of wings in my middle, aware of just how much regret is threaded through my tone.

"No, you don't!" Amira's voice calls from the office. "Alison canceled again."

Simon smiles, still holding my gaze, as if Amira hasn't been eavesdropping on the whole exchange. That smile makes me—and my dumb hyperextended knees—weak. "There you have it. Alison to the rescue. What do you say?"

I open and close my mouth before I can finally gather the language skills to say, "I'll get my purse." And then the studio owner kicks in, and I pick up a spray bottle and clean rag and thrust them at him. "While you wipe off the Reformer."

He smiles and follows directions, and I walk casually to the office where Amira is no doubt pressed to the door frame. Sure enough, as soon as I enter, her eyes go so wide she looks like a cartoon character. "Oh my god," she mouths silently to me. "It really was him."

"Evidently." I feel bad about having blocked him now, but not that bad, given that it brought him to my doorstep. "I don't have anything else this afternoon, do I?"

"You don't have anything else this"—she checks her watch—"next eighteen hours. Have fun."

I make a face at her and roll my eyes, then pull my small crossbody out of my duffel. At the last minute, I remember to swap out my studio shoes for my regular trainers. "How do I look?"

"Pretty enough to date an idol, that's for sure." Amira grins at me and gives me a shove. "Go. Live vicariously for me."

I laugh. As if she wasn't doing all the vicarious living for both of us these days.

When I get back out into the studio, Simon is wearing his joggers and hoodie again despite the warmth of the day, his backpack slung over one shoulder. As soon as he sees me, he sweeps his hair back from his face and settles his hat on in an automatic gesture that certainly should not be that attractive. "Ready? Are you thinking coffee or real food?"

"There's a place right down the street that has both. How concerned do you need to be about being recognized here?"

He thinks. "At the moment? Not very. I'm careful in how I'm photographed, so no one would expect me to be dressed like this. Especially since I posted an airport picture last night hinting I was headed back to Korea." He grimaces. "People will figure it out when I don't show up at Incheon, but I've got another day at least until anyone tracks me down here."

I stare at him for a long moment, then just shake my head. That's right. There are people waiting for him at the airport on both ends whenever he travels. I've seen the videos of him coming off international flights, tired and likely annoyed, mostly covered by a face mask and glasses, but he still manages to sign hearts for the cameras and fans. Maybe our lives aren't all that similar after all.

Simon slips on his aviator shades the minute we step outside—he holds the door for me—and I gesture for him to follow me to the left down the sidewalk. We walk in awkward silence for a few moments until I finally ask, "How did the rest of the tour dates go?"

"Good," he says. "Phoenix, obviously, was a disaster. But Chicago was flawless. Atlanta, it rained, but not enough to cause major problems. The 'Industry' choreo actually looked really cool with the water flying everywhere on stage. New York was the only place we didn't sell out, can you believe that?"

"I don't believe it," I reply, though I really have no idea whether New York should be a good venue or not. "I have to admit, I watched the Phoenix show and I didn't see a single thing wrong with it."

"Really?"

"It was part of what made me sure that you weren't who you said you were. You said you missed lines, but I couldn't see where."

He rubs the back of his neck ruefully. "Yeah . . . I might have exaggerated a bit. You have to remember, we practice with no margin for error, and when something goes wrong, it feels like letting the whole group down. Especially when it's a group of veterans. I was upset with myself."

I can understand that—his audience knows his choreography and lines as well as mine knew the steps to a well-loved ballet. Mistakes stand out. But still. "Your body survived the end of the tour?"

He nods. "I had the therapist working on me every morning just so I could get through the day. I cleaned out the ice maker on my floor at every hotel and lived on painkillers. But I made it."

"You don't seem all that rough today."

"I've been here for a few days, relaxing. My parents still live in Ventura. I would have been here sooner, of course, but it was the earliest you had an opening." He glances at me, that sly, small smile lifting one side of his mouth. It has exactly the effect he intends of almost making my trip over my own feet.

Just when I get lulled into the sense that he's an ordinary guy, I'm reminded that he can make sixty thousand women swoon with a single wink.

Fortunately, we reach Daybreak before I have to say anything else, and we join the short line inside the cool, air-conditioned cafe. This place is only open until 2:00 p.m. and serves both coffee from the bar and a full menu from the kitchen. Amira and I spend an ungodly amount of time and money here, given how close it is to the studio and the fact that I don't have a car.

When we finally get up to the front, I order an iced herbal tea and a toasted breakfast sandwich, and Simon steps up behind me to ask for an iced Americano. He waves me off when I try to pay and slips a credit card from his wallet to tap to the reader. Oddly, it's the Hangul printing on his credit card that causes a moment of dissonance. In his designer sportswear and expensive glasses, Simon certainly stands out, but not so much as a "foreigner." He simply carries himself like someone who's used to attention, who's comfortable with the twenty-thousand dollar watch he wears loosely on his left wrist.

We make small talk about the restaurant while we wait for our orders to come up, then grab them from the bar. I snatch a little paper sleeve of utensils on my way out and we find a free bistro table on the sidewalk outside. He settles himself opposite from me, legs crossed elegantly at the knee while he sips his drink. With the expensive clothes, perfect skin, and collection of titanium hoops in his ears, there's no question that he's not just an ordinary resident out for a quick bite.

I repress a smile as I cut my sandwich in half on the diagonal.

"What?"

"I take back everything I was thinking. You look like a celebrity."

"I am a celebrity," he says easily but there's a little lift to his mouth that makes me think he's joking. "Fortunately, your paparazzi thinks there's only one K-pop group in Korea, and I am not in it."

I snort because it's true, though I note that he says *your* and not *our*, and nudge half of the sandwich toward him. "You want some?"

He shakes his head.

I shrug and take my first blissful bite. I don't eat bread all that often—I find it hard to digest—but this is the one exception I'll always make. Perfectly toasted sourdough, scrambled eggs, shredded cheddar, and homemade, locally sourced spicy sausage. I chew for a minute, then reach for my tea.

"You're not going to hassle me about not eating." A statement, not a question.

I shrug again. "Why would I?"

"Because you're against the unrealistic body standards that the Korean entertainment industry pushes?"

"Yeah, because ballet is known to promote healthy body image." I take another bite, but as good as it tastes, I may actually already be regretting ordering it. I put it aside and sip my tea instead. "Besides, considering your abs have their own fandom, I figure you don't eat random carbs."

He almost chokes on his Americano. "I . . . what?"

I lift an eyebrow. "You didn't know this? There are Instagram accounts dedicated to your six-pack. One of them is literally called *Simon Yang's Six-Pack.*"

His cheeks color and he turns away from me. "Good god."

"That's not even the worst one. Trust me, your fans range from extremely creative to absolutely deranged. My favorite one is *Seojun's Left—*"

"Please do not finish that statement," he cuts in, his tone pleading. "There are many possibilities and I don't want to hear any of them."

I settle back in my chair with a satisfied smile, and even though I can't see them behind his glasses, I'm sure he's narrowing his eyes at me. "Did you . . . actually look at all those photos?"

"Oh, yes," I say deliberately. "Every single one. Very impressive, Simon. You should be proud."

He catches my tone and makes a face. "You did not."

"No, I did not," I relent. "It felt weird. It's one thing to objectify a stranger and another to do it to a . . ."

"To a what?"

I clear my throat. "Someone I know."

"In any case, I probably deserved that. For the naked texting comment."

Now I feel myself blush. "You do remember that then?"

"Remember might be a strong word," he says carefully. "But there was textual evidence the next morning. You know . . ."

"Whiskey," I finish with him.

We fall into silence, and I take another bite of my sandwich before I realize that it's indeed a bad idea. Then it's just drinks for both of us. When the silence stretches, I finally gather up my courage to bluntly spill what's on my mind. "Why are you here?"

"At this table? Or in California?"

"Either. Both."

He moistens his lips, and I have to look away. I have read far too many odes by thirsty fans to his perfect mouth to be strong.

I need to get off the internet.

Finally, he says, "I wanted to see you. Especially when I couldn't talk to you anymore."

"To explain?"

"Of course. I didn't want you to think I'd ghosted you. But I also . . . just wanted to talk to you."

"Why? I mean . . ." I clear my throat for what now feels like the hundredth time. "You meet hundreds, thousands of people a day sometimes. So why am I the one you wanted to talk to?"

Simon toys with his cup on the table. "You're not going to like the answer."

I steel myself. "Try me."

"I thought you were pretty. No, let me take that back. I thought you were fucking gorgeous. With a body that deserved its own Instagram account."

He smirks at the last part, and heat rises to my

cheeks. I guess I can thank Amira for that—the bra top really was the night's hero. "And I'm not going to like that answer?"

"Well, I'm supposed to say something like I was taken by your intelligence or your courage, but on stage, I had no way of knowing any of that. I wasn't actually paying attention to you. Until you smiled at me. Why did you do that, by the way?"

Now I smile again. "You were very convincing, and I'm sure from the audience you looked incredibly seductive. But for a moment, I could see you do all your calculations of where you were on stage in relation to the camera and what you were going to do next and if you were too close to stand straight up or you need to rock back . . ."

He chuckles. "So maybe I really did fall for your intelligence."

Fall for. *Not really what he means, Trina. Don't get stuck on in it.*

"Don't get me wrong, I was truly concerned about you. You still looked out of it when we were taking pictures, and I wasn't sure you hadn't hit your head on the way down or something. And then . . ."

"And then . . . ?"

"You were absolutely genuine. Treated me like a person."

"That's so unusual?"

He lets out a little sigh. "I get treated like a child by fans who have followed me since I was seventeen and like a sex object by those who haven't. I'm a money-making tool to my company and everyone connected to the group. And to everyone else, I'm . . ."

". . . an idol. With all the benefits and drawbacks that entails."

He nods.

"Okay."

"Okay, what?"

"Okay, I accept your answer to that question. I believe you."

"And that's it? No reciprocity?"

"For why I had a week-long running conversation with you?"

He nods.

I smile to myself. "You're an adorable drunk."

chapter seventeen

Simon walks me back to the studio, but just before we reach the door, he stops on the sidewalk. "So."

"So."

"When can I see you again?"

I didn't expect him to be so straightforward. "I'll have to check my schedule. At the moment, I have very few spaces available for new clients."

"I didn't mean I expected you to train me." He looks slightly offended, and I can't help but laugh again.

"I know you didn't. But you've got, what. . .more performances when you get home?"

He hesitates. "We have fan meetings in Seoul and Tokyo and then we start preparing for end-of-the-year music shows."

"Right. So maybe we should use this time that you're in California to get you ready to perform without pain through the end of the year."

I see him go still as he calculates my words. "We?"

"Yes, we." I make a face, as if I'm relenting, but I've planned on offering since we walked out of the studio. "My last session ends at six on Mondays, Wednesdays, and Fridays. Whatever days you can make it, we'll work out."

"And then you'll let me take you out to dinner after?"

"Every night?"

"Well . . . I can't promise that I can make it every day. I have to spend some time with my family and I have appointments set up over the next couple of weeks."

"Then you send me your schedule and I'll put it on the calendar."

"With the accompanying dinner?"

He looks so hopeful that I can't help but smile. "Yes."

"Will you let me take you out to dinner tonight?"

He is making me breathless with his persistence, and when he looks at me with that open, innocent hope, it's almost impossible to resist him. But I do. I need to. "Not tonight."

"Why not?"

"Because I don't want you to think I'm too available."

He chuckles a little. "That's fair."

"Message me," I say, walking toward the door. But before I can reach for the handle he calls after me.

"Can I have your phone number?"

I turn around and hold my hand out. He presses his phone into it, and I tap my name and phone number into the contacts list before handing it back to him. "Nice to see you, Simon." And then I pull the door open and enter the cool interior of the studio. I don't look back through the plate glass windows to see if he's still watching or if he's turned to get into his car, whichever one it might be. Instead, I just walk straight through the space toward the office.

I don't know what got into me. I'm not the type to play hard to get, but I hate the idea of simply being one of a million women—and that may be a gross underestimation—who would do anything to have the full focus of his attention. And while I know it's not fair, I need a minute away from him to order the thoughts that have been spinning in my brain from the moment I recognized him in my studio.

Amira looks up in shock when I walk in. "What happened? Why are you back so soon?"

"Did you think I was going to go back to his hotel with him or something?" It's unnecessarily aggressive, but I hate the implication that there's something wrong with taking an hour for coffee and no more. Like Simon was running away from me.

She picks up on my tone and holds up her hands. "Of course not. The man just came from New York to see you. He avoided going back to Seoul to track you down."

"Technically, he's on vacation, and he came the fifty miles or so from Ventura. I think he's visiting his family."

Amira seems slightly disappointed, and yes, that is less flattering than the idea he crossed continents for me. But I don't need to ask to know that Amira is still thinking of him as Seojun. Simon. . . Simon is a completely different person.

Okay, maybe not completely different. The playfulness, the intelligence, the wry self-awareness—all those come out on stage, but they're amplified into something that's not quite reality, that's beyond it. Simon is a quieter, toned-down version of Seojun, and in some ways that's far sexier than the overt charisma he displays on stage.

"Trina?" Amira cocks her head at me. "Did I lose you?"

Yes. I most certainly got lost in imagination there for a second. "I'm going to train him while he's here. He's got a heavy schedule when he goes back and he can't afford to get deconditioned."

Amira rolls her eyes but she doesn't argue. "Time together is time together, I guess."

Now I narrow my eyes at her. "Why are you so invested in this?"

"Are you kidding me? Did you forget you let me read your conversation? You guys were vibing. It's so obvious that you like each other. For real. And not just because you are two very attractive people the other one would be a fool not to notice."

"It's not like that." But isn't it? I'm not sure what else you could call that exchange at the cafe. Trading sarcastic little flirts, veiled compliments. Clearly, we're both interested, but . . .

. . . he's only here in California for a month before he heads back to Korea, where his life is.

So what exactly do I think is going to happen here?

I rub my eyes and slump down into a chair in front of the desk. Amira takes one look at me and reads my mind.

"Oh no. You're not going to overthink this. Not everything has to be planned out years in advance. Why did you even start chatting with him if you weren't interested in getting to know him?"

"I . . ." I have to think about the answer. "It didn't feel real. It was just words on a screen, and I wasn't even 100 percent sure that it was really him."

"But now he's here in front of you and you have to deal with it."

I bite my lip and nod.

"So what are you afraid of?"

I open and close my mouth. What *am* I afraid of? Finally, I just shake my head.

"If you can't articulate it, than it can't be a real risk, right?"

Amira tends to be very practical with these kinds of things, but then again, she's far less cautious than I am. Her idea of a risk is imminent bodily harm or arrest. Everything else is a gray area. She's never been in a position where a single bad decision—skiing over Christmas break, sleeping with a co-worker—could potentially end her career.

"I can't articulate why I'm afraid of swimming in the ocean either, but there are still real risks involved."

Amira rolls her eyes, but I've got her there. I pick up my bag and shove my purse into it. "I'm going to head home and work on the presentation. Did you send me your comments?"

"While you were having lunch with Simon," she says, a little smile lifting her lips. "It's good. It's really good, actually."

I know she's trying to bolster my confidence, but I appreciate it anyway. "Thanks again. Will you be in tomorrow?"

She gives me a look—of course she will—so I give her a quick hug and then leave the studio. Not for the first time, I have the sense that somehow I'm missing something, that I've vaguely disappointed her, but I don't know how. Her opinion on how I'm handling the Simon thing aside, I know I'm not an easy person to have as a best friend. Which is why I'm under no illusions that I am or have any desire to be her only friend—she has her high school and college friends, most of whom are still living the single party life in LA. She has her business contacts. And unlike me, she has no problem striking up conversation with strangers and accepting offers of dates.

She has no idea how much I wish I could be one of the people who simply accept last-minute invitations without considering whether it will affect my ability to go to work in the morning.

Almost as if my mind is trying to make a point, by the time I get home, I'm breathless and a little light-headed. I make it up my stairs and feed the cat before I collapse onto the sofa with a big cup of water and my laptop. I stretch out so I put less pressure on my stomach, which is already starting to churn uncomfortably from my small lunch, and then set up my computer on a little tray in front of me. I consider for a second, then pop my earbuds in and select an album off my streaming music app.

Helios, this time their most recent album.

I've been listening to their music enough that I instantly recognize Simon's voice—just as clear and true as it was when he began, but stronger now, trained. It's even more evident to me how hard he's worked, not content to rest on his looks and dancing and fan praise. I wonder how Simon feels about his early records now, about the fact that his fans chart his vocal development and discuss it all over message boards and in the comment sections of Helios's videos.

As I've said before, I really need to get off the internet.

I've only just started reviewing Amira's notes—astute and concise as usual—when my phone beeps over the music. A message from an unfamiliar number pops up, but it doesn't take much to guess who it's from, considering it starts with +82 country code.

[UNKNOWN NUMBER]
Hi.

I smile to myself.

TRINA
Who is this?

[UNKNOWN NUMBER]
Simon.

I grin over the fact that he's taking me seriously, as

if I get texted by random Korean numbers all the time. I take a moment to save it before I respond.

TRINA
Prove it.

A second later, the *downloading* alert shows up and then a photo loads. It's a selfie, and it's an impossibly good one, taken in his car so the light slants across his face, making his eyes shine golden and giving his hair a haloed cast. His little half-smile makes my heart do a nervous leap. Before I can think of how to reply, he texts again.

SIMON
What are you doing?

TRINA
Reviewing Amira's notes on
my keynote.

SIMON
Keynote? For what?

TRINA
Pilates festival in Long
Beach.

SIMON
Wow, congratulations!
That's a big deal, right?

TRINA
It is to me. I'm usually
reluctant to do these things.

SIMON
Why? Stage fright?

I hesitate and then tell him the truth.

TRINA
Afraid of a repeat of the
concert situation.

SIMON
Oh. Yeah, that would be
nerve-wracking. Anything
you can do?

TRINA
Have a stool handy?

SIMON
I meant more like...more
sleep, less sleep, hydration,
medication?

TRINA
Beta blocker helps. Usually.

This conversation is getting more serious than I want at the moment, and I smile to myself as I think of a way to lighten the mood.

TRINA
Had I known some hot
stranger would have his
hands all over me, I would
have taken one first.

There's a long pause now, and I grimace. That was too much, too stupid, too close to implying that my episode was his fault. That wasn't what I meant at all; I was trying to make light out of things. Gah. I'm terrible at flirting. But then his reply comes back.

SIMON
How much warning do you
need, then? Just as a matter
of scientific curiosity.

My face heats as a surprised laugh bursts out of me. We're still only in the realm of innuendo, but it's enough to make my imagination run wild. I groan.

TRINA
What are YOU doing now?

SIMON
Absolutely nothing. I
cleared my schedule
because I'd been hoping to
convince you to spend the
day with me.

I feel a momentary twinge of regret, which I shove away. He was so sure that I didn't have plans; now I'm glad I made him wait.

TRINA
I'm sorry to disappoint you.
But you're resourceful. I'm
sure you can find something
to do. You can start by
sending me your schedule.

SIMON
Oh, right. It's right here.

It takes a second to load, but he sends me a screen shot of his phone calendar. Every Monday, Wednesday, and Friday evening for the next three weeks are marked with a single word: *Katrina.*

My gut gives a brutal twist that makes it feel like my insides are rearranging themselves around my heart. It's a clear statement and I'm not entirely sure what to do about it, particularly when it's this hard to catch my breath. I type and erase my response three times before I finally settle on something non-committal.

TRINA
You're on my calendar. I'll
see you tomorrow at 6.

SIMON
Can't wait. Good luck with
your speech.
Any food preferences/
allergies I should know
about?

For a second, I almost think to ask if he's familiar with the area and realize he grew up here, even though he hasn't lived here for decades.

TRINA
Not really. I like almost
everything.

SIMON
It's the "almost" that's
concerning. 😃.
Tomorrow...

Tomorrow. I smile to myself. It was meant to be a reminder, but it feels like a promise.

chapter eighteen

If I take more care in getting ready the next day, no one can blame me. Not only do I have an unusually heavy day ahead of me—none of my clients have canceled on me, which is more rare than you'd think considering I work mostly with entertainment industry folks—and I'm booked from 9:00 a.m. to 7:00 p.m. I put on my favorite pair of black leggings with the mesh insert up the side and a bra top beneath an open-backed sweatshirt. The studio gets cold when I'm not moving much, and these days I'm trying to keep my activity down to the lowest level possible. I rarely wear makeup when I teach and I'm certainly not going to start today, but I'm not sure if I'm going to have time to come home and shower, so while I pack my clothes, I tuck in my makeup case at the same time.

Listen, if you were going out to dinner with a guy who is literally the face of a couture fashion brand, you'd want to look your best, too. I already have to force down the idea that he's way too good-looking to be interested in me, though I know it probably doesn't matter and also that I should get used to it. No, I *shouldn't* get used to it. You only get used to things that are going to last, and I'm pretty sure that for all the intense interest he's showing me right now, this isn't going to go any further than a handful of Pilates sessions and a few dinners.

I'm not even sure if I *want* it to go anywhere. We don't even know each other, and admittedly part of the appeal is the interest from someone who would normally only see me as staff.

And right there is the humiliating crux of this whole situation.

As if he senses my inner turmoil, Misha comes up to me as I'm trying to slip on my shoes and winds his way around my ankles. I bend down and scratch the back of his head for as long as he'll let me. When I stand, I have to blink away stars. I wait, frozen, to see if it's going to come to anything, but it seems to be an isolated incident. I feel okay. Not perfect, but perfect isn't even a standard I try to reach anymore.

Amira is waiting for me when I come through the doors of the studio, the air conditioning already going at full blast in preparation for our near-hundred-degree temperatures this afternoon. If we don't get ahead of it early in the morning, we'll be chasing it all day long. But that isn't the reason for Amira's smug look.

"Regular six o'clock session, huh?"

I look back innocently. "I try to accommodate clients whenever possible, especially when they're only in town for the short term."

"Mmm-hmm," Amira says, but I catch her smile as she turns away. She approves.

I don't have much time to dwell on it. I have half an hour to work out the kinks on the Reformer and stretch thoroughly before my first client shows up. While Wednesday is packed as usual, it's a different roster since several of my clients only come a few times a month. I take the half hour between sessions to lay down in the office with my feet on the wall and take bites of a clean protein bar. Days like this, I can't eat lunch; I can't afford for my body to waste effort on digesting food when I need it to focus on circulating blood through my body. By switching between standing and sitting, I make it all the way through my five o'clock without any concerning symptoms. Pride—or maybe relief—blooms in my chest.

Ironically, my last client before Simon is Alicia—a mononymous pop star known for her three Grammys and her fantastic figure. I have nothing to do with the former, but I can certainly take some credit for the latter. She's prepping for her next world tour and has expressed concern about her stamina, so I spend some time with her on the jump board, focusing on foot and ankle strength for all the choreo she's going to be performing in heels. We're just finishing up with stretches on the Reformer when the door opens with a jingle, letting in a rush of hot air.

I spare only the slightest glance in Simon's direction before I return my attention to Alicia, though my heart gives a little hitch. He dips his head and walks straight to the locker to drop his things, taking a seat out of the way on the bench in front of them.

"Great job today," I tell Alicia when she finishes. "Can you fit a few extra sessions in between rehearsals before you leave?"

"I'll see," she says with a warm smile. "Thanks, Trina."

"It's my pleasure. And thanks for the tickets, by the way. Amira and I can't wait to see the new show."

Alicia beams and picks up her water bottle and towel from beside the apparatus before moving to retrieve her own things from the lockers. I busy myself with wiping down the Reformer, but I'm still aware of Alicia's sudden halt from the corner of my eye.

"Wait. We've met, haven't we?" she asks, frowning.

Now I'm watching the exchange openly. Simon just gives her a slight, wry smile. "Coachella two years ago."

Alicia lets out a big laugh. "My God, you're right. It has been that long. Seojun, right? You're with Helios. That was a monster set. I've never heard a crowd scream that loud in my life. Including my own."

Simon chuckles and cocks his head to study her. "You say that as if you weren't the main stage headliner. I'm flattered you remember us."

"You're hard to forget," she says in a low voice. There's not a hint of flirtation in her expression, but somehow she still manages to make it sound suggestive. Or maybe I'm just reading into it. She opens her locker and pulls her designer bag from the shelf, then shrugs into her sweatshirt. "Have fun. You're in good hands with Trina."

"That I am," Simon says, then gives her another smile and bows his head. "Have a successful tour."

Alicia gives him one last look and then smiles at me before she lets herself out the front door where her car waits. I turn to Simon with my eyebrows raised.

"What?" he asks innocently.

"I said nothing."

A sly smile spreads across his face. "Jealous?"

I shake my head slowly. "That was Seojun, not Simon. Put him away for a bit, will you?"

Simon laughs and pulls off his jacket, then shoves it into his locker. I point him to the metal apparatus bolted to the wall behind a thick mat, springs clipped to its railing. "Tower today. We're going to work on some of those imbalances."

"Yes, ma'am." He bows slightly again, and I'm struck by how much the gesture is ingrained in him despite his

California upbringing. He moves to the Tower, his steps light but his movements careful.

"What hurts?"

"Is it that obvious?"

To anyone who knows what they're looking for, yes. "Where? Your back still?"

He nods. "And my left hip and right shoulder aren't particularly pleased either."

It's a typical compensation pattern, so that doesn't surprise me. "You have to let me know if anything hurts while we're working. This isn't something you should push through."

He just gives me a nod, and when I gesture to the mat, he seats himself facing the wall. Yes, he knows the drill.

There's no set series for the Tower, so I take him through the exercises in an order that will allow him to warm up his muscles and lengthen his spine without putting pressure on his injuries. He doesn't break a sweat, but by the time we're finished with the leg springs, his muscles are trembling. There's no doubt that he's strong and flexible and well-trained, but repetitive patterns always leave invisible weaknesses. When I finally take him through a final stretch grasping the upright rails of the apparatus, he groans.

"What's wrong? Does something hurt?"

"Everything hurts," he says, throwing me a wry look. "You're either a genius or a sadist."

I grin. "Both. Good work today. Now wipe down your mat."

Simon throws me a look full of mock offense. "You didn't make Alicia wipe down her equipment."

"Because she's Alicia," I say, wide-eyed. In truth, I'd just been so distracted by Simon, I'd forgotten to remind her, and when Alicia's in tour-prep mode, she doesn't remember anything she's not specifically directed to do.

He shrugs as if to say *that's fair*, then retrieves a spray bottle and a rag to clean his equipment. I pry my eyes away from him. Technically, I am now off the clock, but it's not good form to ogle a student.

When he's finished, he turns to me and clasps his hands together. "So. Dinner? Do you need to go home and change?"

I shake my head. "I brought my clothes with me."

"Good, me too."

I nod in the direction of the rear hallway. "There's a changing room back there. It's marked. Fifteen minutes?"

"Perfect."

He's grabbing his keys, ostensibly to return to his car, and I go back to the office to grab my bag. Amira is tapping away on the computer when I enter.

"So?"

"So what?"

"Where's he taking you?"

"I don't know." I hadn't thought to ask, and that in itself should concern me. And yet it doesn't. I barely know the man, but somehow I already trust him.

"Okay, text me when you know for sure."

"Weren't you the one dying for this to happen?"

Amira relents. "Yeah, I know, but safety is safety. Though, all things considered, you're probably safer with him than the other guys you've gone out with. He's already risking enough by taking you out publicly."

That's true. I've done my research in my spare time, and while idols of Simon's age and experience aren't banned from dating by their companies, they're also encouraged to be extremely discreet. Fans don't like the idea that their favorites aren't available—the entire industry hinges on that illusion, or maybe *delusion*. He has far more to lose here than I do.

Which again begs the question why he's willing to risk it.

Too much. Too much thinking and questioning when I should be changing. I sigh and slip out the door to the women's changing room.

Fifteen minutes later, I emerge. I have no idea where he's taking me, so I've gone safe in a loose, dark-green jumpsuit that shows off my toned back and arms, my hair twisted into a low knot at the nape of my neck. I've opted for light makeup, just enough to accentuate my eyes and cheekbones and a light coat of gloss. In LA, this should be suitable for just about any place he decides to take me.

Simon emerges from his dressing room at almost the same time, and I do a double-take as I lurch to a stop, suddenly glad I haven't gone more casual. If I thought he seemed like a normal-ish guy the other day, he is show-stopping now in a beautifully cut navy suit with a silky, light blue shirt beneath it. The top two buttons are open to show a silver box chain and a dainty necklace holding the same butterfly pendant I've seen in every photograph of him. Not only is it. . .a lot. . .for a summer evening in California, but this is the man I'm used to seeing on Instagram and in media photos. Expensive, polished, confident.

"Wow," I say, my mouth jumping ahead of my brain, at the same time he says, "You look beautiful."

I blush, and I swear the tips of his ears color again. We look at each other, suddenly awkward, and I flash back to the junior prom that I almost missed because my date canceled on me and I had to take my pas de deux partner.

"Um, let me drop my bag and tell Amira goodbye," I say, ducking into the office.

She lets out a low whistle when I enter. "I see you chose violence."

I set my bag by the desk, shaking my head, though inwardly the words hearten me. I pull out my small black handbag—bigger than a clutch, nicer than my everyday cross-body—and then give her a quick hug. "Wish me luck," I whisper in her ear.

"You don't need luck," Amira says. "Because you're fabulous."

I blow her a kiss, then exit to where Simon is waiting, looking at his phone. He immediately tucks it into his pocket. "Shall we?"

I nod and head for the door, and once again, he opens it for me and follows me onto the sidewalk. "Where are we going?"

He leads me toward the BMW sedan parked a few spaces down at the curb and opens the passenger door for me. "Do you like seafood?"

"Of course."

"Then I'm taking you to my favorite seafood restaurant in Malibu."

There are quite a few of them; I've been to all of them and there's not a bad one in the bunch. I climb carefully into the passenger seat, and he closes the door behind me before he circles in front of the car. I study him through the windshield as he waits for oncoming traffic to pass so he can climb into the driver's side. I joked with him about his alter-ego Seojun, but that was my first thought when I saw him in his designer suit in the hallway of my studio. Now, as he rushes to get into the car through a gap in traffic, he seems nervous.

"Nice car," I observe blandly as he presses the button to start the engine.

He grimaces before he throws on the turn signal and pulls out into traffic. "It's my dad's. I didn't want to take you out on our first date in a Ford Focus with a dent in the rear bumper."

I laugh at his sheepishness before I clock what he said. "Our first date. Is that what this is?"

He doesn't look at me, but I get the sense that's purposeful. "I had rather thought it was. But if you're not interested, then please just tell me now so I don't embarrass myself further."

"I . . . didn't want to make assumptions." It's not an answer to his question, but it must satisfy him, because he throws a tiny smile at me. Still, the silence stretches between us, and I fiddle with the end of my jumpsuit's belt.

"So tell me," I say finally when the silence lingers to an awkward degree, "what exactly is your schedule like when you get back to Korea?"

This must be a safe topic because he relaxes visibly and begins to give me a play-by-play of the last three months of his year. And it's astounding. Video filming, magazine shoots, two fan meetings, and so many end-of-the-year awards shows I lose count. Their expected performances are all songs that they just finished touring with, and the choreography doesn't change, but apparently they do different arrangements and styling for each one.

"So this is literally your only break until next year."

He nods. "Yes."

"And you're spending it doing Pilates?"

"Hey, you were the one who told me I needed help if I was going to make it through all that."

I can't argue with that. It's true, and I'm sure that I can send him back home in better condition than he came here in. At least that's the goal. "I wouldn't put it so bluntly, but yes, we'll do our best."

We've exited the 101 Freeway now onto Malibu Canyon Road and we're starting our descent through the twisty mountain pass toward the ocean. He's concentrating on the road, but mostly I feel like we've run out of things to say to each other. I search for another question. "What's your favorite city to travel to?"

"For performance or just for fun? Because most of the time, I end up seeing the venue and my hotel room and nothing else."

"Let's say for fun, then."

He answers immediately. "Paris. No question."

"Ooh. When were you in Paris for fun?"

"Well, it was still sort of for work, but I was there last summer for Fashion Week with Roger Dupree from Duchene."

That's who he's wearing. I should have recognized it, as much attention as the young French designer is getting in LA these days. Simon is one of their brand ambassadors and now I remember seeing his stunning photos when I was secretly stalking him on the internet. "What else did you get to do?"

"Embarrassingly touristy things. The Louvre. Dinner boat ride on the Seine. Climbed to the top of the Eiffel Tower."

"Sounds fun."

"Have you been?"

"I have, but on tour with my company. And I got thrown into an understudy role, so while everyone else was sightseeing, I was rehearsing at the theater."

"Which ballet?"

"*Manon.*"

He lets out a sound of approval. "That's a shame you missed out, but to do *Manon* at the Paris Opera House? Worth it."

"How did you know it was at the Paris Opera?"

A smile curves his lips. "You're not the only one who knows things."

"Fair enough." I look out the window at the rocky hillside, but the canyon blocks enough sunlight that for a moment, I can only see my own reflection in the tinted window. "Do you miss it?"

"Ballet?" He thinks for a second. "No. I mean, I did wonder if I'd made the right decision, especially during my years as a trainee when I still couldn't speak Korean well and I was struggling to adapt to the culture. Somehow I thought it would be easier than being Asian in America, but I realized that *looking* Korean but not actually *being* Korean was worse. Everyone expected me to know what I was doing and they gave me very little grace."

"In your company?"

He nods. "If it hadn't been for Joon—Jae—I probably would have quit. He was four years older than me, and he took responsibility for me. Things were better then. For a while at least."

"What happened then?"

He doesn't say anything for several heartbeats. "The company moved me to the training squad they wanted to debut as Astra. I was the maknae, the youngest, by almost two years. I trained with them for about six months. On camera, no less. And then one day I was told that I was getting kicked back down. Joon refused to have me in the group, and the company conceded."

My mouth drops open in shock. "Why would he do that?"

"My reaction exactly," Simon says wryly. "The official reason was that my Korean wasn't good enough, and he didn't think I would present myself well to the press."

It may be secondhand indignation, but I can imagine the feeling of betrayal by someone he was close to, someone he probably thought of as a brother. But he'd said *official reason*. "What was the real reason?"

"I didn't learn this for years, not until after I debuted and Joon came to congratulate me in person. He told me that he knew I was destined to be something special, but if I debuted back then—I was barely sixteen, remember—I would struggle for years in full view of press and fans and never reach my full potential. And he was right. I developed my vocals in those two years, improved my Korean, and debuted as main dancer of Hyperion instead of the youngest and least-prepared member of Astra."

Simon falls silent for a minute. "The thing is, I was so angry with him for so long. And it turns out it was all for my own good. He knew it, but I didn't. I just wanted to debut, to be part of something, to know that I hadn't made the wrong decision in leaving America for this wild dream. So when I found out that I was the first member he asked for when they formed Helios . . ."

"It felt like redemption," I say softly.

He throws me a quick smile before returning his eyes to the road. "Something like that. However short-lived."

"Why do you say that?"

"Because our contract is up at the end of this year, and we haven't decided what our future is as a group yet."

I go still, sensing that he's telling me something that no one else knows, that *I* shouldn't even know. His trust in me makes my throat constrict with something that isn't altogether pleasant. "You're taking a big risk in telling me."

"I am. Did I choose wrong?"

"No," I say softly. "You can trust me."

We finally emerge from the canyon, and the Pacific Ocean sprawls out before us, the sun painting it in shimmering gold as it dips beneath the horizon. No matter how many times I see this view, it never fails to astound me. But before I can say anything, the phone rings through the car's speakers. Simon registers the number and grimaces. "This is Joon. I should take this. Do you mind?"

"Of course not."

He clicks a button on the steering wheel. "Yeoboseyo."

I don't recognize the low voice on the other end, and the caller is speaking Korean so I have no idea what he's saying. Simon replies, and the only thing I catch and understand is *Joon-hyung*, until he says, "I'm in the car with a friend right now going to dinner." I realize as I listen that Simon's voice is deeper in English than Korean, and it momentarily distracts me from the fact that their conversation is becoming increasingly more animated.

I watch Simon's face shift from relaxed and open to hard and cautious. He falls silent and for a second, it sounds like he's being scolded. "Ne," he says, resigned. "Okay."

As soon as Joon hangs up, he flexes his hands around the steering wheel and lets out a long, careful breath.

"Problems?" I inquire delicately.

"Team business," he says, then forces a smile, but this time he doesn't quite glance at me.

I have the strangest feeling that the argument was about me.

chapter nineteen

The restaurant Simon takes me to sits on a bluff overlooking the ocean, which is now lit with sunset colors on the horizon. I'm familiar with it, but I've only been here once because it's the most expensive place in the city. It also happens to be one of the most private, and I wonder for which reason he selected it. That question goes away when he escorts me inside and we're immediately met by an older white man with a shiny head and a perfectly trimmed goatee.

He greets Simon warmly with a handshake before he pulls him into a hug, and then he leads us through the restaurant to a small private alcove in the back with three tables; only one of them is set with linen and candles. The man pulls out my chair for me while Simon settles across from me and gives him a grateful smile.

"The owner is a friend of my dad's," he explains. "He understands why I might want discretion."

"That's nice," I say, folding my hands awkwardly into my lap.

I'm happy that the usual restaurant procedures take up time, because now it feels like neither of us has any idea of how to act. We order our meals—lobster ravioli for him, grilled snapper for me—and non-alcoholic drinks, and then we're staring at each other as awkwardly as any fourteen year olds on their first unaccompanied outing.

Simon runs his hand through his hair in a gesture that will never stop being attractive to me, then shoots me a rueful smile. "This felt a lot easier over text. I don't even know where to start."

I smile because I'd been thinking the same thing. "A mentor once told me when you don't know where to begin with anything—whether it be how to approach a role or how to connect to a partner or the audience—you can start with one true thing."

He cocks his head at me, interest piqued. "What's that?"

"One true thing. Something universal that everyone would understand. Something personal that anyone can relate to."

Simon sits back in his chair, thinking. "Okay," he says finally. "How's this? You are the first person I've been in public with who is not a member of my team, my family, or the press in years, and I feel very self-conscious about it."

It's a level of transparency that I don't expect, even aside from the revelation. I lean forward and cross my arms on the table, not realizing what it's doing to my cleavage in the halter until his gaze dips down and then back up again. I straighten a little. "How is that possible?"

"Twelve- to eighteen-hour work days, very little opportunity for anything else. And if I'm not working, I'd rather be alone. The demands feel. . . ." He licks his lips and sighs. ". . . unending sometimes."

My instinct is to empathize, but there are things I want to know. "Friends?"

"Other idols, musicians, dancers. But we still keep up mostly by text because they're just as busy as I am."

"Dating?"

"Define dating."

Now I grimace. "I don't want to know."

He frowns and then laughs. "I just mean . . ." He shakes his head. "It's not like I can just take someone out to the movies. I have to be careful about being seen in public with someone who isn't already associated with me, male or female. So it puts a damper on things."

"Relationships?"

"Of course. But nothing that's lasted very long because of all the other things. If they're in the industry, they have the same issues I do. If they're not, it can be . . . hard to adjust to."

I can understand that. There's a reason dancers mostly marry other dancers, or at least other people who work in theater or entertainment. There's nothing about having a workday that spans noon to midnight that is compatible with a normal life. Though if you're going to live an abnormal life, New York pretty much caters to it.

"I understand," I say finally.

He smiles at me, warmly but a little disbelieving. "Do you?"

"I was seeing someone, but I think we went out maybe a dozen times over eight months. That's . . . it. Since I moved to LA at least."

He goes still. "I find that very hard to believe."

"Let's just say that my life isn't much less focused than yours, if for different reasons."

He catches on quick. "Because of your . . . condition? Is that the right way to say it?"

"That's fine." I toy with my napkin, then take a sip of water. "Just like no one wants to hide inside on your end, no one wants someone who's too tired to go out at the end of the work day. Or you know, who collapses at concerts."

He smiles faintly. "Would it be rude to say that I'm not all that sorry about the last part?"

I give him a mock-shocked expression. "Yes! That's terrible!"

"Even if I say that I was happy to have a reason to contact you?"

My stomach gives a little flutter at the sincere look in his brown eyes as he watches me across the table. "Well, maybe I'll give you a pass on that one." I settle back. "Icebreaker time. What's the most embarrassing moment you've had on stage?"

"Ughhhh." He sits back too and lets out a groan. "On stage or on camera?"

"Both. Either."

"On stage? I split my pants during my center on a dance break. It took some...creative choreography not to show the audience that I was wearing red underwear."

I snort-laugh at that detail, and his surprised look makes me laugh harder. "Sorry. Red?"

He shrugs, unconcerned. "Shows up less under light colors when you have darker skin."

"I did not know that. What's the biggest on-camera mistake?"

"It was right after Hyperion debuted. I was being interviewed on TV—in Korean, of course—and I got flustered and told the host that I was very bored to be there. I meant excited, but I got my words scrambled. There are memes about it now." He grins. "Or maybe it was more of a Freudian slip. It was a terrible show."

"That's what I would have trouble with. I never had an issue talking to journalists, but if they ever wanted to shoot video..." I shook my head. "I'd rather be on stage."

"Yeah," he says. "Me too."

We share a smile as the server returns with our drinks. Simon raises his glass to mine. "To Freudian slips and red underwear, I guess."

I laugh and clink my glass to his. I don't know how he can feel nervous and then say such random things with a straight face, but he's a strange combination of shy and bold. The conversation shifts to performances and touring—for both of us, though he's done far more of it than I have—and gradually the awkwardness ebbs away. We may have different lives, but we understand each other in a way that only other performers can. There's a certain kind of personality that gravitates toward the long hours and sacrifices that come with this kind of career, a willingness to sacrifice yourself upon the altar of your art. So I'm not surprised at the question that I knew was coming eventually.

"Do you miss it?" he asks. "Performing?"

I don't hesitate. "Every day."

"And there's no chance of going back?"

I shake my head. "POTS is manageable but not curable."

I never told him what my condition was, but he doesn't seem surprised, so I guess he must have done his own research. "I'm sorry," he says simply. "That must be heartbreaking."

"It is." I can feel things taking a morose turn, and this is not how I want to spend the evening, so I force a smile. "I do like what I do now, though, so it's not a complete loss."

He stares out the window at the ocean for a long moment, and I think he's working up words of encouragement or optimism. Instead, he murmurs, "I don't want to re-sign when my contract is up."

I go still, not wanting to break into what feels like a very difficult admission.

"That's why I'm here." He finally turns back to me. "I need some distance from it all. I've been doing this for fifteen years . . . and don't get me wrong, in some ways it's more than I ever expected it to be. And in some ways, I'm not sure if it's been worth it."

"Was that what you were arguing with Joonwoo about?" I ask quietly.

He nods, and my cheeks burn at my own arrogance to think I could have been the source of conflict between the two men.

"He wants you to sign?" I guess.

"Not exactly. Joon is . . . all about the group. We've only been together for three years, but he's known all of us since we were trainees. He feels responsible for us. So he's in a bad spot. He knows I want to leave, but Hyunsoo and Jiho and Kai want to stay. If I leave, I hurt the group. Not just because of what the fans will do, but because I'm the dance leader. I work with our choreographers, I drill the routines." He holds his head in his hands, his elbows propped on the table, for a long moment. Then he straightens. "I'm sorry. I don't mean to dump that on you."

"It's a lot," I say softly. "I've been in a situation that was similar where I felt like I held someone else's career in my hands and . . . it's a weight." I swallow and shove down the swell of memory that comes with that admission. We are not talking about my trauma, we're talking about his. "Let me ask you this then. How long do you have left of this career? Realistically?"

"Realistically? A couple of years at most. Even if I weren't in pain, things can start to feel weird as an idol in your mid-thirties. I mean, things feel weird now—I'm a grown man still having to perform aegyo, for God's sake—but if I never hear a twelve-year-old call me *oppa* again, it will still be too soon."

There is so much in that sentence I don't understand, but I get the sentiment behind it. "So if you resign, you're just delaying the inevitable."

"Yes, but the other guys . . . they're not quite ready to throw in the towel. Hyunsoo is only twenty-six, so I get it—he has a few more years before he can even think about retiring. Jiho and Kai were already soloists, but they're doing much better with the group."

I shake my head. "I don't know, Simon. I don't think you can make decisions solely based on what the people around you need. What if you re-sign and your back gets so bad that you can't dance? What does it do to the group then? If you're on borrowed time . . . you're on borrowed time."

He nods slowly, but I don't think there's anything I can say that's going to help him make this decision. There's the weight of years of dedication to his groups, his company, and a culture that I don't understand. For all Simon strikes me as American, he's spent half his life and the entirety of his professional career in Korea. I'm not sure that reinforcing the American belief in rugged individualism is going to help him right now.

Almost as if the universe sensed that we needed a pause, our food comes out and it looks every bit as delicious as I would expect from the lovely setting. We sip our drinks and eat our food in silence for a few moments, then Simon throws me a mischievous look. "Too much heavy stuff for one night. Let's play a balance game."

"A what?"

"An icebreaker. Like *This or That* or *Would You Rather*." He narrows his eyes playfully. "And you call yourself a Hellion."

"I do not, actually. I am an unapologetic Seojun solo stan." I wink at him. "I know the game, I just didn't know it was called that. You go first."

I take another bite of my fish and watch him try to come up with his first question. Finally, he asks, "Would you rather be alone for an entire month or be surrounded by people twenty-four hours a day for a week?"

"Easy," I say immediately. "Alone. As long as I have internet."

"Fair. I should have known you're an introvert."

I laugh and lean back in my chair, face tipped to the ceiling. Oh, I have a good one. "Would you rather split your pants on stage wearing *no* underwear or have to go out on stage wearing *only* red underwear?"

He stares at me. "I give you a softball question and you give me this one?"

I just grin and wait.

"Do I have to do all the choreo as usual?"

I nod.

He winces. "Split my pants with no underwear."

"Really? I thought for sure you'd pick the other one."

"Oh no, you've seen our routines. It would look like a striptease. My mother would never speak to me again. As it was, the first time she saw me perform live, she hugged me and whispered, 'But does it have to be quite so sexy?'"

A laugh bursts out of me, bouncing off the walls of the small alcove, and I clap my hand over my mouth until my shoulders stop shaking. "Oh, the pain of having a child who is a performer. My first role as a soloist had a bedroom pas de deux. The questions my mother asked me about why my partner's hands were where they were. . .I don't think I've ever been so embarrassed in my life."

Simon's eyes glint. "I've seen that one. *Intersections?*"

Now it's my turn to flush. "That's the one."

"It was incredible. But that particular pas de deux was . . . yeah." He clears his throat, but I can see his lips quivering as his smile tries to break free. "I've never been quite so interested in contemporary ballet."

"Yeah, well, you know as well as I do that it feels very unsexy in the moment. Especially considering I didn't like my partner very much."

"Really! I'd never know. You had great chemistry on stage."

"All acting, I assure you," I say. "If we weren't dancing together, we refused to look at each other." Of course, that had more to do with Philip replacing his usual partner with me in the ballet, but I don't tell him that because it would make the story darker than I intend.

Instead, I meet his gaze and we both start laughing again. There's something freeing about commiserating over the utter ridiculousness of our chosen professions, the vast difference between what the audience sees and what it feels like as a performer, and I feel something loosen in my chest that I didn't realize was knotted. I still can't finish my meal, but I do finish my drink, and by the time we walk out of the restaurant, the awkwardness between us has melted away.

When he reaches for my hand on the way to the parking lot, it feels like the most natural thing in the world to lace my fingers with his. I'm surprisingly sad to release him when I climb into the car.

We're mostly silent on our way back down PCH, but it's a comfortable silence this time, and when he places his hand face up on the console in invitation, I don't hesitate to take it again. He has nice hands, strong and slender and well-manicured like the rest of him, and in the dark, leather-scented interior of the car, I can't help but imagine what they would feel like on me, grazing my back or lacing through my hair.

"What are you thinking?" he asks suddenly.

I flush, glad the shadows hide my face. "I was just thinking that for two people who don't date, we managed that pretty well."

He smiles. "I don't think you're supposed to talk about underwear on a first date."

"I don't think you're supposed to talk about naked ice baths via text either." I laugh. "We had an unconventional first meeting."

"That we did. Speaking of unconventional, I want to ask you something, but I don't want to freak you out or have you read too much into it."

"How could I possibly be nervous when you say something like that?"

He throws a glance at me as he moves into the turn lane for Malibu Canyon Road. "My parents want me to be home for dinner on Friday. I was wondering . . . if maybe you'd like to come?"

"Dinner with your parents?" I blink, my stomach suddenly tightening.

"See, that's why I didn't want you to read too much into it. I don't know if this helps or hurts, but Joon will be there too."

"Wait. He's in LA?"

"For a bit. He's flying back to Seoul on Saturday because he has meetings on Monday at the agency."

I think about it for a minute. There's nothing normal about whatever *this* is, and I don't even know if *this* is going anywhere, so . . . what exactly do I have to lose? "Okay. How should I dress?"

"Casual," he says immediately, but I don't think I imagine the relief in his voice. "Joon has requested American barbecue, so you won't even have to eat Korean food."

"But I love Korean food," I say. "There's a fantastic Korean restaurant down the street from me, actually. I order bibimbap or jjajangmyeon practically every other week."

"Some other time, then. So I should tell them to expect us?"

Us. "Yeah, that sounds like fun. Thank you."

He squeezes my hand. "You're welcome."

I'd like to say that I don't analyze every moment and every word on the way back to my house, but that would be giving me too much credit. I might be able to act like a normal human being, but inside I can't quite countenance that I'm holding hands with a pop star I met on stage at a concert less than a month ago. Not that the pop star thing has any bearing on my interest in him—though all we have in common as dancers certainly does—but it lends a certain unreality to the whole situation. Like this is simply a strange dream and I'm still lying unconscious on the side of the stage.

When we get to my place, Simon insists on walking me to my door, but before I can put my key in the lock, he reaches out and gently tugs me back. "I'd like to kiss you goodnight," he says quietly, looking me directly in the eye. "If that's okay with you."

I freeze, then mutely nod. He bends close to me, enveloping me in the light scent of his cologne, and presses his lips gently to my cheek. Then he straightens and brushes his hands down my arms, shoulders to fingertips. "Good night, Katrina."

I clear my throat. "Good night, Simon."

He gives me a little smile and then turns away. He never looks back, but I don't stop watching him until he disappears.

chapter twenty

February 2020, New York City

In the end, like dancers always do, we pull it off.

That's not to say it's easy, because it's absolutely not. Philip is changing blocking up until the last moment when we have our dress rehearsal on the Met's grand stage, tweaking formations for the corps de ballet, giving last minute notes to each of the dancers as they finish their performances.

And yet for me, he's gone completely silent. Even after finishing the Rose Adagio, which has consistently given me problems to the point that I'm not sure I'm going to be able to execute this choreography, Philip merely looks at me for a long moment, then gives me a mute nod. The rest of the company has no more idea what to make of it than I do; I can tell half of them think it's a blessing and a privilege because of our relationship, while the other half thinks it's a sign of something gone completely, utterly wrong.

If I'm pressed, I would have to agree with the latter statement.

Maybe it's just the pressure of the world premiere of an entirely new staging of *The Sleeping Beauty*—along with a wildly different jazz arrangement of the Tchaikovsky score—but Philip has been distant and distracted for the last few weeks. We still leave the studio together most nights, picking up food on the way home, taking taxis more often than not to save me from walking on my still-problematic foot. We still have sex nearly every night, even if I'm so exhausted I can't see straight or he's so frustrated he barely says a word to me. But I can tell his mind isn't completely here. Even if he is being overly solicitous, monitoring the status of my foot, bringing me ice and NSAIDs, giving me massages while we watch the evening news.

I wish I had someone to talk to about this, to tell me if I'm just imagining things. We've been living together for almost a year at this point, so it's natural for things to become rote, right? To be settling into a routine. I never thought I would long for the days when I could barely put down my dance bag before he was all over me, taking me up against the front door of our shared apartment, but now that cooling ardor makes me think that he might be regretting our rash decision to move in together.

But Maddie and I are still barely more than coworkers, and my status as the choreographer's favorite *and* live-in girlfriend doesn't exactly endear me to the rest of the company, particularly the ballerinas I've supplanted. Which means that it's just me and my nagging thoughts, alone, over and over until I'm almost sick of myself. Even Janine, who has been a constant encouragement since *Intersections,* seems to be keeping her distance. I just wish I knew why.

So instead I stand in the wings of the opera house, waiting for my first entrance as the quirky jazz score filters through the heavy curtain while the stage hands switch scenery and backdrop in a decidedly inelegant process. It's a stripped-down staging, with a backdrop that looks like a soaring contemporary mansion, all crystal and marble and heavy draperies, a cityscape visible through the painted two-story windows behind. I cycle through my shoes and bounce on the balls of my feet, trying to stay warm while I wait and quell the panicked flock of hummingbirds in my gut. The audience's gasp when the curtain went up on the prologue propelled the first-act pantomime and brought down the house with applause. And now it's my turn.

The orchestra strikes up the first strains of the next scene, and I move out of the way as the party guests—dressed in quasi-modern costumes that evoke the feel of Jazz Age passed through a fantasy filter—line up in the wings, ready to make their entrance. I have to admit, I've never loved the first-act waltz—a lot of hand-waving and formations, but very little actual interesting dancing—and so now as the lines of dancers prepare to make their entrance in their ballroom attire, I feel myself understanding Philip's full vision. It's a whirl of color and fabric, a true ballroom waltz, and it's mesmerizing. I'm so caught up in the spectacle of it that I nearly miss the cue for my entrance and have to strip off my thigh-high leg warmers so quickly I almost trip over my own feet. But I'm there in the wings on time, plastering a smile on my face before I step onto the stage—not a princess in this staging, but the daughter of a captain of industry, ready to hold court.

It's as exhilarating as it has always been, that first moment I emerge into the lights and feel the expanse of the stage and the opera house over and around me. It's as if I could jump and just keep going, carried weightless into the ornate ceiling, the laws of gravity no longer applying in this rarified space. The nerves give me a touch too much amplitude as I bound onto the stage in my spangled ballet version of an evening gown, and I have to rein myself in before I overshoot my mark.

There really is nothing like it, the feeling of four thousand pairs of eyes fixed upon me, breaths held as they wait for what I'm going to do next.

It's a short entrance, less than a minute, but it's a sparkling, girlish, exuberant minute in which I express how excited I am to be here at my fabulous birthday party with the who's who of society at my beck and call. I've thought more than once that the choreography would suit Maddie better than me, but I'm happy with my execution when I finish my last turn in a deep fourth position and the opera house breaks into applause.

I barely have time to breathe before we're into the Rose Adagio. I pantomime meeting Aurora's suitors with studied boredom, then begin the long series of partnering steps moving downstage. It's going pretty well—I make it through the first series of finger turns and développés with nary a wobble. But when I circle back around to begin the long series of balances and step onto pointe, I hear a crack.

You have got to be kidding me. I feel my balance shift as the shank of my shoe splits across the middle, depriving me of a good part of my support just as I step into the arabesques that have been giving me difficulty this whole time. I have a split second to make a decision, and I make the one that's going to be most seamless to the audience and also get me greatest amount of grief when it's over—I change the choreography.

Instead of holding the balance, I gracefully roll off pointe into a deep, bent-leg arabesque, only rising up to my toes again when the next suitor comes around to support me. And then I do it three more times.

It's not nearly as impressive as the real steps, but I know it looks graceful . . . and I also know the audience has no clue. I finish the rest of the adagio, nail the lifts, and finish to a wild ovation of applause.

I can almost feel Philip's glare from the front row.

Somehow I make it through the first act despite feeling the jab of the broken shank in my arch and a distinct wetness that I'm afraid is not sweat but blood. By now, that foot is so numb from the pointework that I barely feel any pain; all I can concentrate on is getting off stage to change shoes. Fortunately, after I prick my finger on a record player and collapse into a heap, there's not much to do but lie there until I'm carried into the wings. The minute I clear the stage lights and the men set me on my feet, I'm tearing at the ribbons of my pointe shoes to get them off and assess the damage.

Sure enough, there's a small puncture from the nail that worked loose from the shank just beneath the heel of my right foot, but the blood has clotted and dried to my tights, so I just toss the shoes aside and reach for the brand-new pair waiting for me in the wings for Act 2. I've got time now—just not enough time to go back to my dressing room—while the fairies dance and my friends mill around my sick-bed, which is to be revealed later when my handsome prince kisses me to wake me. I test these shoes thoroughly—no repeats of that strange little flaw—and then move off to the side where a dresser helps me out of my first act costume and into the flowing, billowing white gown that's—I suppose— intended to mimic a couture nightgown. It's one of the weirder wardrobe choices in this ballet, and I spend the entire second act in it.

But that's neither here nor there, because the dresser is helping fix my hair for the second act—removing my bobbed wig and smoothing down the elegant half French twist beneath, the lengthened hair meant to indicate the passage of time. I'm on the side of the stage in time to see my prince's entrance—Tony, looking resplendent in a dark suit—and before I know it, I'm making my miraculous recovery, sneaked into the bed on stage behind the cover of Aurora's friends in time to be kissed by my true love.

The act speeds by with remarkable alacrity, and I have very little dancing to do in this act—a short variation and a brief wide-eyed pas de deux before I'm escorted off the stage once more.

"What the hell happened?" Tony asks without any heat. "You changed the first act choreography?"

"Shank broke," I say wryly. "Trust me, I'm going to hear *all* about it tonight."

He grimaces, but I don't have time to think about it. There's plenty to be done to get me into my third act costume, a white spangled flapper-eseque wedding dress, and it requires me pinning my hair up beneath a sequined cap. Fortunately, I have some time before I have to make my entrance since the third-act diver-tissements come before Tony and I rejoin the stage for the famous wedding pas de deux.

I check that my shoes are still good, touch up my makeup, and then high-tail it back to the stage with plenty of time for our entrance. That's not why I'm rushing anyway, and I'm pleased that I hit the wings in time to see Maddie step out, swathed in a tiny, sparkly blue dress to the familiar strings-and-flute opening of the Bluebird Pas de Deux.

My heart clenches in my chest as I watch her and her partner move through the sparkling piece, full of supported pirouettes and balances, lifts and jumps. Of all the choreography that's been redone in this ballet,

Bluebird is probably the one that's gotten the greatest overhaul, and even I can see that Philip has set the choreography to highlight Maddie and her partner Daniel's strengths. Still, I'm holding my breath through the whole thing, willing it to go brilliantly, and when Maddie runs off stage in my direction, I'm waiting for her with a box of tissues.

She blots the sweat from her face, but she manages to give me a smile. I have just enough time to wish her merde before she's back on, rejoining her partner in a long string of fluttering petit allegro, pointework, and turns. Slowly, the knot eases from my stomach. Even though this is the part that has been causing her to cry in the bathroom after rehearsals, you'd never know it to see her now—she's sparkling and magnetic on stage, and the explosive applause at the end of the variation proves it. I'm clapping along, a huge smile on my face, and I'm there to catch her up in a hug when she runs my direction once again.

"You were amazing!" I hiss fiercely. "That's the way to do it."

"My turns were off," she mutters. "And that last lift—"

"No one noticed but you," I reassure her quickly. "You were marvelous."

But I don't have time to stick around and tell her how wonderful she was, because Tony is gesturing frantically from the opposite wing that it's time for us to take our positions. I blow Maddie one last kiss and then scurry off to join my partner behind the scenery that creates the walls of the ballroom, ready to make our entrance through the wide "double doors."

I should be nervous when I take Tony's hand and let him escort me out onto the stage, but with the Rose Adagio behind me, all I feel is excitement. In my opinion, this is one of the most beautiful pas de deux in ballet, and if anything, Philip has made it more beautiful, erasing the formality of the original and replacing it with sweeping romanticism. In many ways it reminds me of *Intersections,* just grander, and I let myself be caught up in the emotion of it, the technical details melting away as I feel the music. This is why I became a dancer, this freedom, when the steps are so ingrained that I can just . . . *be.*

I'm so caught up in the moment that when I exit stage right to give way to my partner's variation, it takes me a minute to feel the pain in my foot coming from both top and bottom. I grimace at the swelling above the vamp of the shoe; it turns to a spike of alarm when I see the spot of blood soaking through the satin near the sole.

"Shit," I mutter. The puncture must have opened again somehow. There's nothing I can do about it now, though, because Tony's variation is coming to an end. I send up a hopeless prayer that the bloodstain won't spread enough to be visible from the audience and rush to the rear wing for my entrance.

I try to will back that flow state when I take center stage for my solo variation, but it's long gone, filled with worries about what might be going on inside my shoe, the throb that's begun around that stupid unhealed injury. *You're a professional, Kat. Suck it up and get it done.*

And I do. Unlike some of the other stagings, Philip's Aurora is not a wide-eyed innocent at her wedding, full of girlish enthusiasm and naive purity. Instead, she's a young woman in full command of her power and sexuality, and I play it that way, giving a coquettish air to the intricate pointework and well-balanced turns. Despite everything flitting around in the back of my head, there's something in me that finally connects to the character. She's got what she wanted. She's triumphed over the plans of the evil fairy Carabosse and the bumbling of her parents and the fairies in handling the curse. And now, now that she has the attention of every single person in the town, she's going to show them what she can do.

It's that burning determination that drives me through the last half minute, where Tony and I trade off the center focus, him for a series of turns a la second, me for a long diagonal of pique turns and jeté leaps, then come together again at the crescendo for one last bit of partnering. His hands skim my waist, tightening around it on the last turn and I strike the final attitude devant, my arm upraised.

It's over.

I gracefully lower my leg and step aside while Tony takes my hand, but all I can hear is the thunderous applause, all I can see is the opera house rising to their feet in a standing ovation. All those brutal rehearsals, the doubts, the pain . . . it's all come to this moment of triumph.

And it is a triumph, minor hiccups aside. Philip has done something astounding in his reimagining of a classic. I wouldn't be surprised if other companies want to stage it as well. And no matter how many ballerinas dance this Aurora after me, everyone will always know that I was the one who originated it. That I was the one who inspired it.

It's a feeling like I've never felt before.

That carries me through the bows with the rest of the cast, then the ones by ourselves, where Tony lifts the heavy curtain so I can step out on the apron for my moment. Errantly, I wish my parents were here to see this, to see what all their sacrifices and demands have brought about. I might have fought against their demands for me to come to New York with Maddie, but no one can ever say that I didn't make the best of it.

The real celebration comes on stage when I step back beneath the curtain. Tony catches me up in a hug and spins me around, then plants a huge kiss on my cheek. I laugh as Damien appears by his side, a mock-reproving look on his face for me before he plants one on his husband. I turn and there's Maddie, waiting with a huge smile.

"You were spectacular," she says, pulling me into a hug. "I couldn't breathe through the pas de deux."

"So were you," I whisper back, holding tight to her. "You pulled it off, sweetie. I'm so, so proud of you."

We make our rounds through our friends and fellow dancers, caught up in the adrenaline of a finished show, but it isn't long before nervousness creeps into my stomach. It's only a matter of minutes before Philip shows up here to accept his well-deserved congratulations. I just don't know if the first thing that comes out of his mouth will be praise or criticism.

But after a few minutes when he doesn't show up, I let myself be caught up in the trickle of dancers leaving the stage for their dressing rooms. I'm already unpinning my feather-adorned headdress as I go, my dead pointe shoes slapping the concrete in the hallway as I make my way back into the bowels of the theater. Now that the adrenaline has worn off, I'm feeling exhaustion in every part of my body. My foot is throbbing and I can feel some strain in my right hamstring that I'll need to get worked out with the therapist tomorrow. Now I'm almost glad that Philip hasn't showed up. I need a few minutes to get myself together before he starts berating me or groping me or both.

These days, I only share a dressing room with one other ballerina and she wasn't cast in this ballet, so I have the space to myself. I strip out of my spangled dress and hang it on the rack, then slip a t-shirt on over my bare torso and flesh colored tights. I'm stalling. I'm dreading taking off my shoe and seeing the damage.

But it's not as bad as I thought. Despite the red bloom on the peach satin of my shoes, the bleeding seems to be localized and already clotting. I cringe as I pour a little water onto some paper towels, then press it to the bottom of my foot to loosen up the blood before I peel my tights back. It takes more water and more paper towels to swab away enough to see the spot.

It's not so much a puncture as a shallow gash, which explains why it bled so much. I let out a long sigh of relief. A couple of days rest and it won't be an issue. I was so worried I was going to have to go to the ER or something, imagining a shoe filled with blood. If Philip were here, he would laugh at me for my wild imagination. "Always going to the worst possible scenario," he liked to say. As if I didn't have reason to believe it might happen.

I remove my makeup, take down my hair, and slide into fluffy joggers and a comfy sweatshirt, all the while keeping an eye on the clock on the wall. I putter around, cleaning up my stuff, stopping at the dressing table to sniff the bouquet of white roses from Philip that were waiting at the theater when I arrived.

When the knock sounds at the door, I let out my breath and prepare a teasing, chiding greeting for him. I open the door. "I was beginning to—"

Except it's not Philip standing there, it's Janine. Ironically, she played Aurora's mother in this ballet, even though she's only thirteen years older than me. Now, she wears a huge smile.

"You were *amazing*," she says, sweeping me up in a big hug. "I am so, so proud of you, you have no idea."

The words are a balm to my nerves, and I let myself sink into her bony arms for a long minute before I pull back. "Thank you. So were you."

Janine waves a hand to blow off the compliment; we both know that her role was more acting than dancing, even if she pulled it off flawlessly as usual. "It was nothing. How do you feel? How's the foot?"

I back off in surprise and plop down on my chair. I didn't know my ongoing problems were so well known; I tried to keep it quiet. But it doesn't take a genius to guess the reason for all the classes I take in flat shoes, why I sometimes skip my right side in exercises.

"It's okay, except for this." I raise my right foot to show her the bandage on the sole of my foot.

She grimaces. "Nail?"

"Yep."

"Brutal." She pulls up the chair at the empty dressing table behind me and plops down on it. "You headed home soon?"

"Yeah, I'm just waiting for Philip to come up." I grab my water bottle and take a long drink. I know it's deflection, a way to signal that I don't want to talk about Philip, but I can't miss the shift in Janine's expression. "What?"

"Sweetie . . ." She breaks off, her eyes pained. "He left."

"What?" I blink at her. "No, I'm sure he's just . . . caught up with Alec."

"I saw him myself at the stage door as I was leaving. I just . . . I knew you'd be sitting up here and I didn't think it was fair."

My breath hisses out from between my teeth and I bend forward to put my head in my hands. "Shit. I knew I shouldn't have done it. I just didn't think I could make it through the balances with a broken shoe. Dammit." Tears swell in my eyes, but it's nothing compared to the self-recrimination that's welling up inside.

Janine is just looking at me sympathetically. "Babe,

I've stayed quiet for as long as I can, but . . . you can't keep going on like this."

I lift my head. This is not what I expected her to say. "What?"

"We all see the way he treats you, sweetheart. I just don't understand why you stay with him."

"What?" I repeat. "No, you've got it wrong. Everything's fine between Philip and me. We're happy."

"Kat, you've lost ten pounds in the last year. You're skeletal. You're in pain because you refuse to take care of your injuries. This . . . this isn't sustainable."

"Ballet is hard on a body," I say. "We all know this. It doesn't have anything to do with Philip."

Janine takes a long, deep breath and lets it out in a stream. Regret threads her voice when she says, "You know he's sleeping with other women, right?"

I know she expects some sort of shock from me, but all I feel is a wash of resignation. The "meetings" have been more frequent lately . . . sometimes he doesn't even come home. I can't summon the will to put any force into my protest. "No, he isn't."

"Darling, there's at least one dancer in the company who's hooking up with him, and even she knows that she's not the only one. Philip Barbier is brilliant, but he's not a good man. We all know this."

All my suspicions, all my worries of the last few weeks come rushing in, but I stubbornly push them aside. "I don't believe it. I know what you all say about me. I know you talk crap behind my back, think that I slept my way into this position. But I earned it."

"You did earn it," Janine says softly. "But I'm not sure you understand what's required to keep it."

I blink away the sting of tears and push myself to my feet, almost crumpling at the stab of pain. "I think you should go now."

Janine stares at me for a long moment, then shakes her head. "Okay," she murmurs. "I tried. Just don't say that no one warned you."

She pushes herself out of the chair and walks to the door. She doesn't even give me a last look before she slips out and shuts the door behind her. And even though I know I told her to leave, it still feels like the last person here has given up on me.

chapter twenty-one

"He invited you to what?"

I wince at Amira's screech. So much for dropping the family barbecue invitation casually in the hope that she wouldn't read too much into it. Now she's staring at me as if I grew another head.

"He's introducing you to his parents."

"It's not like that. We were planning on doing something Friday, but they want him home for dinner. Besides, Joonwoo is going to be there."

Amira clutches her heart and falls into the chair. I think she's mostly playing it up for effect, but it's hard to tell. "You're having dinner with Seojun and Jae."

"I'm having dinner with Simon and Joonwoo. There's a difference."

"Okay, right." Amira shakes herself. "No chance for a friend to tag along?" When she sees my look, she laughs. "I'm just joking. Good for you. It sounds like fun."

"Yeah, I'm sure it's going to be." Except now my stomach is twisted into knots. Mostly I've been replaying every moment from my dinner with Simon last night, second-guessing everything that I said and every way I interpreted everything *he* said. But now I realize that it's going to be double pressure. No, triple pressure. Not only do I not know Simon all that well—certainly not well enough for this kind of event—I'm going to be worried about the opinions of both his parents and his mentor.

"You know," I say suddenly, "I think I'm not going."

Amira jumps up out of her seat. "No, I'm not letting you sabotage this. You like this guy. He likes you. You have all of—what, three weeks?—to decide whether or not you're ever going to see each other again. You're not going to miss out on a family barbecue because you're nervous."

"Yeah, thanks, that really helps take off the pressure."

"Okay, fine. Tell him you don't want to go and you'll see him on Monday instead."

I stare at her. "I can't do that. He's already told them I'm coming. They'd hate me, or at least think I'm a snob. Or worse, racist."

Amira just stares at me with a satisfied look on her face. I sigh.

"Okay. I'm going."

"Good girl. Now go out there and get warmed up for your classes."

I do a good job at pretending like I'm not obsessing for the next two days, and while my clients definitely help—when I'm teaching, my full attention is on them—the knot in my stomach grows with each passing hour. By the time I finish my second-to-last client on Friday, it's grown to a huge tangled ball that presses on my lungs and makes my heart feel like it's too large for my body. Even the casual check-in texts I get from Simon throughout both days do nothing to ease the sensation.

Until Simon walks in the door at 6:03. He takes his sunglasses off, and his eyes immediately focus on me, his face softening into a smile. "Hey."

My heart gives a bump at the same time all the tension drains from my body. "Hey."

"Sorry I'm running a little late." He goes to the locker and puts his bag in, then shrugs off his oversized sweatshirt and shoves it in after.

"You're fine," I say as he swaps out his footwear for studio socks. "Busy day?"

"Something like that." He walks towards me, rolling the kinks out of his neck in a way that should not be sexy but actually is. "Reformer or Tower?"

"Reformer." I step aside to make room for him, but as he passes me, his hand grazes mine.

My heart leaps, and the tiny smile he gives me before he faces the apparatus, ready to start his roll-down, tells me it was no accident.

I force my attention back on what I should be concentrating on—my *client*—and start him into the classical sequence as usual. He's moving better today and when I comment on it, he says, "I swam at the gym this morning instead of running and then got a massage. I'm getting there."

Good. It looks like my lecture on giving his joints a rest got through. I focus my cues on stability today, limiting his range of motion. We work slowly and steadily, and even considering his insane level of conditioning, he's working hard by the end. He steps off the Reformer gracefully and does the final roll-down while I watch his spinal articulation. It's smoother than it was, but he's still clearly feeling pain in his lumbar region. He's probably so used to it, it doesn't even register.

"Good work," I say finally, handing him the spray bottle and rag. "I think we're on the right track."

He beams at me. "Me too. This is the best I've felt in a while."

"I think next time we'll do some mat work. It would really be best if you can keep it up when you're on the road. I know I can feel the difference even when I miss a couple of days." No one who isn't a dancer understands that when you retire, you don't just go back to normal. Even if you've managed to avoid the major professional pitfalls requiring hip and knee replacements or spinal fusions, there's an increased level of daily maintenance. Simon and I will never be free of the need to stretch and work out every day if we want to make it into our twilight years somewhat pain-free.

"That would be great, actually. I haven't done enough to be confident in my technique on the road." He drops his cleaning supplies in their designated bins, then moves to the locker. "Do you need to go home and change before we head to Ventura?"

There they are—the butterflies that professionalism have kept at bay. "No, I brought my stuff. You can use the dressing room if you need to."

"I'll just change at home," he says. "All my things are there anyway."

I swallow and nod. "Then just give me a second."

Amira has already gone for the day; she doesn't stay much after noon on Fridays, so I don't have to hear her play-by-play as I go back to the office to retrieve my things. Simon said casual and the temperature is still hovering around ninety even at 7:30 p.m., so I'm glad that I went basic with a pair of mid-length white shorts, a simple striped t-shirt, and a pair of nautical-looking espadrilles. Even five years after ending pointe work, I don't show off my feet willingly. I smooth the loose tendrils from my ponytail and then take a moment to apply some tinted moisturizer, cream blush, and mascara before I call it good. I don't want to seem like I'm trying too hard.

When I walk back out, however, Simon looks me over from head to toe with a slow smile.

"What?"

"You look nice."

That was *not* what he was going to say, but I don't press. Instead, I just pull my keys out of my bag and start the shut-down procedure for the studio—air-conditioning on standby, lights off, back door locked. When we step out onto the sidewalk, I lock up behind us, and then laugh. There's a dirty white Ford Focus with a dent on the passenger fender waiting at the curb.

Simon grins. "Sorry. Dad needed his car today. It was admittedly easier parking downtown today with this."

I wait until we're both seated in the rental car—its cloth interior inexplicably smells like French fries—before I ask, "What was downtown?"

He pulls away from the curb before answering. "I had a meeting."

"Sorry, I didn't mean to pry. If it's not my business, just tell me."

"No, it's not that." He flicks me a look. "I just . . . It was with an indie record label."

My eyebrows fly up. "Oh."

"Yeah. I actually met their A&R guy back in Seoul a year or two ago, and he invited me to come talk with them should I ever have an interest in making a change. Their CEO used to be an idol, understands the transition."

"Wow." I knew he was serious when he said he was uncertain about extending his contract, but this is a big step. "So, what did you think? What kind of vibe did you get?"

He thinks for a long moment before his face relaxes and breaks into a wide smile. "It was good, actually. I like everything they have to say. They're based here in LA, but they still have strong ties to Korea, so it wouldn't be like everything I built there goes to waste. Small, very collaborative. The artists work together pretty closely. I'd have a chance to co-produce my own stuff, expand into different genres."

I hear the hitch. "But . . ."

"But it's a huge change. I've lived in Seoul for almost fifteen years. It's all I know at this point. Being back in LA feels simultaneously strange and familiar, like I'm . . ."

"Displaced," I say softly.

"Exactly. I would be leaving everything I know. All my friends. All my contacts. Coming back to a place that has changed so much I almost don't recognize it. It would be starting over."

I fall silent as he navigates the small car to the freeway on-ramp. "It's a big decision. I imagine it would be easier to let the group go and stay there as a soloist than it would be to make the move here."

"That's exactly it." Simon's hands flex on the steering wheel and he lets out a soft sigh. I study his profile, rendered soft by the slanted sunlight through the window, and I can see the turmoil there. I don't envy him the decision. I pivoted because I had to; this is his choice. Even though what I said the other day is true— he's working on borrowed time. But just because he retires from an idol group doesn't mean he has to leave the South Korean music scene or the larger entertainment industry. I've done a little research on other idols and now I think he could pretty easily get a gig as a TV show host or even an actor. He's certainly handsome and charismatic enough for it.

"What do your parents say?" I ask finally.

"I haven't told them. And Joon doesn't know either, though I'm sure he suspects that I'm considering my options while I'm here. I just. . ." He shakes his head. "I don't want to disappoint anyone."

Someone is always going to get disappointed in this scenario, but whether it's Simon or everyone else around him is the bigger question. I don't say it, though. You don't shut off loyalty and concern for other people's opinions like a switch, and his entire adult life has been entangled with his company. Still, I saw that spark of excitement when he talked about the indie label—that same thing that lights him up on stage—and I hate the idea of it getting extinguished.

We turn north on the freeway, headed toward Ventura in still-heavy traffic, but we haven't gone very far before he reaches across the console for my hand again. I give it up willingly, lacing my fingers with his as my heart swells with an unfamiliar sensation. It feels like we've finally crossed the threshold of awkwardness for our in-person relationship, and now being with him just feels . . . easy. Relaxed. I haven't felt this way around anyone but Amira in so long that I almost can't place it.

"So tell me what I should expect," I say finally when we're leaving the confines of the San Fernando Valley and heading up the coast.

"For what?"

"For everything. Everyone, rather. Your parents, Joon . . . what do they know about me?"

He takes a moment to answer. "They don't know you're the one in the video . . . not sure if they've even seen the video since I don't really encourage them to watch performance footage. For obvious reasons." He throws me a grin. "I've told them you're someone I met while I was in LA the first time and we already had plans when the barbecue idea came up. Joon, of course, knows who you are, but he won't let on. Not that I'm ashamed of it, it's just . . ."

It's just that he probably don't want his parents' first impression of a woman he's seeing to be a stage performance with such obvious sexual overtones. Got it.

It doesn't answer my question, but I'm not going to get anything more out of him. I'll just have to wait and see how it goes. I'm not all that worried about his parents; I might be introverted, but I can manage polite and respectful without an issue. It's Joon that I'm concerned about. Somehow I'm not convinced he'll be able to see me as anything but a fan who somehow won the golden ticket when Simon pulled me up onstage.

It doesn't take much imagination to know that Joon is the one I have to convince about my innocent intentions.

A tricky task considering I don't even know what my intentions are. Simon has been the pursuer in this relationship, and so far he's been surprisingly low-key. He may have kissed me on the cheek when he dropped me off the other night, but he hasn't done anything more than hold my hand. I can't tell if it's because he doesn't want to scare me off or if he genuinely moves at this pace, but given how open he is about his thoughts and feelings—even without whiskey—he's surprisingly reserved.

Then again, I haven't given him much to work with.

I'm pondering that thought when we exit the freeway and he makes a turn that takes us to Pacific Coast Highway, where we wind up the coastline. Blue-green water stretches out beyond us, sparkling with the light of the setting sun. I barely note the houses that line the coast until he turns on his signal and moves into the center turn lane, waiting for oncoming traffic to pass. Then he turns into a driveway and parks in front of the two-car garage.

It's a typical California home from the sixties or seventies, clad in beige-painted wood siding, two boxy stories with a high gate and an enclosed entry. It's tiny, but it's on the water, so I know this place has to be worth several million dollars. I shoot at glance at Simon.

"I grew up here," he says, answering my unspoken question. "It wasn't quite as extravagant to live on the water back then."

I suspect that's not the entire truth, but he's trying to manage my expectations, so I just nod and climb out of the car. The cool sea breeze hits my skin and I breathe in the scent of salt. I've seen the ocean more in the time that Simon has been back in town than I have in the last year. Everyone thinks of LA as a beach city, but in truth, it's just too much effort to get there all the time when your life is inland.

Simon places his hand on my lower back as he guides me toward the enclosed entrance, and I shiver even though it's not remotely cold out. He holds down the gate latch and swings the wooden door open onto a large paver-clad courtyard overflowing with plants.

"My dad's," he says, nodding at the colorfully glazed pots. "He's the one with the green thumb. My mom kills every plant she touches."

I laugh as he walks up to the ornately carved front door. He knocks lightly, but he doesn't wait for anyone to answer before he pushes it open.

The entrance widens into a tiny living room filled with pale, beachy furniture, but my attention goes to the wall of windows overlooking the ocean. It's a stunning view, and I stand there for a second before I realize that Simon is slipping off his shoes and placing them on a rack in the entryway. Oof. I completely forgot that I'd need to take my shoes off, even though I don't wear them in my own house. I unbuckle the ankle straps of the espadrilles, but I hesitate in stepping out of them.

Simon comes to the rescue with a smile—he hands

me a pair of fuzzy slides from a basket next to the rack. "Here. These should be more comfortable."

Gratefully, I take them and swap my shoes for the fuzzy slippers, even though I feel a little silly. I don't have much time to contemplate, because before we can take more than a few steps, Simon's mom comes around the corner.

I don't know what I was expecting, but this petite woman with hair swinging to her waist, dressed in jean shorts and a tie-dyed T-shirt is not it. She laughs and exclaims in her California accent, "Simon! Finally! Did you bring the drinks?"

Simon puts his arms around his mom—he has to bend to do it—and squeezes, then picks her up off her feet. She laughs gaily, and when he puts her down, she turns to me with an outstretched hand. "And you must be Katrina. Welcome. I'm glad you could come."

I'm instantly taken by her warmth, and when I reach for her hand, she pulls me in for a hug too. She throws an arm around me—I'm not tall, but she still has to stretch—and then starts to guide me into the kitchen. "Simon, grab the drinks. Katrina and I will get to know each other."

Any nervousness I might have had vanishes in the face of the outgoing Mrs. Yang. "Thanks for inviting me. Your house is beautiful."

"Thank you," she says easily. "But it's mostly the view."

I chuckle, because the kitchen she leads me into is decidedly 1960s with a saltillo floor, burnt orange Formica countertops, and dark-stained wood cabinets. A wide array of hamburger fixings are laid out on the peninsula countertop, and several covered bowls wait beside unopened packages of potato chips.

"Well, it's a beautiful view. I don't know what more you need."

Mrs. Yang pulls down a stack of plates from one of the cabinets and hands them to me—I take them automatically, though I'm not sure what to do with them. "Simon told me you were a ballet dancer."

"I was." I finally decide to set the plates down on the kitchen table which stands in front of sliding glass doors that lead out onto a wide wooden deck. It must be the right choice because she hands me a handful of flatware next. "New York Theater Ballet."

Her eyebrows go up. "Impressive. It's been fascinating to watch them go from relatively unknown to a world-class company in only twenty years."

"You know them?"

Mrs. Yang laughs. "Of course I do. Simon was considering that route himself, you know. Well, of course you know. I always loved ballet as a girl, but there weren't all that many Asians to look up to, and of course, I don't have the body type for it." She sweeps her hand downward—despite being so petite, she's also curvy. "I was sorry to hear you had to retire so soon."

Exactly how much did Simon tell her about me? Since she's being open, I figure it's probably fair game to pry on my own end. "Simon sent me a video of him dancing when he was younger. He was very, very good. Was it a hard decision to walk away from ballet?"

"For him?" She thinks and shakes her head. "I don't think so. He wanted to perform, but I'm not sure he much cared how he did it. He was the only kid who never got nervous at his piano recitals. He'd put on little shows, singing and playing guitar in the living room. We all know he was born to be on stage."

The way she speaks of him, fondly and with few regrets, somehow warms me. I got the impression that idol is not exactly a respected job title in Korea, but then again, Mrs. Yang is about as American as I am. I didn't realize that she was born here; now my own assumptions shame me.

The front door opens again, and Simon calls from the other room, "Look who I found!"

When he enters the kitchen, he's followed by Joonwoo, who's dressed impeccably in dark jeans and a button-down shirt beneath a canvas jacket. I realize I've never seen him out of makeup and costume, and while he's just as good-looking as he is on stage, he's far more approachable. Or he would be if the expression on his face were not so wary.

Mrs. Yang goes straight to him for a hug. "Joonwoo. I've missed you."

The man gently gives her a squeeze, but his smile is bright and genuine. "Eomeonim, thank you for inviting me."

She swats him on the shoulder as he straightens. "You don't need any invitation, you know that. You're welcome here any time, with or without Simon. Have you met Katrina yet?"

Simon's dark eyes flit to mine, and I don't think I miss the slight tightening of his face. He bows his head slightly in acknowledgment. "Katrina, good to see you again."

I smile at him. "Same. You're looking well. You've recovered from your tour, I take it?" Internally, I roll my eyes. I'm talking like I'm the heroine of some nineteenth-century novel, but the careful, formal cast of Joon's Korean-accented English makes me feel like we're sparring in a drawing room.

The corner of his mouth tips up and I think maybe he's thinking the same thing when he replies, "Yes, thank you. I'm enjoying the time off, even though I have to return tomorrow."

Our repository of small talk exhausted, we stand

there awkwardly until Simon steps between us. "Is Dad out on the deck?"

"He just put the burgers on," Mrs. Yang says. "Joon, go out and say hello. I know he'll want to see you."

Simon and Joon go to the sliding doors and step out onto the deck; I hover behind, not knowing if I'm meant to follow. But Mrs. Yang just nudges me. "He's protective of Simon, even now. He still sees him as that little trainee without any Korean. I've known him for fifteen years. He'll warm up to you once he realizes you mean Simon no harm."

I glance down at her, surprised by how easily she reads the situation. "It sounded to me like he looked after him for a long time. It was hard for Simon at first, wasn't it?"

Mrs. Yang's cheery demeanor slips a little. "It was. I don't think he ever let on how hard it was, because he didn't want us to worry. He always told me he was fine, he was having fun, he was adjusting to the culture, but he sounded so tired and sad all the time. It took everything I had not to tell him to forget it and come home."

"Why didn't you then?"

"Simon has always been focused. It was his decision to go and it needed to be his decision to stay or leave. You can't make those choices for other people, even when they're your own child." Mrs. Yang stares out on the deck, where the three men are talking and laughing easily—I can only see the back of Simon's dad's head, but he's gesturing with a pair of barbecue tongs. I smile, and when I turn back, she's watching me thoughtfully.

But she says nothing, she just nods toward the table. "Grab the dishes and flatware. We'll eat outside."

When we step onto the patio, the three men are speaking Korean, but they quickly change to English when we appear. After I set down the place settings, Simon summons me to his side. "Dad, this is Katrina. Katrina, my father."

The older man holds out his hand, and I shake it. "Nice to meet you, Katrina. Thanks for joining us."

"Thank you for inviting me," I reply immediately. Mr. Yang has a California accent like his wife but there's a slight inflection that makes me think he probably grew up in a bilingual household. I've never thought so much about the nuances of multi-cultural families as I have today; my dad's family came over from Greece somewhere in the late-1800s, but we lost our connection to our culture a long time ago, until now the only thing Greek about us is our name.

Mr. Yang turns back to the barbecue and starts to move the hamburgers and bratwurst to a platter. "Okay, food is ready. But where is Ella? She was supposed to be here already."

I look to Simon. "Ella?"

He chuckles. "The free spirit of the family. My sister."

chapter twenty-two

Almost as if she was summoned by the words, a young woman slides open the glass door and steps onto the balcony, dropping her mirrored sunglasses down over her eyes. "Sorry I'm late. Traffic on PCH."

"You're just in time," Mrs. Yang says, stepping forward to hug the woman I presume must be her daughter. I study her surreptitiously from my spot across the deck. She's taller than her mom, probably about my height, tanned and slender, with long chestnut brown hair that falls around her shoulders in waves. Even from here with the glasses on, I can tell she's just as beautiful as her brother.

She hugs her dad and then smiles and waves at Joon, who actually looks pleased to see her, before she focuses on me. She pulls off her glasses, revealing a perfectly executed smoky-eye look, and grins. "You must be Katrina."

Before I can do anything, she's pulling me into a tight hug. "I'm so glad you came. Simon never brings home anyone to meet us."

I find Simon's gaze over her shoulder and he's just

grimacing helplessly. I know the feeling. Simon may be irresistible on stage, but Ella is a force of nature. The Yang children evidently got their charisma in buckets instead of drops.

"Sit, eat," Mr. Yang says, waving everyone to the table that I've been busily setting. We shuffle ourselves into order and I find myself sitting between Simon and his sister, directly across from Joonwoo. Great. Now I get to stare at his disapproving face the entire supper. It doesn't take a lot of imagination to guess he doesn't like me, whatever Mrs. Yang might say.

I'm apparently the guest of honor, though, because Simon's dad brings the platter to the table and looks at me first. "Katrina, what would you like? Burger? Brat? Both?"

"Um . . . brat?" He transfers a sausage to my plate before moving on to the others at the table. Simon nudges me and I reach for a bun, surprised by the informality. Ella digs in immediately, but Simon and Joon are both waiting patiently; it takes me a second to realize they're waiting for his parents to begin eating. I clasp my hands in my lap, and only when the two men pick up their forks do I do the same.

I catch a quick exchange of looks between my date and his mentor, but not until Simon brushes my hand under the table do I realize it's approval.

Even so, I can only manage a few bites of the bratwurst and some of the potato salad before my stomach starts to twist, so I put my fork down and turn to Ella. "Ella, what do you do? I'm not sure Simon has mentioned it." He hasn't mentioned her at all, but to be fair, we've been talking far more about our careers than we have about our families.

"I'm a makeup artist," she says easily. "For the fashion industry."

So two children involved in entertainment in some sense. I steal a glance at Mrs. and Mr. Yang, but there's no sense that there's any regret over it, or at least if there is, they hide their feelings well. I turn back to Ella. "That's interesting. How did you get into that?"

"I did a visual arts degree, and for a while, I was an apprentice for a special effects makeup artist. Then a friend from design school asked me to do makeup for her runway show and the rest was history." She throws me a smile. "I found I liked doing avante-garde makeup a lot better than blood and gore."

I laugh. "I can understand that, I guess. Do you travel a lot then?"

She takes a sip from her glass of tea, and I notice that her nude lipstick doesn't leave a single smudge on the rim. I'll have to ask her about that miracle lip color later. "Not as much as you'd think. I do a lot of magazine work in LA, but I do get requested for fashion shows and previews quite a bit. I went to Paris last summer for Duchene."

I lift my eyebrows. "Did you work with your brother?"

She grins. "I did. Nepotism, but I'm not complaining. He was stunning."

I throw a quick glance at Simon and find him ducking his head, his ears turning pink with embarrassment. His shyness strikes me as adorably endearing, and I impulsively reach for his hand under the table. He laces his fingers with mine and squeezes.

Ella tracks the movement, and a small smile curves her perfectly lacquered lips. "In any case, I'm glad to have him back in California for a while. You know I was ten when he left for Korea, right?"

"I hadn't thought that much about it," I admit. "That must have been difficult."

"It was." She leans forward to shoot her brother a soft smile past me. "You're still wearing my butterfly."

"Of course I am." Simon reaches into his shirt and pulls out the delicate charm to show her. "Any time I'm allowed to. I told you I wouldn't stop wearing it until I came back for good."

I feel like I'm intruding on a private moment between the siblings somehow, and when my eyes meet Joonwoo's from across the table, I can see he feels the same way. We look away, disturbed to find ourselves on the same side of anything, and the conversation moves to other topics. After dinner, we all help clear the table, and then Mrs. Yang waves us out of the kitchen. When Ella suggests they go find the torches so we can sit out on the deck as it gets dark, she and Simon disappear, leaving me alone on the outdoor sofa, looking out over the ocean. The peaceful sound of the water hitting the cement breakwater is lulling me into calm, so I barely notice when Joonwoo appears at my side, holding two glass bottles.

"Sparkling water or beer?" he asks.

"Water. Thanks." I take the bottle, and when I fail to twist the cap off on the first try, Joon takes it back and removes it for me without comment. I take a long drink, waiting for him to start. He didn't come out here just to bring me a drink.

But the moment stretches into minutes, and he just leans back against the sofa, his arm extended over the back, taking occasional sips from his beer bottle.

Finally, I can't stand it. "Is this the part where you tell me I'm bad for Simon?"

He throws me a wry smile, and I have the sudden sense that under any other conditions, I'd probably like him. He's a quiet guy, but there's something about him that makes me think there's a lot going on beneath that placid surface. "I don't think you're bad for Simon. He's been happy since he met you."

"But?"

"But I have to worry about more than Simon. I'm responsible for the group. And I have three other members who would be affected if he decides not to renew."

I take a long drink of my water, forgetting it's carbonated, and cough as the bubbles hit the back of my throat. At least it gives me a second to collect my thoughts. "So you're here to ask me to do what? To convince him to stay?"

"I'm asking you not to influence him at all." Joon shifts on the seat, turning his body toward me, even though his gaze still remains fixed on the horizon. "Contrary to what the general public believes, we all date. Discreetly. Everyone except for Simon. He's always been too focused on his career for anything to last too long. Says he has time for that when he retires. But sometimes, I wonder if he doesn't want to meet someone in Seoul and lose his option to come back home."

"And you think he's going to stay here for me."

"I think you underestimate how seriously he takes these things. He doesn't just . . . hook up." The phrase sounds awkward on Joon's lips, and the way he shifts away from me tells me that it feels just as awkward.

There is so much to unpack here, though, I'm not sure where to start. I'm not naive enough to think that Simon is inexperienced with women; he's far too up-front about things. But Joon clearly thinks that we're already sleeping together, when Simon has literally done nothing more than kiss me on the cheek. How exactly am I supposed to take that?

I stay quiet for so long that Joon starts to look uncomfortable. Finally, I twist toward him, tucking my legs up under myself with sigh. "My first instinct is to tell you to go to hell, I hope you know that."

Joon cracks an expression that might actually be a smile.

"But I know you care about him. I know what you did for him by delaying his debut and so does he. But you have to know that this is all going to end sometime. Better than even I do."

"I do. And that's why I know the difference a few more years will make, even for Simon. You can't underestimate the power of our combined fandoms for Helios."

They make a lot more money as members of Helios than they would as soloists, I presume he's saying. And I get it. There's an expiration date on their relevance. So why waste those years on endeavors that won't pay off?

Except there's a lot more to life than making money, and I find it very hard to believe that Simon, with his looks and his talent, won't land on his feet. So this has more to do with the rest of the group than it does him.

"You know that his back is in bad shape, right? And his joints aren't much better."

Joon gives a slow reluctant nod.

I smooth my hair back, give my ponytail a yank. "I'm not influencing him one way or another, but I won't lie to him. If he wants my opinion, I'll give it. But I have no claim on him. Right now, we're . . . friends. That's it. Maybe it will be more later, maybe not. But if he decides to leave Helios, it won't be because of me."

I don't think we've really resolved anything to either of our satisfaction, and there's no more time to do it, because Simon is striding toward us with a smile. He seats himself beside me on the chaise and rests his hand on my knee, his thumb rubbing a back-and-forth path over my skin. It feels like a claim, a statement, and suddenly I feel guilty about my conversation with Joon, like I've somehow betrayed Simon. I rest my hand on his, and he turns it over, palm up, so he can interlace our fingers again.

Joon follows the movement and lets out a deep sigh. Then, as if resigning himself, he pushes himself up from the couch and murmurs something to Simon in Korean.

Simon replies, but his brow is furrowed when he turns to me. "What was that about?"

"He's worried that I'm talking you into staying in California and leaving Helios."

I expect him to be angry or annoyed, but he just sighs. "I'm not surprised. Sometimes I think he thinks that I'm still fifteen years old and can't make my own decisions."

"Well, he's basically your older brother. That tracks."

Simon huffs out a little laugh and scrubs his fingers against his scalp, sending his hair flopping in all directions. He looks so appealingly boyish, looking up at me from beneath his fringe that my heart gives a hard clench I don't entirely understand. I have the impulse to lean forward and press my lips to his, but our first real kiss is not going to be on the deck of his parents' home in full view of his family and Joon, so instead, I reach out and brush the hair out of his eyes with my free hand. Before I can draw it away, he brings it to his lips and presses a kiss against my palm. My bones instantly go liquid.

Well, shit.

I don't think it's a coincidence that a few beats later, he settles back and asks, "So how long do you want to stay?"

"As long as you'd like. I'm enjoying myself. It's a beautiful night."

"A bit longer than and we'll make our escape."

A bit longer turns out to be another two hours, as we sit on the deck in the deepening night, tiki torches lit and flickering in the brackets on the edge of the railing, eating cookies and drinking coffee while the strains of music filter from inside. It takes me a few minutes to realize that it's Hyperion, and I smile at the idea of Simon's parents playing his music as a way to show him their approval. They're such a sweet, close-knit family that I can finally understand what it took for Simon to leave home. Had I been so close to my own parents, I probably wouldn't have been quite as eager to move to Manhattan as young as I had.

When we finally get ready to go, Joon gives me a firm, silent handshake, while Ella pulls me to herself in a tight hug. "Be sweet to my brother," she whispers in my ear. "He's more sensitive than he seems."

I pull back in surprise and then give her a little nod.

Mrs. Yang hugs me goodbye and then presses two containers into my hand, one filled with chocolate chip cookies and the other with homemade kimchi. "Simon says you like Korean food. Next time we'll have ssam. It's Simon's favorite."

"That sounds wonderful," I say. "Thank you again for having me."

Out in the car, enveloped in darkness, Simon starts the car. "Mom liked you. She wouldn't have sent you home with food if not."

"I liked her too," I said. "All of them."

"Even Joon?"

I give a little laugh and look out the window as Simon starts to back out of the driveway and makes the turn to merge back onto PCH. "Joon is looking out for you. And for the other members. I can't really blame him for that."

"You're very forgiving."

"I don't think I have any right to be otherwise. He's been part of your life for fifteen years in one way or another and I've been part of it for fifteen minutes."

"Sometimes time doesn't equate to impact," he says quietly.

I think about that as we cruise down the highway, the moon glimmering on the ocean just beyond my window. It doesn't make any sense, the way I feel right now. We met in a strange way. We conversed over text for a while and then I convinced myself that he wasn't actually real. And yet a few days into our in-person acquaintance, I'm sitting with him in a rental car that smells like French fries, feeling more comfortable than I have with another human in the last five years. As much as I love Amira, there's always an undercurrent of worry that I can't quite discount, as if she's as much my minder as my friend.

Simon seems content just to be with me. Maybe it's a sense of calm at his core that I can't quite understand but still envy, but I never get the feeling that he wants to be anywhere than in this very moment.

"You're an unusual person," I say softly. "I don't quite understand you sometimes."

"On the contrary. I think you understand me better than anyone ever has."

I don't think that's actually true, but I have to admit that deep down, there are things about us—how we look at the world, what we're willing to sacrifice for our dreams—that can't be understood by anyone else who hasn't done what we've done.

That might be why when Simon walks me to my apartment, I unlock the door and open it wide. "Will you come in?"

His eyebrows lift, but he follows me in and shuts the door behind him. "Lock it?"

"Please." I move through the space, pausing to pet the sleepy cat sprawled on the dining table before moving into the kitchen. I put the cookies in the cabinet and the kimchi in the fridge. "Do you want something to drink? I have tea, cold brew, probably some wine somewhere."

"Water is fine."

I pull the filter container from the refrigerator shelf and then remove two glasses from the cabinet, which I fill to the top. I've just put away the container and taken the glasses in either hand when I turn to find Simon standing behind me. Our eyes meet for a long moment, and then very slowly, he takes the glasses from my hands and sets them on the counter. I catch my breath as he raises one hand to my cheek, cupping my face while his thumb brushes my cheekbone.

Dating history aside, Simon is far more experienced than he pretends, because the slow, deliberate way he kisses me makes my knees weak in a split second. Before I can really think about it, I'm pressed up against him, my head spinning, completely consumed by the kiss. He is obviously under far more control than me, because he manages to pull back.

Or maybe not that much more, because he's breathing as unsteadily as I am, his eyes a little glazed. "I . . ." He falters.

I pull his head down and kiss him again. Somehow we end up on the sofa and not long after that, I'm pressed beneath him, his body held lightly above me while he trails a line of kisses from my collarbone down the deep V of my T-shirt. I arch mindlessly beneath his lips, but it's only when his hands begin to slide up the hem of my top that I return to myself enough to realize where we're heading.

I close one hand around his wrist to still his movements. "Simon, stop."

He freezes and pushes himself up to look me in the eye, waiting.

"There's something we should talk about."

His lips curve in a little smile, but it seems more self-deprecating than anything else as he pushes himself off me. I blink off the delicious haze of lust quickly enough to register the expression. Does he . . . does he actually think I'm rejecting him? I push myself up on my elbows and wiggle myself to a sitting position. It takes a few seconds to find my voice. "You should know that I haven't . . . I mean . . ."

Now he looks at me, eyebrows lifted. "You've never . . . ?"

I laugh at his shocked expression, but I sober quickly. "Not since my diagnosis."

Understanding flashes over his face. "And you're not sure how that will go?"

I shake my head. "And this—us—is too new for me to be comfortable finding out."

He nods slowly, then pulls me over him, shifting me so I'm straddling him on the sofa. A wry smile comes to his face again as he looks up at me. "I want you to know that I didn't come in thinking this was going to happen. I mean, I hoped, but I didn't actually expect it."

I laugh at his bluntness. How he can be so shy about some things and expressive about others still surprises me. I lean down to press a kiss to his lips again, and it isn't long before it turns heated. He groans when I lift my head.

"I'm trying to behave myself," he mutters, "but it's impossible when you're this fucking beautiful."

I narrow my eyes at him. "Imagine the view from my direction."

To my surprise, he colors again and averts his eyes. I cock my head and trace a fingertip across his cheekbone, down his sharp jawline. "Why do you do that?"

"Why do I do what?"

"Get uncomfortable when I compliment you."

He sighs and tips his head back against the sofa. "Because it reminds me that you might have certain expectations of me because of who I am." He lifts his head to look me in the eye. "And trust me, I cannot live up to Seojun's implied reputation. I'm much closer to a monk than a rock star."

It takes me a second to register that he thinks he's going to disappoint me. I laugh, and then instantly regret it because of the hurt that surfaces in his eyes. I take his face in both my hands and make him look at me. "I can't promise you much, but I promise you this. It's Simon I'm interested in. Not Seojun." I give him a wry smile. "He's just a bonus."

"A bonus, huh?"

I shrug. "What can I say? I have a thing for guys who wear earrings and eyeliner."

He bursts out laughing and the tension of the moment is broken, at least emotionally. I'm still buzzing with desire and frustration and Simon doesn't seem to be any better off. I shift off him anyway, and he plops one of the sofa pillows onto his lap and pats it. After a moment, I realize he's inviting me to lie down. I scoot down and stretch out with my head in his lap, and he begins to run his fingers through the length of my ponytail.

"So unfortunately, I have plans for the rest of the weekend, but I was hoping maybe we could spend some time together on Monday. What are the chances of you getting the afternoon off?"

"Not good," I say regretfully. "Monday is my busiest day. But we still have your session and whatever time you can spare afterward."

"Not what I'd hoped for," he grumbles, "but I'll take what I can get."

I look up at him, see the genuine affection and regret on his face, and that spot in the middle of me warms again.

And then quickly goes cool when I remember why he's trying to force all this togetherness. We're already a week into his vacation, and time is ticking down to an uncertain future for us.

But I don't want to think about that now. I don't want to think about how this is the happiest I've felt in years, how this is the most like *myself* I've felt since I quit dancing, as if I'm doing more than going through the motions.

"Kiss me again," I whisper, and he's more than happy to comply.

chapter twenty-three

I wake up the next morning smiling, and it takes me a few minutes to remember why. It certainly wasn't because I got much sleep. I was still buzzing when Simon left, and it took me a long time to drift off to sleep with the memory of his hands and lips on me. Even now, a tremor shudders through me at the recollection, and I reach for my phone, knowing what I'm hoping for even if I don't articulate it to myself.

I'm not disappointed. There's a message from Simon.

SIMON
Good morning, beautiful.

It's accompanied by a selfie. Whatever he's doing today, it must be official, because his hair is done and a trio of silver chains peeks from the open throat of his crisp white button-down, the butterfly barely visible. The lurch in my chest is altogether disproportionate to the offering, and that might be what propels me to reverse the camera to snap a pic of myself with my hair spread over my pillow behind me. I look good, mussed and a little flushed, and I know exactly what I'm doing when I press *send* without any caption.

A minute later, his response comes through.

SIMON
You're cruel.

I smile and push myself upright, then swing my legs over the side and jump out of bed. My balance shifts for the briefest moment and I freeze, blinking the sensation away. Just a blip. Nothing more. I move to the bathroom, take a shower, twist my wet hair into a knot at the back of my head as a tiny measure of protection against the blazing day ahead of me. And then I type a quick message to Amira.

TRINA
What are you doing today?

It takes a few minutes for her to respond, and I imagine I can hear her shock though the screen.

AMIRA
I'm scrubbing my bathtub.
It's thrilling. What are you
doing?

TRINA
I'm bored. I want to do
something.

AMIRA
Thought you'd still be with
Simon. 😊

TRINA
He didn't stay.

AMIRA
Wow. I really thought he'd
be the cuddling type.

I snicker, though my face heats at her assumptions.

TRINA
Nothing happened. Much.

AMIRA
Not much is not nothing.
Spill!

TRINA
Only if you can abandon
scrubbing to hang out with
me.

AMIRA
Be there in an hour.

I laugh, knowing that despite what it might look like, Amira would have come over for the sheer novelty of me asking her to. But the impulse for a play-by-play of my evening is definitely too much for her to resist. And sure enough, the moment she knocks on the door fifty-three minutes later, the first question out of her mouth is, "So, is he a good kisser?"

I pause and shut the door behind her, but the look on my face must give me away because she grins. "That good?"

I wave her off. "Do you want something to drink? I just made coffee."

She shakes her head. "You know I don't like decaf." But she moves into my kitchen and opens the refrigerator door, scanning until she pulls out the caffeinated, bottled cold brew. She makes herself a glass with the vanilla creamer I keep on hand just for her, then seats herself on the sofa. "Spill."

"His family is great," I say by way of opening. I settle on the chaise and stretch my legs out in front of me, flexing and pointing my feet automatically, feeling my joints crack. "I hadn't realized they were born here. His mom doesn't even speak Korean."

"I know," Amira says, and I'm jarred by the realization that she probably knows more about my boyfriend than I do.

Wait. Boyfriend?

That stuns me into momentary silence. It's certainly how he's been treating me, how his family treated me. But we haven't talked about it. It feels presumptuous. We barely know each other.

"Trina? You in there?"

I blink. "Right. Anyway. They were really sweet. His sister is great. Did you know that she gave him that butterfly he always wears?"

Amira smiles again. "Of course I do. He revealed it a while back when people were debating whether it was a personal statement or if he was standing in solidarity with his LGBTQ+ fans."

"You know, it's really weird to be dating someone that the entire world knows."

"Not the entire world," Amira says quickly. "Just, like . . . ten, twenty million people. Helios isn't *that* popular."

I stare at her and she laughs. "Sorry. Not helping. Continue. Skip to the good part."

Right, the kissing. "He's good. He's very, very good."

"I knew it! I never believed the *I'm dedicated completely to my career* line."

That gives me a moment of ick, imagining him with other women. "I'm not entirely sure about that. He was a little . . . concerned that I might have unrealistic expectations of him."

"Aww, that's actually kind of endearing, to be honest. So it was him who put on the brakes?"

"Oh no, it was me." I glance at Amira. "You know I haven't slept with anyone since Philip."

From the surprised look on her face, maybe she didn't. "Oh. Since the diagnosis."

I nod.

"Okay, well, that's reasonable. It's way less casual for you than it might be otherwise. I get it. So . . . will you?"

I sigh. "I don't know." Then I shake my head. "Who am I kidding? Of course I will. But the question is when. I'm half-tempted to wait until the last moment possible so that if it all goes badly, he'll leave and I don't have to feel guilty about not seeing him again."

"Or, it could be fantastic and you've deprived yourself of a month of mind-blowing sex and the potential of international booty calls."

I choke out a laugh, and Amira grins. "I'm just calling it like I see it."

"You may be right," I say, but for all my bluntness, I'm not that casual about sex and I never have been. I have to be falling for a guy to even consider it.

And you're not?

Shit. That's really not a possibility I'm prepared to consider this morning, even when it's been hovering in the back of my mind this whole time.

"Regardless, it will not be this weekend because he is busy and I won't see him until Monday. So . . . that leaves the question . . . what should we do today?"

Amira draws her legs up underneath her. "You tell me. You're the one who has suddenly decided to return to the land of the living after a really good make-out session."

I make a face at that, but she's not entirely wrong. "Malibu Seafood for lunch and then beach. For a while. Until it gets too hot."

"Done."

Amira is as good as her word, and as we're sitting on the covered patio at Malibu Seafood an hour later, eating fried clams and fish and chips and overlooking the Pacific Ocean, I'm suddenly overwhelmed by a mix of love and guilt. I reach for her hand and squeeze. "Thank you."

She looks at me, surprised. "For what?"

"For being you. For being patient. I'm not the easiest person to have as a friend. I take a lot more than I give back."

Amira doesn't argue, but she also looks away, embarrassed. After a moment, she squeezes my hand, too. "You know I just want you to be happy."

"I know. It's just taking me a while to figure out what that means."

"Well, had I known what it would take, I would have dragged you to a K-pop concert a long time ago." She shoots me a grin before she draws her hand away and toasts me with a battered clam. "I mean, I know people say their concerts are life-changing, but I really never expected this."

The joking is her way of diffusing feelings she's embarrassed to acknowledge openly—I've always known that—so I let it go. "I have no idea why Simon likes me."

"Oh, because you're gorgeous and talented and—"

I cut her off. "No, I'm not putting myself down. I'm just saying. . .it's kind of nice to be liked just. . . because. He doesn't have any real reason to have felt a connection with me, and yeah, we have things in common but . . ."

I can't put it into words, and I'm afraid if I try, she'll just take it as an insult. The fact is, it's been so long since I've had a relationship that didn't in some way feel transactional that I've forgotten sometimes *just because* is an appropriate answer to *why?*

Before she can say anything else, I just shrug. "Regardless, he's easy to be with and he makes me feel like just me, who I was before all the other crap."

I thought I was being casual, but Amira stares hard at me. "You really are falling for him."

I don't even try to deny it. "I don't know. Maybe."

"Shit." Amira wipes her hands on a napkin, not meeting my eye. "I don't want to be the buzzkill, but Trina . . . just be careful. You don't know what it's like to date an idol."

"I deal with celebrities all the time. They're just people."

"Right. They're just regular people, albeit talented and in this case, insanely pretty ones. But K-pop fans are a different breed entirely. And Seojun has a particularly delusional fandom. A casual hookup is one thing. But if it ever got out that you were actually a couple . . ." Amira shakes her head slowly. "You have no idea that shitstorm that would be coming for you."

My stomach twists. Amira is serious about this. "But surely his company . . ."

"His company won't do anything. In fact, because it's so well known his company won't do anything, their idols deal with sasaengs all the time. Seojun has had at least three stalkers in his career, one of whom actually got arrested because she bribed a hotel worker for a duplicate key and was waiting in his bed when he came back from a show. She truly thought they had a relationship because he smiled at her from stage one night."

"So either the sasaengs would go after me for messing

with their man, or the regular fans would assume I *am* one if they figure out I was the one on stage with him." I let out a long breath. It's a dimension I hadn't even considered.

"I'm not trying to discourage you. I just thought you should know before you get in too deep. It sounds cruel, but you really do need to weigh how much you like him versus how it might affect your life."

There can be no doubt that Amira's bluntness has weighed down the mood, but I do my best to force it to the back of my mind as we throw away our trash and then drive down PCH to our favorite beach spot. It's rocky—not the ideal place to spread out a blanket—so that means it's not particularly crowded even on a hot, sunny day like today. I slip off the shirt that covers my bikini top, kick off my sandals, and walk ankle deep in the surf until my feet are numb and my shoulders are singed. I don't realize Amira has been taking photos of me until a few beep through on my phone.

I pause at one taken in side profile, my shoulders curved forward, my hair flaming in the sun as it blows across my back and face.

"You're gorgeous," she says. "Send that to Simon."

It's a peace offering, an apology, and I attach it to a message without comment once more. I don't get a reply until we're well on our way back to the valley, winding up Malibu Canyon—it's the heart-eyes emoji. I show it to Amira when we come to a stop light on the other side of the canyon, and she sighs.

"He's really sweet, isn't he?"

"Impossibly so."

Amira drops me off in front of my apartment building as usual, but before we go, I reach for her hand and squeeze. "Thank you for everything you've done for me in the last four years. I love you, you know."

Pink colors her cheeks, and she doesn't quite look at me. "I know. I love you too. Now get out of my car."

I laugh and climb out, feeling pleasantly tired as I walk up the stairs to my apartment building. I feel energetic enough to take a cool shower, rinsing off the salt and sweat and feeling the spray sting my sunburned shoulders, and I settle onto my bed with the remote control with the intention of picking up the K-drama that I've repeatedly abandoned for the last couple of weeks. Still, I know exactly what I'm waiting for, and when my phone rings just after six, I don't hesitate to pick it up immediately.

"Hi," Simon says. "You seem like you had a good day."

"I did. How about you?"

"I just took Joon to the airport."

There's something weary in his voice that tells me there's more to the story than just a drive in heavy traffic. "Oh? How did that go?"

"He's going back to talk contract renewal. And obviously, he wants me to make a decision sooner rather than later."

My stomach lurches upwards into my chest. "Any thoughts yet?"

"Not yet. I have a couple more meetings here in LA before I can make a decision. He was . . . not pleased to hear that."

"Did he really think he was going to talk you into it on the ride to the airport?"

Simon laughs softly, but there's something sad in it. "No, but I don't envy him the conversations he'll have when he gets back. Telling them that only four of the five of us have committed to an extension isn't exactly the strongest bargaining position."

"Or maybe it's the best bargaining position," I

counter. "He can tell them you're close to jumping ship and they need to step up their game if they want to keep you there."

"Maybe," he says, but I can tell he's not convinced.

Maybe it's the fact that I've had a good day or maybe it's simply that hearing his voice makes me miss him, but impulsively, I say, "Do you want to come over?"

"I'm meeting Ella for dinner. She wants to introduce me to her new boyfriend. I think she wants me to run interference with Mom and Dad."

I don't think I imagine the regret in his reply, and it matches my own disappointment. "Okay, I understand. What's the problem? I'm thinking it's not because he's a rock star or something?"

Simon laughs. "He's a venture capitalist, actually. Which is pretty hilarious."

"That definitely requires some prep work." And I'm only slightly kidding, because the Yangs are the least pretentious people I've ever met, even considering their mega-famous son.

"Right. And then tomorrow, I'm meeting some old neighborhood friends. We kept in touch after I moved to Korea, but I haven't seen them in person in years."

I hear what he's not saying. He's rebuilding his relationships here in California while he decides whether he wants to stay or go. I imagine that having those connections would make the move back here a lot easier. "I understand. Monday at 6:00. And I was thinking . . . why don't you just come over to my place after? I'll make dinner."

There's a long pause on his end of the line, and I wonder if he's trying to guess exactly what the invitation entails—because I'm trying to figure out the same thing. Then finally, he says, "That sounds nice. It's a date."

"Good. Tell Ella I said hi. And be nice to the boyfriend. Just because he's in finance doesn't mean he doesn't have a lot to offer her."

Simon's laugh huffs softly over the line, and it warms me. "Bye, Katrina."

"Bye, Simon." I punch off the line and lean back against my pillows, wondering about the ache in the middle of my chest. Talking to him fills a spot in me I didn't know was empty while simultaneously opening up a hollow elsewhere. It's a feeling I can't put a name to, one that I'm not sure I *want* to put a name to. I told Amira that I might be falling, but now the question occurs to me—falling into what?

chapter twenty-four

February 2020, New York City

After my talk with Janine, I try to pretend like everything's the same as it's always been, but I feel like I'm living in a fish bowl. Any of the female dancers might be the one—or more—Philip is sleeping with. I imagine every member of the company looking at me in pity or scorn, the stupid girl who got mixed up with her choreographer and is now paying the price.

It doesn't help that Philip and I don't speak on opening night. I leave the theater and go home, expecting that he'll eventually wander in, but in the morning, I wake to find his side of the bed still neatly tucked, unslept in.

Which means, undoubtedly, that he spent the night in someone else's bed. I'm spiraling out over what this means—is he going to break up with me? Am I going to have to move out and find somewhere else to stay?—when a text beeps through on my phone. I pull it out and my heart does a triple-beat when I see Philip's name on the screen. Surely this is an apology or some sort of explanation of his whereabouts.

But when I unlock the phone and click the message,

I find it's only a page of the New York Times Dance section. Not a link. But a screenshot of a review.

I have to blow it up on my phone to be able to read it, but I skim the words quickly. It says complimentary things about Philip's choreography, though it questions whether the jazz age is somewhat overdone in terms of setting. My heart rises into my throat when I get to the section about me:

> The role of Aurora, danced by twenty-one-year-old principal dancer Katrina Barbas, highlights the differences between Barbier's vision and Petipa's. Aurora is no ingenue, needing to be rescued by a man; rather she's an independent woman tossed about by the vicissitudes of fate and forces outside her control. Barbas makes the most of the choreography with a performance that is alternately powerful and flirtatious, desperate and seductive, though her delicacy makes one wonder if she'd be better suited to the traditional Aurora than Barbier's liberated flapper. The only rough spot in Barbier's inventive staging, which reimagines the steps of every role from Prince Désiré to Florine/Bluebird, is the odd choreographic choices made in the Rose Adagio, which swaps a famous and difficult set of balances and promenades on pointe for an awkward penché arabesque sequence . . .

I freeze, the blood draining from my face and sending a chill through my body. Now I understand the reason for the screenshot, even without Philip's use of the highlighter on his phone to mark the last sentence in yellow.

It would have been a perfect world premiere, except for the change I made.

I sink down on the edge of the bed, my stomach churning ominously. Obviously, my intention had been to get through the performance seamlessly for the audience. I never thought about the fact there would be critics there, though I should have. It would have been one thing if no one knew the choreography, but if you're going to keep one thing from the Petipa staging, it would be this sequence. The one I thoughtlessly and impulsively butchered.

I lean forward and put my head in my hands. This is bad. This is so much worse than I thought.

Because now that it's been called out in the New York Times, if I dance the choreography the way he intended it, people will think that Philip changed it in response to a critic. And that is something that his ego will never, ever allow to stand. But if we leave it the way it is—my imperfect, impromptu version—to save face, not only does it mar the integrity of the ballet, but people are going to think that Philip changed it because the steps were too hard for me. Or worse yet, that he's just made a choice in bad taste.

If I were thinking at all—if I were not been blindsided by Janine's revelation—I might have had the presence of mind to put up a post on Instagram talking about my broken shank and the last-minute step change. If I did it before the review came out, it would have been fine. If I try to do it now, it will look like we're making excuses.

This is horrible.

But however horrible it is, it's not an excuse to be late for company class. I pry myself up off the bed and get dressed, then pack my bag for the day. Then I go to the kitchen and pull out Philip's Vitamix to make myself a protein shake to drink on my way, just whole milk, protein powder, and a handful of frozen fruit. I blend the violently pink concoction and dump it into a steel tumbler, then rinse out the blender jar. At the last minute, I take a few seconds to wipe the inside and replace everything back in the cabinet. If I leave it out and Philip comes home before I do, I'm going to hear about it.

Except I soon find that my stomach is too twisted to accept anything, and I arrive at the studio with my drink still three-quarters full and beginning to congeal in the cup. I keep my head down as I enter the building and make my way to the dressing room, not making eye contact with anyone. It might just be my imagination, but I can swear I feel the weight of appraising eyes on me as I pass.

Which is why I don't immediately realize that I'm not alone when I walk into the dressing room. I open my locker and pull out my hairbrush and pins before I notice the slumped form sitting on a bench in the corner of the room. And it takes me a couple more seconds to realize it's my sister.

"Maddie?" I ask softly. "Are you okay?"

She looks up, and I see that her eyes are red-rimmed and swollen. My heart leaps into my throat, and I rush to her side. "What's wrong?"

Her throat works, but her eyes are defiant when she turns to me. "I take it you didn't see the review."

I frown. "About me? I did. But why are you upset about that?"

"God, not everything is about you, Kat!" She shoves her phone at me, and I take it from her with a frown. She has the NYT site up, but there's more to the review than what Philip sent me. I skim it quickly.

Bluebird danced by Daniel Pliny and Madeline Barbas . . . subpar technique inadequate for the difficult, inventive choreography. While the elder Barbas shines in every role in which she's cast, the younger appears to be enjoying a halo effect of her sister's fame that her talent quite can't back up.

My mouth drops open. Not only is it patently unfair—Maddie's performance was good if not *great*—rarely does a dance reviewer resort to personal speculation of this sort. It's shocking.

Maddie yanks the phone back and drops it into her bag, then stomps off to her own locker. I stare after her, and the stress of the last few days crash down onto me. "What is your problem?"

She cocks her head and turns to me. "You're my problem, Kat."

On the heels of my own worries, defensiveness wells up within me and it takes everything I have to squash it down enough to answer levelly. Still, my voice comes out chilly. "How *exactly* am I your problem, Maddie?"

She wheels on me. "You never even wanted this. You're only here because of me!"

I rear back, not because it's untrue or unfair. I simply didn't think she was aware of that fact. Her face twists into a mask, one that I know means she's holding back tears.

"You weren't supposed to stay," she grits out. "You weren't supposed to be good. You were just . . ."

In the light of everything that's happened of late, I can't stop the anger that's boiling up. "That's right. I was just supposed to sacrifice everything for you, Mom's talented little dancer, so you could live your dream, right? Forget what *I* wanted to do." I take a step toward her automatically, and she steps back, her eyes widening.

"I bet you don't know that the summer we came to New York, I gave up a trip to Europe with my boyfriend's family, do you?"

Maddie's mouth drops open, and I can tell by her expression that it's new information.

"No," I snap, "of course you didn't. Just like you have

no idea that I had early admission to Rutgers, which I deferred and then lost in order to become a student here."

Maddie's lips tremble and her eyes fill with tears. It's not what she was expecting, not after years of me forcing down my feelings to spare hers. "But . . . but you wanted to come here. You love dancing."

I drop my voice. "No, Maddie, *you* love dancing. I just happen to be good at it. *I* wanted to be a doctor, but Mom and Dad made it very clear to me that *your* dreams, *your* talents were more important than mine. So you'll excuse me if I don't apologize for making the best of it and trying to squeeze out a career while I can."

My voice is shaking now, my vision blurring with the effort of controlling my voice. And in the end, it doesn't matter. The emotions that have been eating away at me for years burst through the last thin dam I've built around them, spill over into my voice.

"You've been given every opportunity and every advantage at zero cost to yourself. So if you can't hack it here, you've got no one to blame but yourself."

I wrench up my bag from the bench and storm out of the dressing room, shaking. I haven't even reached the studio before remorse comes rushing in. The look on Maddie's face, the stricken horror as everything she thought she knew about our time here in New York got rearranged. I never wanted her to find out this way. No, I never wanted her to find out at all. Because however much I might resent the situation, it's not her fault.

I scrub my hands over my face, feeling a scream rising inside me that I know I will never release. Because I never do. I just do what's expected of me. I suck it up and work harder. I make the people around me proud. I tear myself apart in order not to hurt any of the people who depend on me. And now in one day,

I've disappointed the two people whose opinions mean most to me in the world.

It's a measure of my preoccupation that I no longer notice the stares thrown in my direction as I warm up for class. Instead, my attention is fixed on Maddie's hunched, cramped figure in the center of the studio at the least prized section of the bar, looking like she thinks can disappear if she curls in on herself enough.

And at the empty spot on the opposite end of the room where Philip should be. But isn't.

• • •

When Philip does finally show up, it's not to the studio but to our apartment, acting as if nothing is wrong. Which is even worse than having his fury directed at me, because I have no way to read the situation.

"Philip," I begin when he walks through the door, his duffel bag over his shoulder, but I drift off at the blank look he gives me.

"I'm going to take a shower," he says calmly. "Order whatever you want for dinner. My credit card is still in the kitchen drawer."

I just watch his departing back, my stomach twisting into knots. He doesn't seem mad, and that alone makes me worry. He's usually so transparent with his feelings, this calmness seems unnatural, the lull before the storm.

But it will be worse if he comes out and I haven't ordered anything for dinner, so I pick up my phone and scroll though the options for a couple of minutes before settling on his favorite dishes from his favorite Italian restaurant. I pay with his credit card and settle back on the sofa, my feet drawn up beneath me as if I fear to take up any more space than necessary.

He takes his time in the bathroom, and as the minutes tick by, my stomach twists tighter, awaiting the certain explosion to come. It's only when the food arrives and I start unpacking it in the kitchen that the bedroom door finally cracks open and Philip comes out.

He's wearing a T-shirt and loose-fitting sweatpants that skim his thin frame, his dripping hair leaving translucent spots on shoulders. "That smells good. What did you get?"

"Mama Estella's," I say. "I got the eggplant parmesan you like so much." I turn away to get plates out of the cupboard, so focused on keeping my body language casual that I don't notice him coming up behind me until his hand closes on my waist and his lips find the side of my neck. The plates clatter on the granite countertop as I set them down with trembling fingers.

"Philip," I begin, but my words die when his teeth close on the skin of my neck. My whole body stiffens, rigid beneath his roaming hands, but he doesn't seem to notice. "Can we talk first?"

He must mistake my breathlessness for arousal, because he's unknotting the drawstring on my loose pants and pushing them down over my hips, his breath hissing out when he sees that I'm not wearing panties beneath. And now I know that I have no choice in the matter, that this is going to happen whether I want it to or not, just like he had no say in what I did to his ballet up on stage. I blink away tears, but I make no sounds of protest. I simply grip the edges of the counter until he's done, which is blessedly quickly.

He bends his head to my neck again and kisses the spot that he bit earlier, his breath whispering over my skin. "I forgive you," he murmurs. "I was angry, but I can never stay angry at my beautiful girl for long. You did your best." He draws my pants back up over my hips, and I try not to flinch as he reaches around me to tie the drawstring. "Are you ready to eat?"

My voice comes out in a croak, and I have to clear my throat before I can manage a somewhat steady, "Sure." My hands are shaking when I pick up the plates and carry them to the peninsula where the food sits; I slop sauce onto the counter when I try to dish out the eggplant parmesan, but even though I brace myself for a scolding, Philip just regards me with bemused affection.

Only when we're seated in the living room with the late news turned on low in front of us, our plates in our laps, do I manage to ask the question that's on my mind. I need some warning for what's going to happen in rehearsal tomorrow. "What are we going to do with the choreography?"

Philip slants me a look. "What do you mean 'what are we going to do?' You're going to dance the fucking choreography like it was intended to be danced. You're not going to botch it, and you're not going to change my steps again. I don't care if you bleed out on stage to do it."

I swallow and nod quickly, averting my eyes. It's a blessing that my stomach is too tight to eat more than a few bites of my food; it's either the knots in my stomach now or the pain later. "I won't let you down again. I promise."

He reaches over and ruffles my hair, a soft look coming onto his face, the corners of his mouth turning up. "I know you won't. You were brilliant, by the way. Except for that single problem, you exceeded every one of my expectations. I can't wait to see how you dance the next show."

"It was wonderful. I know everyone is going to perform up to your standards now that the jitters are past."

"I know they will. And I'm looking forward to what Sonya can do in Bluebird."

Cold washes over me. "You're taking Maddie out."

"She'll still dance the matinees," he says. "But I'm changing the casting for the evening performances, yes."

I swallow and nod. There's absolutely nothing I can say about this. He gave Maddie a chance and the critics were less than impressed. This won't look like he's making major casting changes based on reviews, but he's certainly not going to risk an imperfect performance on the nights we most rely on for ticket sales.

"Does Maddie know that?"

"Cast revisions are going up tomorrow. She'll know when everyone else does."

He means she'll find out at the same time everyone else does, so that her colleagues can see the shock and humiliation when she's taken out of every significant evening show and shunted into the half-filled Saturday and Sunday afternoon performances. My stomach twists again and I lean forward to set my plate on the coffee table.

"You don't like it?" Philip inquires, deceptively concerned.

"Not that hungry," I lie. "I had a snack before you got home. I wasn't expecting to eat dinner together."

"Probably the best choice," he agrees. "That first-act costume shows absolutely every ounce."

When Philip is done, I take our plates to the kitchen, scrape off the remnants of the food, and take my time washing the dishes and replacing them in the cupboard. I portion out the rest of the eggplant into small plastic containers to be eaten later this week and put them in the fridge, then do a quick clean-up of the sauce I spilled earlier. The tomato sauce has left a slight stain on the light granite, but I don't have the energy to dig out the abrasive cleaner and fix it tonight, so I leave it. Philip rarely does more than make himself a to-go mug of coffee in the morning before he leaves. Chances are he won't even notice.

By the time I finish my shower, Philip is lying on his side, fast asleep. I quietly creep into our bed and carefully pull the covers up before I turn to put my phone on the charger. And then at the last minute, I pull it back and open up a message to Maddie.

Philip told me tonight you'll only be dancing matinees. I thought you'd want to know before it's posted publicly.

I press send, and then after a hesitation, tap out a second message.

I'm sorry.

I plug in my phone and set it aside on my nightstand, then squeeze my eyes closed. But sleep isn't destined to come. Instead, my mind replays everything that's happened in the past couple of days on repeat. The performance. Philip's angry texts. My blow-up with Maddie. The stinging between my legs. Maddie's punishment for poor performance. Janine's words.

Philip Barbier is brilliant, but he's not a good man. We all know this.

I don't dare make any noise, but it doesn't stop the tears from sliding out of the corners of my eyes and pooling on my silk pillowcase in two wet spots. It feels impossible to deny the facts now. I've explained things away. I've justified his actions. I've just been lying to myself.

And yet, knowing that doesn't make anything easier. Knowing that doesn't change anything.

Because for better or worse, Philip is all I have left.

chapter twenty-five

I know there's something wrong the minute I walk through the door of the studio on Monday morning. Amira meets me in the front before I can even open my mouth. "I know. I've already called the landlord."

I drop my bag and take a deep breath. The lights are still off, but despite that, the interior temperature is already ten or fifteen degrees higher than I'd like it to be this early in the morning, despite the fact I can feel the air circulating from the registers. "Is the AC not turning on at all or is it just not getting as cold as it should?"

"It's cool, but not cold," Amira says. "I have it on full blast, but there's obviously something wrong." She grimaces. "Should we cancel?"

I put my hands on my hips as I look around. It's not *hot* exactly, but it's definitely not as cool as I like to start the day, especially considering we're supposed to hit ninety-five in the valley this afternoon. "Not yet. I think we can make it through the morning sessions if we bring out the big fans. Hopefully it can be fixed before then."

And we do make it through the morning sessions with only a few comments from my clients. Most of them murmur something about how it's going to be a hot one today and then get down to work, immediately stripping off long sleeves or sweatshirts the minute they step onto the apparatus. I position myself in front of one of the large metal floor fans, but by the time my morning appointments are over, I'm glistening at best and sweating at worst.

"You doing okay?" Amira asks me when she walks in with our lunch order—salads and milk tea, both of them designed to cool us down. "It doesn't feel so bad when you come in from outside, but . . ."

"I'm okay," I tell her as I take my salad from her hand. And I am, until I'm not.

The first bit of lightheadedness hits me when I'm demonstrating Swan on the ladder barrel for my 12:30. I blink away stars and drag a stool over to the side while she takes her position on the apparatus, sneaking a quick glance at my heart rate on my watch. Higher than I'd like, but I'm coping. I take ten minutes between this session and the next to wet a rag under the lukewarm water in the sink and press it against my forehead and the back of my neck. Amira gives me a close look when I come back out, but she says nothing.

I'm only halfway through my next appointment when my watch starts beeping a warning, despite me sitting. The initial throb of a headache starts in my left temple and behind my eye. I power through, but I don't even have to open my mouth before Amira says, "I'm canceling the rest of the sessions for the day and taking you home. It's warm in here, even for me."

I don't answer, just carefully lay down on the cool wood floor near the barre while Amira makes phone calls and sends push notifications through our app, locks the front door, and turns off all the lights. Then she comes over to my side. "You need help up?"

I nod, and she helps me sit upright, where I remain for a few minutes while everything stabilizes, then helps haul me to my feet. I let her support me with an arm around my waist as she guides me out to her car, where I slump into the passenger seat.

She turns on the air conditioning immediately and points all the vents in my direction. I blink away starbursts again and pull out my phone, tapping out a message to Simon with difficulty.

> TRINA
> Sorry to cancel.
> AC out in the studio.

> SIMON
> No problem. I understand.
> When do you want me to be
> there?

When I don't immediately reply, a second message beeps through.

> SIMON
> Uh oh. Are you okay? Did
> the heat trigger an episode?

We haven't talked about my condition, but it doesn't surprise me that he knows that's one of my triggers. I had, after all, mentioned it at the concert, and he seems like the kind of guy who would do research. Slowly, correcting my typos as I go, I reply.

> TRINA
> Yeah. Going home to lie
> down.

SIMON
Okay, I'm coming over. I'll
be there by 5.

I stare at my phone. "Simon says he's coming over."

Amira throws me a look as she turns out onto Ventura. "Tell him you don't want him to come if you'd rather be alone."

I can see why she'd think that—most other times, I've told her I'd rather lie alone in a dark room than have her stay with me, but that's more because I don't want her to change her plans for me and also because I don't want her pity.

TRINA
You don't have to do that.

SIMON
I want to. I'll bring dinner.
You said you like Korean.
Does spicy food make
things worse?

TRINA
Sometimes, not usually.

SIMON
Okay, I'll bring options. Just
leave the door unlocked so
you don't have to get up.

I stare at the phone, complicated emotions swelling in my chest, and I can't quite explain why I have to blink tears from my eyes.

"Is everything okay? Don't tell me he's being a jerk about things."

"No," I murmur. "He's actually being really sweet."

TRINA
Okay.

Deep down, I wonder if I'm using this as a test. See how he reacts to me at my worst, when I can give him nothing in return. I haven't wanted anyone besides Amira to see me like this, though it's not like I look any diffcrent in a horizontal position. It just makes me feel weak.

And yet Simon has already seen me pass out off-stage and he pursued me anyway.

I don't say anything to Amira, just shove my phone back into my bag. She helps me up to my apartment, and while I slump on the chaise on my sofa, she gets my giant jug and fills it with ice water. She positions it close to me on a tray with my cell phone and then finds the remote control. "TV on or off?"

"On, please."

She clicks it on. "You need anything else? I can stay if you want."

I smile at her. "No. Thanks. I'll be fine once I cool off. You can crank the AC down a few degrees when you go, if you don't mind."

"Arctic blast coming up." She smiles at me and nudges me with her knee. "Text me later and tell me how you're doing. And call if you need anything."

"I will. Leave the door unlocked, will you?"

She side-eyes me, but she doesn't ask any questions—she's probably already guessed why. "Okay. Take care of yourself."

I keep my apartment cool already and with the AC

turned down, it gets even colder. It isn't long before I have to drag the blanket from the back of the sofa over myself—only partially covering me. I close my eyes against the persistent throbbing of my head and let myself drift.

I'm woken by the buzzing of my phone, and I wince as I turn my head toward it and the room shifts. A message from Simon.

> SIMON
> I'm here.

Already? I squint at the numbers on my phone and see it's already 5:17.

> TRINA
> Okay. Door open.

A second later, the knob turns and Simon steps in, toeing his trainers off at the doorway. He's dressed in a pair of joggers and a close-fitting black t-shirt, his hair tucked back under a baseball cap, and he has a large paper bag in one hand.

"Hey," he says softly. "How are you feeling?"

"Okay, if I don't move." I smile at him. "Thanks for bringing dinner."

"Of course." He drops the bag on the dining table and then moves to my side to press a quick kiss to my forehead. It's so unexpectedly sweet that I smile when he rises again. "Can you sit up enough to eat? Or do you want to wait?"

"I'll try." I push myself upright, blinking away stars, and he quickly grabs a handful of throw pillows to prop behind me so I'm half-reclining. "How was your day?"

"Good. I went shopping."

I laugh. "Where'd you go?"

He's busying himself with the paper bag. "I wanted to check out a couple of new stores on Robertson."

"Oh?"

He throws me a glance. "I might have dropped into the Duchene store on Rodeo for a bit."

I laugh. "For your Instagram, of course."

"For my Instagram."

"Did you go looking like that?"

He looks horrified. "Of course not. I was actually on a run when I got Amira's message, so I went home and showered. It felt like too much effort to get dressed for the third time today." He grimaces. "Sorry. I didn't mean to imply that you're not important enough to get dressed up for . . ."

"No, I get it. If we're just going to be sitting around, might as well be comfortable."

He comes over to me with a recycled paper bowl and hands me both chopsticks and a fork. "I guessed for you. Bibimbap with beef. Is that okay? I got the gochujang sauce on the side in case you thought the spice might be a problem."

I take it from him. "Thank you, that's perfect."

He gets himself some water from the fridge and then brings his bowl to sit next to me on the sofa. "You want to watch something?"

I nudge the remote in his direction while I withdraw my chopsticks from their paper sleeve. The food looks delicious, but I can already tell I'm not going to be able to eat much of it. My stomach is always in knots when I have one of these episodes, and nothing that my doctors or the armchair specialists on Reddit suggested have actually worked for me. It has the benefit of making it so I don't have to watch my weight, but it does put a damper on enjoying my favorite foods.

I figured Simon would select Netflix, but instead

he's navigating to YouTube. He types in a string of numbers and *Astra* and selects a video. Then he pauses. "Okay, I want you to know that I am not playing this because I am a narcissist. I am playing this because you've only seen Joonwoo and Kai as fully-formed grownups and you need to feel the secondhand embarrassment."

I have no idea what's going on, but I like the build-up. "Okay."

He grins at me and presses play. The video is clearly a Korean TV show, but the graphics are splashy and neon-colored and there are a lot of Korean captions overlaid with English subtitles in black boxes.

"What is this?" I ask after I watch for a minute and still have no idea what's going on.

"This is the Astra survival show. Where they selected the members of the group. If we were to watch the entire thing, you'd see where I got eliminated for my poor Korean language skills. But we are only here for Joon's haircut." He fast-forwards to what looks like a dance studio and then pauses the video when the camera focuses on a young, thin boy with a yellow-blond bowl cut and . . .

"Braces?" I splutter. "He had *braces*?"

"Oh yes," Simon says with a grin. "He had braces. And that hair color did not suit him at all." He presses play again, and a familiar song—one that Amira has played for me—comes through the speaker. I watch as nine boys who must still be in their teens move through choreography with varying degrees of success. One of the boys speaks rapid Korean, correcting the group as he demonstrates a section of the choreography. When they start again, my eyes fall on a skinny kid in baggy clothes and his own black bowl cut. Despite the fact he looks like the youngest of the group by a wide margin, he's the one who has picked up on the choreography the fastest, his movements nearly flawless.

I gasp. "That's you. The one in the red shirt is you!"

Simon grins at me. "Okay, so I did want to show off a little."

I watch Baby Simon in rapt fascination. "You were so cute! And so good!"

"I was so lost. I could follow the choreo, which is good because I only had the most basic Korean. Look." He points, and in the back, Joon leans over and whispers something in Simon's ear. "He's translating for me."

Over the course of the episode, that happens a lot. Joon was clearly already the leader of the group, despite the fact they were still just trainees, and as the show cuts between clips of them practicing their vocals and their choreo and finally standing on stage for an evaluation in front of who I guess are the company executives, I see how protective the older boy is of Simon. On stage, as they're receiving a rather harsh critique, Joon stands beside Simon and holds his hand, clutching it hard.

"I want to see the next episode," I say as soon as it ends, and Simon looks surprised, but he puts it on anyway.

I'm not paying that much attention to the format. Amira has already told me that these shows are staged to greater or lesser degrees depending on the company— they're designed to gain the idols a fan base before their debut. Instead, I'm watching the interplay between Joonwoo and Simon—or Seojun, as he's being called in the captions. How carefully Joon translates for him, the way his eyes flick to him in concern when they're being chewed out in Korean and it's clear that Simon has no clue what's being said. The little nudges and words of encouragement. Even here, I can tell how much the older boy cares for his squad's maknae, and my heart twists a little.

"I get it," I say finally. "That's why you wanted me to see this."

Simon doesn't deny it, simply nods. "It's hard to explain what I owe him if you don't see it for yourself. It's not like it would be here. We were isolated. We worked eighteen hours a day. I was finishing school at the same time I was being tutored in the language, sleeping only an hour or two a night. Had it not been for Joon, I wouldn't have survived." He clicks the remote control and fast-forwards it to a scene that makes my gut clench: Simon sitting in the corner with his arms wrapped around his knees and his head tipped down, his shoulders shaking in silent sobs. Joonwoo sits down next to him and wraps both arms around him, holding him tight.

It's not even my decision to make, but I can feel the weight of Simon's current dilemma. This Simon had been so, so fragile. He could have easily been crushed under all the pressure, what Joon had tried to save him from. He tried to make sure that all Simon's talent and potential wouldn't be ground away in the machine of the idol life. Now that they're grown and successful, it's Simon's turn to repay the favor. I reach my hand out and Simon takes it, squeezing my hand hard for a second before he continues eating.

"Yeah. So this is what I always think of every time I consider not renewing."

"I know it's not easy. He understands that you only have a few more years. He's still concerned about you, though maybe a little less than the other members."

"I know." Simon flicks off the app and goes back instead to regular broadcast TV, where the channel is playing a cop show rerun. He hits the mute button. "I don't know what to do."

"I promised Joon that I wouldn't try to sway you, I would just give you my honest opinion."

"And? What's your honest opinion?"

"I think you have to weigh your own wants against your responsibility to your group and your mentor. But I also think you have to consider how he's going to feel if you suffer a career-ending injury under his watch. He's not a dancer. I mean, he's good at choreography, but he doesn't have the ten years of ballet training and the hypermobility and the impact of all those solos for the past fifteen years. You have to admit that you dance at a higher level than all of them, and that takes its toll. How is he going to feel if it ends your career prematurely?"

Simon licks his lips and sets his chopsticks down. He's already considered the possibility of his career ending because of an injury, but I don't think he's considered the impact on Joon. "He'd probably never forgive himself."

"Right." I sigh. "That doesn't help, I know."

"No. But it's a good thing to consider. Disappoint him now or crush him later. Maybe." Simon sighs and holds his hand out for my bowl. "Do you want me to put this in the fridge for you?"

"Yes, thanks."

I pull some of the pillows out from behind me and scooch down on the sofa so my stomach isn't pressing into my ribs, blinking away sleepiness. When Simon returns, he's carrying a black bag that I somehow didn't notice when he entered. "What's that?"

"Laptop. Do you mind? I have to look at choreography submissions for a performance I'm filming when I get back. I won't start rehearsing until the middle of next month, but they have to hire the choreographer and figure out the schedules and rehearse the backup dancers in the meantime."

"How long will you have to learn it?"

He throws me a wry glance. "Three or four days. And I'll probably be in the studio for twelve hours each day to get it perfect."

I grimace. It wasn't unlike me learning *Manon* in Paris, though at least I had had the benefit of a passing familiarity with the ballet. "Okay, let's see what we've got."

I can't deny this might be fun, despite the fact that fatigue is tugging at the edges of my consciousness. Simon sits on the floor at the intersection of the sofa and chaise and angles the laptop screen so I can view it from my reclined position. He opens his email—all in Korean, I notice; I will never get over the dissonance of realizing this California boy lives his life in another language—and queues up the first submission.

The dancer is a petite woman with green streaks in her hair, dressed in a track suit, and there are two similarly dressed male dancers positioned behind her— part of the agency's in-house choreography team, he tells me. The song they've apparently chosen is an upbeat, American pop-R&B number, and the choreo is mostly hip-hop with an unmistakable K-pop flavor. They're unquestionably amazing, but as I'm watching the low stances and pops and body rolls, I'm thinking about the impact on Simon's unhappy lumbar vertebrae.

"It's good," I say. "What's next?"

The second submission he tells me is from an outside choreographer from Singapore with whom he connected when he was with Hyperion. Same song, but this choreo is a sinuous blend of jazz-pop and Broadway—what here in LA we usually call commercial dance. It reminds me a lot of his "Burn" performance.

"Damn," he says quietly. "I like it. A lot."

"It's good," I agree. "It would suit you and your long limbs."

He casts me a look, and I laugh. "What? It's true. You have long arms and legs and you articulate your body so elegantly. This would show off that quality." I grin at him. "Plus, it's way sexier than the first one."

"Yeah, that's what I thought you were going to say." But he winks at me and then launches a third submission.

We don't even get halfway through it before he discards it as entirely unsuitable. "Nope. Not doing it. Too provocative. This is supposed to show off my dancing, not turn into a Chippendales show."

"I would pay good money to see you do that chorus," I tease.

Mischief sparks in his eyes. "You would, would you?"

I look at him. "It was a figure of speech."

"No, it wasn't. What will you give me?"

I lick my lips and watch him track the movement. "Dessert."

"Dessert?" he prompts, eyebrows raised.

"I'll *buy* you dessert. Or rather, I will DoorDash you dessert. If you learn and perform the chorus for me."

"Deal." He jumps to his feet without hesitation and puts the laptop on the coffee table, then clicks the full screen button and starts it from the beginning. I watch in amused fascination as he starts marking out the choreo for the first eight counts of the chorus, his brow furrowed in concentration.

I'm not too proud to say I wanted to see him perform that impossibly sexy choreography, but now I'm struck by just how *good* he is. It takes him almost no time to get the first two bars down perfectly, and then he's moving on to a slinky section of isolations combined with complicated arm and hand movements. He straightens. "Okay, I think I've got it. Give me a minute to run it through before I show you." He stares me down. "Hands over your eyes, and promise me you won't watch."

I sigh dramatically and place both my hands tightly over my eyes. I can hear the quiet shush of wood on carpet as he pushes my coffee table back, and then the music turns on again. His footsteps and the rustle of his clothing tells me he's moving through the choreo at full speed and it takes all I have not to watch him. Then he claps his hands together sharply. "Okay. You can look. I'm ready."

He's grinning at me, rubbing his hands together in something approaching exhilaration. There is no question that he loves what he does. "Ready?"

"Oh, I was born ready."

He winks at me and then darts forward to click on the video, backed up a few seconds into the first verse, then gets into position in the small space in front of my sofa.

When I challenged him to this, I half-expected him to make a joke out of it, but no . . . he's very serious as he launches into a near-perfect facsimile of the submission we'd just watched, flavored with his own style and colored by his very expressive face. I'm trying and failing to keep my expression critical; we're eight counts in and I'm grinning like a fool. Somehow, in joggers and socks, he can make this whole thing look as seductive as if he were on stage in full costume and makeup.

And then he's done with the chorus. Seojun vanishes and Simon reappears, grinning at me like a little boy. He clicks off the video. "So what's the verdict? Did I earn my dessert?"

"Oh," I say slowly, "And then some. That was the sexiest damn thing I've seen in a long time."

I expect his cheeks to color, but instead he just narrows his eyes at me. "Was it really? Maybe I should choose this one instead."

"Oh no. There is no way I want your delusional fans watching *that*. It will give them a heart attack. Keep that one all for me."

He chuckles and drops to his knees next to me on the rug, then presses a slow kiss to my lips. "With pleasure."

The kiss deepens for a brief moment, long enough to make me catch my breath and speed my heart again, but then he's pulling away. "So what do you want?"

"Don't ask me! It's your prize."

"Ice cream," he says immediately. "No question."

"Ice cream it is." I reach for my phone and open a delivery app, then select my favorite local ice cream shop. I quickly tap in my regular order and then hand it over to him. He takes several minutes to peruse the options before he finally selects something and hands it back to me.

"Coffee ice cream with fudge and chocolate chips?"

"Mocha," he says with a grin.

"I approve." I set the tip and send the order, and Simon drags the coffee table back toward the sofa, close enough to reach the laptop. He plops down beside me on the floor, his legs crossed, and opens up his email again.

I watch unrepentantly over his shoulder, and he doesn't object, nor should he since he's typing in Korean on a Hangul keyboard and I can't read a single blessed thing.

"Telling the agency who I chose and why," he explains. "They'll set it up, get the choreographer and backup dancers hired, communicate with the channel that's filming it . . ."

"They do all that?" There has to be a significant cost attached, and I realize that I actually have no much idea how much an upper quarter—but not very top tier—K-pop group can earn.

"Yeah, it's good publicity for me and the group. Technically, I'm a soloist on loan to Helios, my contracts just expire simultaneously."

I watch as he types intently, the geometric letters shifting and reforming syllables and words, and my gaze drifts to his serious profile, the way he bites his full bottom lip. He is unequivocally one of the best-looking humans I've ever seen in real life, and yet there is something so ordinary about the way he holds himself in unguarded moments. I'm not used to this kind of humility. I deal with Western celebrities all the time and even when they're being supposedly transparent, there's always this sense that they know how important they are. I don't know if this is a Korean industry thing or if it's just a Simon thing, but it's refreshing.

I reach out and slide my hand into his hair, watching the strands slip through my fingers. His eyes drift closed as he leans into my touch. "I don't understand how your hair is so soft when you color it so much."

"Very expensive hair masks and heat protectants," he murmurs, sighing again when my fingernails scrape across his scalp. He's as happy as a cat right now, practically purring beneath my fingertips. "And I try not to bleach too often. That's why I did light brown after the pink. I'm going platinum when I get back."

I study him, trying to imagine him with silver-blond hair and decide that it will probably suit him just as well as everything else does. "You'll have to send me a photo. I don't think I've ever seen you with hair that light."

"Not since debut." His eyes are still closed, and I

swear that if I keep playing with his hair, he's going to drift off on me.

"Are you ready to go back?" I ask quietly.

"No. I'd rather just stay here like this forever." He opens one eye and shoots me a wry side-glance. "That was your cue not to stop."

I smile and resume the motion of my hand through his hair, letting the strands fall from it like silk, but the fact he made a joke out of it doesn't change the underlying truth of his words.

And once more, for reasons I can't quite explain, my chest aches in a way that has nothing to do with my condition.

chapter twenty-six

I wake up the next morning to a flashing green light on my phone and a message from Simon.

SIMON
How are you feeling today?

I smile to myself and push my mussed hair from my eyes as I hold the phone above my head and type out a response.

TRINA
Not sure. Haven't gotten out
of bed yet. Will know in 5
minutes.

I know I'm being mean by putting the image of me in bed in his head, but we've somehow hit a strange level of comfort where the flirtation and suggestiveness is completely divorced from our actual level of intimacy.

SIMON
You teaching today?

TRINA
No. Amira canceled my
sessions. She knows I need
a day to recover.

SIMON
Can I come over? I'll bring
breakfast.

I pause. I literally saw him seven hours ago and he's asking to come over again. After he finished his work last night, he climbed up onto the chaise, settling me between his legs and against his chest, and we watched a movie with his arms wrapped around me. It was the happiest and most secure I've felt in years, and even now that feeling lingers. I'm trying not to let the knowledge that we're living on borrowed time taint the memory. Neither of us are talking about what will or will not happen when he goes back to Seoul in two weeks.

TRINA
Give me an hour. I'm moving
slowly today. I'll leave the
door open for you.

I soon learn that I probably should have said more than an hour, because it takes me thirty minutes just to summon the energy to get up. I can never tell what the aftermath of an episode is going to be. Sometimes I'll wake feeling energetic but like my muscles have been through three hardcore weight workouts in the same day. Other times, my body feels fine but I can't summon the effort to move. Today is the latter, and when I finally do get upright and take my blood pressure and heart rate—both jacked up to an unreasonable level from the mere action of changing position—it takes me another twenty minutes to get to the front door and unlock it. I've used up all my energy by the time I get to the bathroom, so I turn on the shower, sit in the tub, and let the water beat down on me from above.

When I finally get out, dry off, and slip into the least restrictive items in my wardrobe—joggers and a tank top—I hear the faint strains of music coming from my living room. It takes me a few moments to realize that it's not the radio, but rather Simon's *singing*. Slowly, I open my bedroom door and lean in the door frame, listening to his smoky, flexible baritone lift and dip over what sounds like a R&B song turned low on my portable speaker. I would stand there longer, hidden from view by the kitchen's half wall, but Misha realizes that the door is open and jumps from his position on the bed to make a bid for freedom. I know the second I've been found out, because the singing breaks off.

"Katrina?"

Slowly, I move into the living room and toward the kitchen, glad that I'm steady even if I feel like I'm trudging through molasses. "Morning."

I must look worse than I think, because he's rushing toward me, slipping an arm around my waist. "Where do you want to sit?"

"Breakfast bar."

He supports me as I walk to the breakfast bar and sit on one of the wicker barstools. Only then do I realize he hasn't brought pastries or burritos like I expected, but he's actually *cooking*. I blink at the ingredients spread over my counter.

"I took a chance," he said. "I wanted to make you breakfast."

I don't object. "Korean?"

"Filipino, actually." He throws me a curious glance. "Did you know my mom is half-Filipino?"

"I didn't," I say. "Is that why she doesn't speak Korean?"

He nods and moves back around to the other side of the island, where he uses tongs to transfer some thinly sliced meat to a hot frying pan. The delicious smell of searing marinated beef immediately fills the kitchen, and my stomach rumbles in response.

"Yeah, her dad is Korean, but her mom is Filipino. Her parents met in Manila and emigrated here, so Mom grew up hearing Tagalog and not Korean at home."

"Do you speak any then?"

He flips the meat with the tongs and casts a look over his shoulder at me. "Only a little. I understand more than I can speak. But my Japanese is considerably better. It was my priority after Korean since the Japanese K-pop market is so important."

The longer I spend in his presence, the more inadequate I feel. He's gone from being an English-speaking ballet dancer to a multilingual vocalist/dancer/pop star in less than fifteen years, and I can't help but be aware of how much time I've wasted in comparison. Add the fact he can actually cook, and it seems impossible that this man is still single.

And he *can* cook. The food he finally puts in front of me—garlic fried rice, thin-sliced beef he calls *tapa,* and fried eggs—is every bit as delicious as any restaurant meal I've ever had. Even though I know I'm going to regret it later, I eat everything on my plate. "You are officially the perfect man," I say lightly. "Can I keep you?"

The joke spills out accidentally, and when I see the sharp, questioning look he sends me, I worry I've said too much. But he responds with a wink in my direction. "I thought you'd never ask."

When we've finished eating and he's cleaned up the kitchen and placed the dishes in the dishwasher—he really is the perfect man—he looks at me. "What do you feel like doing today?"

The answer, really, is *nothing*. I don't have the energy to do anything but sit in one place, and for the first time in a while, it fills me with frustration. I can deal with the realities of my condition when I have nothing better to do—after all, I'm an introvert at heart and it's not exactly a hardship to sit on the sofa and read books and watch movies when I'm feeling unwell—but knowing that the clock is running out on our time together makes me furious that I can do no more than my rock impression.

"You don't have to hang out with me today," I say finally. "I know you have things to do."

"Not really," he says. "I'm on vacation. And I'd rather spend time with you than do anything else."

"Simon," I say softly, "I can't really do anything but *sit*."

He thinks for a second. "Want to go for a drive?"

"Where?"

He smiles. "Just trust me."

I do. And going for a drive with him sounds a lot more fun than sitting around here and watching TV. "Okay. Let me get changed and grab some things."

I'm feeling a little better as I walk back to my bedroom—now that I think about it, I haven't eaten a lot in the past couple of days—where I change into a pair of shorts and a loose-fitting tank top with a lace overlay. I put on my favorite pair of sneakers and grab a denim jacket in case I get cold. When I come back out, Simon is filling up my big jug with water and ice. It sends a pang straight into my chest to realize how closely he's been paying attention when he's with me.

I stretch up to kiss him lightly and then brush past him to take down a couple of energy bars and a package of beef jerky in case we can't find anything suitable on the road. I pause to give Misha goodbye hugs and kisses until he squirms away from me and runs under the sofa and then fill his food and water bowls again. "Okay, let's go."

Simon has his dad's BMW again, which I have to admit will make for a much nicer ride wherever we're going. "You sure he's not going to mind you putting the mileage on his car?"

"No." Simon casts me a little smile as he pulls away from the curb in front of the building.

I study his face. "You bought the car for him."

He doesn't say anything, but I know I'm right. No wonder his dad doesn't mind him driving it when he's here. And now that I think about it, this idea might have been planned from the beginning. I settle back into the seat, not sure how I feel about that, and then decide I don't care. I've been clear that I like him, that I'm attracted to him, that I want to spend time with him. What's the point in playing hard to get?

I'm not surprised when he heads back down Malibu Canyon and turns north onto PCH. This coastal route is one of the prettiest drives in California, and only a few miles down the road, I reach up to open the sunroof.

"You pick the music," he tells me. "Passenger's prerogative."

"Funny, I thought the driver got to pick."

"It's my car—sort of—so I make the rules."

Instead of tuning the radio, I take a minute to connect my phone to the car's sound system and then scroll through my playlists. A smile stretches my mouth when I punch the button to randomize one particular artist.

The minute the strains of the first song come through the speakers, Simon laughs. "Really. Of all the things you could choose, you pick Hyperion?"

"I happen to like Hyperion. Particularly this one really good-looking dancer. Maybe you've heard of him?"

He shakes his head. "At least play our most recent album. I can't stand hearing myself on our early stuff. I was terrible."

"You were not terrible," I say, but it answers my earlier question about how he feels about his progress. I flip over to something else and press *play*, giggling to myself.

Simon rolls his eyes. "Helios. I take it back. Your selection privileges have been revoked." When we stop at a stoplight at Kanan Dume, he takes my phone from me and taps in a quick search. The smooth sounds of an R&B song pours out—an early 2000's-inflected style with Korean lyrics.

"Was this what you were singing this morning?"

He seems surprised that I remember. "Yeah, he's one of the artists under the label I met with."

Now I understand why he doesn't want to listen to his old work, and it has nothing to do with his perfectionist tendencies. Today is a day to forget about the things he's trying to escape—the things that we're trying to escape—and I resolve to stick to that myself. It's a beautiful day with blue skies above, the sun shining down, and the stunning expanse of the Pacific Ocean out the window. I reach for his hand and he laces his fingers with mine. It's natural. Comfortable.

The conversation flows just as easily as we wind our

way north. Turns out that we knew some of the same people back in our ballet days and took class from some of the same teachers, at least during the period of time he trained in New York. I talk about my experiences as a student at the New York Theater Ballet and how it felt to go from corps de ballet to principal dancer in less than four years. He talks about the tough early days as a trainee with his company and the many missteps he made as he learned the language and culture of his new home.

I'm struck once more by the similarities of our experiences—not the daily details, but the pervasive feelings of fear, pressure, incessant perfectionism. The obsessive self-analysis and the determination to work harder each day than the last. Neither of us pretend that it's healthy or desirable, but it's the reality of our chosen professions—or at least my old chosen profession. Somehow, though, talking about it feels like exorcising those demons, putting the overly rosy memories in perspective.

"How can you love something so much even as it destroys you?" I murmur.

He sighs and throws me a glance. "Trust me, I ask myself that all the time."

"Do the other members feel the same way?"

"Joon, for sure. Jiho loves every minute of being on stage, but he's such an extreme introvert, the fan stuff is hard for him. Everyone else is some shade in between."

We stop in Carpinteria, a charming small town about an hour north of Malibu, for snacks, gas, and a bathroom break—more for the novelty of stopping on a road trip than actual need—and I'm pleased to find that I'm feeling steadier as the day goes on. I'd like to believe that it's the effect of Simon's presence, but in reality, I probably just caught my episode before it turned into full-blown syncope and therefore it's not taking me as long to recover as it did last time. I inform Simon that Carpinteria has the world's safest beach, which tempts him for a moment to park and go down onto its fine beige sand, but we decide to continue on instead and climb back into the car.

The further north we get, the more overcast the weather becomes, giving the ocean a greenish cast instead of the bright blue of hours before, and the conversation gets quieter and more serious. I tell Simon how Amira and I met and became friends shortly after I started teaching Pilates in Los Angeles, how Amira offered to become my partner in the studio and then bankrolled it for eighteen months until we were profitable, how her connections were what gave me the clientele I have now.

Simon tells me about his roommate, Taehyun, in Seoul, who is currently fulfilling his military service. "We've lived together since our Hyperion days," he says, "but he's always been biding his time. His family's wealthy and he wanted a way to make his own mark. He invested every last dime into property in Busan, so he'll go back to manage his real estate when he gets out."

It's a fascinating idea, the idol career simply as a way to build wealth for other things, and while I suppose it's not much different than Western artists who get into show business for the money, it seems like a difficult road to choose if you don't love performing.

"I don't mean to be indelicate," I say, "but can you afford to quit right now?"

He shrugs. "I mean, I'm not obscenely wealthy, but I've made good investments. And I barely spend any money when I'm home in Korea. So yeah. I could afford to quit and live pretty comfortably. It's more the question of what am I going to do with my time if I quit? I've been working so hard for so long, I wouldn't know what to do with myself if I didn't have a goal."

I get that. It was why I launched myself into the highest level of training when I shifted from ballet to Pilates. Something to occupy my mind, a goal to reach, a justification for my path.

We're about three hours north of our starting point, approaching Pismo Beach, when Simon looks at the clock regretfully. "I'm thinking we should probably stop for a bite to eat and then turn around."

The disappointment that fills me surprises me, as does the wild impulse to be irresponsible and run away. "And if we don't?"

He looks at me longer than he should, considering our speed on the coastal highway. "The drive all the way to Big Sur is pretty spectacular. I haven't done it in years. But it means we'd have to stay overnight or get back very late."

My heart is beating hard in my chest now. "Let's keep going."

"Really?"

I nod. "I'll tell Amira to cancel my sessions tomorrow. She won't question it."

"Can you do that?"

"I'm going to do that," I say. Forget the fact it's completely irresponsible. Forget the fact that I've canceled on my clients too much already. I've been doing nothing but surviving and immersing myself in my business for years. And right now, I just want to . . . live. Be. Enjoy the man beside me while I can, because today has just reinforced the fact that even if he stays, things between us will not be the same. Even if he moves back to California, he'll be recording and touring and performing. I'll be teaching.

This is a sun-blessed, protected bubble of time that we're never, ever going to get back and I'm not strong enough to give up this fleeting bit of happiness.

chapter twenty-seven

In Pismo Beach, we find parking a block or two off the boardwalk, and Simon takes my hand as we stroll in the deepening afternoon light. He snags a passerby to take a photo of us together in front of freestanding lettering that spells out *Pismo Beach* and halfway through the impromptu photo session, he bends to kiss me. When we get his phone back, he swipes through to one of the last photos. His head is tipped down to mine, a smile on his face; mine is turned up in an expression of delighted surprise. It takes me aback to see my adoration written all over my face; my feelings seem even clearer in imagery than they do in my head.

Simon winks at me and sets the photo as his phone background before he takes my hand again and we start walking.

"A little dangerous, don't you think?" I murmur, tucking in close to his body.

He kisses the top of my head. "I'll risk it. Besides, you can only see it if you get past my lock screen."

I laugh at the practicality coming directly after the romanticism; he is far more aware of the realities of his life than I am anyway.

We find a nearby restaurant with patio seating and get a table right away, where we order seafood pasta and drink sparkling water and chat about our childhood memories of beach vacations in our home states—him in California, me in Florida. And then we're back in the car, winding our way north as the sun begins to dip lower and lower toward the ocean. It's starting to edge toward twilight when we finally reach Big Sur and I pull out my phone.

"I'm going to try to find us a place to stay," I say, opening a booking site.

"Look for something with an ocean view," he suggests.

I check the box for *views* and my eyes practically bug out at the prices. "Simon, the only one that has rooms available is like eighteen hundred dollars a night. I can't afford this."

He throws me a look, and I realize he knew exactly how expensive hotels would be here.

"I can't—"

"You can," he says easily. "And no, we don't have to share a room just because it's expensive."

I'm not sure if that makes it better or worse. Either way, it's a subtle way of telling me that he's not expecting anything from me tonight, and I appreciate it even though I hadn't thought otherwise.

"Okay, there's a three-star hotel in Carmel with beach access or a five-star hotel on the bluff in Big Sur with wood-burning fireplaces. I don't think I need to tell you that the second one is astoundingly expensive, but also pretty cool."

"You choose. I don't care either way as long as the beds are comfortable. And I don't mind driving to Carmel. It's only another thirty minutes or so."

The five-star hotel is tempting—it's not fancy, but it feels like a getaway in the mountains—but I can't bring myself to make him drop almost two grand on a single night, especially on a whim. "The first one," I say finally. "I want to listen to the water."

"Oceanfront it is. Put the address into my phone."

He unlocks his phone screen and hands it to me, and yes, I take a moment to study the photo of us in the background. Then I open the map app and put in the address.

When we pull into the charming beach town of Carmel-by-the-Sea and find our hotel a few blocks off the beach, I'm happy that I picked this location. It's a beautiful, sprawling Spanish-style structure with black iron balconies, stuccoed porticos, lavishly landscaped grounds. Beyond, through breaks in the mature trees, the Pacific Ocean spreads out in breathtaking majesty.

"Good choice," he murmurs in approval when we pull up to the front and a valet immediately comes out to take the car. The attendant opens my door and helps me out before circling to Simon's side. They have a quick conversation, probably about our lack of luggage, and then Simon is taking my hand as we walk up into the saltillo-tiled portico and through the heavy wood double doors.

The marble-tiled lobby is cool, relaxed, and cozy, giving a sort of old-world luxury feel. Simon goes straight to the front desk clerk and asks about availability.

"Of course, sir," the woman says with a pleasant smile. "One room or two?"

"One," I put in before he can answer. "A king if you have it, please."

She looks between the two of us and smiles, and I wonder what she's thinking about us arriving at a hotel this fancy, dressed casually with no luggage. Whatever she's thinking, it's probably correct. In minutes, Simon has handed over his credit card and secured our room.

"Is there a grocery or drugstore nearby?" I ask before we walk away.

"There's one a few blocks north of here." She pulls out a tourist map of Carmel and circles our current location, then puts a big X on the map several blocks away.

Simon smiles and thanks her, then takes the map. "It's not far. Walk or drive?"

I take stock of my body and realize I actually don't feel bad. Not as energetic as usual, but I've been more or less resting in the car all day, so I think I can handle a few blocks on my feet. "Let's walk. It's a beautiful night."

I've never been to Carmel. In fact, I've never been this far north in California, and it has a completely different feel than the southern part. The town is vaguely European with steeply sloped shingled roofs and stuccoed buildings, though it becomes a bit more turn-of-the-century as we move away from the water and deeper into town. The drug store is just where the desk attendant said it would be, in a white-washed brick building with a cheery scalloped awning out front. We step through and it's like we've gone back in time to a 1950s soda fountain.

"I'm going to grab us toothpaste and toothbrushes," I say. "Any preference?"

"No, you choose." His attention has already been grabbed by the wood-framed cosmetic counter, where there's a selection of expensive-looking skin care products behind glass. I chuckle to myself—of course he's not going to go an evening without his alpha-hydroxy-whatever, a habit I really should adopt considering his skin is way better than mine—and then wander through the store, picking up the necessities for the unexpected overnight. I hover in the family-planning section, uncertain, before I snag a box off the display and add it to my basket. I've already checked out with my purchases in a paper bag by the time he finally selects a cleanser and moisturizer and goes to the counter.

It's not exactly dark by the time we exit the store, but it's definitely edging toward twilight—the route up the coast took much longer than I thought, and I'm glad we decided to overnight it. Only then do I realize I need to let Amira know that I'm not coming into work. I tap out a quick message.

> TRINA
> I'm not going to make it into
> the studio tomorrow. Can
> you send out cancellations?

Amira must have been waiting for this message, because she doesn't even ask why.

> AMIRA
> Done. Feel better.

Guilt floods me for misrepresenting the situation to my best friend, but I'm honestly not sure what she would say. Would I get a virtual high five and a pat on the back for doing something impulsive and putting my personal life first? Or would she warn me that I'm headed for disaster in a relationship that can't possibly last? She's been frustratingly difficult to read the past two weeks, and I don't know if it's because she knows things I don't about the realities of dating an idol or because she's just not used to me having anything else in my life but the studio and her. It's an uncharitable thought, but I can't discount the possibility that she might not like the idea of no longer being my only friend. She's definitely been more support to me than the other way around, but I am the one stable thing in her world.

"Problem?" Simon asks, squeezing my hand.

I shove the phone into my purse again. "No. I just feel bad not telling her why I'm really canceling."

"Then tell her." He casts a look my way. "Unless you're ashamed?"

I huff out a laugh. "Ashamed of you? Not possible."

He actually looks relieved, and once more, I can't fathom what goes through his head. How on earth could I be ashamed of dating the kindest, best-looking, and most talented man I've ever met? True, there might be some recency bias involved, but if you stack him up with the few men I've been with, he absolutely does not come out as lacking in the comparison.

I haven't explained why I didn't tell her yet, though, and I struggle to find the words. "Maybe I just want to keep you to myself for a little while. Without having to hear other people's opinions. I mean, if Joon were here, would you tell him?"

His silence is the only answer I really need. We may be surrounded by people with our best interests at heart, but that doesn't mean that we want their opinions on every aspect of our personal lives. Sometimes we just want to live.

By silent agreement, we decide to go back to the room and relax before finding someplace to eat dinner later, and I'm not disappointed when Simon opens the door to our room. It's not exactly luxurious, but it's beautiful and traditional and furnished in shades of cream and beige and pale blue that echo the colors of the building and the ocean beyond. I go straight to far side of the room and open the sliding glass door so I can step out onto the balcony and breathe in the sea air. We're high enough in the hotel that we have almost one-hundred-eighty degree views of the ocean, trees and buildings spread out before us in the few blocks to the beach. A cool breeze ripples the tendrils that have pulled free of my ponytail, and I drag the rubber band from it so I can shake the wavy strands free around my shoulders and feel the wind blow through it.

I'm aware of Simon approaching me, but I don't turn, even when his hands close on either side of my waist. My heartbeat ratchets up when he bends to kiss the sensitive spot where my neck meets my shoulder.

My knees go a little unsteady, and I tip my head back against him, bringing with it the fleeting memory of the night we met on stage. The hum in the back of his throat—not quite a laugh—makes me think that he's remembering the same thing, but his hands don't move, even when I twist to face him and pull his head down to kiss him full on the lips.

The heat that flares between us tonight is a slow burn, as if we're both trying to draw out these moments for as long as we can, and I lose track of how long we kiss on the balcony. I'm the one who breaks away first, and I smile at the surprise in his eyes as I place my hands on his chest and gently push him backwards into the room. I'm still not sure he knows what I have in mind until I grasp the hem of his shirt and let my fingertips brush his torso as I slide the garment slowly upward by inches.

He shudders beneath my touch and bows his head so I can pull the shirt off, but he grasps both my hands before they can resume their exploration. "Katrina, are you sure? I promise you, I'm don't expect anything from you."

I let out a long breath, then nod. "I'm sure. Just...let's take things slow. I don't know how this might go."

Something shifts in his face, as if he realizes the amount of trust I'm placing in him, choosing him to be my first in so long. Part of me thinks this is too much of a risk, that I'm flinging myself down a disastrous path that I'm going to regret. But when he bends to kiss me with aching tenderness, every touch careful, almost reverent, I know I've made the right choice.

chapter twenty-eight

It's pitch black over the ocean by the time we summon the energy to discuss dinner. I lie with my ear pressed against Simon's bare chest, listening to the steady thud of his heartbeat while his fingertips trace lazy circles across my back.

"Room service," I murmur, pressing a kiss to his skin. "I don't want to move from this spot."

"I'm sure that would give the hotel employee a shock."

"They've seen worse. It feels like too much effort to get up."

He raises his head to look me in the eye, concerned. "Are you okay?"

I just close my eyes and snuggle closer into him. "I'm good. Happy. Satisfied." I would never have dreamed that I could feel this comfortable with anyone, but Simon proved to not only be attentive and patient but surprisingly uninhibited. I shouldn't be surprised. He communicates so well that it only makes sense it would carry over into bed.

"Me too," he says, kissing my temple. "Thank you for trusting me."

I nod, and for a second I'm drifting. Then I say, "French fries."

"What?"

"I want French fries."

He chuckles, and I feel his abs contract beneath my fingertips. God, I would kill for these abs, but I struggle to eat enough to maintain the muscle I already have these days. I can't even fathom his diet and workout routine. I trace my fingers over the smooth ridges until he captures my hand on its downward path.

"You need to stop that if you want your French fries."

"Okay. French fries first."

He extracts himself from me with a laugh, and yes, of course I take the opportunity to get another look at his beautiful naked body when he crosses to the phone. "Is that all you want?"

"I'll just take a bite or two of yours if you're willing to share."

"Jagiya, you can have anything you want."

I don't need the translation to know from his tender tone that it's an endearment. I close my eyes and let myself drift while he orders room service, not paying much attention to what he chooses. As soon as he puts down the phone, I pat the bed next to me, but I don't know if he ever comes back because I'm drifting until the brush of fingertips over my arm wakes me.

"Food's here."

I blink and stretch. He's in a bathrobe, apparently as loathe to dress and return to the real world as I am, and there's a tray beside the bed. I push myself up on one elbow and blink away dizziness, waiting, but nothing else comes of it. I focus on the food. "Steak frites?"

He plucks a French fry off the plate and feeds it to me, and I almost groan at the hot, crisp exterior and light sprinkling of salt. These are without a doubt my greatest weakness. I push myself up and let the sheet fall, see the widening of his eyes.

"I can put on clothes," I tease.

"Oh, I'd rather you didn't."

I like the glint of interest in his eyes, but I still go and retrieve a robe from the closet, then perch on the edge of the bed and nibble French fries off the plate. I steal a couple of pieces of steak, too, but my body is already reeling and I don't want to confuse it any more by drawing attention to my stomach. Instead I stretch out on the bed, the robe open to mid-thigh—purposely and rather effectively, I might add—and watch Simon as he eats his meal. He's as focused and graceful doing this as he is at everything else, and I let my eyes roam every angle of his face and body as if I can commit him to memory. When he's back in Seoul, I want to be able to summon the sharp slant of his cheekbone, the way his hair falls over one eye, the almost compulsive way he runs his fingers through it when it doesn't lay the way he wants.

Just like I want to remember how he kisses me and skims his hands over my body and smiles in satisfaction when I arch beneath him.

I can't tell if the sudden pang inside me is affection or heartache.

When he's finished eating, I push off the bed and start for the bathroom, which a quick glimpse has told me is half again the size of the room. "I'm going to go take a bath." Halfway there, I untie the robe and let it fall from my shoulders. "Would you like to join me?"

By the time we wake late the next morning, I'm tired and sore and sated, and in a strange way, I feel like I'm an entirely different person. This was the feeling I expected when I lost my virginity to one of the few straight boys in the NYTB school, a perfunctory experience that left me wondering what the big deal was. Surely that couldn't wasn't the thing that inspired rapturous tributes from singers and poets and novelists. And my relationships since that one have been . . . complicated . . . at best.

So it surprises me, this depth of affection I feel as I study Simon in the driver's seat while we wind our way back down the coast toward home. I don't know if I'm in love with him. But no matter what happens, I love him a little for helping prove that my condition hasn't taken everything from me. That I can expect more from my life than merely accommodating my weaknesses and managing my episodes. That I can *do* and *feel* and view my body as something other than a constant form of pain and disappointment.

"What are you thinking?" he asks when he catches my gaze on him for what feels like the hundredth time.

"I don't know. I'm just happy."

He reaches for my hand and brings it to his lips. "Me too."

Our talk this time is light, unimportant. We argue the relative merits of various flavors of potato chips. Whether or not an actual bar form is required for something to be considered a candy bar. Which foods, drinks, movies, and songs we can't live without. It's all a concerted effort to avoid talking about the future, what lies ahead of us when we get back to LA, a way to stay in this little bubble that we've created for the two of us.

And yet real life intrudes when we're about three hours outside of Los Angeles, with the electronic ring of Simon's phone through the car's speakers. He blinks at it in surprise. "It's Hyunsoo."

"Take it," I say immediately.

Simon clicks a button to accept the phone call and answers with a string of Korean, I assume to inform his team member that he's not alone in the car. I don't need to understand the language to recognize the tight, worried tone of the man on the other end, nor to feel the sudden tension rolling off Simon. "Okay," he says finally. "I'll call you back."

He clicks off, swearing repeatedly under his breath, then puts on his signal to pull onto the shoulder. My stomach lurches into my throat when he slams the car into park and fumbles for his phone. He clicks on a link from a message, bringing up a website, all in Korean. "Shit shit shit shit."

"What is it?" I brace myself. Was he recognized? Were *we* recognized? Am I about to find myself in the middle of the dating scandal that Amira warned me about?

When Simon shoves the phone in my direction, it takes me several seconds to reorient my expectations around what I'm actually seeing. Instead of a photo of us making out on the balcony (or worse), it's a snap of two men on the doorstep of what looks like an expensive house, heads together in what can either be intense conversation or the moments before a kiss.

My chest squeezes when I recognize the longish undercut and stack of silver bracelets. I jerk my eyes up to Simon's. "Joon?"

He nods solemnly. "With Lee Dohyun. He's an actor."

My mouth opens and closes while I try to think of what to ask first. The photo is ambiguous—Joon's hand on the back of the other man's neck might just be his way of emphasizing whatever he's saying—but there's something about the body language that says otherwise. I finally decide to go with bluntness. "So Joon is gay?"

Slowly, Simon nods.

"Does anyone know?"

"Outside of Astra and Helios?" Simon shakes his head emphatically. "No."

I let out a long breath. "What happens now?"

"The company issues a statement and denies everything, I suspect. I'm surprised Joon was so indiscreet. They've managed not to be caught for the past three years. Dohyun is out, so it's not an issue for him, but this could destroy Joon's career."

I wipe my hand over my face. It's such a foreign idea to me, given how accepting the dance world is about sexuality and gender expression, that the idea of it causing a scandal is incomprehensible. I appreciate the fact that Simon doesn't feel the need to tell me to keep this to myself—because of course I will.

"Do what you have to do," I say finally. "Don't worry about me."

Simon throws me a grateful look and dials, the contact name hidden to me in Hangul. It takes several rings before someone finally picks up.

"Joon-hyung, naya."

It's all Simon says before I'm lost in the string of Korean on the other end of the line. I watch Simon's body get stiffer and tenser as he listens to his mentor unload. He takes a long, deep breath, considering before he replies.

Whatever was said, it feels like something's been decided, because Joon sounds relieved when they hang up. Simon, on the other hand, looks troubled.

"What is it?" I ask quietly.

He swallows. "I'm going back."

The news vibrates through me as an unpleasant shock. "When?"

"Tomorrow."

I catch my breath. "Oh."

He throws me a pained look. "I'm so sorry, Katrina. I have to been seen with him. Considering I haven't been posting about my vacation on social and technically no one knows where I am, it might look like I'm distancing myself from him. Which in turn makes it seem like there's truth to the speculations."

"And he can't just come out?" I ask, knowing the answer before I voice the words.

Simon shakes his head. "Our company is very conservative. They'll battle the rumors, but admit to them? If he came out, they either wouldn't renew our contract or they'd remove him from the group. South Korea has come a long way in the last few years, but not that far."

I just concentrate on the breath in and out of my lungs while I think. "You know I have to say it, Simon. If you don't go back . . . the decision is out of your hands."

"And you know why that's not even an option."

I do, and I'm not going to argue about why it should be. Simon already showed me what he owes Joonwoo, why he would do anything for him. And if Simon turns his back on him now, neither of us could ever respect him again.

"Okay," I say softly. "I understand."

He lifts my hand to his lips again and kisses it, and I don't think I imagine his look of gratitude. Did he expect me to demand that he stay? Did he think that just because we slept together, I would want him to choose me over his closest friend? No, that's probably exactly what he expected, and I can't even be mad. Yet the knowledge that our two weeks has been reduced down to a single day hits me with a force I don't expect.

"Can you stay with me tonight or do you need to go back home?" I want to wring every last minute with him from our remaining day.

Regret colors his voice. "I need to go back and spend the evening with my parents. I haven't seen them in two years and I'm already cutting my visit short by weeks."

And that, too, I understand. There's nothing I can say. So instead I just take his hand across the console and hold it tight all the way back to LA.

Simon walks me up to my apartment and silently follows me inside. There, he takes my face in his hands and kisses me, long and sad and deep. I feel the words swell up inside me, *I love you*, but I don't say them because I don't know if they're true.

Instead, I just smile at him. "Call me when you get to Seoul. No matter what time it is. Okay? I want to hear your voice. Know that you're okay."

He nods, then bends and kisses me once more. "I'll be back as soon as I can. I promise."

"I'll hold you to that."

I'm sitting alone on the edge of my bed, my fingers making trails in Misha's soft fur while he purrs contentedly, when the message comes through a few minutes later from Simon. It's the photo of us about to kiss in front of the Pismo Beach sign. I set it as my phone wallpaper just as he did and stare at it as tears roll down my cheeks. I'm still looking at it long after they dry.

chapter twenty-nine

I feel oddly calm when I wake the next morning. I'm not at all surprised to find a selfie from Simon still in bed, shirtless with the silver butterfly chain splayed across his golden skin, his light brown hair mussed on the pillow. The roots are already growing out with a dark shadow, reminding me that in a few weeks, he'll be platinum and this version of Simon will be gone. I stare at the photo for a long moment, remembering how he once refused to send anything of the sort because of the risk of hacking, and recognize the offering for what it is. But instead of responding in kind, I just tap in a "blowing kiss" emoji and press send before swinging my legs over the side of the bed.

Ironically, the two days off on our adventure seem to have done me some good. I feel only a shadow of the fatigue from the weekend and all my stats are back where they should be. I go through my morning routine and walk out the door with my smoothie as I always do. The heat has finally broken in the Valley—we'll only hit low-eighties today—and there's a coolness in the air that I haven't felt since early spring. Somehow, it seems like a benediction, like the universe is sending me a consolation prize for the fact that the first man who has made me feel something in years will be winging his way back across the Pacific this afternoon.

It takes exactly thirty seconds after I step the studio for Amira to figure out what's going on. "You look rested," she says immediately, looking me up and down. "And happy. Oh my god, you slept with Simon!"

I blink at her. "How on earth did you figure that one out?"

She makes a face. "I take it you haven't seen the group Instagram." She pulls out her phone, taps a few icons, and brings up a post on Helios official . . . a long series of photos of the sea and the beach, captioned, *I'll miss you, California. See you soon. #Seojun #Helios*

I catch my breath when I realize the multiple statements he's making in that single post. Not just telling his fans where he is so they know to expect him back in Seoul, but making a statement to me, a reiteration that he intends to be back.

"I don't know how you got me sleeping with Simon from that one post."

"Because that is definitely not Southern California and you called in sick without any notice. It was obviously a last-minute romantic getaway." Her expression changes and her voice gentles. "How was it?"

I know she isn't asking about Simon's prowess in bed, because she knows of my fears about sex with my condition. "It was . . . good. No issues. I feel like I've been worried for nothing. Not that I will necessarily get a chance to test that theory. He's flying back to Korea tonight."

"Shit. It's the Jae thing, isn't it? It's been all over the media. It's a huge scandal."

I shouldn't be surprised that she knows about it, considering how closely she follows the group, but I know that even if she asks, I can't tell her what I know. Simon trusted me with the information and I'm not going to break his confidence. "Yeah, they're rallying the troops. It would look bad if Simon were missing and silent while this all goes down."

To say that I'm distracted for the rest of the day would be an understatement. And yet I'm too busy to do much more than check my phone compulsively during my breaks between clients. Simon keeps up a running commentary on text, which I can barely find the time to respond to.

> SIMON
> Packing up now. Dad is
> driving me to the airport
> later.

> SIMON
> Last brunch with the family.
> They say hi.

That one came with a group photo of the Yang family on the outdoor patio of a restaurant I don't recognize, Simon once more swathed in a hoodie that's mismatched to the weather. I now recognize it as his subtle disguise— taken side-by-side, barefaced Simon in oversized streetwear only bears the slightest resemblance to fully made-up public Seojun in designer menswear. That one, I do take a moment to reply to, even though I suspect I'm a bit too late.

> TRINA
> Tell them I said hi back and
> it was nice meeting them.

I get a smiley face in return.

The inconsequential messages continue through the day, but it's not until I come across a recommended video on Instagram, thanks to my previous Seojun-heavy browsing history, that I understand the full extent of his plans. Simon appears on the curb at the international terminal at LAX, dressed casually and yet elegantly in jeans, a button-down shirt, and a baseball cap with those aviators, while fans crowd around him, screaming and calling his name. The airport police are having a difficult time holding back the fans until they get to the security line, two beefy bodyguards doing most of the heavy lifting in clearing the way for him, but Simon still smiles and makes finger hearts toward all the cell phones pointed at him. When he finally makes it through security, he turns back and gives a little wave before disappearing beyond the barriers.

I put down my phone and let out a breath. I know this is his life, I've seen the videos, but somehow it hits different after the time we've spent together.

Amira appears over my shoulder, clocking what I'm watching. "It's wild, isn't it? I wonder how they found out he was going to be there. They're usually pretty discreet about their travel plans when they're on vacation."

"I'm sure his company tipped them off," I say. "They want everyone to know where he's been and that he's coming home."

I get a string of photos from the airport from him—another feet-on-top-of-luggage shot, this time in an expensive pair of Italian leather boots instead of Converse, a goofy selfie of him eating a sandwich, a shot of *Rolling Stone* on a newsstand, the cover featuring Helios, the guys all in full glam, looking seductively at the camera. But it's the last one that gets me, taken from his first class seat, hat and glasses off, gaze soft, with the caption, *Miss you already.*

I blink away tears and shove the phone into my pocket. We have not known each other long enough for this. And yet I pull the phone right back out and type back, *Miss you too. Call me when you land.*

"Can you do dinner?" I ask Amira at the end of the day, when my empty six o'clock slot—Simon's spot— rolls around. "I don't want to go home by myself."

She looks at me in surprise and gives a little nod. "Sure. Sushi?"

"I know just the place," I say.

Less than an hour later, we're seated at the bar in the same sushi restaurant I went to with Jackson—something that feels like it happened a lifetime ago—slowly eating California rolls and nigiri without conversation.

"So what happens now?" Amira asks finally, broaching the question that's been hovering unspoken in the background this whole time.

I take a moment, but I have no good answer. "Right now, it's important for Simon to be with Joon in Seoul."

"Are you in love with him?" she asks softly.

I lick wasabi-infused soy sauce from my lips. "I don't know."

But I do know. My heart teeters on the edge of that complicated emotion, waiting for something to tip it one way or another. Waiting for Simon's decision. Because once I let myself fall, I'm committed, to all that entails for good or bad.

Amira stays quiet, her usually effusive mood dimmed by the uncertainty. I nudge her. "It's not like I'm never going to see him again. He just had to cut his vacation short. True, the next few months are going to be insane for him, so I can't imagine when he'll have time for me, but . . ."

Amira laughs now. "If that's your attempt at being positive, I don't want to hear you being negative."

I'm not exactly counting down the hours of Simon's flight, but I'm not surprised when I get the message the next morning as I'm getting ready for work.

SIMON
Touchdown Seoul.

And I absolutely do not delay my departure to the studio, refreshing my Instagram, looking for the inevitable video of Simon walking through Incheon Airport. It pops up just as I'm about to leave—the idol flanked by two of his company's bodyguards, his leather duffel slung over one shoulder, looking somehow even less rumpled than he had when he left LA. He plays to the cameras, smiling, waving, throwing finger-hearts. I do not replay that video over and over just to see his face and his smile.

I am a liar.

"Did you see?" Amira asks as soon as I walk through the door of the studio.

"Yeah, he texted me when he landed." And not since, because I imagine he's been on the phone with his members or his company since the minute he climbed into his car at the airport. They'll be in a full-scale publicity press now to mitigate the effects of the scandal. "Anything new on Joon?"

"Minor fan-wars about whether or not Jae's actually gay or this was a set-up to discredit him. About half of the fans support him, whether it's true or not. Another quarter believe it and want him removed from the group. Last quarter is just unhinged and trying to track down the person who took the photo so they can doxx them."

"And which camp are you?"

Amira hesitates. "The first. I've always thought it was a possibility."

"And that doesn't bother you?"

She snorts. "Like I had a chance with him if he were straight? Honestly, I just hope he's happy and that he comes out of this okay. No one deserves this shitstorm."

I bump her with my shoulder, surprised at how protective I feel over a man I don't even like. But he's important to Simon, and via the transitive property of relationships, he's now important to me. Especially since I instinctively know this adds another layer of complication to Simon's decision.

I'm grateful that it's Thursday and I only have a handful of sessions, because my mind is focused on the phone stashed in the office and not my clients. I need to get it together. My clients are understanding, but only to a degree . . . they're paying exorbitant fees for my full attention an hour at a time, and I owe it to them to give it my best. I make it through the morning with a good semblance of focus and then Amira and I shut down the studio, leaving the now-fixed AC on for the afternoon classes. "Lunch?" I ask. "We can walk to Dorian's."

She stares at me in surprise. Dorian's is almost half a mile away, and I always suggest that we drive in case I can't make it back. But she doesn't argue, just follows me out of the building. We don't get far before she nudges me with her shoulder. "Had I known all it would take was getting you laid, I would've set you up earlier."

I shoot her a look filled with half-hearted reproof, but inwardly, I know it has nothing to do with the sex. I mean, it does, but it isn't like hooking up with a random stranger would have been the solution to my problems.

I'm feeling tired by the time we get to Dorian's, but the inside is cool and not as crowded as I expected, so we only have to wait a few minutes until two seats open up at the bar. I suppose this place is probably California fusion or something given the casual, diverse menu, but we only come here for loaded nachos and margaritas—virgin, in my case. We're halfway through both when I realize I've been so fixated on my own issues that I never asked Amira about the blond man from the club.

She just laughs, though, when I bring him up. "I don't even remember his name."

I lift my eyebrows at her.

"Oh, relax, I didn't go home with him. We drank too much, we made out a little bit, and then he passed out in the booth in the corner and his friends had to carry him out. He was cute, though, wasn't he?"

"He was," I agree, though this is just another place where Amira and I diverge. No surprise that I'm dating a guy who claims to be more monk than pop star. I don't *quite* believe that—he's way too good in bed to think he's some innocent virgin—but I also don't think he's the type to hook up with random women. Or maybe that's my own wishful thinking, my desire to think I'm special.

When we're finished with our food, I pay the bill and then we step outside into the waning sunlight. But we only make it half a block before I stop and pull out my cell phone. Amira looks at me questioningly.

"Rideshare," I explain. "I ate too much."

She doesn't need further explanation, and I'm grateful that she doesn't question it as we plop down on the edge of a planter and watch the little icon move across the map as our ride approaches. But it's only after we climb into the backseat of the car that she looks at me. "You never would have done that before."

"Call a rideshare? I use them all the time."

"Call a rideshare without being embarrassed and apologizing up and down."

I blink. She's right. My usual wash of shame over my inability to walk half a mile back to the studio is completely absent. "I guess I don't think there's anything to be embarrassed about."

She nudges me with her shoulder. "That's exactly right."

But her proud expression gives me far too much credit. When Amira drops me off at my apartment, I stretch out on my sofa and check my phone, hoping for something from Simon. Nothing. Then again, it's early morning in Seoul, and I hope that he's actually getting some sleep and not sitting up all night hashing out strategy with Helios's management team. I putter on my phone for the next several hours—which really means watching video after video of Simon and Joon and the rest of the members, collectively and apart, even though my eye immediately goes to Simon in any group situation. Finally, a little after 6:00 p.m. when I'm heating up a natural frozen meal—more for something to do than any real hunger—my phone beeps.

It's a selfie in front of Simon's bathroom mirror. He's wearing a dress shirt and slacks, his hair done and his face free of makeup. Clearly going into the office rather than to an official schedule.

SIMON
Headed to work. Wish me
luck.

I type my reply multiple times and delete it before I finally settle on the only thing that feels appropriate.

TRINA
화이팅

He replies with a blowing kiss emoji.

I sigh and retrieve my food from the microwave, even though between my regular eating issues and the sudden nervous twist of my stomach, I know I won't be able to force down more than a few bites. This isn't my scandal, my decision, but I'm self-aware enough to know I'm too invested in my relationship with Simon to not worry about what it might mean for me. For us.

And yet for the next six hours, I hear absolutely nothing. I crawl into bed with my phone, turn on the same K-drama episode I've now unsuccessfully watched three times, and keep one eye on my message notifications. It's after 1:00 a.m. when I finally get tired enough to sleep, and I'm plagued with restless dreams that I can't remember.

Maybe my subconscious was onto something, because when I wake up, there's a text message waiting.

SIMON
Call me when you wake up.
Don't worry what time it is.
I'll be up.

A wash of dread rushes over me. Because even without knowing what happened in his meeting today, I know I'm not going to like what comes next.

chapter thirty

I delay the inevitable by taking a shower, doing my hair, and getting dressed for my day before I finally summon the courage to press the *call* button. It only rings twice before Simon picks up, and when he does, there's audible relief in his voice. "Katrina."

"Simon." The dread slips away, replaced only by a sense of relief that I can't quite explain. "Are you okay? Is Joon okay?"

"It's a mess," he says wearily. I hear rustling in the background and the sound of a door closing, and I sense that he's changing locations. I suddenly realize he might still be in the office and not at home. "Joon finally convinced the company not to put out a statement about the photo, said if they acknowledged it, it would just be feeding into the drama. But really, I think he didn't want to publicly deny his relationship with Dohyun. Joon loves him. He doesn't want to do that to him."

I can understand that, but it's still a bold move. Surely Joon's boyfriend would understand why it's necessary to do damage control, whether the statement is true or not. Then again, if it were my relationship with Simon that was outed, how would I feel if his company put out a statement that I was nothing to him? No, Joon is doing a courageous thing, accepting the risk to his career in order to save someone he loves pain. My respect for him rises a notch. I might not exactly like the man, but I can't deny that he has principles.

"So what now?"

The long pause that comes next brings the jitters back to my stomach. "I don't really have any choice."

"Simon—"

"I already agreed. I'm signing the contract extension. I owe him, Katrina."

My head falls forward and my voice catches in my throat before it can be released. "What does that mean then? For your plans here in California? The indie label? Me?"

He sucks in a breath. "I hadn't made any commitments to the label. I'll have to put that off. Obviously, I'm scheduled heavily until the end of the year, and we'll be starting work on our next comeback right away. But I'll have some time in December. I was thinking maybe I could fly you to Seoul right after Christmas and we could spend the week together before I have to get back to work."

It's tempting, so very tempting that I have to stop myself from saying *okay* right now. "And after that?"

The hesitation tells me what I need to know before he says the words. "I'm not sure what it will look like. We should get a short break in February or March before we start shooting videos and promos. We're doing an Asia encore tour, but that won't be for more than a couple of weeks in the early fall."

"So, I'll get to see you in December and maybe in February or March and then . . . October?"

Simon lets out a long breath. "Yeah. Something like that."

I stare up at the ceiling, studying the pattern on the plaster. In some ways, what would it matter? It isn't as if I do much besides work and sleep anyway. We started out with a long-distance correspondence via messenger and text, and I was the happiest I've been in ages.

But that was before. That was before Simon showed me what I've been missing by living my life so small. How little I demand for myself. And this might be the happiest I've been in years, but am I really going to waste more time sitting around and hoping for some slim possibility of a future with Simon? What happens when he gets talked into signing another contract extension? And another? Am I going to wait for a man who will continually put his career first, his group first? I may be able to understand why he feels he needs to do it now, but what's to say that will ever change?

"Katrina, are you still there?"

I draw in a long, deep breath and let it out as slowly and silently as I can. "I need to think about it."

"Okay," he said quietly. "I just thought—"

"You're asking me to put my life on hold for you, Simon."

"I'm not. You know I'm not."

"So I'm free to date? To sleep with other guys?"

A beat before he answers. "Of course."

I shake my head at the choked sound of his voice. He may say that, but he could never deal with it. Just knowing there's a possibility of another man in my bed would tear him apart. Pop-star persona aside, Simon is traditional at his core. "You don't believe that any more than I do. You're asking me to wait for you with no guarantee you're ever going to come back. After knowing each other for a couple of weeks."

"I know." His voice sounds small, shamed. "But I care about you. Believe that I do. This wasn't just . . . a way to pass the time."

"I know it wasn't. And it wasn't for me either."

"Katrina, please. I don't want to lose you."

I press my fingertips against the sting of tears in my eyes. I knew this might happen, I knew this was only short term, and yet I let myself be sucked in anyway. I let myself ignore all the reasons why this probably wouldn't work. I even believed, somewhere deep inside, that what I could offer would be enough—combined with the lure of a new independent life in California— to make him stay. And now faced with the truth, all I feel is my own foolishness and a gaping emptiness in my middle.

I have to say it, even though I know what the result will be. "Simon. I was never yours to keep."

Now it's his turn to let the silence stretch, and I swipe away the swell of tears beneath my lower lashes while I wait for his response.

"I see," he whispers finally. "I . . . I guess you're right. Thank you for . . . everything. Know that I only wish you well."

And before I can give into the impulse to take it all back, to try to make this work no matter the cost, he ends the call.

The call screen disappears from my phone, defaulting back to the wallpaper of us in front of the Pismo Beach sign, and it's that photo and the deliriously happy look on my face that does me in. I crumple around myself like I've been punched in the gut and sob as if my heart is breaking.

But that's ridiculous. Because my heart broke a long time ago, and all Simon did was give me one small piece of it back.

● ● ●

I'm relieved when I arrive at the studio and find it dark and locked. I'm not sure that I can face Amira so soon, while I'm still trying to get a handle on my emotions. I stayed so long, frozen and staring at that stupid, gloriously happy photo of Simon and me that it was only the prospect of being late for my first client that got me up and out the door.

Now, I move through the space automatically, unlocking doors, flipping on lights and air conditioning, checking voice mail messages. I have just enough time to take a five minute stretch on the barre before my first Friday client walks in. For once, I'm grateful it's another heavy day, because the constant stream of clients into the studio gives me something to focus on other than the knot in my middle, the gaping spot where happiness resided just days before.

Amira cruises through the door just before noon with a paper sack in her hands, no doubt our lunch, and gives me a surreptitious wave before disappearing into the office. I steel myself and turn back to my client, correcting his form on the ladder barrel, even though my stomach churns with dread. It's that dread that makes me putter around the studio even after he leaves, straightening up things that don't need to be straightened and pushing a mop around the space.

But finally, I can't delay the inevitable any longer. I walk through the door of the office. "Dare I guess that's lunch?"

"I got bibimbap from that place you like," Amira says, handing me a paper bowl. "Gochujang on the side."

I force a smile, even though the words are like a hammer's blow. "Thanks. I appreciate it."

Amira doesn't buy it. She narrows her eyes at me. "What's wrong?"

I slump down into the chair in front of the desk and pop off the lid to the bowl, but the smell of kimchi turns my stomach. "I spoke to Simon this morning."

Amira's expression turns wary. "And?"

"He's decided to renew his contract with Helios. He felt like it was the only way he could show his support to Joon."

She nods slowly. "I can see that. The press has been vicious, and the company still hasn't issued a statement."

"Nor will they. Joon refuses to throw Dohyun under the bus."

"Wow. I have to say, that ups my respect of the guy a few notches, and I say that as a fan who thinks he can do no wrong." She studies me closely, and I must be doing a better job of hiding my feelings than I think, because her brow barely furrows. "What does that mean for you and Simon?"

"It means nothing. Simon and I aren't together. We never were." I snap apart the disposable chopsticks and dig into my rice for something to do, a reason not to look her in the face.

"Trina . . ."

"Listen, I knew it had to end at some point. It was fun. He's a good guy and I don't regret anything that happened at all. Besides, how many girls can say—even if they can't really say—that they had a wild fling with an idol? I'm just not willing to be his beck-and-call girl."

I know that neither my flippancy nor my movie reference lands when Amira just shifts a look full of sympathy at me. "I'm sorry, Trina. I really wish it turned out differently."

I lever another bite of rice into my mouth. "Thanks. You did try to warn me."

"That doesn't mean I wanted to be right."

I shoot her as much of a smile as I can manage, grateful that she's going to let it rest. I only eat a few more bites—I know that today's stress already makes the chance of an episode higher than usual without adding my wonky digestion to the mix. Then I snap the lid back onto the bowl, hand it to Amira to put in the mini-fridge behind the desk, and grab my toothbrush from my duffel bag to freshen up before my next client.

And if I have to fake my way through the rest of my day, plastering a pleasant, untroubled expression on my face, it's hardly worth mentioning. I've been trained to hide my real feelings my entire life.

chapter thirty-one

I would like to say that now that my decision is made, I move on seamlessly with my life, having learned an important lesson about how I have undervalued myself and allowed my condition to dictate too much of my fate. But I would be lying.

No, instead, I spend the next couple of weeks wallowing in misery and self-pity.

But even that's not entirely true. I show up to work and give my all, trying to transmute that constant ache in my heart into energy to help my clients meet their goals. They seem pleasantly surprised at how wholeheartedly I throw myself into their training, making suggestions about where we should go next and how they can cross-train for better effects. By all external markers, I'm doing just fine.

But Amira knows different. There isn't an afternoon that passes that she doesn't invite me over for dinner or out to grab a mocktail after work, not wanting me to go home alone. Sometimes—and I surprise myself with how often it is—I accept. Other times, I beg off, citing the need to rest, assuring her that I'm fine alone.

She doesn't need to know that any time I'm alone, I'm following the Helios scandal for new crumbs of information, combing social media for some clue about what's happening inside. That's ridiculous, of course, especially since I could get the actual, accurate and un-filtered news if I were just willing to pick up the phone. But instead, I spend all my time on social media trying to get a sense for how public opinion has shifted.

As always, it's a mixed bag. There are plenty of fans in the LGBTQ+ community excited to see representation within one of their favorite groups, and the fan edits and speculations have already blown up social media. It's only now that I learn that Jae and Seojun are a popular ship and that there's an ocean of romantic fan fiction about the two of them; apparently, with the revelation of Jae's relationship, their enthusiastic writers have now shifted to angst and poly relationships.

Then there are the ones leaving hateful comments under Helios's posts and videos, denouncing Jae and claiming to have burned all their CDs and merch in protest. (Somehow I doubt that—I know how much all that stuff costs.) Between the extremes is the middle ground, the Hellions trying to calm everyone down but often starting fights between the two factions instead. I can only imagine Joon and Simon watching this go down, helpless to speak out about it however much they might want to. There's no good way to handle this but to stay out of the limelight and wait for the furor to die down on its own.

It reminds me so much of my old experiences that after a few weeks, it becomes difficult to follow without anxiety swelling in my chest, and I delete social media from my phone so I won't constantly doomscroll.

And yet without that distraction, I'm aware of how empty my days feel. Yes, my schedule is packed. Yes, I'm still working on my presentation for the Pilates conference. And Amira and I spend far more time together than we ever did before, something I can tell alternately pleases and worries her. It takes me another month of following this same unvarying schedule for me to realize the truth.

It's not that my life feels empty. It's that it feels meaningless. I've been working to build this new life for five years since I retired from dance, and up until now I've thought it's enough. I'm using what I'm good at. I'm using my contacts. I'm making a difference to the performers I work with, making it easier and safer for them to go out in the world and create their art. Even now, when I think about my part in that, I feel nothing but pride and satisfaction. I've built something special and important out of the wreckage of my former existence.

It's simply that spending time with Simon, seeing how much he loves his career, as difficult as it is, has shown me how little my heart is actually in this. Doing the next logical step, making the best out of things isn't the same as loving what you do.

I'm now not sure that I even know what that feels like. There were things that I loved about dancing—I enjoyed performing, I thrived on the energy I received from the audience. But was that because I loved dance? Or was it because that was the only time I was ever seen, acknowledged?

Simon *saw* me. All of me, bad and good, and showed me that person was worth loving.

And now that I've experienced that, I'm not sure I can go back.

But these aren't thoughts that I can say out loud to Amira. She's sacrificed a lot to build this business with me, and it's not something I can just walk away from. It wouldn't run nearly as well without her, but it wouldn't exist without me. If I change course now, it means she has to start over from scratch at the age of thirty.

No, I'm in this, whether I like it or not. So I give my all every day in the studio. I make sure I eat as well as I can, take my vitamins and supplements, rest enough. By all exterior indications, I've bounced back from a minor disappointment.

Until one morning I walk into the studio to find Amira waiting for me with an odd look on her face, her phone clutched in one hand. I stop just inside the door, the chime still hanging on the air. "What is it? What happened?"

She just holds out the phone to me.

I take it and frown at the screen. It's a photo of Helios, the five of them on stage, dressed in leather and satin and a lot of BDSM-inspired straps.

No, scratch that. Not the five of them. *Four* of them.

I look up at Amira in alarm. "What was this from?"

"Fan meeting in Seoul today. The company put out a statement that they regretted Seojun would be unable to perform and they would update with more information at a later time."

My stomach drops into my feet at the cold crawl of dread down the back of my neck. I know what she's saying. I've seen enough of these statements to read between the lines. Typically, Titan Entertainment over-explains to a laughable degree, attempting to put fans' fears to rest. This is shockingly light on the details. Does Simon have a cold? Was he in a car accident? Or is he in the hospital being treated for some terrible virus? It could be any of those, and the lack of specificity tells me that it's bad enough they'd rather cause speculative panic than actually give the real story.

My own phone is out and in my hand before I even

think about it. I don't even bother with text. I find Simon's number and press call. Never mind the fact that it's 10:30 at night in Seoul right now. I'm not going to be able to breathe until I hear his voice.

Except the phone goes straight to voice mail, which means it's off or dead.

I swallow hard and tap out a message.

TRINA
Simon, is everything okay?
Please just let me know. I'm
worried about you.

And then I'm scrolling through Instagram, hoping that someone might have more information. It's not until Amira pries my phone from my hand do I realize that I'm shaking and there are tears running down my face.

She takes me by the shoulders and gently forces me look at her. "Trina, this isn't just worry about Simon being injured. What's going on here?"

I lift my eyes to her and blink through my tears. Somehow the question slows my panic, and I suck in a long breath. "Tell me he's alive, Amira."

Her eyes widen in surprise. "Of course he's alive. He's probably either injured or sick and they don't know if he's going to perform for the rest of the fan meeting." Her hands tighten on me. "Please, Trina, what's going on?"

I swallow down my panic and focus on her eyes. "Did I ever tell you that I used to have a sister?"

chapter thirty-two

February 2020, New York City

Philip is gone in the morning, and I'm glad. I need time to gather myself and prepare for a day in the studio, pretending that everything is fine and that my world isn't collapsing around me. I feel like everything that I've been trying to ignore, all the ways I've been lying to myself, are rushing in now, making me realize how stupid I've been.

He is not a good man.

And yet my trajectory in this company is inexplicably linked to Philip's. I am his muse. He's the reason I've gotten the opportunities that I have here. And if I break up with him now, those might dry up. I've done far too little of value for the director of the company and linked myself far too strongly to a single man. Breaking up with him essentially means I would have to move companies, and I'm not entirely sure that's realistic. I've been trained, groomed, molded into a particular style—not bravura, not hummingbird-quick. My style is best suited for European companies like the Paris Opera, but I'm not delusional enough to believe they'd take a look at me for anything but a guest artist slot to dance a Barbier ballet.

I am stuck here.

But I'm not sure you understand what's required to keep it.

I have the fleeting thought that no matter how humiliating it would be, Janine might help me, give me advice. She cared enough to warn me, to tell me what was going on behind my back. It's not like she's going to be able to dig me out of this hole that I've made, but she knows the dynamics of this company better than I do. She would at least know what the chances of me keeping my job once I break up with Philip are.

Once I break up with Philip. It's the first time I've put it into words, and it fills me simultaneously with terror and the wild hope of freedom.

I shower again for no other reason than the unreasonable feeling I can wash away my doubts with scalding hot water, get dressed, make myself a smoothie that I know I'm not going to be able to finish. I pack my lunch for the day, shove it into my dance bag, and walk out the door, my heart fluttering in my chest. Now that the thought has taken root, it's all I can think about. My exit.

The looks are less speculative when I move through the company's space. I stop by the call board in the hallway to look at the posted cast changes—Maddie has been removed from all but six performances. The realization of how this is going to hit her smashes that fragile hope in my chest and replaces it only with pain. I wish now I was more kind the last time we talked. Yes, she was out of line, but can I really blame her? It has to be torture to have everything just within your grasp, but not quite be able to reach it. Worse yet to know that your older sister who doesn't even want it has had it all handed to her so easily.

The thought stuns me, and I stumble over it in the carpeted hallway.

I don't want it.

I have to try on the thought to ascertain its truth. What would happen if I just walked away? What would happen if I broke up with Philip and got kicked back to corps de ballet roles? Do I love dancing enough that I would be happy to remain?

Or would I just quit, turn down my next contract renewal, and walk away from everything related to my ballet career?

My heart beats frantically with the realization that it might not just be Philip I could leave behind.

And yet, as I warm up in the main studio minutes later, I know there are things that I love about this world. I love the predictability. I love knowing I belong. I like the feeling of pushing my body to its limits, of accomplishing something difficult that most people can't. I like the music, I like the discipline, I like the incremental gains that show that I'm making progress. I like being able to express my feelings through my body, and I love the response I get from the audience when they feel those things as strongly as I do.

But is it impossible to believe that I might be able to find those things elsewhere?

My focus is turned so inward that it's not until the ballet mistress, Diana, enters the studio to start company class that I notice Maddie's space at the barre is empty. Technically, company class is not a requirement in the same way that rehearsal is, though it's rarer than rare for a dancer to skip it. It's what allows us to maintain our baseline classical technique and fitness, especially when we might be spending our rehearsal time in contemporary movements. Did Maddie decide to skip in order to save herself the humiliation of checking the cast board? It wasn't what I had in mind when I texted her, but I suppose I can't blame her if she did.

Between barre and center, when most of the women are putting on their pointe shoes, I pull out my phone and quickly text her: *Is everything okay? Why aren't you in class?*

I leave the phone on the floor next to me while I stretch—I'm still not doing pointe in company class—but Maddie doesn't respond before it's time to start tendus in the center. I shove the phone back into my bag and the bag back under the barre before I take my place in the left front section of the studio.

I perform terribly in class, falling out of pirouettes and forgetting the combinations. I don't really care. My mind is pulled into too many directions to really be concentrating on my technique today. I barely notice the knowing looks exchanged between the cattier members of the company, as if they're witnessing something they've been waiting for. Like I've finally crashed and burned.

I shove all my stuff into my bag as quickly as possible so I can accost Delaney, Maddie's roommate, before she leaves the room. "Why isn't Maddie here today? Is she sick? Did she decide to skip because of my text?"

Delaney's brow furrows. "I don't know. Her door was closed when I left. I thought she would already be at the studio. She's been leaving early to work out before class."

"Well, she's not answering her texts."

The look Delaney gives me makes me think there's probably a reason for that; I'm not all that surprised that Maddie doesn't want to talk to me. But she still pulls out her phone and dials. I can see her confusion deepening into worry the longer the phone rings. "She's not picking up," she says slowly. "Do you think we should—"

"Yes," I say immediately. "I have some time before my first rehearsal. Do you?"

"I'm not on the schedule until four." She meets my eyes as we make the decision simultaneously.

I quell the nervousness in my stomach as we change into street clothes, shove our things into lockers in the dressing room, and get ready to leave the studio again. It's only about twenty minutes to their apartment and back, so I should have plenty of time, but still I bounce between worry and annoyance that she's making me go after her. She's probably pouting or sulking or crying—she hasn't exactly handled a lot of the last year or two with professionalism. And then I instantly feel guilty for those thoughts. She was just been more or less removed from a major role after a scathing review; if I were in her place, I'd probably want to hide out too.

I wouldn't *do* it, but I'd want to.

Delaney and I don't have much to talk about as we traverse the city streets to the subway and then ride the train to the stop nearest their apartment. Twenty-five minutes later, we're entering a brick, five-story walk-up, the younger woman already fumbling keys out of her pocket to open their apartment.

My heart plummets into my stomach at the stillness inside. Maddie isn't huddled on the sofa with her blanket and the cat like I expected her to be, ready to scold us for being stupid enough to worry about her. Instead, the place sounds and feels completely empty.

And then I hear a faint meow from somewhere in the apartment.

Delaney and I exchange a look, and I follow the sound to Maddie's door. I knock on the door. "Maddie? It's Kat and Delaney. Can we come in?"

I expect Maddie's angry voice, but all I hear is a frantic scrabbling on the other side of the door. Misha. I don't hesitate. I grasp the door handle. Locked.

"Do you have a screwdriver? A small one?"

"I think so?" Delaney hurries off, and I go back to pounding on the door.

"Maddie, open up please. We're worried about you."

Delaney reappears with a small plastic toolbox in her hand. I open it on the floor and select a small skinny screwdriver, then insert it into the hole in the doorknob. The privacy lock pops open easily—thank god for a cheap modern replacement and not the original pre-war hardware. I toss the screwdriver back into the toolbox and twist the knob, but still I enter quietly, tentatively.

"Maddie?" I whisper. The minute the door opens wide enough, Misha shoots off like a rocket, disappearing into the far reaches of the apartment. My heart rises into my throat when I open the door wide enough to see the motionless shape beneath the blankets in Maddie's bed.

"Sweetheart, are you sick? Are you okay?" I slowly approach the bed, my eyes flicking between her back, turned toward me, and the nightstand beside her. An orange plastic pill bottle sits there, neatly capped and standing next to a half-full bottle of vodka. Guilt strikes me with each step. This is because of my message last night. She got drunk and crashed out and missed class.

"Time to wake up, sweetie," I say, fondness creeping into my voice despite myself. "You know you can't hold your liquor. This is gonna be an epic hangover."

I reach out to shake her, but the minute I touch her, I know something is wrong. Gooseflesh rises on my arms; the hairs on the back of my neck spring up. "Maddie?" I whisper.

Delaney's quavering voice comes from the door. "Is she . . ."

In an instant, I'm around the bed and on my knees, gripping Maddie and shaking her. "Maddie, wake up. Maddie, sweetheart, you need to wake up."

Except I know she's not sleeping, because she

doesn't loll back on the bed or spring to alertness like I expect. She's rigid, fixed, her eyes closed and unmoving, her chest still. Like a doll.

I scramble away from her, and my tailbone hits the wood floor with a thud. I don't recognize the sounds that escape my mouth, the ragged wail that rips out of me between my frantic breaths.

It's Delaney's quiet crying from the doorway that brings me back to the present. "Call 911," I say hoarsely between sobs.

"Is she . . ." Delaney struggles to get the words out.

I can't take my eyes from the lifeless form of my sister, almost as if I'm still expecting her to wake up, to tell me that it serves me right, that I needed a lesson. And yet she just lies there, a discarded porcelain figurine, the life escaped from her body.

And I know, without a doubt, that I'm responsible.

chapter thirty-three

Amira cancels my morning sessions. I don't even try to protest. I'm lost in memories, huddled in the chair in the corner of our office, wrapped in Amira's sweatshirt, trembling. It's like everything I've been keeping a secret for the past five years was the only thing holding me together, and now that I've spilled it, I'm just a pile of disconnected bone, muscle, and nerves. I could sooner teleport myself back home than I could gather myself enough to stand up from this chair.

And yet I'm sorry for what I've just dumped on Amira. I can see by her horrified expression that she has no idea how to deal with the fact that I found my own sister dead in her apartment. Even worse, we both know it was my fault, that I'll never be able to forgive myself for letting Maddie down. She might have been selfish at times, she might not have understood how much I gave up for her, but she was my little sister. That was her privilege. She never should have had to pay the price for my career.

I sit there while Amira closes up the studio, and I follow numbly when she pries me up from the chair and shepherds me out to her car. By the time we park in front of my apartment building, I've come back to myself enough to say, "You don't have to come up. I'll be okay."

Amira stares at me like I'm utterly mad. "Of course I'm coming up."

I don't have the energy to resist, nor do I really want to. Somewhere in the back of my mind, I'm worried that if there's not someone to anchor me, I might just float away, never to return. It's an illogical thought, and it amuses me that I'm logical enough to realize that it's an illogical thought. I smile, and Amira shoots me a look that feels remarkably like terror.

"I'm okay," I tell her, but we both know that's not the truth.

Amira is treating me like I've had another syncope episode, holding my arm as I go up the stairs, supporting my weight. But I don't need it. My body is functioning just fine; it's my mind that has decided to take a temporary vacation. Inside, she settles me on the sofa with a blanket and then hustles off to the kitchen to make me a cup of herbal tea. When she returns, she presses the mug into my hands and huddles at the end of the chaise, staring at me.

"I don't know how to help you," she whispers. "Is there anyone I can call?"

"You can find Simon," I say, but we both know that I've done everything that can be done on that front. If I had Joon's number, I would call him and he'd probably answer, but we never really reached that level of comfort, Simon and I, where we exchanged emergency numbers. Besides, with the way we parted, there was the unspoken understanding that we would not be communicating any further.

Amira pries the phone out of my hand and taps on

it for a few seconds before she sets it aside on the coffee table. "What can I do for you, hon?"

"You can leave," I say quietly. "I love you, but I just want to be alone."

Amira hesitates.

"I'm not going to kill myself," I say, my voice stronger than it feels. "If I were going to do that, I would have done it a long time ago. I just need some time alone with my thoughts, without worrying about you too."

"Okay," she says quietly, rising from the sofa. "But if you need me, you call me. No question. I will be here in twenty minutes. Promise me."

"I promise," I say, though we both know that I'm lying.

As soon as Amira leaves, I lock the door behind her and then take my untouched tea and set it in the sink. Then I wander into my bedroom, taking my phone with me, and crawl into bed, where I open YouTube.

It's not Helios that I search out, but *Madeline Barbas, New York Theater Ballet.* I scroll down until I find the video clip I'm looking for, the ill-fated Bluebird from the opening night of *Sleeping Beauty*. I've never watched these performances; in fact, I never rewatched my performances at all. I know some dancers like to review their clips, but it's always been the ephemeral nature of ballet that I love, the idea that every performance is a little different.

So I don't know what to expect from the video when I cue it up, having only my memory of six years ago to work from. I remember being so proud as I watched from the wings, marveling at how well she pulled it off. And I remember how angry I was at the criticism the next day, even though it was that argument that put the final nail in the coffin of my relationship with Maddie.

And yet as I watch it, somewhat detached and

dispassionate, I have to be truthful with myself. It's . . . not great. She was magnetic because her personality showed through in everything she did—she was a dancer who gave her all on stage, who poured her soul out through the steps. But if I'm being honest now, her technique was sloppy, unformed.

Not only was the reviewer correct, but even I can see now that she should never have been cast.

Somehow the realization hits me even harder than it might have back then. Philip was a terrible person, but I have to believe that he actually did care about me at one point. And now I wonder if he cast her as a favor to me, one I never asked for but which he gave all the same. Perhaps he saw that same magnetic quality and thought she would rise to the challenge; perhaps it was straight-up bias. I'll probably never know, and I'm not going to approach Philip just to satisfy my curiosity.

But now that I've seen it, I can't go back. It *was* all my fault. Not in the way that Maddie seemed to think— I wasn't eclipsing her and taking the focus from her; for all her talent she was never going to be a principal dancer. But because she *did* rise higher in the company than her talent could support, and she knew it. She felt that weight of knowing she was only there because of me, that what I said was true.

Yes, Maddie had made the decision to take her own life—or at least make the decisions that led to her death; I still don't know if the overdose was intentional or accidental—but no one could question that I helped pave the way. When my parents asked me to give up everything for her, I should have said no. I should have said that if she had the talent and the drive, she could do it on her own. I should have said that my own dreams were as important as hers. I should have let Maddie have the satisfaction of knowing that succeed or fail, at least she'd done it on her own efforts and her own talents.

It's the reason I reacted so strongly to the idea of Simon sacrificing what he wanted to do for his friend and older brother; not because I related to Simon but because I know what it feels like to see someone you're supposed to protect suffer. And I know what the cost is on the other end of that sacrifice.

Almost as if there's some sort of cosmic tie between us, a message preview flashes up on my phone, and my heart rises into my throat. Simon.

His reply is perfunctory, but it's unquestionably him.

SIMON
Injured in rehearsal,
couldn't perform today. In
hospital but ok. More later.

Relief slams into me with the force of a sledge-hammer, cracking the last bit of control that I've maintained over my emotions. My sob bursts out of me like the cry of an injured animal, and the tears keep coming in gulps and bursts as my body rejects every last bit of pain that I've carried. Somewhere in the back of my mind, I'm glad I made Amira leave because I don't want her to see me like this, unraveled, inarticulate sounds pouring out with my pain.

I'm sorry, I think over and over as I cry with the ragged abandon of a broken heart. *I'm sorry.*

But I'm not sure if the words are meant for Maddie, Simon, or myself.

* * *

I float in a half-conscious state for the rest of the day, only moving from my spot in bed to use the bathroom and refill my water cup. Food is the last thing on my mind; my stomach wouldn't take it anyway. Instead, I exist in an endless cycle: nap, cry, scroll YouTube. Now that I've watched the Bluebird performance that I've been avoiding, I find myself seeking out every video of Maddie that I can find. I don't know whether I'm looking for evidence to support or refute my conclusion, but it doesn't matter. At some point, I stop watching the videos as a dancer and start looking at them as her sister.

Maddie is . . . was . . . beautiful. Magnetic. Joyful. I remember the fun that we had in New York, before my burgeoning career began to drive a wedge into our relationship. We explored Manhattan, from the tourist traps to the locals' recommendations, reveling in our freedom. We thought ourselves so grown up, still in our teens, still with our enthusiasm born of naivete. We made it to the New York Theater Ballet. Nothing could stop us from reaching the top together. Every time I think I've exhausted my tears, I summon more from the capped well of my grief, until my eyes are so swollen that I can barely see the screen.

Still, I watch.

Amira texts me every couple of hours, and I ignore them until she threatens to come over and check on me herself.

TRINA
I'm fine. Reminiscing.

Fifteen minutes later, my doorbell rings. I ignore it, not budging from my bed until a follow-up message comes from Amira.

AMIRA
Food at the door. Go get it.
I mean it.

Shame washes over me, but there's an underlying warmth that comes with it. I'm not the easiest person to be friends with, but Amira never gives up on me, never stops taking care of me. I peel myself out of bed and stumble to my door, outside which sits a soggy paper bag. Carefully, I bring it inside and find a quart of wor wonton soup from my favorite Chinese restaurant. This is one of my sick meals, one of the few things my stomach can handle when it's acting up, and tears prick my eyes again, stinging my already swollen eyelids.

I pour the entire thing into a salad bowl and take it back to my bed with a spoon, where I eat it very slowly with my phone propped up on my knees in front of me. After a few minutes, I come to my senses and text Amira.

TRINA
Thanks for the soup.

I get a smiley face emoji back and nothing else.

And then, late that night, pushing eleven o'clock, my phone rings. I blink at the contact card that flashes onto the screen, sure that I'm hallucinating it. Simon.

I surprise myself with how long I hesitate to pick up the call, but at last I hit the green button and raise the handset to my ear. "Hello?"

"Hey, Katrina. Am I calling too late?"

Simon's deep, familiar voice washes over me, making my heart clench in my chest. "No," I croak out. "I was awake."

His tone shifts to alarm. "What's wrong?"

I give a hoarse laugh. "You're asking me what's wrong and you're in the hospital?"

"I'm fine," he says. "Everyone goes to the hospital for everything in Korea. I'm being discharged later today."

"What happened?" I'm running on autopilot, letting my mouth bypass my heart, which is screaming out things like *I miss you. I'm sorry. Don't leave me behind.* "You said you hurt yourself in rehearsal. Is it your back?"

"No." His low laugh hits me in the chest and spreads outwards. "You did your work too well. My back is feeling pretty good, actually. It was my ankle. I landed wrong in rehearsal. X-rays show it's only a sprain, but I'm going to be out for a few weeks."

"I'm so sorry," I say sincerely. I don't remember their comeback schedule exactly, but I know that's going to throw a kink into their performance plans.

"It's okay," he says quietly. "I feel like I need the time."

I freeze, my heart rising into my throat. This is already a surreal conversation considering I expected to never speak to him again. My voice sounds distant to me when I ask, "Why is that?"

He falls silent for a moment. He has to clear his throat before he speaks, but even then, his voice is husky, choked. "I miss you. I hate the way we ended things. I . . . I don't want to be here."

I close my eyes and harden myself against the swell of hope that rises in my chest. "Then why are you?"

"You know why," he says.

I can hear the misery in his voice, and it makes me ache for him. I know how he feels. I warned him about this when he was considering the impact of staying or leaving. I know the pull of that obligation and the pain of knowing you can't follow your heart without damaging someone you love. The brutal likelihood that no matter which decision you make, someone's getting hurt.

"I can't tell you what to do," I whisper into the phone.

"But . . ." He clears his throat. "Please. Just say what you feel. If I knew you—"

I have to stop him, even though my heart is throbbing in my chest so hard I feel like I need to call an ambulance. There's nothing I want more than for him to choose me. To choose a new life, a chance for us. But I can't let him finish that sentence.

"You can't make this decision for me," I whisper. "Because if we don't work out, if this was just a . . . a temporary thing . . . you'll always resent me. You'll always be angry at yourself for letting down your family—your real family—over a woman. I don't want you to have any regrets. And if I'm the only tipping point in this decision, then I'm not sure it's the right one."

I hear muffled sounds on the other end of the line and my breath catches. Is he . . . crying? I'll never know, because when he finally speaks again, his voice is steady and sad. "You're right. I know you're right. I just . . . Katrina, I fucking hate it. I hate it all so much."

"I know," I murmur, forcing words out around the knot in my throat. "I do too."

"Can I still call you?" he asks hopefully.

It kills me to answer, but I do it anyway. "If you're going to stay in Korea indefinitely, I don't think that's a good idea. I . . . I don't think I can handle it."

"I wish I could tell you what I'm going to do," he whispers. "All I can tell you is that I'm committed here for a year."

"Then," I say slowly, as gently as I can, "the decision has probably been made. I wish you the world, Simon, I truly do. And I'm so grateful I got to be in yours for a little while."

"Katrina," he breathes, but I can't stay on the line

because we both know that no matter how much it hurts, the lines have been drawn between us. We've made our choices on what we can bear. He can't let down his best friend and mentor. I can't hinge my future on the decisions of a man who will put his career first, however altruistic those reasons might be.

"Goodbye, Simon," I say, then click off the line. And before I can talk myself out of it, I press *block*.

chapter thirty-four

If this were a story, the closure with Simon would give me a new lease on life, a melancholy but hopeful view of the future. The reality is nothing like that.

I cry. For days. I cancel all my sessions for the week and weep until my eyes and throat are raw and every new round of tears makes me want to throw up the very little food I manage to ingest. It's not just the situation with Simon. It's that the past few months have stripped away all the barriers that I've erected my whole life, and without them, I have nothing to buffer me from the flood of feelings.

Over the weeks that follow, I have to face the fact that I gave up what I really wanted in life for my sister, but my ambition to make something out of it killed her. That my relationship with Philip might have been consensual, but it was still abusive and inappropriate and my view on relationships will probably always be affected to some degree. And I have to admit to myself, finally, that my career was over before COVID shut the theaters and took away my ability to perform. That Maddie, however twisted and battered our relationship had become, was my reason for dancing. Without her, I would never have been able to continue on.

It was far easier to mourn my career than my sister.

I recognize now that my business was built the same way, out of the feeling that I had no other choices, but I also recognize how lucky I am to be working with my favorite person on the planet. Without Amira, I couldn't get through this. Some days, I think she's turning out to be the love of my life—even if it's in a distinctly un-romantic way—and I regret how long I've spent keeping her at arms' length.

"You should write a book," Amira says one Saturday in November when we're huddled on my sofa beneath one large blanket, sipping hot cocoa. The weather has finally broken into fall after a long, hot, prolonged summer and has gone straight into a damp cold that sinks into my bones and makes my ballet-scarred body creak in every joint.

"Write a book about what? Like, a novel?" I shake my head. As it turns out, I'm not such a bad speech writer, but I've never really thought I have the imagination to write stories.

"No," she says slowly, "About your experiences. About dance. About Maddie."

I frown at her. "Who would read something like that?"

"A lot of people. You had over a million followers on your ballet account at the height of your career. You haven't been forgotten. Your name comes up in hushed tones any time they stage a Barbier ballet."

I manage to repress my flinch at Philip's name—it's getting easier these days after spilling every detail to Amira, however horrified she might have been to hear them—but I still shake my head. "Just because I originated those roles doesn't mean anyone cares."

She pulls out her phone, taps around a little bit, and

then shoves it at me. "Six thousand comments seem to disagree."

I take the phone with a frown. She's pulled up a YouTube video of a performance of *Intersections*, which ironically, has just been restaged at the Paris Opera Ballet. I expect rave reviews of the ballerina who performed my role, which there are, but as I scroll down the comments section, I'm shocked to see how many are some variety of *Nice, but doesn't compare to the original.* People talking about how Katrina Barbas brought a freshness to the role that hasn't been seen since. How it was my technique combined with a complete lack of guile that made the ballet so magical.

I can't disagree. I was too young and clueless to know what the ballet world was about, to understand that men like Philip clutched at the youth and naivete of women like me to salve their own insecurities. The ballet wasn't about the triumph of love over life; I should have known from the last step, where my partner leaves me hanging in mid-air, frozen in the moment before the lights go down, without any support. A snapshot for the consumption of others without any care for the crash that came afterwards. It was an ironic foreshadowing of the way that he discarded me as soon as I was no longer useful to him.

I hand the phone back. I say nothing and Amira doesn't push, but the suggestion lingers in the back of my mind for weeks. I focus on my students and Amira and Misha and a new diet and supplement routine that my doctor has recommended for me. I delete my old Instagram account in favor of a fresh one and train the algorithm not to show me K-pop. I find a therapist at a nearby practice within walking distance, courtesy of Jeremy Kane, and start seeing her twice a week.

It's agonizing work, and I learn to schedule

appointments on Tuesday and Thursday afternoons so I have the rest of the day to recover before teaching the next morning. But . . . I think it's working. I'm learning to forgive myself for the decisions that I made under duress or with incomplete information. Learning to forgive myself for Maddie's death is going to take longer. I guess I have a way to go in seeing Maddie as a fully realized person who made her own decisions. But the fact I can anticipate a day where that might happen . . . that's progress.

I'm still fooling myself, though, like a cartoon character creeping up on her own shadow, because I don't admit to myself why I'm collecting newspaper articles and blog posts related to the key points of my career. I tell myself that I'm simply trying to make sense of my past, fill in the blanks that I don't remember or that I've misinterpreted. I gather it together in a folder on my laptop called *ballet stuff* in case I want to look at it later.

It's only when I dig up Janine's email address at her new gig—she's the artistic director of a small ballet company in New Jersey—that I finally admit to myself what I'm planning on doing.

I don't, however, tell anyone but my therapist as I quietly up my sessions to three times a week.

I expect the work to be soul-crushing and devastating, and it is. Thanks to therapy, I'm having to recast my memories in the light of my older, wiser self and I'm often horrified at what I see there. How easily deceived I was. How much abuse I accepted as normal. How much fear and self-hatred had lingered beneath my drive to be perfect, to rise through the ranks of my company. And how utterly unprepared I was to support Maddie as she went through the same thing.

Only now do I truly understand that we were kids, sent off alone with little support, doing our best to make it through each day. Perhaps our parents deserve some of the blame for thinking my presence could replace their guidance, but mostly we were just doing the best we could with what we knew.

And what we knew was how to dance.

It takes me six months of focused work to finish the first draft of my manuscript, and even then, I know it's not publishable. It's too raw, too honest, and it includes too many details of my relationship with Simon to ever put into the world. I realize now that he never asked me to sign an NDA, which is somewhat standard for relationships in his industry, but even without one, I could never betray his trust. For now, this is a project just for me, to let me work through my feelings and traumas on paper, to grope around the edges of my past and make sense of the shape of my life now.

"We should celebrate!" Amira says when I call to tell her I've finished.

"I'm going to celebrate by going to bed," I say, slumping back in my desk chair to prop my sock-clad feet on my desk. "I'm exhausted."

"No, we're going out, even if it's just for a little bit. You've written an entire book. How many people can say that?"

"I don't know. Millions maybe?" I'm grumpy for reasons I can't explain. Maybe it's because I was hoping to have a happy ending for my story and really, all I have is more of the same. Same work, same job, same doubts about my future. Just with a finished manuscript I can't show anyone for the sake of a man I haven't spoken to in almost a year.

Amira ignores my grumbling. "Take a shower and get dressed. We're going out for margaritas."

"I can't drink."

"Virgin for you. I'll take your tequila."

I laugh, finally; when Amira is like this, there's no dissuading her. "Okay. Margaritas it is."

I shower and dress in jeans and a T-shirt, and I'm just twisting my wet hair up in a knot when Amira knocks at the door. She's dressed up tonight in a cute skirt and tank top with a strappy pair of sandals. I take one look and turn to go back to the bedroom.

"Noooo . . ." Amira grabs my arm before I can get too far and swings me back around. "You look cute. And it doesn't matter because we're just eating chips and salsa and drinking margaritas. A quiet little outing to celebrate a huge accomplishment."

I roll my eyes at her and sigh, but I grab my purse and slide my feet into ballet flats. Fifteen minutes later, she's dragging me into a packed Mexican restaurant, the din of the crowd just below deafening. I throw her a reproving look, but she seems as surprised as I am.

"It's usually so quiet!" she protests.

We find out why in a moment when we hear someone belt out the first line of a Celine Dion song from the bar.

"Karaoke," we say simultaneously.

I'll admit I usually stay away from noise levels like this, but we're celebrating tonight and people seem like they're having fun, so I let myself be led into the bar where professional equipment has been set up in the corner, complete with a screen for the lyrics. We find a spot at the bar top and order our margaritas along with chips and salsa and then spin on the stools to watch the (mostly drunk) patrons take turns at the mic.

"I'm going to do it," Amira says finally, hopping off the stool. "You should too."

"No way." I shake my head vigorously.

"Why not? You have a nice voice."

"In the shower!" I protest. "Not in front of a bunch of people."

"Fine, then we'll do a duet. And you can sing quietly." Amira pulls out her phone and scans the QR code on the tent card on the bar to bring up the song list. She thrusts the phone at me. "Pick something."

I fumble the device as she passes it over and somehow close the browser. When I tap it again, it instead opens to her last tab. I'm about to scan the QR again when I catch the title of the article.

K-pop idol announces departure after world tour.

I blink for a second as my brain processes the headline; it takes another second to realize the photo underneath is a publicity photo of Simon.

"What is this?" I ask shakily, holding out the phone.

Amira immediately looks guilty. "I'm sorry. I know you didn't want to be reminded—"

"He's leaving Helios? He's retiring?" I pull the phone back and scroll down to the beginning of the article.

"You—you didn't know?"

"No! How would I know? I don't follow him! I've removed K-pop from my life completely."

Amira looks conflicted, but I'm already reading. It's a lot of speculation and vague platitudes from the company, followed by a single quote from Simon:

I've been blessed beyond measure to be a part of first Hyperion and then Helios, and I can't imagine a better experience for a Korean-American kid moving overseas to live his dreams. I wish all my members the best, and I'm excited to pursue new opportunities for my career in America."

I lower the phone slowly. "He's coming back."

Amira freezes, then gives a tiny nod. "It sounds like it."

I open a new browser window and scan the QR code again, aware of Amira studying me with concern. I scan the duets section of their list and pick a song that I know. I swivel the screen toward her. "This one okay?"

"Sure," she says without looking. "Trina . . ."

"I'm fine," I say. "What he does isn't my concern anymore. I'm just happy to see that he's doing what he really wants to do."

Except, obviously, I am not at all fine. I somehow make it through the duet with Amira, her carrying us the entire way with her surprisingly good singing voice, and go back to the bar to devour chips and salsa and my virgin margarita. If I weren't doing so well with my condition lately, I'd be tempted to push my luck and order something with a little kick to it.

I'm not fooling Amira, of course. She knows my enthusiasm is fully put on, just like she knows that my mind is centered somewhere in Seoul and not here in Los Angeles.

Funny how all it took was a single article to unravel all the progress that I've made in the past year.

Except, as we drive home two hours later, I don't think that's true. The sharp, unbearable pang of loss that I expect, that I remember, is only the dull ache of regret. I have enough distance to know that I fell in love with Simon when we were together. And I've gained enough self-awareness to recognize that there's still a little part of me that loves him. But I also know that some connections are only meant for a short time, to launch us into the next stage of our lives. Without having met Simon, I never would have questioned my past or my present or for that matter, my future—and I can only hope it's the same for him. While I might have no idea where I want to go next, at least I don't feel trapped by my decisions. I can recognize that doing something you enjoy that pays the bills with someone you love is often the best you can hope for.

Someday, other opportunities will open up, and at least—I hope—I'll be healthy enough to pursue them.

Amira pulls up in front of my apartment building, but leaves the engine running. "Will you be okay?"

I look her in the eye and think before I answer. "Yes," I say finally. "I'll be fine."

She looks like she's going to squeeze my arm, but she changes her aim mid-reach and pulls me into a hug instead. "I love you, Trina. I'm so proud of you."

"I love you too," I whisper into her hair. "I'm so grateful for you."

"I'm going to remind you of that," she mutters.

I quirk a look at her. "What?"

"Never mind." She shakes her head. "Get your ass inside."

I laugh, grab my purse, and climb out of the car. I make it upstairs, into my apartment, and into my bedroom before the feelings hit me. I sink down onto the edge of my bed.

He's quitting, coming back to Los Angeles probably, and he didn't tell me.

I suck in a breath and let it out in a long stream, trying to calm the hurt. We broke up. I cut all ties. I blocked his number and dumped my Instagram account. Even if he wants to, he can't get in contact with me. I made it very clear that things were over between us and I wanted to be left alone. It's simply some unreasonable leftover desire to be seen, to be wanted, that has me feeling like he should have tried harder.

I let out a laugh and scrub my hand over my face. I'm so pathetic.

I want to go online and search out every bit of news I can find; I want to look up this world tour the article mentioned. I want to see his face, hear his voice, even if it's only through a screen.

Funny how quickly that small spark of regret whips into an inferno.

But I don't do any of those things. Instead, I wash my face, take my supplements, and change into my pajamas. And then I climb into bed where Misha has already made himself at home and put on my headphones.

There's simply no amount of soothing music that will ever drown out the roar of my thoughts.

● ● ●

I make a pretty good show of not being distracted to everyone but Amira, but blessedly she says nothing. She knows the news about Simon has thrown me for a loop. I know this feeling of hurt is unreasonable. We discussed that he wouldn't be free to make any decisions until his contract extension was over; it seems that he's finally made peace with Helios and Joon. I stopped following the furor over Joon's "gay dating scandal," so I have no idea how that all shook out. I actually feel a little guilty about that, but I can't bring myself to look into it now.

About a week later, I've just finished up my ten o'clock client when a uniformed courier walks in through the front door of the studio. He smiles at me and pulls a sealed cardstock envelope out of his bag. "I have a delivery for Katrina Barbas?"

"That's me," I say, holding out my hand.

He hands me the envelope, taps something on his phone and then holds it out for me to scrawl my signature on the screen. "Have a nice day."

"Yeah, you too," I say absently, picking up the envelope. It only has my name and the studio information on it, but no return address. Frowning, I pull the strip to open the top. It looks empty.

No, not empty. I shake it, and a small white envelope falls out. My stomach twists as I slide a fingernail beneath the flap.

Inside are two tickets. It takes a long time for me to register what I'm seeing. Even longer to understand why.

"Amira," I call in shaky voice. "Can you please come out here?"

Amira pops out of the office immediately, then skids to a stop when she sees me clutching the tickets with what must be a look of utter confusion—or maybe terror—on my face. "I can explain."

"You can explain why I'm holding two tickets to see Helios tonight in downtown LA?" I check the printing again. "VIP tickets, even? Was this your idea of a gift? A surprise?"

Now Amira is frowning. She strides towards me and picks up the envelope, pokes around inside. "Well, you'd think there would at least be a note." She sees my look and holds up her hands. "Trina, they're not from me."

I swallow as a sudden wash of cold comes over me, starting at the crown of my head and moving downwards. "Then who are they from?"

She smiles softly. "You know who they're from."

It hits me in the gut, and a little noise that sounds suspiciously like a whimper slips from my lips. "Amira . . ."

"His manager left a message for me on the studio phone, asking for my personal number. Simon called me."

I jerk my eyes to hers. "You—you talked to him?"

"Briefly."

"And?"

Amira relaxes a little now that she knows I'm not going to chew her out for keeping this from me. At least not now. Depending on what she says, all bets might be off. "He wanted to know if you were available to come and if it would be out of line for him to send us tickets."

I forget I'm still holding the tickets, so when I go to rub my face, I almost poke my eyes out instead. Amira takes the tickets from my hand and puts them aside.

"But . . . tonight? It's so soon."

"I don't think he wanted to give you time to overthink it."

I fix a look on Amira. "He didn't or you didn't?"

"I don't think the details matter all that much," she evades. "Listen, if you don't want to go, I totally understand, and I think he would too, he just—"

"I'll go." There was never really any question, from the moment I saw the group name printed at the top of the tickets. I was just thinking about how he couldn't get in touch with me, wondering why he hadn't made any attempt to reach out. This is his attempt. It would be surly to ignore it.

And yet I have to temper those thoughts, be reasonable. Just because he's asking me to come to the concert doesn't mean anything. When he called Amira and got her phone number, he could have asked her to relay a message, asked her to have me unblock his number, but he hadn't. I have to consider that this might simply be a nice gesture, an apology. A no-hard-feelings for breaking his heart. Because I'm not so selfish to think I'm the only one who got bruised in this scenario. I can still recall the pain in his voice as he begged me to say I loved him, to give him a good reason to turn his back on his responsibilities. No, I can't allow myself to believe this means anything at all.

I just can't shove down the surge of hope that comes along with it.

chapter thirty-five

I'm lucky that it's a Thursday and also that I didn't have more time to obsess over the concert. As it is, I'm distracted through my remaining two sessions of the morning, so much so that my clients ask me if I'm feeling okay. I smile and admit, "I'm seeing an old friend tonight and I'm a little nervous about it." They simply give me knowing looks and smile to themselves if I miss a cue or have to consult my notes more than usual. I've opened up a bit more about my personal life these days, and these two at least know that I went through a rough breakup that took me time to recover from.

I have just enough time to walk home after my last session, take a shower, and then try on every last item in my closet. Compared to the first (and only) time I saw Helios live, I have both the luxury and the motivation to consider what I look like. I finally settle on jeans, comfy Chelsea boots, a black halter tank, and a canvas jacket. I take my time doing my hair and makeup, but more than once I have to pause because I find myself holding my breath.

No, I don't have any kind of anxiety or anticipation surrounding this concert *at all*.

When Amira texts me that she's waiting outside, I grab my purse—a sling pack to keep my hands free—give Misha a little scratch where he's sleeping in a patch of sunshine near the front window, and then bound downstairs to meet her. As soon as I climb into the car and shut the door behind me, getting a full blast of air conditioning, she sends me a searching look. "We're doing this?"

I inhale and exhale slowly, then give a definitive nod. "We're doing this."

I try not to think about the last time we made this trek as we crawl through traffic on the 405 Freeway; it's just as bad as it ever is, but at least today we've left ourselves plenty of time to get there and park. Still, the closer we get, the more I fidget; my foot taps the floorboard in time with the drumbeat of the music Amira is playing—J-rock this time instead of K-pop— and I pick fitfully at my cuticles. Finally, Amira reaches over and grabs my hand.

"It'll be okay, babe," she says, giving it a squeeze. "No matter what happens, you'll be okay."

"I know I will," I say, and I mean it. I shift topics, not wanting to dwell too much on what awaits us. "What does Jamal think about all this?"

She looks away from the freeway long enough to grin at me. "Honestly? He's kind of pissed that there's not a ticket for him."

I laugh. Amira has been dating Jamal for about four months now, and from what I can tell, it's getting serious. For one thing, he's an absolutely gorgeous set designer with as weird a schedule as Amira's, so he's unperturbed by the fact she has zero work boundaries with me. For another, he used to play guitar in a rock band in college, so he shares Amira's wild enthusiasm for music of all kinds. I've only met him twice—once at the studio when he came to pick Amira up and another time at dinner with a larger group—but so far I like him. More importantly, he makes Amira happy.

Seeing her living her own life instead of being so worried about me that she prioritizes my happiness has let me take my first deep breath in longer than I can remember.

Which are admittedly in short supply tonight. When we get to the arena, parking is predictably a nightmare and we have to park in the back-forty and walk in—something that would have been unimaginable for me a year ago. Once we get there, the line for entry snakes out from the side gate, curving back and forth in a cramped ribbon. Amira leads me past the line and straight to the VIP entrance, which is considerably shorter. I see a couple of curious glances leveled our way from fans as we hand over our tickets, no doubt wondering who we are that we get special treatment, above and beyond what they've paid for.

It isn't until we start to wind our way to our seats that I have to laugh. "Really?"

We're in the same section we were last time, except closer to the stage. Conspicuously, most of the people in this section are Korean, which makes me think they might be family and friends of the band. I hold my breath for a second as my eyes search the faces near me, waiting for them to resolve into the Yang family, and I let it out in relief when I don't recognize anyone. The girl next to Amira looks at me curiously, noticing my scrutiny, but thankfully she doesn't say anything.

The buzz of the crowd grows as time ticks toward start time, and then music begins. Soon the entire crowd is singing along with their favorite Helios songs, and

I'm among them. I might not have had the heart to listen since Simon and I called it quits, but that doesn't mean the lyrics—the English parts, at least—aren't emblazoned permanently on my brain. And then the lights go down on stage and the lasers begin, flashing in red-and-white patterns across the stage. I forget to breathe again and reach for Amira's hand. She grips it hard and shakes me back to the present. It hardly matters. Because the minute that the guys appear on the stage, a nice little slight of hand involving a cloud of dry ice that resolves into their leather-clad figures, I couldn't think about anything else if I tried.

The costuming is new, of course, the hair colors shifted from the last time I saw them, but the moment I zero in on Simon, the rest of them might as well not exist. He looks. . .healthy. Not as thin, a little more muscular than before, like he's been eating well and hitting the gym. I realize with a jolt that I've never seen him with his natural dark brown hair, and my heart squeezes at just how beautiful he looks.

Not just beautiful. Heartbreakingly familiar. My eyes immediately swim with tears.

"You okay?" Amira asks as they shift into the opening choreo for a song I don't recognize—it must be off the new album, which I completely ignored.

"I'm fine," I whisper, even though I don't know if it's at all true. I convinced myself that I'm fine without him, and maybe I've even proved it. Or maybe seeing him in the flesh, even wearing the Seojun mask, just reminds me that I've merely pushed him into a far corner of my mind and locked him away rather than releasing him completely.

The concert is a surreal experience. I'm there but not there, my present self and my former self together like a double-exposed film negative. I take in the whole performance, songs I know and songs I don't, but always my eyes return to Simon, the lines of his body and the sound of his voice still so familiar. I'm sure my longing and pain is written all over my face, but I can't even manage to care what anyone around me might see. Let them think I'm a desperate fangirl. At this point, I might as well be. He's nearly as out of reach for me as he is for any of the other screaming Hellions in the audience.

I do my best to let myself get caught up in the performance and not my racing thoughts. About a third of the way through, when they come back out after a costume change, they perform one of their songs that has no choreography, instead spreading out on the edges of the stage to engage with fans, waving and reacting to signs. It feels not at all like a coincidence when Simon, now in ripped jeans and a white tank top, strides down the thrust stage and plops himself on the edge of it, his legs swinging casually while he belts his lines with impressive ease. He smiles into the crowd, scanning faces, returning hand-hearts and blowing kisses, the Seojun persona firmly in place—confident, basking in the adoration of his fans.

And then, finally, he looks my way. My heart climbs into my throat as our eyes meet, and his mask slips for the barest second, giving way to relief and happiness so plain that I feel it like a physical blow to my very core. He raises his hand mic to sing his part of the bridge, Korean lyrics I don't understand, but his eyes never leave my face. For a second, it feels like the arena has shrunk to only the two of us, connected by that single glance.

So much so that he seems to forget where he is in the song. As the music shifts into the chorus, he snaps back to himself in horror. He hurriedly levers himself off the edge of the catwalk and sprints back to the main stage while his members laugh at him. Around us, fans erupt into cheers and laughter, acknowledging his mistake, but I'm frozen there, my limbs going numb.

"You okay?" Amira shouts into my ear, squeezing my hand hard. "Do you need to sit down?"

I shake my head, even though my knees do feel weak. It's not syncope; it's emotional shock. She nods and bumps my shoulder with her arm, but she doesn't let go of my hand.

I blank out. Stages pass without my notice while thoughts swirl in my brain, wild hopes and second-guessing hand-in-hand. Until the lights go down for another costume change and the screens flash a new VCR. When the stage lights come back up, it's not the whole group. It's a single figure.

Simon.

The delicate opening, piano and guitar only, fills the arena, and Simon slowly walks downstage with a microphone in his hand. I'm so taken with the first notes in his beautiful baritone that it takes me a second to realize the lyrics are in English.

"Oh my god," Amira says beside me.

I drag my eyes away from Simon long enough to look at my best friend. "What?"

"This is new. I've never heard this song before."

I drag my eyes back to Simon where he's stopped on the apex of the thrust stage, his hands closed around the mic, his eyes closed as his voice rises into the soaring notes, emotion coloring lyrics about divergent destinies, the pain of parting. It's undoubtedly a love song, one so beautiful it crawls into my chest and takes up residence there, setting my heart aflutter. Surely I'm misunderstanding . . . surely he isn't . . .

And then he slowly walks down the thrust stage, his eyes sweeping the audience until he lands on me again at the exact moment he starts into the chorus. There can be no mistaking his intentions as he sings the lyrics, *I don't need a perfect path, just your hand in mine,* our gazes locked, never wavering. And then too soon, he's moving back upstage, even though his eyes linger on me until the last minute when he has no choice but to turn away.

I feel like he's taken a little part of my heart with him when he does.

"Holy shit," Amira murmured, slipping her arm around my waist for much-needed support. "So that happened."

I nod blindly, following him around the stage even though my brain feels like the victim of a power surge. I must be destined to miss the last third of any Helios concert, because I barely process anything that happens after the end of Simon's solo. I clap and shout when I should, I laugh at the jokes during their "ments" where they chat up the audience and take a break from their choreography, but that's simply me on social autopilot. Rational thoughts have ceased to exist since that eye contact, replaced only with a soft, endless litany.

What if, what if, what if. . .

I must be doing a pretty good job of acting normal, though, because other than a few searching looks, Amira doesn't seem worried about me. Instead, she's enjoying the rest of the concert, screaming Jae's name when he comes to our side of the stage, waving at him with both hands while wearing a brilliant smile. Her enthusiasm breaks through my endless rumination, and I laugh in delight when he looks her way and holds up his hand in a half-heart, which she completes with her other hand. I really should have arranged a meeting for her before Simon and I broke up.

What if, what if, what if. . .

And then somehow, it's over. They take their final bows and run off stage, then come back to perform one of their recent title tracks for an encore. I half-expect someone in the group to acknowledge Simon's departure, to wish him well or allow him to say goodbye to the fans one more time, but it seems like that's a topic they're not going to touch on stage.

The stage lights go down and the field lights come on, bathing the arena in blinding yellow light, while background music blares from the speakers, a final send-off. My chest feels tight, my stomach twisted. I'm unmoored. There's no reason to stay, and yet I can't bring myself to turn around and walk out to the car after that. Amira seems similarly conflicted, but as the crowd starts to thin slightly around us, we begin to edge toward the aisle.

Only to be met by a man in black with a headset, one of the tour staff. "Ms. Barbas?"

My heart rises into my throat, throbbing, cutting off my ability to speak. "Yes," I croak. I clear my throat and try again. "Yes, that's me."

"Seojun would like to see you backstage."

Behind me, Amira lets out an excited squeak.

Everything around me goes still, and suddenly my mind is crystal clear, as if all the noise has been suddenly shut off. I sound calmer than I feel when I say, "Okay, when?"

"Whenever you're ready."

I twist to look at Amira behind me.

She grabs both my hands and leans in to kiss my cheek. "Go get your man, babe. Don't worry about me. I'll be here if you need me."

I slip my hands from hers and then wrap my arms around her in a big hug. "Thank you, Amira. I love you."

She actually looks emotional when I pull away, but she just rolls her eyes. "You should go now. You can't keep the super famous idol waiting. What would he think?"

I laugh softly and gather myself before I turn back to the staff member, who looks completely baffled by what's just happened in front of him. I take a deep breath.

"Okay," I say quietly. "I'm ready now."

author's note

When I started to write this story, it was a light-hearted K-pop romance inspired by a well-known stage solo by a member of a popular boy group (veteran fans will probably know exactly which one I mean). I'd been casually exposed to Korean pop music for decades, thanks to my days in Korean martial arts, and I had a fan girl phase with a boy group in the mid-2010s, but life and raising children and building a writing career had me listening to almost no new music for almost ten years.

My younger son got me hooked on K-pop again about four years ago, and in typical *me* fashion, I wanted to know how it functioned behind the scenes. Yet the more I learned about Korean entertainment companies, the trainee process, and how restricted idols' lives could be, the more shocked I became. Not because it can be abusive—which it can be—but because of how familiar it felt. Things that fans decry as unhealthy and manipulative were just a daily part of my life as a ballet dancer, so normal that I simply accepted the brutal criticism, long hours, poor body image, disordered eating, misogyny, and abuse as part of the gig.

The novel started to turn, then, from a romance to a story of two people coming to terms with what they had to give up to follow their dreams . . . and the lasting damage those sacrifices left behind.

Much of this book, then, is taken from my own personal experiences. While I have never been diagnosed with POTS, I did (and still occasionally) suffer from dysautonomia as a result of long COVID. Katrina's experiences reflect my own and aren't meant to represent the daily lives of all POTS sufferers. Likewise, both Katrina and Simon's hypermobility reflect my own experiences as a dancer with a possible (but undiagnosed) soft-tissue disorder and isn't meant to speak for the larger EDS/HMS community.

I also feel the need to address the attitudes around food displayed in this novel. Disordered eating can occur within and outside of full-blown eating disorders. The lack of direct attention in the story to this issue is not meant to minimize the harm or concern about disordered eating; rather it simply wasn't the focus of the book, but something I used to illuminate the mindset of performers who rely on their looks and their bodies for their livelihoods.

If any of the themes in this book resonate with you, and you would like more information or you feel you're in crisis, please reach out to one of the many hotlines and organizations that are available to you.

National Suicide Prevention Lifeline
988 | 1-800-273-TALK(8255)
National Association of Anorexia Nervosa and Associated Disorders (ANAD) Helpline
1-888-375-7767
Dysautonomia International
https://www.dysautonomiainternational.org/

discussion questions

1. Katrina goes by *Kat* in her dance days and *Trina* in the present. Yet Simon is the only one who calls her by her full name. What do you think the use of two nicknames and her whole name signifies?

2. We see Katrina with three different men in *Afterlight*: Philip, Jackson, and Simon. How do her relationships, including her physical relationships, with each of them illuminate her internal journey? In what way?

3. Philip is alternately caring and cruel, concerned and dismissive. Is this a bad relationship or an abusive one? How does the disparity in their ages (thirteen years) affect your answer? How do the ballet expectations of being obedient and submissive, as well as the acceptance of constant criticism, carry over into that relationship?

4. In chapter six, why do you think Philip pushes to out their relationship right after the ballet's debut? How does your knowledge of how it affects Kat's

place in the company change your perspective by the end of the book?

5. With Philip, and even Jackson, Katrina pushes herself to put on the façade she thinks they want to see, particularly around her physical needs and wants. Why is it significant that she doesn't do that with Simon and instead allows him to see her at her "worst?"

6. Katrina and Simon fall in love but they don't know much about each other. Why do shared experiences and trauma create such a powerful bond, even when it's unspoken?

7. Out of all the characters in the book, Katrina spends the most time with her best friend, Amira. How does her relationship with her change over the course of the book? Why do you think she calls Amira the love of her life by the end?

8. One of the running themes in Katrina's backstory is wondering when her sacrifices will feel worthwhile. How does that tie into Simon's dilemma? When do the benefits of following your dreams outweigh the sacrifices? And how do you decide when the balance tips the other way?

9. Compare how Simon was held back from debut by Joonwoo for his own good and how Maddie was pushed beyond her abilities. What kind of parallel do you think the author meant to draw? How does that play into Katrina's understanding of Simon's responsibility to his group leader?

10. There are various discussions of disordered eating throughout the book: Katrina's teen client, Simon's lack of "random carbs," the fact that Katrina won't let herself gain weight, Maddie's struggles with her growth spurt. Even though it's not addressed directly, how does their easy acceptance of the realities of physical standards in the entertainment industry illuminate the mindset and traumas of their careers?

11. Katrina realizes she's just following the next step rather than finding something she truly loves to do as much as Simon loves performing. But by the end of the book, she has concluded that doing something you like with something you love might be the best one can hope for. What do you think this says about how Katrina's priorities have shifted and what she now values?

12. Why do you think the author decided to make the outcome of Katrina's relationship with Simon open-ended rather than providing an on-page happy-ever-after?

13. Why could Katrina be considered an unreliable narrator?

content warnings

While this book does not contain explicit material, it contains content pertaining to the following themes, which may be upsetting to some readers:

Ableism
Body dysmorphia
Bullying
Chronic illness
Coercive relationships
C-PTSD (unnamed)
COVID-19
Death of a family member
Disordered eating
Emotional abuse
Grief and loss depiction
Homophobia
Intimate partner abuse/violence
Sexual abuse/assault
Suicide/apparent suicide

about the author

Cassandra Pine is the award-winning author of over twenty books under various pen names in multiple genres. She now writes thoughtful and angsty contemporary fiction from her home in Colorado, fueled by a raging boba and mochi donut habit and helped-slash-hindered by her feline office assistant, Willow.

www.ingramcontent.com/pod-product-compliance
Lightning Source LLC
Chambersburg PA
CBHW021402310726
48971CB00005B/1170